CW01391231

New York Times and *USA*
B.J. Daniels lives in Montana
and three springer spaniels. When not writing, she quilts,
boats and plays tennis. Contact her at bjdaniels.com, on
Facebook or X @bjdanielsauthor

Debra Webb is the award-winning, *USA Today* bestselling
author of more than one hundred novels, including those
in reader-favourite series Faces of Evil, the Colby Agency
and Shades of Death. With more than four million books
sold in numerous languages and countries, Debra has a
love of storytelling that goes back to her childhood on a
farm in Alabama. Visit Debra at debrawebb.com

Discover more at millsandboon.co.uk

RECKONING WITH THE COWBOY

B.J. DANIELS

WITNESS TO MURDER

DEBRA WEBB

MILLS & BOON

All rights reserved including the right of reproduction in whole or in part in any form. This edition is published by arrangement with Harlequin Enterprises ULC.

This is a work of fiction. Names, characters, places, locations and incidents are purely fictional and bear no relationship to any real life individuals, living or dead, or to any actual places, business establishments, locations, events or incidents. Any resemblance is entirely coincidental.

Without limiting the author's and publisher's exclusive rights, any unauthorised use of this publication to train generative artificial intelligence (AI) technologies is expressly prohibited. HarperCollins also exercise their rights under Article 4(3) of the Digital Single Market Directive 2019/790 and expressly reserve this publication from the text and data mining exception.

® and ™ are trademarks owned and used by the trademark owner and/or its licensee. Trademarks marked with ® are registered with the United Kingdom Patent Office and/or the Office for Harmonisation in the Internal Market and in other countries.

First Published in Great Britain 2025
by Mills & Boon, an imprint of HarperCollins*Publishers* Ltd
1 London Bridge Street, London, SE1 9GF

www.harpercollins.co.uk

HarperCollins*Publishers*
Macken House, 39/40 Mayor Street Upper,
Dublin 1, D01 C9W8, Ireland

Reckoning with the Cowboy © 2025 Barbara Heinlein
Witness to Murder © 2025 Debra Webb

ISBN: 978-0-263-39730-7

1025

MIX
Paper | Supporting
responsible forestry
FSC
www.fsc.org
FSC™ C007454

This book contains FSC™ certified paper and other controlled sources to ensure responsible forest management.

For more information visit: www.harpercollins.co.uk/green

Printed and Bound in the UK using 100% Renewable Electricity at CPI Group (UK) Ltd, Croydon, CR0 4YY

RECKONING WITH THE COWBOY

B.J. DANIELS

This is dedicated to my friend Joanna Wayne,
who we lost while I was writing this book. I've never
met anyone with so much joy for living. She was always
up for anything, so full of energy, so creative and so fun.
I loved being around her.
We had so many adventures with our good friend
Amanda Stevens.

Amanda and I were both relieved when Joanna was at
conferences to stay up drinking till closing time with our
editor since we just needed to get some sleep.

This one is for you, Joanna. You will be dearly missed.

Prologue

My Angel,
Thank you for writing to a guy like me. I can't tell you how much it means to hear from someone on the outside. I get so lonely here, especially knowing that I'm locked up for something I didn't do and may never get out.

Tell me about your life, your friends, this town where you live. I always wanted to go to Montana. Do you have a boyfriend? I had a girlfriend before I got locked up. I had dreams. I want to hear yours.

I'll stop. Please keep writing me and I will write back. I live for your letters.
Your prison pen pal,
Shane

Chapter One

Josephine Brand's head jerked up, her attention drawn to the dirt road past her house. She took a whiff of the air as if trouble had a scent. Maybe it did because she felt the hair quill on the back of her neck.

Her rocking chair creaked on the worn boards of the front porch as she sat forward to see better. The road seemed to remain stubbornly empty as the large bowl of unsnapped green beans shifted on her lap.

A breeze played at a loose lock of her long dark hair. Unconsciously, she tucked it behind her ear, her focus on the road that led into the town of Dry Gulch. It was another beautiful late fall Montana day. She could hear the rustle of the dried leaves on the aspens next to the old farmhouse, smell the odor of burning weeds and feel the shadow overhead as a flight of geese made a dark V against the cloudless sky.

"Those beans won't snap themselves," her baby sister said from the other side of the screen door.

"Sorry, Amy Sue." Josie went back to work snapping beans to be canned for the long winter ahead. "Just gathering wool." It had been her grandmother's expression. The reassuring memory of Nana sitting out here on this very porch had always been like a touchstone, just not today.

Try as she may, she couldn't shake off a sense of foreboding. Her grandmother had told her it was a gift, this sensing things. Josie had never tried to put a name to it. Sometimes she sensed trouble, although hers was never as strong as Nana's, never as clear. Amy Sue had always been skeptical, saying she didn't believe Josie had inherited anything except their grandmother's bossiness. But Josephine knew better. While she often couldn't see what was coming, she felt an uneasiness—just as she did right now.

"You need to learn to trust it," her grandmother used to say. "You also need to stop being afraid of it."

She knew Nana had been right. Josie was skeptical about her so-called gift and wished she were instead happily oblivious and never had a sense of what would come. Like now. She could feel trouble on the wind, sure as the devil. As she continued snapping the beans, though, she kept checking the road as if expecting what was coming.

Several thoughts skittered through her mind, but she couldn't formulate a clear vision. She never had been able to. Nor did she want to. Yet she couldn't shake off the foreboding she felt. Even if she refused to see, she couldn't help the *knowing*.

What she was sure of… It wasn't *something* coming. It was *someone*—and it was personal.

CLANCY ROBERTS OFTEN complained that nothing ever happened in the sleepy rural town of Dry Gulch. Even that old familiar community rhythm had slowed to a crawl, she thought as she came out of the drugstore to look down a deserted Main Street.

A dust devil picked up dried leaves from the gutter, sending them whirling down the street. She watched, feeling the wind on her face, as a large tumbleweed sailed past like in an old Hollywood-movie-set ghost town.

This was her life, she thought with a groan. Dry Gulch was in a slow-motion death spiral. But no one seemed to notice or care. While other parts of Montana were booming, one glance in either direction of Main Street told you this town wasn't going anywhere but down.

And that was the hard part for Clancy. She knew she would have to pack up and leave soon if she hoped to make anything of herself.

"I've already stayed too long," the nineteen-year-old said to the wind, then shielded her eyes as she saw raised dust on the road. Looking closer, she could make out what looked like a pickup pulling a rented trailer. The rig didn't look familiar. As it drew closer, she saw why. The vehicle had out-of-state plates. Curious, she squinted into the wind and dust trying to make out what state. Texas? Florida?

For the life of her, she couldn't remember the last time anyone new had moved into town—let alone to the area. The local population had been dropping for some time, with older folks passing on and their kids moving away for more education or better jobs.

She got only a glimpse of the driver behind the wheel and felt her pulse jump even as she told herself it couldn't be.

WIND ROCKED CORDELL LANDER'S pickup as it rumbled into town. A tumbleweed blew past, cartwheeling across the street ahead of him like a warning. People would know soon enough that he was back, he thought with a grimace. Even if he'd let someone know about his impending arrival, no red carpet would have been rolled out. Far from it. In fact, he was expecting just the opposite given the way he'd left Dry Gulch.

He had been planning to return soon—just not for the reason he was now, he thought as he pulled to a stop in front of the former car dealership, now empty with a for-sale sign in the window. He'd been driving for two days almost straight through and was beyond exhausted. But there hadn't been time to stop.

Now, though, he wanted to get out and walk the rest of the way. He'd needed to stretch his legs and prepare himself for what was about to happen.

The wind threatened to steal his beat-up lucky Stetson as he shoved it down harder on his thick head of sandy-blond hair. As he did, he caught his reflection in the car dealership window. Should have at least gotten a haircut, he told himself. Too late now, he thought as he continued down the street toward the sheriff's department.

Yep, coming back here filled him with so many emotions he felt choked up. It was the exhaustion, he told himself. Just the thought of seeing his brother filled him with regret over the past and fear about the future. If they had a future, he thought as he passed the drugstore, glad to see it was still open. So many small towns in Montana were dying. He couldn't bear the thought that Dry Gulch was headed in that direction.

He caught a glimpse of a young woman standing just inside the door of the drugstore. She looked vaguely familiar, but then again, unless Dry Gulch had changed a whole heck of a lot in the six years he'd been gone, he knew everyone in this town and most of those in the county around it.

Chapter Two

Cordell pushed open the door to the sheriff's office on a gust of wind. He saw his brother look up from the small glassed-in office set back from the dispatcher's and deputy's desks. Out of the corner of his eye, he saw the two them freeze.

Seems they had already heard he was in town but hadn't expected him to walk into the mouth of the lion, so to speak. His brother rose slowly from behind his desk and opened his office door to step out. He had the same sandy-blond hair as Cordell except his had been recently cut. Still, it was longer on top than Cordell remembered, making Max look more boyish. The one thing that never changed were the faded-denim blue eyes. They were the same as his, maybe a little more piercing, but definitely not friendly.

"Deputy, arrest this man," Max Lander said.

The deputy looked confused. "Sheriff?"

"He's got several old warrants out for him in this county. Cuff him, read him his rights and lock him up."

The deputy rose slowly from his chair, picked up his cuffs and moved cautiously toward Cordell the way he would a rattlesnake coiled in the middle of the path.

"Max, we need to talk," Cordell said, holding up both

hands in surrender. "I'm serious. You need to listen to me. I have some news you aren't going to like."

Max picked up his Stetson from the hook by his office door. "It's my lunchtime. I'm going down to Goldie's for the daily special. Rance, I expect you to have this man behind bars by the time I return."

"Max," Cordell said as Bobby grabbed his arm and pulled it behind him, then snatched the other one. He felt the familiar bite of the cuffs as Max walked right to him.

"What did you think was going to happen?" Max whispered as he continued to the door and stepped out into the blustery fall day.

IT WAS NEARLY impossible to keep a secret in a small town in Montana. Josie had gone back to snapping the last of the green beans from the garden when she heard the landline ring inside the house. Her sister answered it on the second ring even though Amy Sue was busy putting up the last of the beets.

From the porch, Josie listened to her sister's side of the conversation through the screen door. She'd been expecting a call and now tensed as she waited with some trepidation to hear what this one was about. Hard to tell with her sister's one-word responses to whatever was being said on the other end of the line.

"Well, I'll be," Amy Sue finished. "Sorry to hear that. Thanks for letting us know." She hung up and walked to the screen door again. Josie didn't move, hardly breathed as she waited for the bad news.

"Appears Cordell Lander is back in town," her sister said quietly. "Clancy just called. Says he's driving a pickup and pulling a rented small, enclosed trailer. Sounds like he's back to stay for a while."

Josie closed her eyes for a moment. She could tell her sister was waiting for a reaction. While Josie had done her best to hide how devastated she'd been when Cordell had left Dry Gulch six years ago, she figured everyone in town knew. She and Cordell had been best friends, then sweethearts, then lovers. She'd given him her heart, knowing that if he broke it, she'd never love again.

And sure as the devil, that's what he did.

Rising, careful not to spill the beans, she turned to her sister. "You need some help with the beets?"

"That's all you have to say?"

"What would you like me to say?" Josie asked. The wind whipped her hair into her eyes as her sister stepped back to let her enter the house.

"Aren't you the least bit curious as to what he's doing back here?" Amy Sue demanded.

"Nope. Whatever it is, he won't be here long," she said as she carried the bowl into the kitchen and began digging out a large pot from under the counter to put a scald on the beans before freezing them. She could feel her sister watching her, looking for any remnant of feelings Josie might have for the bad boy who everyone in town, including her sister, thought would ruin her life.

That seemed like a lifetime ago, but really hadn't been all that far in the past. The pain certainly hadn't decreased any. Nor had those old feelings. Not that she would let her sister see either if she could help it.

But as she turned on the faucet to cover the beans with water, she couldn't help the thump of her pulse in her ears at just the thought of seeing Cordell again. What was he doing back here? Had he changed much since the last time she'd seen him? Did he plan on seeing her before he left again?

Her hands shook as she put the pot on the burner.

"You don't have to pretend with me," Amy Sue said, standing watching her. "You know you want to see him." The landline rang again.

The two of them looked at each other. Josie shook her head to indicate she wasn't picking it up. Her sister folded her arms and let it ring another three times before she couldn't take it any longer and answered the call.

"If you're calling to tell me that Cordell Lander is back in town, you're too late," Amy Sue said into the phone. She listened for a moment, her gaze going to Josie, then she said, "Thank you for letting us know," and hung up.

Feeling her sister's gaze boring into her, Josie sighed. "What?"

"That was Tammy down at the sheriff's department." Tammy Brooks was a former classmate and the daytime dispatcher. "If you wanted to see Cordell, he won't be hard to find. He's in jail. Max arrested him."

MAX LANDER SWORE the moment he was outside the sheriff's department. The last person he'd expected to see walk through that door was his brother. He shook his head as he started down the street toward Goldie's Café. No longer hungry, he still couldn't stay in the office. He wasn't up to dealing with Cordell yet.

Whatever ill wind had blown his brother back into town, it spelled trouble. It always had, always would, he told himself. If Cordell thought he would get preferential treatment in his hometown, he was sadly mistaken. Max had done everything he could to keep his brother from jail before Cordell had left town. He couldn't protect him anymore, he told himself as he pushed open the door to the only café still open in town.

When his brother had left six years ago, he hadn't

wanted him to leave. They'd been safe here in Dry Gulch now for years. Max knew it didn't make a lot of sense, this fear of his, but he'd worried about Cordell getting into serious trouble away from here. This was their safe haven. He feared his brother didn't understand that.

His mood, however, picked right up when he spotted Goldie Shaw behind the counter. Her long blond hair was pulled up into a ponytail, her bangs just above her big brown eyes. The warmth of her smile had always been his undoing. His heart did a cartwheel in his chest at just the sight of her.

He headed for her, needing a kind word. Bad-boy Cordell Lander's return would soon be all anyone was talking about. Max hoped to put that off as long as possible.

"Hey, Goldie," he said, already feeling better as he slipped onto a stool that had seen better days.

"The special?" she said, returning his smile with a wink.

"You know it."

She chuckled and headed into the kitchen to tell the cook. Goldie knew just how he liked his meat cooked and what sides he'd want with it. She tried to make everything special for him. She'd put up with him for almost six years. She was too good for him.

"When are you going to marry that girl?" Tanner Frost demanded from down the counter. The older bearded man was hunched over his soup, spoon suspended as if he'd read Max's thought and felt the need to ask the question the entire town had been asking for years now.

"Just eat your soup, Frost," Max said with a groan as he looked through the open serving space to the kitchen to see if Goldie had heard. She was busy talking to the cook, a teenage boy named Ronnie Dean. Max was sure she was distracted. He didn't want her to be offended by his harsh remark. But he knew Frost wasn't the only one wondering about his intentions with everyone's favorite café owner.

Goldie returned, smiling as soon as her gaze fell on him. Damn, he loved this woman, couldn't imagine living without her. How could he explain to her what was taking him so long to make her his wife? He could barely explain it to himself. But his wild brother showing up certainly brought the reason home, didn't it?

"Is it true?" Goldie whispered. For just an instant, he thought he'd been wrong and that she'd heard what that fool Frost had said. "Is Cordell really back?"

CORDELL LAY ON the bench in the smallest of the cells, the drunk tank. It wasn't like he hadn't been here before. But he couldn't help feeling impatient. He'd driven almost straight through from Florida to get home to warn his brother. All the driving, all the worrying, all the second-guessing himself had worn him out. He drifted right off, startling awake to find the sheriff banging on the bars.

Pushing himself up to a sitting position, he leaned his elbows on his knees, before shifting his gaze to his brother. "Enjoy your lunch?"

"What are you doing here?" he said, sounding exasperated.

Cordell rose, stretched, yawned and walked slowly over to the bars and his brother. He had come to warn Max, but it was a hell of a lot more than that. He knew his brother was going to need his help and that Max would fight him on that. That's if his brother even believed what he was about to tell him.

Max passed a sandwich wrapped in waxed paper through the bars to him. Cordell took it, tearing off the paper and devouring it in a few bites as his brother watched. "When was the last time you ate?"

"It's been a while," he admitted. "I didn't want to take the time to eat. Grabbed something only when I bought gas for the truck. Goldie make the sandwich? It's really good." He paused before he asked, "You two still together?"

Max sighed. "If you need money—"

Cordell shook his head. "It's not that."

"So why would you take the chance, coming back here, knowing you have warrants out on you?" his brother demanded.

He wiped his mouth with his sleeve and swallowed the last bite of the sandwich as he wadded up the waxed paper. Max reached through the bars for his brother's trash as Cordell cleared his voice and said, "I was down in Florida in this motel on the Gulf side. The TV was on. I wasn't really watching it until I recognized his voice and looked up and—"

"Is this going to be one of your long-winded stories?" Max interrupted.

He met his brother's gaze, his mouth suddenly dry. "I recognized our stepdaddy."

Max snorted. "He wasn't our stepfather. Now you're telling me you drove all this way because you thought you saw a dead man on the local TV news?"

"He'd not dead. That's only part of what I came here to tell you," Cordell said.

Max shook his head and looked over his shoulder to make sure they were alone before he lowered his voice. "Roger Grimes is dead. Don't you think I should know that?"

Cordell continued as if his brother hadn't spoken. "This TV news story was about some men who were being released early from prison for whatever reason. Couldn't have been good behavior knowing Roger. The newsman was asking each of them questions as they came out. Asking them what they were going to do now." He took a breath, even now questioning if he'd really seen and heard what he thought he had. "Roger looked right at the camera and said, 'I'm going home to look up my stepsons. It's been too long.'"

His brother shook his head and started to step away. "You're mistaken. It was just some man who looked like Grimes."

"Max, you don't think I remember him? There was that familiar glint in his eyes that I still see in my nightmares."

"You still have nightmares?" Max asked, looking concerned.

He brushed the question aside, wishing he hadn't mentioned it. Max liked to think that once they'd escaped, his little brother had been able to put the past behind him. "That look gave me chills even before Roger..." Cordell cleared his throat again and said, "added, 'Can't wait to see the oldest. I owe Max my life.' He'd looked right into the camera and smiled. You remember that smile, don't you? No one smiled like that but the devil himself."

He could see that his words had shaken his brother—just as they had rattled him—but Max being Max, he didn't want to believe it. It's why Cordell had come with the news in person, rather than calling to let him know that he was on his way.

"I'm not sure what you saw or think you heard, but you're obviously mistaken," his brother said. "There is no way he's still alive, let alone on his way here."

Cordell watched his brother grab the cell's bars and squeeze until his knuckles turned white. "It was him, Max.

It was thirty-six hours ago. I drove straight through except for gas and one quick stop to pick up a rented trailer to haul a couple of things I'd left with a friend."

"A couple of things?" He shook his head. "I don't want to know."

"I couldn't come back to town empty-handed," Cordell said.

Max let go of the bars, waving his hands as he tried to dismiss what his brother was saying. "I don't have time for this foolishness."

"Wait, you can't leave me here. I didn't just come to warn you. You're going to need my help. Anyway, Roger isn't coming after just you. I suspect the man knows I helped you that night. He's coming for us. This time, he's going to kill us. You know it as well as I do."

His brother turned and walked to the door before stopping to look back. "Where'd you leave your truck?"

"Down in front of the old car dealership. Max—"

But his brother didn't answer as he stepped out, the door closing behind him.

ALL THE WAY down to the former car dealership, Cordell's keys jangling in his hand, Max refused to even think about what his brother had told him. Instead, he kept replaying the argument he and Goldie had at the café earlier.

"I can't believe you jailed your own brother," she'd said, angrier than he'd ever seen her, though she'd kept her voice down. "Sometimes I wonder about you, Max Lander."

"Cordell has three outstanding warrants on him, all misdemeanors, but I'm the sheriff. It's called doing my job." She had turned her back on him to go wait on another customer. She hadn't come back by the time he'd eaten what he could choke down of the daily special and left a generous tip. He was almost to the door when she came after him, following him outside.

For a moment, he had thought they were about to make up. Instead, she shoved the wrapped sandwich into his hands. "I would imagine your brother might be hungry," she said and turned on her heel, leaving him to return to work in an even worse mood than Cordell's sudden appearance had caused.

Now, as he reached his brother's truck, he saw the rented trailer and felt his irritation with his brother growing. He hated to think what might be inside. This was so like Cordell. A peace offering?

Max knew his mood wasn't really about his brother or the damned trailer and its contents. Cordell couldn't have seen Roger Grimes. Maybe the released prisoner had looked like Grimes, but whatever the man had said that this brother had taken as retribution hadn't been about him and Cordell. Max was a common name. His brother was wrong, and Max hated being reminded of that time and how it had ended. Grimes was dead. No way could he have survived after what Max had done to him that night.

For years, he'd tried to put it all out of his mind. Now, though, like in his nightmares, he saw himself pulling their so-called stepfather off Cordell. Grimes and his mother hadn't been legally married, not that it mattered since by then his mother was gone, leaving them with this monster.

Like most nights, Grimes had come home from work drunk and out of his mind with meanness. He had grabbed up the baseball bat by the door. Cordell lay on the floor in pain from the beating the man had already given him with rubber tubing. Max, seventeen, had watched Grimes lift the bat to swing at his already injured and bleeding twelve-year-old brother on the floor. In a few years, his younger brother would grow into his height and weight and would be able to make it a fair fight, but not that night.

Max had known he was going to have to cross a line that would change everything. It had been a long time coming. He and his brother had feared for their lives from the moment their mother had married the man. But the beatings had gotten much worse after their mother disappeared. Grimes had gotten much worse. He hated his job at the state penitentiary down the road from their isolated shack of a house in the middle of nowhere out in southeastern Wyoming. The man had a streak of meanness that ran deep through him, and he took out his disappointments on Max and Cordell.

Max had rushed Grimes, taking the bat away from him and doing what he'd wished he'd done long before it had gotten so bad. Grimes fought like the animal he was. But by seventeen, Max was strong. Not as strong as his stepfather and probably not as determined, but strong enough since he'd known that he wasn't just fighting for his own life, but for his brother's.

He closed his eyes for a moment as the memory shook him to his boots. He'd killed Roger Grimes. That's why he knew Cordell had to be mistaken. He remembered crawling across the blood-slick floor to check the fallen Grimes for a pulse. Not finding one, he and Cordell had loaded his body into the back of Grimes's old pickup and driven miles through the night to Big Horn Canyon. If their stepfather had been somehow alive, the fall from the cliffs would have killed him even before he hit the lake water far below.

That night was why Max had gone into law enforcement. He wasn't going to be like the law who listened to Max's and Cordell's claims about the abuse by their alleged stepfather and then promised to help by calling Grimes and having him pick up his stepsons. The beatings that followed had laid both him and Cordell up for a week. Max still had the scars, both inside and out. He hated to think that his brother still did, too, along with the nightmares.

Now, standing next to Cordell's pickup and trailer, he tried to shake himself from the past that had haunted him for eighteen years. No one in Dry Gulch knew about their past and that was the way Max wanted to keep it. He'd been determined not to let the shame of what had happened define him, yet he knew it had. Otherwise, wouldn't he have already married Goldie? They might even have a couple of kids by now.

He pushed away that painful thought as he walked around to the trailer and searched the ring of keys his deputy had taken from Cordell until he found one for the padlock. Turning the key in the lock, he removed the padlock, half-afraid of what he was about to find.

The doors swung open in the wind, startling him, but not half as much as what he saw standing inside the trailer. He swore under his breath, before quickly slamming the doors and relocking the trailer.

Chapter Three

"Your brother's asking to speak to his lawyer," Deputy Rance Fletcher said as Max returned to the sheriff's office.

"Of course he is," the sheriff said.

"Who's his lawyer?"

"I'll take care of it." Max tossed his brother's keys onto his desk and headed for the cellblock, snatching up the keys to the cells on the way.

Cordell was where he'd been earlier, snoozing on the bench, his Stetson cocked over his eyes, his legs crossed at his boots. "Comfortable enough?" he asked sarcastically. Cordell had always been able to sleep anywhere under any circumstances since they were kids—unlike Max. It was something Max had resented for years, but especially right now. After what his brother had told him, he wondered if he'd ever sleep again.

"Rance tell you I wanted to talk to my lawyer?"

"You sure your…lawyer wants to talk to you?"

"Doubtful, but I need a lawyer and there's only one in town." Cordell swung his boots off the bench and sat up, casting his hat aside as he raked a hand through his hair. There'd been a time when people had thought the two of them were twins even though Max was older by five years.

"You do know it's Saturday. The law office is closed today."

"I still have the home number on speed dial," his brother said with a wry smile.

Max could only shake his head.

"I wouldn't mind making the call in private, all things considered," Cordell said.

Max just bet he would. He thought about the fight he'd had earlier with Goldie. Why was he being so hard on his brother when he'd missed Cordell like one of his own limbs and had worried about him the whole time he was gone?

Relenting, he pulled out his brother's cell phone and held it through the bars. "You have three minutes."

"I doubt it will take that long."

CORDELL DIALED THE familiar landline number and listened to it ring. Once, twice, three times before it was picked up with an aggravated, "If this is about Cordell Lander, we already know."

It had been so long since he'd heard a familiar voice, it made him smile. "Hey, Amy Sue." Silence. "Sounds like good news travels fast." More silence. "I find myself in need of a lawyer. Is Josie close at hand?" He knew she was. She spent every chance she got out at her grandmother's old farm even though she had a combo apartment–law office in town.

When she came on the line and he heard her voice after all this time, his heart swelled as if filled with helium.

"I figured you'd be calling."

"Josie." He uttered her name like a prayer. She sounded so good that his eyes filled, and his chest ached. "Sure would like to see you."

"Amy Sue said you need a lawyer. These old charges

against you? Or are they new ones?" she asked, sounding like the attorney she was.

"Old."

She made a dismissive sound. "I can probably get them thrown out, if I can tell the judge that you'll be leaving town right after you're released."

"I can't promise that. I need to help Max with something."

"Do not tell me that you've involved Max in your trouble."

"I don't have time to go into it on the phone, but Max is in more danger than I am. That's why I'm back. I'm not leaving until my brother is safe. That's why I need to get out of jail."

"Did Max buy this story of yours?"

"Oh, you know Max. He thinks he's invincible and I'm just a screwup."

"Uh-huh," she said, clearly agreeing.

"He probably doesn't think he needs me. But this time, he does, trust me." The moment he said it, he knew it was the wrong thing to say. "You used to trust me," he added quickly.

"And look where it got me," she said.

He heard the cellblock door open, and footfalls headed his way. "Max only gave me three minutes, but there's so much I need to—"

"I'll see you Monday morning."

"That might be too late." He thought she had already hung up.

"What kind of trouble are you in, Cordell?" Her tone sounded almost warm, concerned, definitely caring, giving him hope. "Never mind, I don't want to know. I'll be right there." Just like that, this time she really was gone.

He disconnected and turned to see Max waiting for his phone. "She going to represent you?" He sounded doubtful.

"She's coming right in," he said, holding out the phone. "We can't waste any time with Grimes on his way here."

Max shook his head, clearly refusing to believe anything Cordell had told him as he took his cell and pocketed it. "You all right about seeing her again?"

"Seriously? You want to talk about how I feel about Josie?" He sighed since the answer was simple. He felt as if he'd been kicked in the chest by a horse at just the sound of her voice. "She's not married, is she? Seeing anyone?"

"Married? No. Dating…?" He shrugged. "You can take that up with her when she gets here," his brother said and started to walk out.

"You can try to convince yourself that I'm wrong, but Roger is still headed this way," he called after his brother.

Max slowed and turned as if he'd changed his mind. Walking back, he said, "I'll move you into a cell with a bed."

Cordell sighed. "How gracious of you. That sandwich was great, but what time's dinner? I really didn't take time to eat on the road."

Max unlocked his cell and opened another one with a narrow cot-like bed. "It's Saturday so the special is Goldie's fried chicken, mashed potatoes and corn. I suppose you'll want pie. Your favorite still banana cream?"

His grin broadened. "You remembered." He was actually touched by that. "Boy, is it good to be home, bro. I just wish it was under different circumstances."

"Yeah," Max said and locked the cell after Cordell entered. "I can't wait to see what happens when the town finds out what's in the back of that trailer you brought."

"I told you. It's a peace offering."

"You serious?" his brother said, shaking his head. "I can't imagine what you were thinking. You aren't going to have to worry about our dead phony stepfather killing you. The town's people will be showing up with pitchforks demanding your head on a stake." With that he walked out.

"About dinner? What time did you say it is?"

His brother didn't answer as he let the door slam behind him.

"You're going to represent him?" Amy Sue asked in horror. "After everything Cordell did to you?"

"He didn't do anything to me that I didn't want to happen," Josie snapped. She'd been more than a willing participant. She'd fallen for the town bad boy, and she'd fallen hard. When he'd broken her heart and left town, no one blamed her—the good girl—for getting involved with him. It was all Cordell who caught the community's wrath. Josie was their pride and joy. The girl who had made good and come back here after passing the bar.

"It's bad enough that he's in town, but if you get him out of jail…"

"It's my job. Strictly business."

Her sister laughed. "You can actually say that with a straight face? No wonder you're such a good lawyer." Amy Sue had never understood why Josie had come back to Dry Gulch to open her practice.

"You have all kinds of job offers," her sister had cried. "You could get hired anywhere, start your own practice anywhere, why would you come back here? I thought you were trying to get out of Dry Gulch."

"It's you who wants out, Amy Sue," Josie had said in exasperation. "You're just too scared to drive out past the city limits. Don't blame me for my choices when you have never let yourself make one."

Amy Sue had never understood that Dry Gulch, their grandmother's farm, this part of Montana was Josie's home. It's probably why their grandmother had left the place to her in a trust so it would be handed down to Josie's children. Their grandmother had never thought Amy Sue would stay around and she didn't want the property ever sold. She trusted Josie to make sure it wasn't.

Even though Josie had left for college and gotten her law degree, she'd always planned to return home. The area needed a lawyer.

"You'll go broke," her sister had contended. "Or get bored to death."

"Good thing I don't need much money, and I'm not easily bored," Josie had told her. "Sis, I know what I'm doing."

But Amy Sue had dug in her heels, determined it was Cordell Lander's fault Josie hadn't left for greener pastures. "You want to be here when he comes back. You really think he's coming back to farm this property?" They had the land leased, which brought in more than enough for them to live on even without Josie's law office income.

She wondered now if Amy Sue remembered those words. Josie would have denied she was here because of Cordell to her dying day. But now she had to wonder if at least there had been some truth to it. Was she that foolish that she'd been waiting around all this time for Cordell to return? No, she thought. As to whether or not she was still in love with the bad boy, that was her own burden to carry since it appeared that he hadn't changed one iota. Maybe worse, it seemed that whatever had brought him back, he was involving his brother in it.

"I'm sure that once I get him out of jail, he'll be gone,"

she told her sister now. "Can you finish up the canning? I have a client I have to see and take that damned phone off the hook." Cordell was back and everyone thought they needed to warn her. The town's people were determined to protect her heart from getting broken again. As if a heart once broken could be that easily repaired for another bout of heartbreak.

Given how the town's people felt about her, she hoped Cordell wouldn't give the residents of Dry Gulch any more reason to want to run him back out of town.

AMY SUE WATCHED her sister leave. Oh, she would finish the canning, but she wasn't happy about Cordell Lander being back. Of course he was already in jail. Why couldn't Josie see that the two of them had no future?

She looked around the farmhouse kitchen. Her grandmother had been wrong. She loved this place. She didn't want to leave. She was the obvious one to keep the farm going—not her sister. Josie thought she was the only one with plans. Little did she know.

Smiling, Amy Sue reminded herself that one day she would run this farm with her husband, a man who wanted to work the land as much as she did. She would show her sister. Josie thought she knew her so well. She had no idea. Wouldn't she be surprised to learn that Amy Sue had a man in her life?

She looked forward to the day when Josie got to meet him. She couldn't wait to see the expression on her sister's face. All the residents of Dry Gulch who thought Amy Sue Brand would be an old spinster out here on the farm alone raising cats would realize how wrong they'd been.

But the main person she wanted to show was her grandmother, who'd left the farm to the wrong granddaughter.

Chapter Four

Josie put on her game face as she pushed open the door to the sheriff's office. She was only there as an attorney, she told herself. If Cordell thought it was more, he was wrong, and she would set him straight right away.

The fact that he'd even had the gall to call her to begin with made her shake her head in wonder. If he gave her any trouble, he could try to find someone else to represent him—if he could get anyone to come to Dry Gulch on his behalf.

But even as she thought it, she had to admit that she was anxious to see him again, curious if he'd changed any, afraid he wouldn't be the same—and just as afraid he would be.

Max looked up as she entered. She could tell by his expression that he questioned her judgment. Nothing new there. Everyone in this town had when she'd hooked up with Cordell years ago. Good girl gone bad. There had been a collective sigh of relief when Cordell had left before he'd done something ruinous like talk her into marrying him. Or worse, impregnated her with his bad seed.

Not that he'd ever asked her to marry him, she reminded herself. So she'd never know what her answer would have been. The thought made her stifle a laugh. Whom was she kidding? She would have married him, had his children and followed him to the ends of the earth if he had asked.

Max nodded to her, rose from his chair and handed her the key to his brother's cell door without another word on her decision. His expression relayed everything he had to say on that matter. "You know your way. Holler if you need me."

She nodded back and braced herself for seeing Cordell after all this time. She wasn't sure what shape she wanted him to be in. A lot could have happened to him over the years he'd been gone—probably mostly bad. But one look into those faded-denim blue eyes and she knew it wouldn't matter if he'd gone to pot, as her grandmother would have said.

The moment she opened the door to the cellblock, he looked in her direction. Clearly, he'd been waiting for her. She tried not to meet his eyes, but it was impossible as she let the door close behind her and walked toward his cell.

It wasn't the first time she'd seen him behind bars. She'd always doubted it would be the last. He'd never been arrested for more than a few misdemeanors. He wasn't criminal material. Instead, he grinned at trouble and dared it to take him on. Often it did, winning, not that he seemed to care.

"I've checked the warrants against you," she said as she approached his cell with his paperwork. "I spoke to the judge. He's willing to make the deal I told you about. You pay a fine and go free—as long as you leave the county."

"You look…amazing."

She glanced up from the paperwork she was holding, not surprised by his words but by the joy she heard in them. Her gaze met his, something she'd been hoping to avoid.

The look in his eyes threatened to buckle her knees. Damn, but he looked good. She would have thought he'd have aged more than he had.

She'd hoped he would have lost that mischievous twinkle in his eyes that kept her awake so many nights. She'd hoped that when he smiled, he wouldn't have that one dimple in his right cheek that made him look like the boy she'd fallen in love with.

He still had a full head of sandy-blond hair. It was actually shorter than it had been the last time she saw him. But everything else about him looked the same, from his broad shoulders, slim hips and long legs to that knee-buckling look in his eyes. Even the nonchalant way he stood was the same. He used to joke that nothing bothered him. And it had appeared that way, like water off a duck. Nothing ever stuck. She certainly hadn't, she reminded herself.

But even when they were very young, she'd sensed something dark under the surface with Cordell that felt to her like hurt and pain and disappointment, if not fear. After all, she only knew the twelve-year-old boy who'd shown up in Dry Gulch one day with his seventeen-year-old brother and a questionable story about where they'd been and why they were there alone.

"I just need you to sign the agreement and you're free to go," she said now, dragging her gaze away as she shoved the paper and pen through the bars. She could understand this man no more now than she could as a teenager. She just needed to steel her heart from getting battered again.

He took both the papers and the pen, looked down at them, then up at her again. "I've missed you," he said quietly. "I needed to leave to make my fortune, but I told you I'd be back so the two of us could be together." He grinned, that dimple in his cheek making her go soft inside.

She shook her head. He didn't look like a man who had made his fortune, but that had never mattered to her. But had he really thought he could walk back in and everything would be just as it was before he left? "Just sign the form, Cordell. You'll be leaving again soon anyway because that's what you do." She wished she had bitten her tongue and stopped herself from saying anything personal.

"I'm not leaving. I just have to help Max with something. I have some big plans."

She stared at him, reminded of that intense feeling she'd had on the porch. Something dark and dangerous. *Someone.* She'd thought it was personal and realized that if it had something to do with Cordell or Max, then yes, it was very personal.

"Unless you're planning to spend your time in Dry Gulch behind bars, sign the form. I'll tell the judge you need just a little time to get your affairs in order and then you'll be gone."

He looked as if he wanted to argue the point but nodded as if resigned. "Thank you for doing this."

"You'll be getting a bill for my services."

Cordell smiled at that, exposing that dimple again. But it was the glint in his blue eyes that made her weaken. "You do that, Josie. Good to see you."

"Just be careful," she said, making his smile broaden, his dimple deepening.

His gaze locked with hers. "I feel the same way about you, Josie. Just want the best for you. Maybe that's why I left. But now I'm back." He turned then to the papers.

She leaned against the cell bars, watching him sign, hating that hope tried to pry open her heart. Was he really back? As he handed her the papers and pen back, his fingers brushed hers. She did her best to hide the shiver that ran through her. But she felt her face flush and knew that he'd seen both because that dimple was back.

"Take care, Josie," he said as she walked out of the cell-block, closing the door behind her.

It wasn't until she handed Max the signed papers so he could release his brother that she saw her hand was shaking. She dropped the pen on his desk, avoiding his eyes.

Max glanced from her to the paperwork, then swore. "Did he say he was leaving town?"

"He said he wasn't. I'll tell the judge he needs a little time and then he will be gone. I already assured the judge I would make sure he leaves." She looked up then to meet the sheriff's gaze. "Why is he back?"

"Cordell didn't tell you?" he asked, sounding surprised, but also almost relieved.

She shook her head. "And I don't want to know." A lie. "He said it had to do with you."

Max grimaced. "You should know my brother by now. He tends to get carried away pretty easily."

Josie smiled at that, realizing that was something she loved about Cordell. "He definitely can be determined when he puts his mind to it." They smiled at each other for a few moments. "But I don't want him dragging you into whatever it is, Max. You've made a good life here. I plan to officiate at your wedding to Goldie one day."

He smiled at that, though it wasn't as bright as earlier. He was handsome like his brother but more serious and responsible. "You all right, Josie?"

"Why wouldn't I be all right?" she snapped and instantly regretted it. She liked Max. She'd always wished that Cordell was just a little like his older brother. "Sorry."

"We're all on edge, believe me."

She did. She stood, feeling the need to say something

more, but half-afraid of what might come out. If Cordell got out of jail and right back into trouble, he'd be calling her. All she had to do was wait.

Giving Max a nod, she headed for the door. The moment she stepped outside, she felt the dark malevolence even stronger now. With a chill, she knew that feeling was back again. Haranguing and haunting her like a demon. She just knew someone was coming for Dry Gulch. Coming for the two men she loved, one like a brother, the other like the lover he'd been. She couldn't bear to think she might lose them both.

Chapter Five

Max didn't know why he'd been putting it off. A lie. He knew exactly why. He was terrified that his brother might be right. The repercussions if true didn't just threaten his job and the life he'd built as well as Cordell's. If Roger Grimes was alive, then it threatened everything and everyone Max loved, including Goldie and the people of this town. If Grimes came to Dry Gulch, there would be collateral damage.

As he sat down at his computer, his fingers fumbled at the keys as he typed in the man's name. He'd hoped he'd never have to hear that name ever again—let alone go looking for him in the system. Roger Grimes was dead. Period.

He'd dreamed about that night for years. Each time, he relived the horror of what he'd felt forced to do. The problem was, in his nightmare when he went to check the man's pulse, he felt a heartbeat.

Max knew it was only his guilt. It was just a bad dream. It meant nothing. He kept telling himself that Grimes was dead and gone. He and Cordell had lived with what had happened that night as they'd tried to start a new life and heal from the past. Not that Max had ever forgotten. Nor had he healed. But he did everything he could to hide the fact.

He would regret what he'd had to do to his dying day. That he could act in such a cold-blooded way still terrified him and made him question what kind of man he was. It didn't matter that he was protecting his brother or that he hadn't meant to kill Grimes. It was what he and Cordell had done after the man was dead that still shocked him.

Instead of calling the law and making public the horror he and his brother had endured for years because of Grimes, Max had taken care of the situation in a way that went against everything he believed about himself. But the law hadn't helped them when they'd tried to stop the abuse. The law hadn't helped them when they'd been fighting for their lives, often not even bothering to drive out to where Max and his brother and mother lived with Grimes. The one time the cops did come out, Grimes assured them what he also told their mother. The boys needed discipline. He was just trying to step in and help their mother.

Now as Max typed in Roger Lloyd Grimes, he found himself praying that his brother was wrong. He'd spent all these years believing Grimes could no longer hurt them. That wouldn't be true if the man really was still alive.

The first thing that came up were old reports of Grimes and a series of small-time arrests for disturbing the peace, brawling outside a bar, threatening his former boss. There was his history of working at the state prison, then nothing, until he was arrested, did some jail time, then finally a seventeen-year prison sentence after he was convicted of bank robbery in Florida along with several accomplices.

Bank robbery? Max stared at the screen. This couldn't be right. Grimes was a small-time criminal at best. Some other criminal must have stolen his identity, robbed a bank and done the time. He knew there was only one way to verify it. Reluctantly, he called up the latest mug shot from

Florida hoping to see the face of a man pretending to be Roger Grimes. Instead, he felt ice water race up his spine.

There was no identity theft. Cordell was right. Max would know that face, those eyes, anywhere. Roger Grimes was alive. The bastard had somehow survived. Max couldn't imagine how it was possible. Only out of pure hatred and meanness, he thought. It was the only thing that made sense.

But why hadn't Grimes come after him and Cordell before now? He'd been behind bars for almost all of the past eighteen years except for one.

With a start, Max realized he probably had looked for the two of them during that time. But they had disappeared and there was a good chance that Roger hadn't involved law enforcement because he much preferred to operate under the radar. He'd always been involved in criminal behavior of some kind.

Which meant he'd gone on with his life, surviving the only way he knew how. Only now he was out of prison, a free man and, according to what Cordell had heard, he was coming for them after all these years.

Max had thought they were safe. They had gotten rid of Grimes's old pickup and taken off after that night with just the clothes on their backs. They'd borrowed some clothing off a clothesline at a farmhouse and then hitchhiked their way north. They had no idea where they were going. They were just running. Their last ride landed them in the out-of-the-way town of Dry Gulch, Montana. The small town in the eastern part of the state had seemed like the perfect place to start over, and it had been.

Max still found himself holding his breath as he scrolled down looking for the man's discharge date from prison. A part of him refused to believe Grimes was loose. When the date came up, he felt his stomach drop. Grimes had been released only days ago—just as Cordell had said—and without parole. The man was free and could be on his way to Montana.

The old familiar fear and loathing rushed at him, making him physically ill. Roger Grimes was alive and, even if he hadn't admitted to the world what his plans were for the future, Max knew he was coming for them. The only thing that had saved him and Cordell it seemed was that Grimes had gotten into trouble with the law before he could find them before now.

How he'd gotten to Florida from where they'd dumped his body, Max had no idea. Just as he had no idea how close Grimes might have gotten to finding them that year before he was arrested in Florida. Had a judge not thrown the book at Grimes and sentenced him to seventeen years, their stepfather might have found them sooner.

But had he found them? Max told himself that even though Cordell swore the man said he was going to look up his stepsons, that didn't mean he knew about Dry Gulch. Max quickly searched online for the interview of the released prisoners, needing to hear exactly what Grimes had said. His heart in his throat, he found the link and opened it.

He was instantly taken aback as his stepfather's face appeared. Max quickly froze the shot and turned down the volume. His heart raced at just the sight of this Roger Grimes, so different from his mug shot. The man had aged, looking rougher and meaner, but not that much. Then again, he hadn't been but twenty-five when he'd hooked up with their mother, who was twenty-nine. Max had been eleven, Cordell six at the time. They'd been told that their biological father had died in a mining accident. Max never knew if that was true.

Grimes had immediately convinced their mother that her boys needed discipline. She'd looked the other way as her husband taught her boys how things were going to be from that moment on. At some point, Max knew she must have known that if she crossed Roger, she'd get the same treatment her boys were getting. She'd only tried to leave him once—the night she disappeared.

Max closed his eyes, remembering his mother's fall down the stairs. He'd thought for sure Grimes had pushed her and there would be an investigation into her death. But Grimes had chased them back up to their room and locked them in, saying she was fine. The next morning, he told them that their mother had just been knocked out and when she'd come to, she'd decided to take a break from her always-misbehaving sons. He said that he'd helped her pack up her things and had given her a ride to town.

Max had known it was a lie, but there had been no sign of their mother. He figured Grimes had buried her and what few belongings she had somewhere on the property since there wasn't another house for miles out where they lived. He'd told the principal at school, who had called the authorities.

They came out, listened to Max's and Cordell's story and then Grimes's account. As they left, Grimes walked them to their car. Grimes had always been a large man who prided himself on being able to talk himself out of anything. Max never knew what else the man had told the law, but that was the last night the cops ever came out to the house.

He clenched his fist at the memory, so filled with hatred for the man that he felt sick to his stomach. On screen, Grimes looked as if he'd been lifting weights his entire sentence. His arms were massive. He stared into the camera as he spoke—just as Cordell had said.

It felt as if he were looking right at Max. His brother was right. Grimes was coming for them. A gauntlet thrown down, all of it directed at Max.

He closed the clip of the interview and put his head in his hands. He'd thought this was all behind them. He'd thought they were safe. But now Grimes wasn't just alive, he was out of prison and he and his violent temper and hatred were most likely making a beeline for Dry Gulch—just as Cordell had said. Retribution had shown in the man's dark eyes, a promise to destroy them and the lives they'd made for themselves.

Swearing under his breath, he tried to think. When they'd arrived in Dry Gulch, they'd told everyone that their mother had abandoned them. When she'd brought Grimes into his and Cordell's life, she had abandoned them to the violent man. It had cost her life. He hated to think what it had done to him and his brother.

On their own in Dry Gulch, a nice lady who ran a boardinghouse had taken them in and given them jobs around the property for their rent. She'd enrolled them in the local school and suggested that Max become his brother's guardian once he was eighteen, which he'd done. They'd been lucky to find a safe, soft place to land. They hadn't changed their names because they'd believed Grimes was dead.

Now Max realized how easily they could be found. He'd gone to the police academy and become the local sheriff. All through school, Cordell had excelled at sports, with newspaper and television stories highlighting his success across the state. A stranger in town asking about either of them would probably direct the man straight to the sheriff's office and Max.

Max had been smart enough not to take his stepfather's pickup after they'd dumped his body. They'd abandoned the truck and walked for miles, afraid even to hitchhike until they were out of Wyoming. But after that, they'd thought they were safe. Until now.

He thought of all the ways a man obsessed with vengeance could have continued to search for them while in prison with too much time on his hands. Max let out a bitter laugh as he realized that they'd put targets on their backs thinking Grimes was dead. Now the man could be headed for Dry Gulch. Hell, he thought, the man could already be here.

Standing, Max looked out at the main street as if he wouldn't have been surprised to see him standing on the sidewalk out front.

"You want me to get our prisoner dinner?" his deputy asked, startling him.

"No, I'll take care of it." Max had to see Goldie. For eighteen years, Max had kept his and Cordell's past a close-held secret. Not that he'd tell Goldie about any of this now. He couldn't help the shame and embarrassment he felt, for his mother, himself and his brother. No one could understand what their childhoods had been like, nor did he want them to try.

Yet people kept wondering why he hadn't married her and started a family. They didn't know how dark his past was. Ashamed of that time, Max had never wanted anyone to know what Grimes had done to them. Nor could he have proved Grimes had killed their mother and gotten rid of her body. He'd been a kid, helpless to do anything but try to survive. He'd felt he had no options even after that night. Go to the law in Montana back when he was seventeen? How could he when he couldn't prove any of it. Not to mention, at the time he believed he'd killed Grimes.

Max realized that he still had no options. Grimes had

been released. He hadn't threatened either Max or Cordell. Yet. The only way to prove just how dangerous Grimes was would mean that one or both of them were already dead.

All Max could do was wait. But as he did, he had to ask himself: How far was he prepared to go to protect himself and his brother as well as this quiet little town he called home—and the woman he loved?

He already knew the answer. It was why his brother hadn't come back just to warn him. Cordell knew they were in this together—just as they'd been as kids. They both knew how this would end.

Chapter Six

Max couldn't get the image of Grimes out of his mind. Cordell was right. Grimes had looked as terrifying as he remembered. Was there any doubt he was on his way to Montana—or what he planned to do when he got here?

Max sighed and headed for the cellblock. He'd made a point of giving Cordell some time to himself after Josie left. One look at his brother, though, and there was no doubt that seeing his old flame after all this time had hit him hard. Max had never understood how Cordell could have walked away from everything good in his life, this town, his brother, let alone Josie—the best thing that had ever happened to him. He couldn't imagine what it had taken Cordell to do that—let alone come back now.

He suspected, though, that Cordell had thought he was doing what was best for everyone. That, at least, Max could understand. His brother hadn't been ready to commit to anything, let alone anyone, even Josie.

After Cordell had left Dry Gulch six years ago, Max had been shaken, afraid the solid ground they'd found here wasn't as solid as he'd thought. He was sure that was why he'd picked a fight with Goldie and tried to break it off then, thinking his brother was right. How could either he or his brother get serious about anyone and not tell them the truth?

Goldie had listened patiently to all the reasons they couldn't be together and seemed to take the breakup well enough. Then three days later, she'd cornered him and told him that everything he'd said was pure bull.

"I'm not going anywhere, Max Lander, and one day you're going to marry me."

He'd tried to argue, but she wouldn't hear it.

"I love you and nothing can change that," she'd said. "At least you didn't leave town like your brother. But he'll be back. I have no idea what the two of you are so afraid of, but I'm sticking by you whether you like it or not."

A week later, she'd stopped by his place with a piece of his favorite pie. A week after that, she'd brought over a stray dog she'd found and asked him to just take care of it until she could find a place to live that allowed dogs.

By the end of that month, she and the dog were living at his place. He couldn't even say exactly how it had happened, yet he hadn't tried to push her away again. But nor had he asked her to marry him.

There had been moments, though, when he'd wanted to so badly to give her the one thing he knew they both wanted. But marriage and a family were the two things he had feared he couldn't offer. How could he give her that knowing that his life since seventeen had been a lie—let alone what he'd done before showing up in Dry Gulch.

Now looking at his brother, he still didn't want to believe that Grimes was alive. It felt surreal, a nightmare in the harsh light of day. Worse, he didn't know what he was going to do about it. Hadn't he always known that if the man had lived, he would come after them with blood in his eye?

Goldie couldn't be around when that happened. Neither could Josie. If Grimes even thought that he and Cordell had women they cared about, he'd make them his targets.

His brother looked as bad as Max felt. "You didn't tell her, did you?"

Cordell shook his head. "Josie wasn't interested in anything I had to say."

"I figured it might be rough seeing her."

"I've been through worse," his brother said but Max didn't buy it.

"I'm glad you didn't say anything to her about Grimes. We need to talk about that, but first I'm going to go get your dinner. You cozy enough?"

"Like a bug in a rug. Max, we may not have much time."

He nodded, feeling the clock ticking. "You need to stay put for now." He started to turn to leave, but his brother's words stopped him.

"You can't keep acting like this isn't happening. And you can't leave me in here to be killed like a fish in a barrel. I've been thinking about it. We have to find Grimes and take care of him."

"You do realize you're talking to an officer of the law, right?"

"I'm talking to my *brother*. You know as well as I do what will happen if he finds us. No one we care about will be safe."

Max shook his head, even though he knew his brother was right. Cordell had come back to face his past even with several warrants against him. His brother thought they were going to do this together—just as they had as boys.

"You know there is only one way this can end," Cordell persisted.

"I thought that last time and look how that turned out," Max said.

"Another reason it makes sense not to wait until he turns up in Dry Gulch. We need to catch him down the road. We need the element of surprise on our side," his brother said.

Max thought of the large violent man who'd beaten them almost to death when they were younger. After seeing the new and improved Roger Grimes after years in prison, he doubted the outcome even if they had the element of surprise on their side.

Worse, while the man had aged over the years, Grimes had always been as strong as he was mean. And now he looked in better shape. Add to that, their so-called stepfather was a dirty fighter, wily and vicious. Now bloodthirsty and full of vengeance, nothing could stop the man except lead, maybe a lot of it, Max thought.

"If we just happened to catch him between here and Florida?" he asked his brother.

"Maybe we'll get lucky, Max. We know he's coming. All we have to do is figure out which route—"

Were they really talking about catching Grimes somewhere on his way to Montana from Florida and killing him? Last time had been self-defense. If Max hadn't stopped Grimes, he would have killed Cordell, then him. He'd never seen the man that out of control.

Over the years, Max had told himself that he regretted not convincing the authorities and taking his chances all those years ago. But back then the stakes had been too high. He'd had to protect his brother, who had no one but him. Not to mention the cops had let him and his brother down before. He'd been afraid he and Cordell could go to prison for life. So, they'd gotten rid of the body. Or at least thought they had.

"Max, we need to go, and we need to go soon if we're going," Cordell said.

Cordell's plan was nothing short of harebrained. But at least it was a plan. Max wished he had one, other than waiting for Grimes to get picked up by the law and never reach Montana. It felt like wishful thinking at best. But calling in a BOLO without a reason would only make Max look suspicious.

"Isn't he on parole?" his brother asked. "Won't he be arrested the minute he's caught leaving Florida?"

Max shook his head. "Not everyone who is released from prison is put on parole. He served all of his sentence, so now he's free."

"So nothing can be done about him until he kills one of us," Cordell said. "With a record like his, how could they let him go like that? They must hope he leaves Florida and isn't their problem anymore."

What Max found odd was that the money from the bank robbery had never been retrieved. If Grimes knew where it was, he could have made a deal for a shorter sentence. Unless he was planning on getting out and spending the money. Was it possible Grimes didn't know that would get him sent back to prison?

It was the not knowing what the man had planned that would keep Max up at night. "I'll be back," he told Cordell, feeling the same urgency he heard in his brother's voice. The last thing he wanted was for Grimes to get to Dry Gulch. If there was a way to stop him… "I'm going to pick up dinner. We can talk when I get back with our meals." He started to turn and leave. Having second thoughts, he tossed his brother the key to his cell.

Cordell caught it and smiled. "I'll be here when you get

back. I'm not going anywhere, but thanks. It's at least a step up from being a dead fish in a barrel."

As Max left, he realized that if Grimes somehow got to his brother in jail, it would mean his deputy and dispatcher were already dead.

There would no doubt be collateral damage if Grimes ever reached Dry Gulch. He told himself that if Grimes had done what Cordell had and driven straight through to Dry Gulch, he wouldn't be fool enough to attack during the day on a main street. But after dark, all bets were off.

Not that Grimes couldn't be close by. He could be waiting just outside of town at Max's house for him.

The same house he shared with Goldie.

GOLDIE COULDN'T HELP her smile as Max walked into the café. Just the sight of him always made her smile. He was a big handsome man with a heart bigger than Montana and she loved him just as much. But she was no fool. She knew he had demons. She'd lain next to him afraid to wake him from the horrible nightmares that had him screaming.

She'd never mentioned the nightmares to him. Max liked to think he was a mystery to her and everyone else. Whatever haunted him had something to do with his brother, as well. She had seen the worry when Cordell had left. Now he looked even more concerned. Because of Cordell's return?

The two Lander men had a past they never talked about, one Goldie feared would eventually catch up to them. Was that why Max looked so scared, the weight of whatever it was riding on his wide shoulders? Or did it have something to do with Cordell's return?

Max loved his brother but the two of them had gone in separate directions, Cordell wanting to break every rule, his older brother determined to make himself a law-and-order life. He'd started out as a deputy and then run for sheriff. Everyone in town loved him, so he'd won by a landslide. He was the only law in this part of the county and took his job sometimes more seriously than he did Goldie.

But she loved him for it, she thought as she watched him take a seat in an empty booth away from everyone—instead of a spot at the counter like he normally did. Worried, she joined him. Did he just want peace and quiet? Or did he want to continue their argument from earlier?

"Get you something to drink?" she asked quietly.

He raised his head to look at her and what she saw in his eyes made her stomach drop. "I need you to move in with your cousin."

She stared at him, the words not making any sense. Not this again. She'd hoped after their last breakup that they were moving in the right direction toward marriage and kids and a life together. She'd given him some time, then they'd found their way back together. She'd moved a few things into his house and soon she was living there again. He'd certainly not said anything as they'd gotten closer.

Until now.

Was that what he was afraid of? How close they'd gotten living together? "Are you going tell me why?" she asked as she dropped into the booth across from him, her legs shaking.

He looked so pained it made her heart hurt. "I just need you to move out as soon as possible. Today."

She tried to find words, only coming up with, "Is this about Cordell? Is he moving in?"

Max shook his head, then his gaze met hers and held

it. "As much as I hate doing this…" She saw him swallow before he finished. "I need you to give me some space."

"For how long?" she asked, her words heavy with emotion.

"I don't know. I don't know what the future holds, but I need you to do this. I'm sorry."

She leaned back in the booth across from him, her pulse a thunder in her ears as her heart threatened to break. She fought to keep her voice down when she wanted to yell to the rafters. She'd been so patient with him. She could only guess at the life he'd had before arriving in Dry Gulch, he and his brother looking like the orphans they apparently were.

She cleared her voice. "We've been going out for years, living together the last four. How much slower could we have moved, Max?"

"Goldie, please don't—"

"Please don't what, Max? You've had plenty of time. Why don't you admit what's really happening here. You're breaking up with me. *Again*."

"I don't want to keep doing this to you," he said, his voice rough with emotion. "I should have never let it get this far."

She took a ragged breath as the impact of the words hit home. *This man is never going to marry you.* She'd only been fooling herself thinking he needed time. While she didn't know everything about his dark past, she knew enough from the horrible nightmares she'd witnessed and always pretended she hadn't.

Letting out the breath, she rose from the booth and looked down at this man she'd loved from as far back as she could remember. "You're right about one thing. You can't keep doing this to me."

CORDELL HAD BEEN looking forward to Goldie's dinner special, so he wasn't thrilled when his brother entered the cellblock empty-handed. Then he saw Max's expression and knew. "What did you do? You broke up with Goldie."

His brother merely grunted in reply as he motioned him out of the cell.

Max had always been the coolheaded one, the person he knew he could trust with his life. "I'm so sorry." Cordell hated this. Goldie and Max belonged together, yet he understood why his brother had held off on marriage. "In all this time together, you've never told Goldie the truth about your past?"

His brother shot him a look that made it crystal clear he had not. Nor did he ever plan to tell her. "I'd suggest you keep your distance from Josie, as well."

Cordell let out an amused laugh. "Like that is going to be a problem. She doesn't seem to want much to do with me. If anything."

"It's for the best right until this is over," Max said.

He wondered if Goldie would feel that way when it was over. "I can see this is tearing you up," Cordell said. "Couldn't you have at least told her what's going on?"

"No," Max snapped. "She'd want to get her gun and be part of a standoff against the man. I don't have to tell you, do I, that Josie would be the same way. Everyone in this town has to believe that I broke it off with Goldie. It's the only way I can protect her."

He could see that there was no changing his brother's mind. "I'm sorry, but I really wish you'd told her *after* you picked up our dinner."

Max cursed in answer. "You can really think of food at a time like this?"

"Yeah, I've always been like this, hungry. I think it's

from going without in the past." He fell silent for a moment. Like Max, he'd thought all of this with Grimes was behind them. "You know he's on his way here."

Max sighed, thinking about his brother being like a fish in a barrel locked up here. "Come on, you're coming with me," he said, and led the way out of the sheriff's department and into the twilight. The sky around them darkened as they walked down the nearly deserted street.

Cordell felt his stomach growl as he matched his brother's long-legged steps with his own. "Max, everyone is going to know about our past if Grimes comes to Dry Gulch for us." His brother grunted in answer. "Where are we going?" he asked, moving fast to keep up. As hungry as he was, he said, "I'm not sure going to the café's a good idea all things considered."

"*We're* not going to the café. *You* are."

Cordell shot a look at his brother. Max tossed him the keys to his pickup with the rented trailer still parked on the street.

"When you get through eating, drive up to my house. Park it in the back. But I don't want to see you for at least thirty minutes."

He felt a jolt. "You think he's already here, maybe waiting for you at the house?" He started to argue that he didn't want Max going alone but changed his mind at the steely glint in his brother's eyes as well as the star on his chest and the weapon on his hip. The sheriff's look said he'd lock him in a cell again if he gave him any trouble. "I am hungry."

Max shook his head. "I can hear your stomach growling from here. Thirty minutes, Cordell. Park in the back."

THE SHERIFF WAITED until Cordell disappeared into the café before he started back up the street. Max figured that if

Grimes was already in town, he'd be waiting for him at the house. He'd started toward the sheriff's department, where he'd left his truck that morning when he got the call.

"A man who says he's your father is on the line," the dispatcher told him. "Says it's urgent."

Max felt as if he'd been punched in the throat. For a moment, he couldn't speak. "I'll be right there." He hurried the last few yards, pushing through the door and heading straight for his office. "Put the call through," he said to the dispatcher.

His phone was already ringing as he closed the door and headed for his desk. He tried to steady himself, to breathe, but it was as if all the air had been sucked out of him. "This is Sheriff Lander," he said as he took the call, surprised how calm his voice sounded.

The raspy voice on the other end of the line let out a chuckle, bringing back a nightmare of horrible memories. "How ya doin', son?"

"I'm not your son."

Grimes's laugh still had that promise of imminent violence. "I think we should meet and talk about old times."

"Why would we do that?" Max asked as he slowly lowered himself into his chair, all the time aware of the danger looming at the other end of the call. "I've spent years trying to forget you and those old times. I want nothing to do with you."

"Funny, but I just can't forget the last time I saw you and your brother," the man said.

"Too bad it really wasn't the last time."

The laugh this time had an edge to it that told Max that Grimes was about to get to the point of the call. "You know I never told anyone about that night."

"I would imagine not. Who would believe you given your criminal record?"

A tense silence followed, then Grimes quit trying to be friendly. "Guess you don't want to know where your mama is, then?"

Max gripped the phone so hard his fingers ached. "You're finally admitting that you killed her and buried her where she couldn't be found?"

"I told you she was fine when she left that night. She'd had enough of the two of you. But I did track her down while I was in the slammer. I can tell you where she is. But you'll have to come home since I really want to see you and your brother. We have some issues to resolve, don't you think?"

"*Home?* You can't mean that shack in the middle of nowhere, Wyoming, where you took your meanness out on us, keeping us prisoners there so you could terrorize us." Grimes had picked the place, he realized now, because there wasn't another house for miles. They'd been alone and trapped with a psychopath.

"I guess we remember it differently, but you were young." Did Grimes worry that Max was recording this call? Was that why he was being so careful? "Son, I really want to see you. Why don't you and Cordell take a ride down here? Or I can come to Dry Gulch. I'd like to meet Goldie. And now Cordell's back. Heard his high school sweetheart, Josie, is an attorney? I would imagine they'll get back together, don't you?"

He knew about Goldie and Josie? Max felt his heart threaten to burst from his chest. Had he really thought getting Goldie out of his house would protect her? It hit him again. Where the hell was Grimes getting his information?

"I think the two of you should come home for this reunion," the man was saying. "I can meet your girlfriends later. Unless you're inviting me to Dry Gulch." He chuckled. "It's just as well. I'm not planning to stay long down here so I hope to see you at the old homestead by tonight. Otherwise, I guess I'll have to make the trip up to Dry Gulch."

"You do know that threatening an officer of the law will get you sent back to prison, right?"

"Threatening?" He howled with laughter. "I just want to see my boys one last time. I'm not as young as I used to be. That's why I'm heading out to the West Coast after our reunion. I liked the sunshine down in Florida but that was about all." He chuckled again. "See you soon."

Max started to speak but realized Grimes had already hung up. He slammed down the phone and swore. Grimes had been so careful not to threaten them outright, but he'd gotten his message across loud and clear.

Chapter Seven

"Max broke up with Goldie," Amy Sue announced the moment Josie returned to the ranch with the news. *"Again?* What is wrong with him? Clancy called to say that she'd help Goldie get her things out of the house and now Goldie is staying in her cousin's spare room. That poor woman. I can't understand why she puts up with him."

Josie nodded, upset with the situation, as well. "She loves him," she said simply. Goldie had been in tears when she'd called. While upset with Max, Josie was more worried about the premonition that still swirled her like a storm cloud. "We should hold off on criticizing Max until we know what's going on."

Her sister made a rude noise followed by a curse word that would have sent their gram looking for a bar of soap to wash out her mouth. "This happened when Cordell left. Now he's back. What a coincidence."

Josie agreed this had something to do with Cordell and why he'd come back and said he couldn't leave, but she didn't share it with Amy Sue. Nor had she told her that she'd felt trouble coming. Her sister had always mocked her premonitions. Foolishly, it was probably out of jealousy. Josie only wished she would be blissfully unaware.

What worried her was the strength of her knowing had been so strong and had felt so personal. She should have known it had something to do with Cordell, the man who'd stolen her heart and broken it. What she hadn't expected was that whatever trouble he'd brought back would sweep up Max into the maelstrom, especially this quickly.

It could only mean that Max was now somehow involved in whatever was going on. She thought about Cordell's pickup and the enclosed small trailer that he'd brought back. They'd already had a call that he'd moved it from where it had been parked along Main Street. It was now apparently parked behind Max's house. Max and Cordell had been the topic of conversation from the moment Cordell had driven into town.

"I suspect you know what's going on," Amy Sue said, squinting her eyes at Josie. "You spoke with Cordell at the jail earlier, right?"

"All he told me was that he was staying in town. He indicated he had something he had to do and couldn't leave." He'd wanted to talk more, but she hadn't let him.

Her sister made another rude noise. "Well, I heard Max told Rance that he might be gone for a couple of days. Why would he tell his deputy that if he wasn't leaving town? Come on, Josie, you know it must have something to do with Cordell. Everyone is blaming him since Max and Goldie were fine—until your old boyfriend shows up." Her sister made the relationship Josie had with Cordell sound like puppy love. He was the love of her life. But after he left, she'd been afraid that he would never return.

Now she'd sensed something dark was still haunting both men and it was why neither of them had settled down with the women they loved. Seeing Cordell today in the jail, she'd known that he still loved her as passionately as she did him. It had broken her heart since while she was capable of getting him out of jail, she hadn't been able to heal the wounded past inside him that made him want to run away.

"Everyone is blaming Cordell for whatever is going on," Amy Sue was saying. "I can understand why you're worried about Max. Who knows what his brother has gotten him into."

Of course the town was blaming Cordell, Josie thought. He had been blamed for everything for years. Not that he'd made any effort to mend his ways. She smiled despite herself. There had always been that devilment of a twinkle in his eye from the first time she laid eyes on him. It had been his bad-boy persona that had attracted her like metal to magnet.

He and his older brother had just appeared in town as if blown in by the wind. They'd both just been boys with apparently nothing to their names. They'd moved into elderly Iris Mason's boardinghouse on the edge of town. Iris had a habit of taking in strays and she and her sister, Esther, ran what today might have been called a bed-and-breakfast. With Iris's help, the brothers started school and had been in Dry Gulch ever since—until Cordell had left six years ago. Max had stayed, gone to the police academy and come back to go to work as a deputy, then sheriff.

Josie often had forgotten that they hadn't lived here their whole lives. She felt as if she'd always known the two of them. Maybe because she'd always sensed their pain. Fortunately, the community had taken them in just as Iris had. As far as she knew, no one had ever heard anything about their family—if they had any—or why they'd shown up, just the two of them, alone. Cordell had never been forthcoming about his life before Dry Gulch.

Amy Sue was right. It was Max's behavior now that caused Josie the most concern. It wasn't like him. Maybe worse, Cordell was involved. It spelled the worst kind of trouble and made her even more anxious than she had been. Had it been legal trouble, Cordell would have to come to her, and Max would have had no reason to break up with Goldie, her instincts told her.

She felt that darkness she'd sensed grow even heavier. What kind of trouble were the Lander men in? Something from their past.

"I'm sorry," her sister said as if sensing how worried and upset Josie was. "At least you got to see Cordell before he leaves again. You know you're right about him not sticking around long. Clancy Roberts called to say Cordell's truck and trailer are no longer parked on the main street."

She heard a told-you-so in her sister's voice but ignored it. "I'm more worried about Max right now," she said truthfully. Maybe Cordell was in more trouble than she knew and now he'd dragged his brother into it. She mentally kicked herself for cutting Cordell off when he'd tried to talk to her.

"How's Goldie doing?" Amy Sue asked.

"She's heartbroken and angry. She went to Max's house, where she'd been living, and took what she needed to stay with her cousin for a while. Clancy has room and will see that she's okay. I'll help anyway I can."

"She's lucky to have such a good friend in you," her sister said.

Josie glanced out the window at the mountains in the distance, wondering what was nagging at her. She knew how Goldie must feel since Josie had been left behind by the younger Lander brother. She considered what to do. Her workload was never very heavy even though she'd taken to doing pro bono cases from across the state. They kept her busier than the paying ones, which was fine with her. She had everything she needed or wanted. She thought of Cordell. Maybe not everything, she amended.

At the sound of a text, she checked her phone and froze. Max had sent her a message along with a mug shot of a man who turned her blood to ice.

"I know it's late, but I'm going to go into town and check on Goldie," she said as she reached for a bottle of wine from the cupboard. "I'll probably stay the night there."

By the time his brother finished his meal and drove his truck and rented trailer out to the house, Max had searched the area, as well as inside. No Grimes. Yet he still felt jumpy.

He kept replaying the phone call. Was he really waiting for them down at the old homestead? With a sigh, Max knew he couldn't take the chance that the man hadn't been lying. He knew what his brother would have said, "Let's go get him!"

With a shake of his head, he made the call to the Rawlins, Wyoming, Sheriff's Department. He had to trust that the law wouldn't fail them like it had when he and Cordell were kids.

"You have a BOLO out on a Roger Grimes," he said to Deputy Hal Green. "I think I know where you can find him." He gave all the information to him on how to get to the old homestead.

"So out in the middle of nowhere miles from here," the deputy said with a sigh. "Sounds like a long drive. How exactly did you come by this information?"

Max had known the question was coming. As badly as he wanted to stay completely out of this, Grimes hadn't left him any choice. "He called me."

"He *called* you?"

"He lived with us when I was a kid. He was abusive to my brother and me. I have every reason to believe he killed my mother and buried her out there somewhere."

Silence, then, "You told all this to the sheriff at the time?"

"Unfortunately, the sheriff sent deputies out to our place several times. They believed Grimes, not us boys, so no, I didn't call him. I had no proof and, quite frankly, I didn't trust him." He feared he might have said too much.

"I see that this perp just got out of prison a few days ago," Deputy Green said. "You really think he's been driving up here all this time?"

"I do." Max feared the deputy was trying to talk himself out of driving up to the homestead to see if Grimes was there. "I believe he is driving a gray van. He'll be armed. If you check Grimes's rap sheet, you'll only see his criminal behavior. I'd take another deputy with you. This man is dangerous."

The deputy chuckled. "Never ran across a dangerous one before."

Max bit his tongue. "You'll let me know when you find him?"

"Yep," the deputy said, and the connection went dead.

Chapter Eight

Cordell opened the back door of Max's house and stopped short. His brother had been on the phone, but now turned abruptly and went for his gun. Recognizing him, Max relaxed, but Cordell had seen the fear on his face.

"What's happened?" he demanded as he stepped in. He could tell that his brother didn't want to tell him. "Max?"

He watched him sigh and remove his hand from the weapon strapped to his hip. He said, "I'm going to tell you, but you can't go off half-cocked and go racing down to Wyoming, guns blazing."

Cordell listened as his brother first told him what he'd learned about Roger Grimes, ending with the phone call.

"What? That son of a— We have to go get him."

"Easy. Don't you think I want to? But I'm the law and I'm taking care of it," Max said.

"How?" Cordell demanded.

"I called the Rawlins Sheriff's Department."

He scoffed at that. "I remember how helpful they were in the past."

"The sheriff's out for a week, but a deputy named Hal Green took the information. I'm hoping he'll go there and check."

Cordell shook his head and moved to drop onto the couch. "So we do nothing but wait for him to come after us?"

"I know you'd rather go to Wyoming and get yourself killed."

"Or wait here like sitting ducks," he offered as he reached for his phone. "After what you told me, I need to warn Josie."

Max stopped him. "Let's give the law down in Rawlins a chance first. If they pick him up for spending the robbery money, he'll be sent back to Florida. No reason to worry Josie."

"But for how long? He's already served his time for the actual robbery."

He could see that his brother knew he was right. But Max was digging his heels in. "I'm going over to the office, then patrol town. Stay here. Keep the doors locked. This could all be over in a matter of hours. Call me if there is any trouble."

Cordell shook his head and got to his feet. "I'm not sitting here and waiting. But first I am going to call Josie. She needs to know. I'm telling her everything."

"No," his brother said, stepping to him. "Why frighten her when it could be over soon?"

"You just don't want anyone in Dry Gulch to know," Cordell said. "Max, people are going to find out about us and Roger Grimes. I know you've always believed it would just be our terrible secret, but the truth is going to come out now."

"Let's not forget what we did," Max said.

"Let's not forget what he did to us!"

"I haven't forgotten, as hard as I've tried," his brother snapped.

"Then you know what he's capable of doing. Roger knows where we are and who we love. We have to warn them." Cordell hated the way his voice cracked with the fear he felt to his very core that his past might harm the woman he loved, had always loved. "That psycho threatened Josie and Goldie."

"I told you. He didn't."

"Only because he's smart enough to worry that you might be recording the conversation. Max, you know what he was saying. He's coming for them just as he's coming for us."

He saw the muscle jump in his brother's jaw, an expression of fury on Max's face. "Of course I know. I've already stuck our necks out by sending the sheriff's department in Rawlins out to the homestead."

Cordell shook his head. "There's no keeping a lid on this." He looked down at the phone in his hand. "Josie needs to know and you can't—"

"Give me your phone."

His gaze shot up to his brother's. "You seriously going to do this?" He and his brother hadn't wrestled for years, let alone fought, but there was no way he was handing over the phone.

With a sigh, Max said, "I promise we'll warn them, but let's wait to see what the deputy down in Wyoming finds out at the homestead, okay?"

"And if Roger isn't there?"

"Goldie probably isn't taking my calls," Max said. "But I'll call Josie myself and warn her. She'll tell Goldie. Let me tell her what I hope will keep them both safe until we know more."

"You need to tell them *everything*. They have to know how dangerous Roger Grimes—"

"They'll believe it when it comes from the sheriff."

Cordell took a breath, reminding himself that his brother the sheriff was respected in the community of Dry Gulch. He, on the other hand, was the kid-brother screwup who'd left town under extenuating circumstances. He had to let him handle this. "That deputy better call soon or I'm going to find Josie and tell her everything," he said as he pocketed his phone.

His brother looked relieved.

"You do realize I'm not staying here to wait, right?"

Max sighed. "Come on, then."

"DON'T WANT TO talk about it," Goldie said when Josie showed up at her door. "I don't need any help, either. But I might take a glass of that wine you brought."

She'd been in a daze for hours wandering around her cousin's house, unable to concentrate. Clancy had a date she'd threatened to cancel to stay home with her, but Goldie wouldn't allow it. "Go, have fun. I'm fine."

But she wasn't fine, so she'd been glad to see Josie drive up. Her best friend knew what she needed. Wine and company. The breakup had come out of nowhere. She and Max had been doing so well together for so long. She hadn't pushed him about making it permanent because she hadn't wanted to rock the boat. She'd felt they were headed in that direction, and she didn't want to corner him with an ultimatum.

It wasn't her style. She'd told herself that she didn't need a ring on her finger or a marriage certificate on her wall. But now she knew there had been something she had needed. A sign that he was as invested as she was in this relationship. Clearly, if he'd given her one, she'd missed it.

She blamed herself for not getting that clarity she

needed. Had she, Max wouldn't have been able to blind-side her. She would have known he wasn't in it for the long haul. She blamed herself. She'd been too afraid to find out how he really felt about her and he'd been afraid to be honest with her a long time ago. They were both cowards. Maybe he wasn't the man she'd thought he was. Or the woman she knew she could be.

Josie held the wine bottle up. "If there's anything else you want…"

Goldie shook her head as she watched her friend get glasses from the kitchen and pour them both some wine.

"I saw Max leaving his house on my way in, Cordell with him," her friend said and handed her a glass.

Goldie held it up, frowning at how little wine was in the glass. She looked to her friend for an explanation.

"Cordell's rented trailer is behind the house," Josie said and drained her glass. "I really want to see what's in that trailer now while they're gone."

It was the last thing she'd expected her friend to say. "I really don't want to get caught out there."

"Me, either," Josie said with a laugh. "That's why we have to move fast."

"I don't even want to ask what you're suggesting," Goldie said and downed the wine. "Isn't there a padlock on that trailer? You aren't seriously going to break in."

"We're just going to take a look. Your cousin must have a hammer and a crowbar around here, right?"

Armed with the hammer and crowbar, Josie drove them out to Max's house. Goldie used her key to go in and turn on the back porch light, but she'd also brought out a flash-light that Max kept by the door. She now held the beam on the padlock as Josie went to work.

She made a point of not looking around the house. Earlier she'd come over when she knew Max wasn't home and had taken just what she needed for a few days. She told herself Max would change his mind by then.

Now, outside shivering in the cold, she watched her friend break the lock. As Josie removed the padlock, she looked over at her before she opened the door.

As it swung open, the flashlight beam illuminated just enough of the cavernous dark interior to see what was inside. *"What?"* was the only word Goldie got out as her flashlight beam fell on the statue of the town's most famous horse. *"How?"*

"Cordell," Josie said with a curse and laugh. "I suspected he stole Big Blue before he left town for whatever reason at the time." She was shaking her head still looking amused.

"I don't think it's that funny. That missing statue had almost caused a turf war with our neighboring rival county, as I recall. What I don't understand is why he'd bring it back," Goldie said, feeling confused and wishing she'd had either more wine or a lot less.

"Because he's Cordell." Josie said, still smiling. "It's his way of saying he's sorry. He's trying to make amends for being Dry Gulch's bad boy."

"You mean he's trying to get back in your good graces," her friend said.

"Maybe a little of that, too," Josie admitted.

"So what are we going to do now?"

"We're going to get a couple of men in town to help us put Big Blue back where he goes tonight and never breathe a word of this to anyone." Josie pulled out her phone. "I have a favor," she said into the phone when it was answered.

Goldie tuned out the rest of the phone conversation as

she hugged herself against the cold night. She would never understand men, she thought.

It wasn't until the trailer was empty and they were alone again in her cousin Clancy's living room that Josie filled their glasses with wine and sat down.

"I don't know exactly what is going on, but I think it has something to do with before Max and Cordell showed up in Dry Gulch," Josie said. "Max sent me a message earlier along with a photo and a warning I know he wanted me to share with you." She pulled out her phone and handed it to her friend.

Goldie's eyes widened as she looked at the mug shot. "Who is Roger Grimes and why would Max send you this?"

Josie shook her head. "All I know is that he's dangerous and he might be coming to Dry Gulch."

Goldie shivered and looked away from the man's face. "You think that's why Max wanted me here with Clancy instead of at the house?"

"I do. Max might be trying to protect you." Josie took back her phone and pocketed it. "He wants us to watch out for this man just in case." She picked up her glass and took a sip of her wine, hesitating before she asked, "What did Max tell you about his life before he and Cordell came here?"

Josie's question made her realize how little she actually knew about Max. All evening, she had kept telling herself Max wouldn't do this to her. She knew him, really knew him. But did she?

She remembered that teenage boy who'd shown up in Dry Gulch out of the blue with his little brother and little else. There had been a haunted look in his eyes. She'd seen that same look earlier at the café when he'd broken up with her.

THE TOWN OF Dry Gulch was small and quiet normally, Max thought as he and Cordell patrolled. Tonight, though, it felt like a ghost town. Max couldn't shake how anxious he was feeling waiting for the sheriff's department out of Rawlins to call with news.

The two of them had driven around the area looking for a van with probably Florida plates. He had wanted his brother to stay at the house, but it was clear he wasn't going to. Also, Max had realized he couldn't leave him alone—not until Grimes was caught.

They'd been coming down the main drag when the call was patched through to him from the Rawlins Sheriff's Department.

"Went out there," Deputy Green said. "Hell of a long way up there. What a desolate place. You lived *there*?"

"Did you find Grimes?" Max said impatiently.

"No sign of anyone. Didn't look as if a soul has been there for a very long time."

His hope died as he disconnected. Max had known this would have only put off the inevitable. If they had found Grimes, arrested him and taken him back to Florida, he would eventually get out of prison again. If he made a deal and returned the money, he might be out even sooner and then he'd be coming for them. This nightmare wasn't over.

Cordell must have seen how defeated he felt. "What are we going to do?"

"I'm already out on a limb," Max said as he drove down the street, pulled up in front of the sheriff's office and parked.

"I'm afraid to ask," Cordell said, looking from the sheriff's department to his brother. "You're not planning to lock me up again, are you?"

Max shook his head and opened his door. "I'm going to deputize you."

It wasn't until they returned to the house that Max saw the broken padlock and the empty trailer, the door standing ajar. For a moment, he thought Grimes might already be here. But he couldn't imagine the man taking Dry Gulch's famous horse statue. Then he looked at his brother and swore as the truth hit him. "This has Josie's name written all over it," he said.

"Josie?" Cordell echoed.

"The woman you call when you're in trouble. The woman who's always been there for you." Max shook his head. "Want to bet where we're going to find Big Blue?"

"How could she pull something like that off?" Cordell asked but he was smiling.

"Because she's Josie Brand, a woman who has proven quite capable of looking out for those she cares about—including you. Let's go see if I'm right."

Back in the patrol pickup, they drove down to find Big Blue had been returned to its resting place.

"Josie is something, isn't she?" Cordell said quietly. "It's why I have to warn her about Roger."

"I already sent Grimes's mug shot to her," he said as they drove back toward the office. His brother started to argue, but he cut him off. "I've been sheriff for most of the time that you've been gone from town. Let me handle this." He made the call, terrified of what could happen to the women if they weren't prepared for what was coming since he feared he wasn't going to be able to protect them.

"Josie, it's Max."

Chapter Nine

Josie knew the moment she heard Max's voice. It had taken her a moment to answer the call because Goldie had been shaking her head, whispering, "If it's Max, I don't want to talk to him." She nodded and waved her friend off as she stepped out of the living room. Since arriving back at Goldie's cousin's house, Josie had been waiting for Max's call after the text and mug shot he'd sent earlier.

Her vision had gone dark when she looked into the man's eyes. Was this what she'd seen coming? Was he what they all had to fear? "Tell me who Roger Grimes is." She heard Max hesitate. "It's about yours and Cordell's past, isn't it? That's why you sent me the mug shot. He's whatever you've spent your life running from."

Max sighed. "He was recently released from prison. He might be coming after me and Cordell. Unfortunately, he knows about you and Goldie. Rance and I will be watching for him. But this man is the kind who will come out of the dark like the dangerous animal he is."

She'd feared it was something like this. And still her stomach dropped, her heart aching. She could hear the fear in Max's voice; it melded with her own. She swallowed and fought back tears as she heard Max's pain. "Cordell is with you," she said, knowing it was true, just as she knew Roger Grimes had done something awful to the man she loved as well as to Max. "You're still in town?" She feared that the man would lure the two of them away. But she didn't even try to talk him out of whatever he was planning to do. She knew Max, knew he would do what he thought was right. "Tell Cordell—" She wasn't sure what she was going to say, but the sheriff didn't give her a chance anyway.

"I know how you feel about him. Just stay safe. Are you with Goldie?"

"Yes. I showed her the mug shot of Roger Grimes and warned her."

"Thank you." With that, Max was gone.

Josie looked up to find her friend standing in the doorway.

"It's bad, isn't it?" Goldie whispered.

Josie's heart was in her throat so all she could do was nod. "But you know Max. He'll do whatever it takes to keep us safe, to keep Dry Gulch safe." To keep Cordell safe, she told herself.

"ARE YOU SURE Max never mentioned where he and his brother came from? Family? Anything?" Josie asked Goldie later when the two of them sat on separate ends of the couch, feet up, another bottle of wine on the coffee table between them.

"He never talked to me about his life before he came to Dry Gulch," Goldie said. "It was obviously something he wanted to forget so I never pushed him on it. The only thing he said was that they were orphans, their parents dead and no other family."

"Did you believe him?" Josie asked.

"Isn't that the same story Cordell told you?"

"I didn't believe it, either."

"I wonder if Iris knew more," Goldie suggested. "She took them under her wing. The whole town did. I guess we all knew that they'd had a rough life before they landed here. But if they're in trouble now, what can we do?"

"Pray for them to be safe," Josie said. "And be careful ourselves."

"That man in the mug shot gives me the willies. What do you think he was to them?"

"Someone who hurt them from their past who might be after them, might be headed for Dry Gulch. Max is worried that it has put the two of us in danger."

Goldie frowned. "This man knows about us? How is that possible if he's been in prison?"

"That's what I want to know," Josie said. "Someone has to know about their past and who might have told this man where they can find Max and Cordell."

"I wish Iris were still alive," Goldie said. "If anyone knew something that might help about Max and Cordell, it was her."

"Or her sister," Josie said.

Goldie looked up in surprise. "*Esther?* You think she knows something?"

"If there was dirt to be dug up, Esther would have been manning the shovel. She always was the worst old busybody," Josie said.

"But if she'd found out, she would have told everyone. The only reason she wouldn't was if there was something in it for her." Goldie flushed and put down her half-empty wineglass. "I shouldn't have said that, but that woman would have eaten her young. I was surprised that Iris put up with her as long as she did. You know that expression, 'If you don't have anything nice to say, then say nothing at all'? Esther wouldn't have been able to get a syllable out." They both laughed, but it sounded hollow. Max's text, then his call had left them both subdued. Not even the wine seemed to help. "What was her problem, anyway?"

"I heard she got her heart broken when she was young and never got over it." Josie's sister had warned her that she was going to turn into Esther Mason if she didn't get over Cordell. "I think I might drive down to Grass Range tomorrow and pay her a visit."

Josie knew she wouldn't be able to sleep—even after the wine. She kept trying to see into the darkness for what was coming. Outside, the town of Dry Gulch seemed unearthly quiet tonight. It unnerved her almost as much as the images she kept seeing. Flashes like in a dream on a dark highway, the rattle of a pickup, sagebrush and more darkness. She tried to see more but it made her head ache.

"Mind if I stay here tonight?" she asked, not wanting to drive in her condition out to the farm, but also not wanting to leave Goldie alone. "I'll call Amy Sue and tell her." She stepped away to make the call even though she'd told her sister she would be staying the night. What she really wanted to do was warn Amy Sue to keep the doors locked tonight.

When Josie returned to the couch, Goldie said, "Are you sure you want to drive all the way down to Grass Range? You know how Esther is."

"I'm sure she'll be happy to help," Josie said sarcastically, and they both mugged faces. Esther had never made it a secret that she didn't like Max and Cordell living in her sister's boardinghouse. She'd started all kinds of rumors about the boys until Iris kicked her out.

But it would be just like the woman to want to prove she

was right about the Lander men, Josie thought. Esther did love seeing the worst in everyone.

If she knew about this man from Max's and Cordell's pasts, she was keeping it to herself for some reason.

Josie was determined to find out.

LEAVING HIS HOUSE AGAIN, Max patrolled the town as usual with his new deputy. He made a point of driving past Clancy Roberts's house, glad to see both Goldie's vehicle and Josie's parked outside. All the lights were on inside. He told himself that both women were safe. At least for now.

"I was thinking," Cordell said. He'd always needed to talk things out while Max preferred to mull them over silently inside his head alone. "We know Grimes stopped long enough to buy a van. Which means that he didn't have everything he needed when he got out of prison. He had to pick up the bank robbery money, which probably means he has access to guns and ammunition. Maybe more worrisome, he might not be traveling alone."

"I've already thought of that," Max said. He could just imagine the kind of men Grimes befriended behind bars or out. Maybe even the men he'd pulled off the robbery with who hadn't been caught.

"If there are two of them traveling together, then they can trade off drivers and make even better time than I did getting here. Maybe he is bringing some equally psychotic friend with him."

Max had been worrying about the same thing. The last time he checked, no more of the stolen bank money had shown up and neither had Grimes or his van.

"Maybe he changed his mind or got picked up and his arrest hasn't gone into the data bank yet," Cordell said. When Max said nothing, he asked, "Going to the homestead when he might be waiting for us… That's probably the worst idea ever, huh?"

"Nope, the worst idea was our mother letting that jerk into our lives," Max said wearily. He drove in silence for a few blocks. His brother fell silent for so long, he wondered if he had fallen asleep. Cordell could sleep anywhere, under any circumstances, he'd proved that.

"You know he killed her." His brother's voice was a whisper as if afraid to say something they had suspected for years.

"Unfortunately, without a body we can't even prove that she's dead, let alone that he killed her," Max said, sounding like the law enforcement officer he was.

Cordell didn't bother to argue the point. They both knew Grimes had killed her. They'd both told the cop who'd come to the house not just their suspicions but how the man had abused her and them, as well. They'd both gotten beaten after the cops left for even suggesting Grimes could do such a thing.

"Either of you ever talk to the cops again, you'll be finding yourself at the bottom of the stairs like your mother—or worse," he'd said as he'd picked up the piece of rubber tubing he'd use to beat them and looked as if he just might go ahead and kill them.

When Max didn't answer now, Cordell said, "I've often thought about finding those cops, you know?"

Max nodded. He did know. "We got away. There's no looking back." Those words had been a mantra he'd repeated those weeks they were on the run and even later when they'd settled in the boardinghouse in Dry Gulch.

Cordell scoffed. "Are you serious? We didn't get away, because here we are. This sure as hell feels like looking back."

Max couldn't argue that. He recalled the one time he'd told anyone about his youth. It had been a man he'd befriended in the academy. "My so-called stepfather killed my mother and got away with it."

"Didn't you go to the cops?" his friend had asked innocently.

"My brother and I told the cops. They didn't believe us. We also told them what the man was doing to us with the same results."

"Wait. Are you saying you don't trust the cops?" he'd laughed. "Then what are you doing becoming one?"

"I wanted to be a better lawman. If anyone came to me with the same kind of story, I would believe them. Or at least find out if it was true."

"You're an avenger," his friend had said. "Good for you. But your stepfather got away with all of it? Didn't you ever want to right that wrong?"

"You aren't sure what you're going to do when we come face-to-face with him again, are you," Cordell said, dragging him from the memory.

Max didn't answer. Instead, he thought about the night they'd finally run away, Grimes's pickup's headlights cutting a swatch of gold down the two-lane highway, the man's body wrapped in a tarp in the bed behind them.

He'd been so sure that Grimes would never hurt anyone ever again. But he'd been wrong. He couldn't repeat that mistake.

Chapter Ten

Josie fought sleep until she'd finally gotten up and gone downstairs and out on Clancy's porch. The night was cold enough that she wished for one of her grandmother's quilts. Wrapping up in the threadbare fabric always made her think of her grandmother tucking her into bed. She could have really used that feeling right now.

She looked out into the night. Town was so quiet that it unnerved her. She spent most of her nights out at the farm where it was always quiet. But not like this. The blackness she sensed hung on the horizon like an approaching thunderstorm. She wondered where Max and Cordell were and feared for their safety. The oblivion seemed to grow denser as shadows shifted before her eyes. He was coming. The man in the mug shot. He was on his way.

"What are you doing?" Goldie asked as she joined her on the porch, dragging a blanket behind her before curling up beside Josie and sharing the warmth.

"Couldn't sleep."

"Me, neither." They sat in silence for a moment.

"How are you doing?" Josie asked.

"Confused, upset, worried. Do you know what's going to happen?"

Josie shook her head. "I've never had Nana's sight."

Goldie looked toward the road. "Good, 'cause I was afraid that you could see into my mind like your grandmother could. She knew what I was up to." She let out a chuckle. "True, I was always up to something."

"She couldn't see into your head," Josie said with a laugh. "She just knew you, knew how you thought."

"Maybe." Goldie sounded skeptical even after all these years. "But once I knew that you might have some of her gift, I thought you knew everything about me and that I could never keep anything from you."

"That's good," Josie joked. "Keep thinking that. I've got my sister buffaloed into believing it, as well."

She could almost hear Goldie smile in the darkness. "I'm glad you can't read my thoughts."

"Me, too. I have enough trouble without looking into that mind of yours." She was joking—but only in a way.

"I'm thankful for that," her friend said as she rose, leaving the blanket. "Good luck saving the world. I'm going back to bed."

"Night," she said and listened as Goldie went back inside. For a few moments, she quit worrying about what was coming and considered what she sensed in her best friend. Fear, but something more that was almost like…unrest. She feared Max had pushed Goldie away too many times. What would Goldie do if he really meant it this time?

Chapter Eleven

Early in the morning before he'd had a chance to go to the office, Max got a call from Deputy Green. "Got some news for you," the deputy said between bites of apparently his breakfast. "Got a call from Cheyenne. They picked up Grimes on his way north and are running him back to the sheriff's office there. Thought you'd want to know."

Max couldn't help the flood of relief he felt. "That's good news."

"That's not the only reason I called," the deputy said. "I told one of the other deputies about what you said about your mother. He ran back out there. He found a shallow grave down the road from the house. There was quite a bit of clothing that was still intact in the grave along with the remains. Might be the only way we can get a positive ID. Would help if you came down to the coroner's office, see if you recognize any of the clothing and make a statement."

Max felt his stomach lurch. He'd known his mother hadn't left. He'd known she was dead, that Grimes had killed her, yet… He felt as if he was going to be sick.

"Yes, we'll come down," he finally managed to say. "I suppose he couldn't tell how she died."

"The coroner said the back of her skull was caved in."

Max had been standing but now dropped into a chair and put his head in his hand. He couldn't imagine how he was going to tell Cordell. "We knew that Grimes killed her, but now we know what he did with her body."

"We'll take your statements when you get here," Green said. "If Cheyenne has Grimes and your statements convince a judge, he'll be looking at murder one. That should keep him behind bars for a while." With that, the deputy hung up.

Max disconnected, his hand shaking. There was no statute of limitations on murder. After all these years, Grimes could be going down for killing their mother. He couldn't help his relief that the man had been picked up in Cheyenne. He hadn't been at the homestead, but he'd been headed that way.

For now, though, the man wasn't a threat.

The news of their mother had taken his breath away. He thought of the dress his mother had been wearing that night, the last time Max had seen her. Was it possible the deputy had found their mother's remains? If they were treating it as a crime scene, they must be taking his accusation seriously. Finally, maybe there would be enough to put Grimes away for good.

Max called his deputy. "I have to leave town for a day or two. You're in charge, Rance. I'll keep in touch, though," Max told him and disconnected.

"What?" Cordell asked as he walked into the room. "Where are you going?"

"Grimes was picked up down by Cheyenne." Max looked into his kid brother's face. "One of the deputies noticed something when he was looking for Grimes out at the homestead. He found a shallow grave down the road a bit from the house. They think they might have found Mother."

To his credit, Cordell didn't even flinch. "We knew he killed her, but we never thought he'd pay for it."

"Maybe he still will. I need to go down there and see if I can identify what she was wearing the last time we saw her."

"Not without me," his brother said quickly. "Out at the homestead?"

Max heard Cordell's voice quaver. His brother had sworn he'd never go back there. "No. We need to ID her clothing at the coroner's office. If it's her, then they want our statements. They treated the grave like a crime scene, but it's been so many years, there wouldn't be much if any evidence to find."

His brother looked relieved they wouldn't be going near the homestead. "I can't believe we might finally get some justice for her murder."

Chapter Twelve

Josie had gotten hardly any sleep last night. But just near daylight, she'd dreamed about Cordell, that gleam in his eyes, that dimple when he smiled at her. She'd awakened with a start when her cell phone rang. Overshadowing the sweet dream she'd had was the darkness looming on the horizon. It felt denser somehow, more threatening this morning, as if getting closer as she picked up the call.

The news from Cordell had come as a shock and a relief.

"We heard from Wyoming that the man I warned you about has been picked up," Max said. "Sorry if I worried you for no reason."

She thought the dark foreboding fog of danger would lift, but she could still feel the weight of it. "You're sure?"

"Everything is fine," the sheriff said. "Cordell and I are going down there. We'll probably be gone at least until tomorrow."

Everything wasn't fine, but he didn't give her a chance to argue the point before he said, "Hold on, Cordell wants to say something."

"We're heading out now," he told her. "Maybe we could talk when Max and I get back? Got to go. Wish us luck."

"Be safe," she said and let him go. Inhaling a breath,

she tried to take it all in. Both men had been in a hurry so she'd only gotten the abbreviated update. Grimes had been caught and Max's and Cordell's mother's remains had been found, which they hoped would prove that Grimes had murdered her all those years ago.

Josie closed her eyes, feeling the brothers' pain. She had only sensed what they'd been through before. Now she knew at least some of it. Her heart broke for them. As she silently wished them a safe trip, she sensed that it wasn't over and feared what might be waiting for them down in Wyoming.

Then she put in a call to Esther Mason to make sure she was going to be home.

"Just heard from Cordell," she told Goldie when she got up. "They caught the man from the mug shot Max sent. But still be careful. Why are you up so early? I thought you didn't work until the afternoon shift?"

"I'm going to have to work a double," Goldie said as she dumped two over-the-counter pain pills in her palm and got herself a glass of water. "My waitress is sick, and Clancy has to work at her real job. Don't worry, I've got it. Also, it appears Max sent his deputy to walk me the few blocks to my job. He's so thoughtful," she said sarcastically.

Her friend had gone from hurt to anger. "He's worried about you and I'm sure he's upset that he's responsible for the danger."

Tears filled Goldie's eyes. Josie could see that she was more frightened for Max than for herself. "If it's over, then why am I still worried about him?" She didn't wait for an answer. "See you later?"

"I'm going down to Grass Range to talk to Esther," she called after her. "I'll stop by the café when I get back."

"Good luck," Goldie said. "You're going to need it with that old battle-ax."

From the window, Josie watched her friend and Rance go down the street to the café. The deputy was strutting more than a little and laughing as they walked. He didn't look worried. But Josie couldn't shake her apprehension.

She sensed just the opposite of everything being all right. It wasn't until she saw the open sign come on down at the café and the deputy leave to head back in the direction of the sheriff's office that she headed for the family farm.

As she drove up in the yard, her sister came out of the house. "I'm surprised to see you."

"I came by to pick up a few things before I head out of town."

"I made some lemonade," Amy Sue said. "Want some?"

Josie reached into her SUV for her insulated coffee mug. "Would love some in here." Her sister took it and they both headed for the house, her sister turning toward the kitchen while Josie ran upstairs to her room, where she grabbed her large purse she often took when leaving town. She had dropped her handgun in the bag, telling herself as she always did that she wouldn't use it unless it was a last resort. But she didn't want her sister to know that she might need it.

"Where are you headed?" Amy Sue asked as she handed over the container as they walked back outside.

"Grass Range."

"I'm afraid to even ask, but does this trip have something to do with Cordell?"

"He could be in trouble."

"Isn't he always?"

"This time, it feels…serious for both brothers." On impulse, she said, "I need to show you a photo."

Her sister recoiled as she took Josie's phone and saw the man. "Who is he?"

She shook her head. "If you see him, call the sheriff's department. Don't confront him." She knew what Max had said, yet the darkness she saw coming was now here and she couldn't explain it.

"Fine," Amy Sue said, handing back the phone. "I can't imagine why he'd come out here, can you?" Josie couldn't since Max had said the man had been arrested, but whatever had her scared was still lingering. If not this man, then someone maybe even more dangerous. "What, or should I ask who, is in Grass Range?"

"Esther Mason."

Her sister laughed. "Why would you want to go see that old crone? Iris was the nicest person I've ever known and even she couldn't stand her sister. Didn't she throw Esther out of the boardinghouse after years of carrying all the weight?"

"Sisters don't always get along."

"Very funny. You know it was more serious than that. Esther was always carrying tales, butting into everyone's lives, spreading lies and suspicion everywhere she went. She was walking misfortune and misery. I bet she's spinning conspiracy theories now that they're the rage." Her sister frowned. "You think she knows something about this man I should watch out for?" She nodded toward Josie's phone.

Josie shrugged and shook her head. "Won't know until I ask her."

Her sister glanced down at their vehicles parked side by side. "Well, you aren't going anywhere in your SUV."

Josie looked and felt her heart drop as she saw that her left rear tire was flat.

"Take mine," Amy Sue said. "I'll see about getting your tire fixed while you are gone."

"Are you sure?" Josie had a bad feeling about all of this. The tire hadn't felt as if it was going flat on the drive there. She found herself questioning if she should even go now. "Maybe I should—"

"For once will you let me do something for you instead of you always having to do for everyone else," her sister snapped.

She had never been good at taking help, she knew. "Fine. Thank you."

Her sister smiled. "Now, was that so hard?"

It was hard. "I just have this feeling—"

"Oh, don't start with the vibes, please," Amy Sue said. "My car's insured if you're worried about wrecking it. Just drive carefully and don't worry for a change. Can you do that?"

She nodded, even as she knew she couldn't. But her sister was right. Josie needed to go. She needed to talk to Esther. That feeling was stronger than the one that made her hesitate. "I'll try not to wreck it. You…just be careful," she said, looking around.

Amy Sue laughed and shook her head as she handed over the keys. As Josie climbed behind the wheel of her sister's SUV, all she could hope was that Esther's prying and meddling would be an advantage this one and only time.

"Be careful," her sister said before she could start the engine. "You're the one with the ESP, but Esther gives me the creeps."

Josie started to explain for the hundredth time that she didn't have visions, but she wished she did. Instead, she smiled and promised to be careful as she started the engine and left.

She felt off-balance, suddenly scared as her vision darkened for a moment and she had this feeling that Amy Sue was in trouble. It was so strong that she almost turned around and went back. Instead, she called her, using her cell since she wasn't hooked up to her sister's hands-free calling.

Amy Sue answered giggling. It was strange to hear. Not as strange as hearing a male voice in the background. "What now, Josie?" she demanded.

"Is there someone there with you?"

"What if there was?"

"Amy Sue, I'm going to turn around—"

"Don't be ridiculous. It was just the TV. I turned it off."

Josie listened, hearing nothing in the background now. "I know you think I'm silly."

"Silly is putting it mildly. I have something on the stove," her sister said. "I have to go."

She disconnected, still afraid, but knowing if she turned around and went back, Amy Sue would be furious with her. Whatever was coming, it felt as if it was already here. But her second sight had never been very precise. Still, she hurriedly called Goldie.

"Can't talk right now, swamped," Goldie said when she answered. "Call me later." With that, she was gone.

Josie tried to relax. Goldie was working a double at the café since the other waitress had called in sick so she'd probably be busy all day. Still, she wished she'd talked Goldie into coming with her and blowing off work. Not that her friend would ever do that since it would mean closing the café. Goldie couldn't let anyone who needed a meal go away hungry.

But Josie had one of her feelings she often had that made her anxious. She reminded herself that her friend wasn't at the café alone. Her teenage cook, Ronnie, and it sounded like half the town was there, as well.

Still, unable to throw off her uneasy feeling, Josie called the Dry Gulch Sheriff's Department and asked to speak to the deputy. When Rance came on the line, she said, "Could you keep an eye on Goldie? She's working a double shift down at the café today."

"The sheriff already has me keeping an eye on her," the deputy said. "Had breakfast down there. Ronnie's there cooking. The place is hoppin'. Not sure what you think is going to happen in broad daylight. Anyway, I thought Max told you. Everything is fine now."

If only she could believe that, Josie thought as she thanked him and disconnected. The Grass Range turnoff was ahead.

ESTHER LIVED IN a senior apartment complex. The smell of boiled cabbage this early in the morning made Josie wrinkle her nose. According to the mailboxes and directory by the entrance, Esther's apartment was on the fourth floor. Josie only half-heartedly considered the small elevator, before taking the stairs.

She could hear the sounds of radios and televisions turned up too loudly as she made her way down the hallway to the last apartment. She thought she heard voices and what sounded like a woman and a man talking as she knocked on the door. The voices inside the apartment silenced.

When no one answered the door, Josie knocked again. She heard the slow thud of footfalls inside a moment before a harried-looking gray-haired woman opened the door.

Josie couldn't recall the last time she'd seen Esther. She remembered her as being a large, stocky woman with a stern, unyielding disposition and a permanent frown. Esther had aged, gotten a little heavier, and if anything, her frown had gotten deeper. She'd never looked like a happy woman, but now her expression was as sour as if she'd just bitten into a lemon on her way to the door.

For a moment, Josie thought Esther didn't recognize her. But then the woman laughed and said, "What are *you* doing here? I was just talking to a friend about you."

That didn't sound good. "I can't imagine why my name would come up."

Esther only laughed again as she stepped back to let Josie into the entryway hall. From what Josie could see of the too-hot cramped apartment, it was cluttered with knickknacks, making Josie feel claustrophobic. She found herself looking around, expecting to see whomever Esther had been talking to before the woman had opened the door. But the small, cramped place was empty.

Out of the corner of her eye, she spotted a dead plant in a pot on a small table just inside the door. There was a cell phone lying next to it. Esther must have had the phone on speaker, which would explain the male voice she'd heard.

"I was hoping you could help me," she told the elderly woman, realizing this was as far into the apartment as Esther was going to allow her. "I recall you had such a good memory when it came to people." Wanting to make this as quick as possible for so many reasons, she hurried on. "Esther, you have a keen ability to dig deeper, see more than other people tend to see."

The older woman seemed touched by what she took as a compliment, as Josie had intended. "I like getting to the root of things," the woman said primly.

"Yes, you do. That's why I knew if anyone could help me, it would be you."

Esther beamed as Josie ran out of flattery. "I bet you know the secret of Max and Cordell Lander." She saw the change in Esther's expression at once. Her face closed up, her eyes narrowing. She even took a step back. She almost looked frightened.

"You do know they're in some kind of trouble, don't you?" Josie said even as the woman shook her head. "Because of something in their past. Esther—"

"You need to leave." The words came out on a ragged breath as the senior citizen motioned toward the door.

"What are they running from?" Josie persisted. "You can tell me."

Esther's gaze shot to her phone on the table by the dead plant. But as she reached for it, Josie snatched it up. "Hello? Hello?" A deep male chuckle sent fear shuddering through her. The sound manifested into the evil, darkness and horror headed for Dry Gulch. She felt it all in that simple sound.

"Josephine Brand, is it? You sound delightful. Cordell certainly must think so."

Fingers shaking, Josie took the phone off speaker. She looked at Esther, who avoided her gaze. "I'm sorry, who are you and why are *you* interested in Max and Cordell?" she asked, surprised her voice didn't give away the terror making her heart pound.

"Why wouldn't I be interested in Max and Cordell? That's why when the cops offered me one call, I told them I wanted my lawyer, Josephine Brand."

"I didn't get your call."

He laughed. "I bet not since I called Esther, who it turns out knew your boyfriend and my stepson Cordell really well."

"Stepson?" Her voice found only dead space and she

knew he'd disconnected. Feeling suddenly dirty, she dropped the phone back on the table and turned to Esther. "What have you been telling him about Cordell and Max?"

"You need to get out of my apartment," Esther said.

"You sold them out, didn't you?"

Looking indignant, the woman glared at her. "What do you know about it? Nothing. You have no idea what Max and Cordell are really like, what they did before they came to Dry Gulch. Now get out."

"Tell me who he is," Josie said through clenched teeth, even though she knew he was the man in the mug shot Max had sent her.

Esther raised her chin, defiance in her glare. "His name is Roger Grimes. He has every right to see his stepsons, especially after what they did to him. Left him for dead, after they tried to kill him. Iris thought they were such nice boys. I tried to warn her. I never trusted them."

Josie shook her head, trying to rein in her anger and disgust. "How did you get in contact with this man?"

"I didn't," she said smugly. "He contacted me. He's one of my prison pen pals. Don't look at me like that. I get lonely. Those poor men get lonely, too."

She had to bite her tongue at how naive Esther was. "Roger Grimes will soon be going to prison again."

"Will he?" Esther asked innocently.

Josie saw the answer in the woman's eyes. "Are you telling me he's not behind bars?" If Esther had told Roger Grimes all about them, then he also must have told her things about himself. "Esther, if you know something—"

"I'm not telling you anything," she snapped. "Judgment is coming to those boys. After what they did to that poor man, they are going to pay dearly. Told everyone those boys were no good, but no one would listen. All thought they knew better. Ha!"

"Esther, you have no idea what you've done." Josie started for the door.

"He's really looking forward to meeting you." There was a snideness to her tone that made Josie stop at the door and slowly turn to look at Esther.

"You told him all about me…me and Cordell." The woman smiled. "Why would you do that, Esther?"

"He wanted to know about his stepsons and the women they were involved with."

Max and Goldie. Josie clenched her hands into fists. Of course he did. "And you were more than happy to tell him. What is wrong with you, Esther? The man is a dangerous criminal." Iris had always been so kind and gracious, so caring. How could two sisters be so different? "You want to get us all killed?"

Looking defensive, Esther said, "Roger isn't like that."

"You have no idea what he's like and now you've given him a loaded gun to come after not just Max and Cordell but Goldie and me."

The woman clamped her lips shut in a thin line before she said, "You are the one who fell in with Cordell Lander, not me. You're the one who knew nothing about him. You know what they say about sleeping with dogs."

Josie turned and rushed out the door, unable to stay in Esther's presence a moment longer for fear of what she might do to the miserable woman.

She had to contact Cordell and Max before it was too late. Something was wrong. It hadn't sounded as if Grimes was calling from jail.

But first she had to make sure that Goldie was all right. The moment she was out of the apartment complex, she called Goldie's cell. It rang five times before it was picked up by voicemail.

Telling herself Josie must be too busy to answer, she quickly tried the café's landline. It began to ring and ring. Even as she tried not to panic, she was.

Disconnecting, she called the sheriff's office only to find out from the dispatcher that Deputy Rance Fletcher had been called down to the café for some kind of emergency and she hadn't been able to reach him.

Goldie! She drove even faster, afraid that she would reach Dry Gulch too late to save her friend.

GOLDIE WOKE, HEAD ACHING. She sat against a metal wall, her wrists zip-tied together and attached to a metal bar along the inside of what she realized was the back of a van. Rock music blared from the car's speakers, but the van wasn't moving. The engine, though, was running.

As she tried to sit up, she saw through the driver's side window the man she now knew was Roger Grimes. Her capture came back to her along with a growing sense of panic. The man had lured her into the back of the café, where she'd found Ronnie injured and bleeding. Grimes had grabbed her and covered her mouth with a rag wet with a substance that knocked her out as he dragged her to the alley behind the café. Max and Cordell's stepfather, the man she'd been warned to watch out for, had taken her captive.

Now he stood outside the van talking on a cell phone. She couldn't hear what he was saying over the music vibrating the windows in the car. She tried to free herself from where her wrists were bound to the van wall, but quickly had to give up. She still felt woozy from whatever he'd knocked her out with.

Just the sight of the man from the café had her pulse in

overdrive. Josie had shown her his mug shot and warned her that he might be coming to Dry Gulch, that he was somehow connected to Max and Cordell. Where was he taking her? What was he going to do with her?

As he finished his call, he opened the driver's side door and peered in at her. "Finally awake, huh?" he said with a deep chuckle as he slid behind the wheel.

"Where are you taking me?" she managed to ask, her throat dry, her tongue feeling too large in her mouth. How long had she been out?

"I thought you'd like to see where Max and Cordell grew up," he said. "But first we need to pick up your friend Josie and then we're on our way."

She felt her pulse jump in alarm. "Josie?"

"Don't worry. Max and Cordell will also be joining us."

She was determined not to let him see how terrified she was. She could tell he liked her being frightening. He enjoyed seeing people suffer, that much she'd figured out for herself. Still, when she spoke, her voice was too high. "Why are you doing this?"

He looked surprised by her question. "I thought you knew. I want to see my stepsons. Having their women there will only make it a more special reunion." His laugh held no humor as he turned up the volume on the radio and began to sing along, horribly off-key.

Goldie closed her eyes, wishing she could send a message to Josie. Her worst nightmare was coming for her. Not far up the highway, he turned off the road, cut the engine and got out without a word.

JOSIE FEARED SHE was driving the narrow highway too fast. She couldn't help feeling anxious. The deputy hadn't called her back. Nor had she been able to reach Goldie or the café.

Something had happened. She knew it, the way she knew the man she'd spoken to on the phone was responsible.

Her blood turned to ice as she thought about him having Goldie. She reached for her phone, desperately needing to talk to Cordell as she felt the darkness approaching her so quickly that—

Her hand brushed her phone lying on the passenger seat as her windshield exploded, the sound like a gunshot. She felt something hitting her face and arms. Instinctively, she hit her brakes as her gaze flew up. She caught only a blur of whatever had slammed into her windshield as it careened off to the side.

She had inadvertently yanked the wheel in her surprise and now felt the tires on the right side drop over the edge of the narrow pavement. The back of the SUV dug into the soft dirt. She had to fight the wheel to get the SUV back up on the road and to a stop.

Her hands shook as she clung to the wheel, relieved that she wasn't in the ditch. Even more relieved that she couldn't see any other vehicles coming from either direction. She tried to get control of herself as she looked out through the webbed windshield and willed her heart rate to slow.

She was all right. All she could figure was that she'd hit a large pheasant. Her bare skin began to burn where tiny pieces of glass had cut her. She eased her grip on the wheel, trying to decide if she could see well enough to get the rest of the way to Dry Gulch. Her worry about Goldie convinced her she had to try.

Something caught her eye in the rearview mirror. She'd been expecting to see a dead pheasant in the road behind her. But what she saw looked like a large rock. How would a rock that size have—

Her side window exploded. Something hit the side of her

head. She smelled strong body odor the moment before the man grabbed her and hauled her out of the car. She tried to fight him off, but he was too strong. As he cupped a wet rag over her mouth and nose, all the fight went out of her. Darkness closed in.

Chapter Thirteen

Josie awoke bound and tied to a metal bracket on the floor of what appeared to be an old panel van. The light was dim but across from her she could see one cut zip tie lying on the floor next to a similar metal bracket.

She couldn't hear anything but the wind that now rocked the van. But she knew Goldie had been here. She could still feel her friend's fear in the van. But she couldn't rise high enough to see out the windshield as to where they were or where Goldie might have been taken. Unlike her grandmother, visions were never clear and the harder she tried, the less she could see. Which was why she'd never trusted this so-called gift. It hurt because she'd never needed it as much as she did right now.

After a few futile attempts to free herself, Josie suddenly stopped. She'd forgotten about the gun she'd put in her pocket after leaving Esther's. She could feel the weight of it and was surprised that Grimes hadn't noticed it. Leaning forward, she managed to get the gun out of her pocket and into the waistband of her jeans. She'd almost dropped it when she heard someone approaching.

Hurriedly, she pretended to still be unfocused from the drug he'd used on her, closing her eyes and slumping over a little, as the side door rolled open and she felt him step inside. She smelled him as he grabbed her arm, forcing her to look at him.

"Wondered when you'd come around," he said as he pulled out a knife. "I'm going to cut you free from the floor, but if you try anything, your good friend Goldie will suffer. Got it?"

She nodded numbly, letting him yank her to her feet and shove her through the open doorway of the van. She felt the gun bite into her flesh at her waist as she stumbled but managed to stay on her feet. Unfortunately, she felt her phone also still on her.

"Wait!" he bellowed in a voice that made her freeze. Grimes grabbed her and shoved her hard against the side of the van as he snatched the phone from the back pocket of her jeans. As he spun her around to face him, Josie got her first good look at him.

He was big and muscled, his tattooed throat corded like his massive arms. Surprisingly, he wasn't as ugly as she'd pictured him, though he had his share of scars, including the one that made his right eyelid droop.

The real ugliness she saw was inside him and shone in his eyes. They were like looking into something dark and deep and revoltingly malevolent. She shuddered as she felt those dark eyes rake over her.

"Ain't you a little thing," he said with a deep, hoarse laugh. "At least my stepsons have good taste when it comes to women. Come on, let's go see your friend."

She glanced around, feeling a chill as she took in the dilapidated old two-story house sitting alone on the hillside apparently miles from anywhere. A feeling of pain and hate and horror rushed at her. She didn't want to go in there. Horrible things had happened there. "What is this place?" she asked, her voice breaking.

"Home," Grimes said with a chuckle that made her gag.

Home? This man and this house were what Max and Cordell had run from. She felt sick to her stomach as he dragged her toward the house. She sensed the hell the two had gone through here and had to fight to block the sensations she knew she would feel once inside as she cursed her second sight. She tried to think of anything but what Max and Cordell had lived through in this place.

As they reached the nearly falling-down porch, Grimes dragged her up what was left of the steps and shoved open the door. Bracing herself, Josie told herself to be strong. For Goldie. If Goldie was still alive.

Where were Cordell and Max? Did they know what was happening?

Josie knew that she couldn't plan on them finding her and Goldie. Grimes hadn't checked her for a weapon. He'd already misjudged her because of her slight build and her gender. Her grandmother had taught her how to use a gun, so she'd also learned to respect the weapon. "Never pull your gun unless you're going to use it. Never use a gun unless you've tried every way but Sunday to talk yourself out of a situation."

She glanced at Grimes. There was a ruthlessness about him that told her everything she needed to know about why Cordell and Max had ended up in Dry Gulch alone. She'd seen Grimes's kind before, usually in a courtroom or a jail—on their way to prison. When she pulled the gun, she *would* use it since she had a bad feeling there was no way to talk herself out of this.

He was right on her heels, not that she was going to run. She flinched at the sight of the battered old house that looked as if it was fighting to stay standing. He shoved her toward it. Goldie would be inside, but she had no idea what shape her friend might be in as she stumbled up the rotting porch steps.

She felt the gun but didn't know if Grimes was alone. She had to bide her time until she knew exactly what she and Goldie were up against. Not that Grimes was ever far enough away from her for her to pull the weapon and fire, not with her wrists still bound.

When Josie saw Goldie tied to a chair, her heart broke for her. She could see her friend's fear, feel her own as the cold shadowy darkness made her shudder.

Grimes seemed to be alone except for his hostages. Josie wished she knew for sure that no one else would be coming through the door at any moment. But the man had stayed close to her, as if expecting her to try something. He hadn't given her sufficient room to draw the gun and fire with any chance of doing more than wounding him.

"Have a seat," Grimes said, pointing to the worn wooden floor next to an old radiator as he pulled a couple of zip ties from his jacket pocket. Josie knew that arguing the point would be a waste of her breath. She could feel the gun biting into her waist as she sat down, hoping he didn't notice her grimace.

As he came over to her, she held out her wrists to make the job easier for him. She could see him watching her suspiciously. He used the second zip tie to attach her wrists to the radiator with no slack. She had no chance to draw the gun unless she could free herself from the radiator.

"You think you're tough, don't you?" Grimes said when she didn't flinch at how tight he did the zip tie. "Just like your friend. Probably need to be because of those two worthless boyfriends of yours."

Josie didn't take the bait, but Goldie started to respond, then caught herself.

"I need to make a call," Grimes announced. "You two stay right here. Don't do anything that will make me angry. You really don't want to see me lose my temper." He laughed. "My stepsons can tell you what happens when I lose my temper."

With that, he pulled out his phone and left them alone.

"Are you all right?" Josie asked her friend the moment he was gone. She didn't know how much time they had before he returned. Goldie only nodded.

"Is Grimes acting alone or is there someone else he's working with?"

"Alone, at least I think so. He makes a lot of calls. Max and Cordell are coming, aren't they?"

Josie couldn't tell if Goldie was hoping they would come and save them or stay away so they weren't harmed. She understood that feeling since she was experiencing it herself. "I don't know what is going to happen, but I don't think he will harm us." At least not yet.

"Unless he can't get his hands on them," Goldie said and looked away as her eyes filled with tears. "All I've ever wanted was to marry Max, have his babies, make a life for the two of us in Dry Gulch."

"I'm sure that's what he's always wanted, too."

Goldie didn't look so sure about that. "I guess he really did break up with me to try to protect me, for all the good it did."

"Roger Grimes already knew about you and Max, about me and Cordell. Esther. She became his pen pal while he was in prison. She told him everything about everybody, but especially the four of us."

"That horrible woman."

"That's putting it kindly," Josie said. "Can you see Grimes?"

"He's outside on his phone. You think the reason Max hasn't asked me to marry him is because of his past?"

"I suspect so." She also thought it was why Cordell had left town, left her, and why he'd come back. Josie knew that he loved her, but sometimes love wasn't enough.

"Grimes still has the phone to his ear," Goldie said. "He's pacing. He doesn't look happy."

MAX HAD BEEN lost in the past as he drove toward Rawlins, Wyoming. For years he'd held the awful memories at bay, fighting desperately to put them far behind him. He'd known that Grimes had killed their mother, but now that her grave had been found just past the homestead—

He started when his cell phone rang, pulling him out of the past. He saw that they were almost to Rawlins and shot a glance over at Cordell, who appeared to be sound asleep, curled in the corner of the pickup. His brother stirred as the phone rang again.

Not recognizing the number, Max let it ring another time before he picked up. "Sheriff Lander."

Silence. Then he heard a low familiar laugh that made his blood run cold.

"Weren't expecting a call from me, I take it?" Grimes asked.

"You used your one phone call from jail to talk to me?" the sheriff said, trying not to let Grimes hear his shock. "I'm honored."

Again, all he heard was that miserable laugh. "Afraid the new deputy picked up the wrong man, though my friend Dave looks enough like me and is a hardened criminal, so you can understand how the young deputy made the mistake, especially with Dave driving a van with Florida plates," Grimes said. "Knowing Dave, he had no trouble getting arrested, especially since he gave the cop my driver's license." Another laugh. "Once they run his prints, they'll let him go, so don't worry about Dave." The line seemed to crackle. "What? Nothing smart to say?"

Max hit the brakes, knowing as his heart sank what was coming next. Cordell sat up and looked around in surprise as Max pulled off the road. The only reason they'd left Dry Gulch was because Max had believed Grimes was behind bars. If it hadn't been him…

"Let me save you some brain cells. Yes, I have Goldie and her good friend Josie. They're fine—at least temporarily. Their safety will depend on you and Cordell. We'll be waiting for you at the homestead. But Max, don't be foolish enough to call the Rawlins cops or I will kill both women. I think you know I will enjoy it. You and Cordell need to come alone. If you don't—"

"Got it, Grimes."

"If you leave now, you should be able to get here by dark. I wouldn't dally if I were you."

The man didn't know how close they were to the turnoff to the homestead. Nor would Grimes know about what had been found up the road if the coroner had already taken the body into town. They already knew that it wouldn't be much of a crime scene given how long ago it had happened. The cops also already had a pretty good idea of whose remains they'd found—and who'd buried their mother there.

"I need to hear Josie's and Goldie's voices to make sure they are all right," Max said as he waved off his brother's demand to know what was going on.

"Don't trust me, huh? Hold on."

Max listened as a door opened. Moments later, Goldie

came on the line. She got out a few high-pitched words before Grimes gave Josie the phone.

"We're fine," Josie said, almost making him laugh. He knew better than anyone that they were far from fine.

Grimes came back on the line. "Satisfied?"

"We're on our way." He started to tell Grimes not to hurt either of the women. He started to threaten him. Instead, he saved his breath and disconnected without another word and turned to his brother.

"Grimes has both women at the homestead." His brother started to ask how that was possible since he should have been in jail. He quickly explained, seeing how scared Cordell was for Josie, before he tried to soften the blow. "He apparently doesn't know about the remains found past the homestead. Nor does he know that we are already down here in Wyoming. We have the element of surprise since he isn't expecting us until dark."

Cordell didn't look all that relieved. "I swore I would never set foot on that homestead ever again."

"Look, if you—"

"I came back from Florida because I knew this had to end." He let out a bitter laugh. "I guess I also knew where it would end."

MAX WISHED HE hadn't brought his brother down here, but he knew in his heart that the only way he could have left him behind was locked up in one of the cells. Nor, as hard as it was to admit it, he didn't think he could stop Grimes on his own. The hardened criminal had both women. Max was well aware of what the man was capable of doing to them.

As he drove toward the turnoff to the homestead, Max also admitted that he was guilty of still thinking of Cordell

as a kid. His brother's antics growing up had made him
think that Cordell would never grow up. A part of him still
felt that way, right or wrong. Cordell had driven almost
straight through from Florida to Dry Gulch to warn him,
making him wonder what he'd been thinking.

"You know you should have just called to tell me about
Grimes."

"Seriously?" his brother said now. "Do you really think
I wouldn't come back, knowing you were in danger and
needed me?"

Knowing that Cordell was risking his life for him upset
Max. "What were you doing in Florida anyway?"

"The weather? The Gulf? The lifestyle? I had a job
working for a private detective doing stakeouts. It was a
good-paying gig."

"So, you wouldn't have ever come back if you hadn't
seen Grimes on TV?"

He felt Cordell shoot him a look. "Are you trying to
pick a fight?"

Max cursed because he had been. "I just feel like I don't
know you anymore."

"I haven't changed, if that's what you're thinking. But if
you're worried about me not being able to back you up—"

"I'm worried about getting you killed," he snapped. "We
could be walking into an ambush. Hell, even if we're not,
this won't be easy."

"You said he doesn't know we're already down here,"
his brother pointed out. "We'll have the upper hand. This
is good news." Cordell had always been like this, seeing
the best outcome in every situation, every person he stumbled across.

"It's Cordell's superpower," their landlady, Iris, always
said. "He's determined to enjoy life believing the worst

is over." She'd looked at him over the top of the glasses perched on her nose. "It's not a bad attitude."

What she'd meant was that Max could be a little more like that. Instead, he realized that he'd been waiting his whole life for the other shoe to drop, for things to get worse, knowing it was just a matter of time. And he'd been right. The shoe had dropped. He'd always feared that what he'd done that night with his brother's help was going to come back on him. Now it had.

Chapter Fourteen

Cordell stared out the window as his brother drove the narrow highway, terrified of what they would find once they reached the homestead. They hadn't passed a town in hours or seen a house in fifty miles. The terrain outside the pickup windows had flattened and become barren. The wind howled, pelting the truck with dirt as the high desert stretched out endlessly ahead of them, filled with nothing but sagebrush in this desolate part of Wyoming.

With each mile, he felt revulsion at the thought of returning to the place where they had grown up. His only good memories were after they'd moved to Dry Gulch. Still, it had taken him a while to shake off the past. His nightmares had always been about Roger coming back to life.

"Maybe everything on the property blew away," he said, glancing at Max. His brother drove with an intense look on his face as if he, too, was wishing that they were going anywhere but the old homestead.

"It's still there," Max said as if, like him, he could never get the image of the place out of his head.

"I just remember it being the windiest, coldest place in the state. Remember when Roger used to make us use the outhouse during blizzards. Said it was to see if we knew how to get back without getting lost and freezing to death. You know he was hoping we'd die out there."

"Let's not take a ride down memory lane, okay? We survived it, made a life for ourselves."

Until now, Cordell thought but didn't voice. There was no need to. They both knew what was ahead for them. "You know, living in fear for that many years, it's bound to have done something to us."

"You think?" Max scoffed. "You're not that messed up."

They rode in silence for a few miles before Cordell said, "I'm sorry that I made your life harder growing up. I always worried that I was like him, not the violent part, but the worthless part."

"He was our so-called *stepfather*, not our blood, so you didn't inherit anything from him," Max said.

"But he was the only father I knew. You don't think we could have picked up something from him?"

Reaching over, his brother squeezed his shoulder. "There is nothing about you that's anything like Grimes. Nothing." His voice broke. "Do you have any idea how much I love you?" His brother reached up and squeezed his hand.

He put his hand back on the wheel. "I swore I would never be like that sorry son of a—"

"You're not, Max," Cordell said. "You never could be."

"I guess we'll soon find out," Max said under his breath as he braked for the turnoff to the old homestead.

Cordell swallowed the lump in this throat as his brother turned onto what looked like a dirt path through the high weeds. "Max, you know we're going to have to kill him, don't you?" he whispered as the wind howled louder and the sky seemed to darken around them as if a storm was blowing in. "That's if he doesn't kill us first."

"He won't kill us outright," Max said without looking

at him. "He'll do what he always did, take his time so he can get as much enjoyment out of it as he can."

"Oh, that makes me feel so much better." He glanced ahead. He remembered the road down to the place being longer, but in no time at all, his brother was slowing again.

He held his breath as Max turned down the short, rutted dirt road filled with dried weeds. In the distance, the lone cluster of dilapidated buildings came into view on the horizon, sending a shudder through him.

What few trees had been planted years ago around the homestead were now misshapen like arthritic fingers. Through the dark twisted branches, he caught sight of the house. Wind and weather had stripped the structure of any color. Now it matched the high desert dirt that formed dunes along its lea side. Windows, dark with dirt and grime, peered out unseeing.

Max came over a rise, the house disappearing, and pulled off the road. Cutting the engine, he looked over at him for a moment before he reached in the back to pull out the weapons he'd brought. "I'm going up there alone to check things out and I'll—"

"I'm going with you," Cordell said.

His brother swore. "I'm trained for this. You aren't." He seemed to recognize Cordell's expression because he sighed. "All right, but we do it my way." He handed him an automatic rifle. "You ever shot one of these? I didn't think so." He pulled it back and handed him a hunting rifle.

Cordell didn't object. He'd seen the damage a weapon like that could do. Also, he was familiar with the hunting rifle since it was his that he'd left behind when he'd gone to Florida. He began to load it as Max laid out his plan, surprised that his hands weren't shaking.

He thought of only one thing. Josie. No matter what he had to do, she had to walk away from this today.

ROGER GRIMES COULDN'T seem to shut up. All he'd done since the call to Max was talk about himself and how life had dealt him a bad set of cards. For a man set on revenge, he seemed more excited than vindictive, overly so. Josie wondered what he was on.

"No one's ever cut me any slack," the man said. "My stepsons had it good compared to the way I was raised. My old man beat me daily. Beat my mother, too. We learned to keep our traps shut and just do as we were told. Didn't want to even look sideways at him or you were going to get the back of his hand."

"That's your excuse for the way you mistreated Max and Cordell?" she asked.

He made an ugly face, and she'd feared for a moment that she'd gone too far. "Nothing wrong with a little discipline. Those boys had been spoiled by their mother. She was pretty enough but mealy-mouthed, if you know what I mean. No backbone, especially when it came to those boys of hers. I told her I'd straighten them out, but she was always crying and screaming for me not to hurt them."

Josie's heart ached at what Max and Cordell must have gone through. "No wonder they ran away."

"Is that what they told you?" He let out a bitter laugh. "First their mother died. Clumsy woman fell and hit her head. Had to bury her down the road. I tried to spare Max and Cordell by telling them she ran off, but they turned me in to the cops for my effort." He shook his head. "After all I'd done for them, taking them and their mother in, giving them a home and feeding them. Ungrateful little—"

"Don't tell me," Josie said, not wanting to hear what he'd

done to them. She couldn't imagine how bad their lives had been with this man.

"How about what they did to me? Didn't tell you that, did they?" He was smiling at her, his smile more disturbing than his words. "I was teaching Cordell what happens when he talks to the cops about me when his brother jumped me. Both of them jumped me, grabbed my baseball bat and knocked me clean out. Which explains why they're still alive. If they'd done a better job of dumping my body after they thought they'd killed me…" He laughed. "Well, then we wouldn't be here right now, and you wouldn't have to pay the price for what them boys did."

She watched him rise to look out the window before checking his watch. She could see storm clouds gathering, smell the coming rain. She had no doubt that Cordell and Max were on their way. Her heart broke at the thought that they would come, and this man would hurt them before he killed all of them.

Shifting a little, she felt the reassuring pinch of the gun. *Bide your time,* she warned herself. *You're going to get your chance.*

Thunder rumbled in the distance. Suddenly, Grimes turned to look at them. His eyes had grown darker, she noticed, as he said, "Change of plans." He grabbed his phone and stepped away to bark out an order.

Heart dropping, Josie realized there were two of them.

Chapter Fifteen

The wind howled, pelting Max with dirt as he cut a swath through the sagebrush, winding his way toward the back of the house. He could feel a storm rolling in, the sky already blackening to the east. He could smell the approaching rain as the day darkened around him.

He kept low, keeping an eye on the house. A threadbare ragged curtain blew out one of the windows, snapping in the wind. Jagged glass edged all but one window that seemed to have miraculously remained. It was that window that worried him because there was darkness behind it, making him unable to see if Grimes was standing there watching him approach.

Max told himself that the man wasn't expecting them until after dark. But that didn't make him any less anxious. Out here in the sage, he was too visible even with the change in light from the storm. Once he got to the house—

He ran the last few yards and pressed his back against the house, listening. But it was impossible to hear anything inside with the wind and the storm coming in. Stepping to one side, he reached over and turned the knob. The back door swung in with a groan, and a rancid smell wafted out, but nothing else happened.

Maybe he was overreacting. Maybe Grimes had lost his touch. Or maybe the man hadn't arrived yet. He stepped in, moving quickly through the long narrow house, a shotgun house, as they used to call it.

While there was no sign of Grimes or the women he'd taken captive, memories ambushed him at every turn, making his stomach roil. He'd reached the living room and just seen the cut zip ties lying on the floor next to the old radiators when he heard the sound of a vehicle.

As first he thought it was Grimes leaving with Goldie and Josie. But as the roaring grew louder, he realized it was someone coming up the road. Not Cordell, surely he wouldn't—

He had only a second to make the decision. He ran for the back door as automatic-weapon fire burst across the front of the house. He heard the path of gunfire tear through the house, splintering the old, dried wood and burying itself in the walls.

Max threw himself toward the back door and almost made it. He felt the bullet rip through his side in searing pain. He was hit! He crashed out the back door and started to turn toward where he'd left Cordell.

But as the gunfire continued to ravage the house, all he could do was throw himself down on the ground next to the foundation. As the gunfire continued, decimating every inch of the house, he lay bleeding in the dirt, terrified that he was going to get them all killed.

CORDELL HAD TRIED to stay behind as his brother asked—until he heard the roar of the vehicle barreling up the road out of the darkness of the storm.

He'd grabbed the handgun he'd loaded and picked up the rifle before slipping out of the truck. The van sped by so fast, he doubted the driver had even seen the truck parked back in the gully where his brother had left it.

When he heard the gunfire only moments later, he'd taken off at a run after the van. He could still hear it. What he hadn't heard, though, was any return fire.

His first instinct was to get to find Max, but he knew he stood no chance of getting near the house, not with the van idling outside and Grimes still firing.

His only hope was getting behind the vehicle without being noticed. The sky darkened around him, the wind growing stronger. Running crouched down, he raced toward the back of the van and realized that the shooting had stopped. He half expected the van to take off before he could reach it.

All he could see of the driver was a large dark shape behind the wheel and the black of the AK sticking out the driver's side window facing the bullet-riddled house.

WHEN THE BOMBARDMENT of gunfire ended, Max lay still, his weapon drawn. He wasn't sure how badly he'd been shot. His side felt on fire, and he was bleeding badly, that much he knew. He waited to hear the sound of a van door opening and whoever had been behind the wheel to come make sure he was dead. Instead, all he could hear was the idling engine.

Sliding over to the edge of the house's foundation wall, he could see the swath of light from the van's headlights. Nothing moved through it.

Where was Cordell? He knew his brother. There was no way he had stayed put in the pickup. Max just hoped he didn't put himself in Grimes's line of fire. Even as he thought it, he knew Cordell was probably doing just that.

With a curse, he lay back in pain and did what he could

to stop the bleeding. He was trapped here. If he tried to run in either direction away from the house, he would be seen by whoever was sitting in that idling van. He figured it was Grimes patiently waiting for him to show his face.

But Max couldn't stay hidden knowing his brother was out there about to do something. He just didn't know what.

STAYING LOW, CORDELL ran through the sagebrush half expecting to hear gunfire again and feel the burn of bullets. But as he dropped to the ground again some distance from the van, he heard nothing.

Catching his breath, he knew what he had to do. Max could already be dead. He had no idea where Josie and Goldie were. Maybe in the back of the van. Hopefully, they hadn't been in the house now full of bullet holes.

Cordell had never wanted to come face-to-face with Roger again. Now he had no choice. He'd also never wanted to kill another human being. But then again, Roger Grimes was a monster. All he could hope was that Max was still alive and that they would be leaving here together with the women they loved.

He broke from his cover and sprinted the last few yards to the van to drop down in the back, hoping he hadn't been seen. Another burst of gunfire erupted from the van. Leaning the rifle against the back of the van, he pulled out the handgun. He would have to make sure his shots counted as he stayed low and moved along the passenger side of the long vehicle until he was crouched under the passenger side door, noticing that the window was down.

The gunfire had stopped again. He listened, half-afraid Grimes had seen him approach and was sitting behind the wheel waiting for him to stick his head up.

On the count of three, he rose suddenly, raised the gun

and fired into the cab of the van at the driver. He quickly dropped back down as a spurt of AK fire erupted and stopped just as quickly. He felt deaf from the close reports of gunfire. He could barely hear the low-idling rumble of the engine.

There was nothing beyond it but silence. It would be just like Roger to be playing possum, waiting with that AK in his big hands, his finger on the trigger.

MAX HEARD THE sound of a handgun, then a blip of gunfire from the AK, then nothing. He waited, expecting to hear the AK fire again. The pain in his side was excruciating but all he could think about was getting to Cordell.

When he didn't hear any more gunfire, he eased out from behind the house, moving swiftly along the side before he broke into an awkward run toward the back of the idling van. He could feel blood running down his arm, his hand holding his weapon slick with it.

Lightning split the sky open, followed almost at once by thunder. He felt the first raindrops hit him and for a moment thought Grimes had opened fire again. Then he saw his brother come around the back of the van, the pistol still in his hand, and noticed his expression. Cordell looked shocked and physically ill. Max couldn't help but think of the night he thought he'd killed Grimes.

Without a word, his brother opened the back of the van. Even in the growing darkness of the storm, he could see that it was empty before Cordell closed the door. "Where are Goldie and Josie?" he said more to himself than to his brother.

"I don't know." Cordell sounded like a sleepwalker. "I'd hoped they would be in the van. But neither is Roger."

"What?" Max thought he must have misheard. "The man

behind the wheel wasn't Roger Grimes?" His voice broke as the pain in his side tried to double him over.

His brother's eyes widened. "You're hit!" Cordell swore as he moved his brother's coat aside to see the blood-soaked clothing beneath. "You need to sit down." He reached to help but Max shook his head.

"We have to find Grimes. We have to find the women."

"I think I killed that friend of Roger's, Dave, the one you told me about who was picked up down in Cheyenne in a van with Florida plates."

Mind whirling, Max only had an instant to consider what to do. Cordell seemed out of it and Max feared he was almost too weak to keep standing, let alone fight off Grimes as he heard the sound of another engine start up, then saw headlights flash on and sweep toward them through the rain. Engine revved, a second van roared toward them.

CORDELL FELT DAZED. Still, he tried not to let his brother see how shaken he was. He'd just killed a man. It didn't matter that the man had been trying to kill them. He stuffed the handgun in his waistband, then looked at Max as he heard the other van roaring toward them.

His brother was leaning against the van trying to lift his weapon, clearly hurt much worse than he'd said. Cordell felt as if he were on autopilot as he heard the van coming down the bumpy road, its engine screaming as it rocked toward them.

"Go get him," Max said and gave up, letting his own weapon drop to the ground. "You can stop him. It's up to you now."

Cordell reached for the hunting rifle and moved to the passenger side of the van. Dave's van was still running, its headlights cutting through the storm like a signal for

Roger to follow. He laid the rifle over the side mirror and for a moment he was blinded by the headlights of the van racing toward them.

Did he dare take the shot? Josie and Goldie might be in that van, he told himself as Roger opened fire. The windshield blew out on the van. The bullets were coming wild, but Roger was still too far away. As he got closer, his aim would improve.

Take the shot, Cordell told himself.

JOSIE HEARD THE glee in Roger Grimes's laugh as he put down the van window, held the automatic rifle out and pulled the trigger. The man had quickly gotten them out of the house, ushering them into the van and hurriedly zip-tying them to the wall of the van again.

It was his need for speed that had made him sloppy and Josie was now taking advantage of it. Her wrists were looser than they should have been, allowing her to begin wriggling free the moment he slammed the van door. Next to her, Goldie was doing the same thing.

But Josie feared they wouldn't be fast enough. She got one wrist free, then the other and immediately went for the gun at her waist. The van rocked as it roared down the road. She had to brace herself against the side as she worked her way forward and got her first look at where they were headed.

She could see another van parked in front of the house. Its headlights were on and it appeared to be running. She couldn't see Max or Cordell, but the fact that Grimes had opened fire on the van told her at least he thought they were either in it or nearby.

Stepping up behind him, she pressed the gun barrel to the back of his head. "Stop," she said.

He kept driving, but he slowed a little. He also quit firing on the van ahead of them. "You aren't going to pull the trigger or you would have already," he said with a scoff and started firing the AK again.

Josie moved the barrel of the gun from his head and fired a shot into his right thigh. Grimes let out a scream of pain, his foot coming off the gas. At the same time, though, he pulled the rifle inside and turned to fire over his shoulder into the back of the van. Josie had seen the move coming and grabbed it with her free hand to shove the barrel away. The passenger side window blew out.

Goldie had gotten loose and rushed to help her as he jerked the rifle free and swung it, catching her friend in the side of the head. Josie's attention was drawn away as she saw Goldie go down.

"Bitch!" Grimes said and stomped on the gas again, thrusting the AK out the window and opening fire on the van.

Josie lost her balance as he hit a bump in the road. She tumbled to the floor next to Goldie, losing her grip on the gun. All she could think was that she should have taken the kill shot. Now they were all going to die, she told herself as she climbed to her feet and saw that they were about to crash into the van head-on.

CORDELL COULDN'T SEE inside the van careening toward him. He didn't know if Josie and Goldie were in there. That's why he didn't want to shoot. He was afraid to take a chance.

But he also couldn't wait any longer as the van headed directly for him. He took aim where he figured Roger's head would be behind the wheel, took a deep breath, held it and pulled the trigger.

He saw the windshield explode. In the headlights of the van, he saw Josie's face as she grabbed the steering wheel and pulled it hard. The vehicle swerved, rocking on two wheels, barely missing him and the van where he stood as it roared toward the old house.

Cordell watched in horror as it crashed through the outer wall and disappeared inside. Pushing off the side of the van, he dropped the rifle and sprinted toward what was left of the old homestead house.

It was the place where Roger had made his life hell, but Cordell was no longer afraid of the ghosts. He was terrified of only one thing. Losing the woman he'd always loved.

THE VAN WAS buried in the building, the engine no longer running. Instead, it was deathly quiet in the former living room. Parts of the walls hung off the van in splinters.

Cordell stumbled through the debris, working his way to the passenger side of the van because it was the most accessible. As he got closer, he could hear the tick of the engine—and smell gas. The scent set his heart thundering as he felt his fear rise dangerously. If Grimes wasn't already dead, he'd kill him.

At the side of the van, he jerked the door open. At first, all he saw was Goldie on the floor. He reached in, checking for a pulse. Finding one, he breathed a sigh of relief. But where was Josie?

He glanced into the front of the van. He still didn't see Josie, and that terrified him. He tried the passenger door and saw her. She'd come over the van's bench seat and now lay crumpled on the floorboard. Rushing to her, he heard her moan painfully as she tried to get up.

Cordell shot a look at Roger. He wasn't moving in the

driver's seat, his head bent to his chest, which was soaked in blood.

"Easy" he said, helping Josie. "How badly are you hurt?"

She shook her head. "My shoulder," she said as he got her out of the van. There was a goose egg of a bump on her forehead, but she was able to stand. "Goldie—"

"She's still breathing," he told her. "I'll get her. But you have to get out of here. Max is outside. Go to him."

She met his gaze before she limped out into the darkness of the storm. The rain had stopped. He barely noticed. Roger was still slumped behind the wheel. There was also no sign of the weapon he'd been firing. That should have worried Cordell more than it did as the man lifted his head and looked right at him. The smell of gasoline was much stronger. It burned his eyes, making him aware that it could catch fire and blow any minute.

"Pipsqueak!" Roger's voice was hoarse with pain and yet that mocking sick humor was still there as he called Cordell by the nickname he'd given him all those years ago. "You've grown up."

He saw that his shot had been low, hitting the man in the chest rather than the head. But from the labored breathing, he suspected Roger wouldn't make it even if he got to the hospital in time.

"You need to get me out of here," Roger said. "This place is going to blow sky-high. Help me with my seat belt. I can't get it to release."

Cordell ignored him and went to the open side door of the van, lifting Goldie out. As he started to carry her toward the huge hole in the side of the house, he heard Roger call after him.

"Son! You can't just leave me here to die."

He didn't turn around as he carried Goldie out toward

the van where his brother and Josie were waiting. Almost there, he heard the explosion behind him, felt its heat and kept walking as Goldie began to come around.

Ahead, he could see his brother's relief as well as his pain. All Cordell could think about was getting everyone to safety and Max to the nearest hospital.

Josie rushed to him, her face lit by the burning building behind him. The homestead was gone. So was Roger Grimes.

Chapter Sixteen

Max opened his eyes and blinked. The curtains were drawn, the room dim, yet he knew he was in a hospital room. Just as he knew he wasn't alone. He could make out the shape of a figure standing on the far side of the room. His pulse jumped, making the machines he was attached to come to life.

It wasn't until she turned that he recognized her, startling him.

Esther Mason made her way to his bedside. "You're awake." Her smile did nothing to change her dour expression. "They said you almost died. Lucky for you, the bullet went right through. Seems you're going to survive."

His mouth was so dry he could barely get the words out. "What are you doing here?" He saw then that she had picked up something. A pillow. She had a pillow in her hands as she moved closer.

He tried to lift a hand, but he was so weak from the gunshot, the surgery. He looked around frantically for the call button, but he couldn't find it. He opened his mouth to call for help, but it was too dry. Barely a sound came out.

It had been Esther. She'd told Grimes about them. How did he know that? Had Cordell told him that? It didn't matter. He had to stop Esther. The pillow dropped over his face. He couldn't breathe and yet he couldn't fight her off. She was going to kill him.

The door of his room opened. He jerked awake and blinked. A nurse stood silhouetted in the doorway. "Nurse!" He'd barely gotten the word out. But even the sudden light she turned on couldn't chase away the nightmare. "She was here. She was—"

He looked around frantically. There was no one in the room. Had Esther hidden under the bed? "There was a woman here," he said as the nurse came over to attend to the devices attached to him. "She—" Was Esther really going to smother him with a pillow? He felt so weak and vulnerable, he wasn't sure he could have stopped her. It was that feeling that had followed him so much of his life because of Roger Grimes.

"There was no woman here. You aren't allowed visitors," the nurse said. "Your brother was in earlier, but there has been no one else. I suspect it was just a bad dream."

He closed his eyes, feeling foolish, but still wanting to ask her to check the bathroom and under the bed. He hadn't felt this insecure and afraid since he was a child living with Grimes.

The nurse got him a cup of water and a straw. He took a drink, cleared his throat and handed it back. "Maybe she went into the bathroom," he said.

She patted his arm and smiled. "Let me check." As she moved to the closed bathroom door, he wanted to warn her that Esther could be dangerous. She opened the door. "Empty."

"Then I guess she's not under my bed, either," he said, pretending it was a joke.

She laughed. "Not there, either. That must have been some bad dream."

She had no idea.

JOSIE STILL FELT as if she were in a fog. She remembered being checked over in the ER after they'd rushed Max to surgery. Her shoulder had been dislocated and she had a slight concussion. She'd given her statement to the state police. By then it was daylight.

The nightmare was over. Grimes was dead. Cordell and Goldie were safe. Max was still in the hospital, but his condition had been upgraded from critical to stable. Both she and Cordell had been questioned at length. He'd saved not just Josie's life, but Goldie's, as well.

Rumors ran wild in town. No one really understood why it had happened except that Roger Grimes had been Max's and Cordell's stepfather and had spent most of his life behind bars.

"You aren't going to work? Surely you can take a day off after almost being killed!" Amy Sue said, shaking her head as Josie came downstairs dressed to go to the office.

"I'm fine." But even as Josie said it, she knew she wasn't. It was as if everyone in Dry Gulch had taken a relieved breath—except her because she knew better. Everyone kept saying at least it was over.

But it wasn't over.

Josie couldn't explain it, the danger she still felt looming on the horizon. She wanted to blame her concussion. She kept waiting for the frightened feeling to go away, but it still had her looking over her shoulder, jumpier than she'd ever been.

She kept reliving what had happened. Her grandmother would have been disappointed in her. She had the chance to stop the man. If Cordell hadn't taken the shot he had, they could all be dead.

Cordell had saved her life. But he'd also endangered it by having loved her. She told herself that he'd no doubt be gone once the state police were through with him.

"You're just going back to work at your office as if nothing happened?" her sister demanded as she watched her reach for her coat and purse.

"What would you have me do? Take to the couch?" Josie demanded, knowing she was more irritable than usual, but unable to help it. She didn't know what to do until the next horror hit town. All she knew was that it was coming. She'd tried to see more, desperately needing to know so she could warn everyone and prepare this time. It felt closer, more personal, and that scared her even more.

At the same time, she kept hoping she was wrong. Maybe this was just an aftershock to how close she'd come to dying. How close she'd come to losing her best friends and Cordell.

As she reached for her purse, she misjudged how heavy it was now. It slipped from her fingers and hit the floor hard. She saw her sister's eyes widen as she looked from Josie to the purse.

Amy Sue got to the purse first, picking it up and not even bothering to look inside. She knew by the weight of it what made it so heavy. *"You're carrying a gun now?"* There was fear in her voice, the same fear that pressed against Josie's chest, making it hard to breathe at every waking moment because her "gift" told her the threat wasn't over. She was afraid and hated it.

Grimes had been a bully, a big man who took his misery out on his wife and his stepsons. He liked hurting and tormenting people, but nowhere on his long list of crimes was there the portrait of a cold-blooded killer. Although according to Cordell, Grimes had pushed his wife down the stairs. He hadn't purposely killed her, but he had lied and buried her in a shallow grave up the road. Max and Cordell had gone to Rawlins and identified the dress she'd been wearing the last time they'd seen their mother alive. So it should have been over.

But the danger Josie saw coming now was different. This person was a cold-blooded killer—and it was personal—just like she'd seen that first day out on the porch. It was still coming and, for the life of her, Josie couldn't understand it—let alone see who it was. How was it possible after what they'd already been through?

"I have to go," she said as she took her purse from her sister and left the farmhouse.

Amy Sue followed her out to the porch. "You're scaring me."

She was scaring herself. How could she explain the sense of foreboding she still felt, the blackness, the evil? Unlike her grandmother, she couldn't give it shape or reason. All she could do was sense the horror that was about to be unleashed. She couldn't even warn anyone. All she could do was wait.

When she reached her office, she found Cordell sitting on the front step. They hadn't had a moment together since the Grimes nightmare. He'd been taken into custody, questioned and released. Grimes's history and their statements would help to get the investigation closed quickly, they'd been told.

"Good morning," Cordell said as he rose. One look at Josie and he didn't have to inquire how she was doing.

He could see it in the dark shadows under her eyes, in the haunted look.

She pulled her purse to her and dug out her keys. "I thought you'd be gone by now."

"About that," he said. "That's why I'm here. I need some legal advice."

"If it's about the shooting, you need a criminal lawyer."

"Nope. It's about those old warrants. I'm afraid I'm not going to be able to leave town after all."

She had drawn out her office keys but was having trouble getting the key into the lock. Cordell took the key chain from her and opened the door. "After you."

Josie entered, realizing she was glad he was here. She turned on the light and looked around before she stepped in. It felt cold and uninviting compared with the farmhouse. She wondered why she'd insisted on coming here today.

"We had a deal," she said to Cordell as she went behind her desk, put her purse in the second drawer and, after removing her jacket, spread it on the back of the chair before she sat down.

"I can't leave because I bought the hotel."

Her gaze shot up to his.

"Why would you do that? That place has been boarded-up for years."

"Because I need some form of employment and I'm looking forward to the challenge of bringing the place back to its earlier grandeur, or at least getting rid of the dust and mice."

She shook her head. "That's a terrible idea. The smartest thing you could do is get your money back and return to Florida or even somewhere farther away from Dry Gulch."

He stared at her. "Wow, it almost sounds like you want me gone."

"I'm serious." Her throat ached and she felt as if she might cry. "You don't want to stay here. For whatever reason, this is a dangerous place."

"Is this about Big Blue?" he asked as if hoping to lighten the mood. He knew her, knew she was fighting tears, and she hated it when he moved behind her desk to comfort her. "You know why I brought the horse back. I wanted to show you that I've changed. I'm determined to prove myself to you."

"Oh, Cordell, you already have," she cried. The moment he drew her up from her chair, she was in his arms again. She leaned into his chest as if needing this as desperately as he did. She didn't want him to leave town. She never wanted him to ever leave again. He could feel it in the way she hugged him back. She seemed afraid of what would happen if he stayed. She was fighting this for some reason he didn't understand.

She stepped out of his arms and sat back down. "The judge isn't going to be happy about this."

"Josie, I'm not leaving. Please, do whatever you have to do, but I'm here to stay."

JOSIE REALIZED HOW desperately she had wanted to hear those words. She swallowed before she turned to look at him. He'd grown into such a handsome, strong man. Most of his bad-boy persona was gone, but there was still some mischief in that gaze. It pulled at her heartstrings, playing them like a symphony. She wanted him to stay. She loved the idea of him opening the hotel, although she couldn't imagine he would make any money. Few people had a reason to come to Dry Gulch.

What she also saw in his gaze was stubborn determination. That made him even more handsome. She desperately wanted him to succeed as she met his gaze and nodded. "I'll talk to the judge."

"Thanks." He grinned, exposing that darned dimple again, and she felt herself weaken. They'd survived Roger Grimes. Wasn't it possible that together they could survive even worse as long as they all stuck together?

"I'd better get to work and let you do the same," he said. "Maybe we could have dinner one night." He held up a hand to keep her from answering right away. "Just think about it."

With that, he left her with her heart aching. Wasn't this what she'd always dreamed of? Cordell coming home, settling here, making a life, being the man she needed in her life.

GOLDIE HADN'T BEEN allowed in to see Max. *Family only.* Those words broke her heart. After giving her statement to the state police, she went down to the café and began to clean up the mess Grimes had left. Max was going to live. She took strength in knowing that, even though she felt as if she were sleepwalking through her day.

The fact that he might not want to see her lodged itself in the back of her mind. She told herself she would visit as soon as she was allowed. She had to make sure he was going to be all right. At least that's what she told herself. In truth, she wondered if any of what had happened had changed his mind about their being together.

Ronnie had suffered a concussion and would be back to work soon, she was told. In the meantime, his mother had volunteered to cook until her son recovered.

Maggie was already in the kitchen cleaning up when Goldie arrived.

"I didn't expect you in today," the woman called to her.

"I can get my daughter Lindsey to work if you need more time off."

Goldie shook her head. "I need to get back to work." It felt surreal, what she'd been through. It had happened so quickly and ended just as fast, leaving her feeling off-balance. She couldn't imagine how Josie was feeling since it had to be much scarier for her. The two of them had talked a little earlier, but both were still a little shaken.

Dry Gulch had always felt so safe. Hardly anyone she didn't know came into the café unless a tourist had wandered in off one of the main highways in the state and gotten lost.

But now she knew she'd never feel safe here again. It didn't help that she couldn't see Max and that no one knew when he'd be back to work. The state police had left. Things should have felt normal again, but they didn't.

Goldie felt as if she was waiting for the other shoe to drop.

"You okay?" Maggie asked.

Letting out the breath she'd been holding, she smiled at the older woman. She realized that she'd been standing staring at the mess, unable to move. "I will be," she said, though she wasn't sure that was true as she shook herself. "I just need to work."

Across the street, she caught a glimpse of movement and stopped. Cordell was removing weather-grayed sheets of plywood from the front of the boarded-up abandoned Dry Gulch Hotel. Vaguely, she wondered what that was about before she went to get a broom and a dustpan.

Chapter Seventeen

Max thought he would feel less off-balance once he knew that Grimes was really dead this time. From what Cordell had told him, he had wounded Grimes enough he would have died but the fire and the explosion had finished him off.

He felt such a rush of pride in his brother. Cordell had stepped up in a way he'd never expected. Max couldn't help but wonder if things would have gone worse had he been there. He would never know, but he was glad when his brother walked into the room later that afternoon.

"How's it goin'?" Cordell asked as he moved to the side of Max's bed and took his hand.

"The doctor said I'm going to live."

"Was there any doubt?" his brother joked. "I told Goldie not to worry because you're the strongest man I know."

Just the sound of her name was a stab to his chest. He didn't feel strong right now. He felt anything but. "How is she?"

"She went back to work today at the café." Max nodded. "She wants to see you."

"That's not a good idea," he said and felt his brother's gaze narrow on him.

"I thought you'd be anxious to see her," Cordell said.

He shook his head, unable to explain this awful feeling he had even to himself, let alone to anyone else. "I think she's better off without me."

"Is this about Roger? He's gone. Nothing came out about our pasts. No one would care anyway. It's over."

So why didn't it feel that way? Because he was sheriff and he'd be facing the next threat that came to town? Living in Dry Gulch, he'd never thought about how if he married Goldie, he might be putting his wife and children in jeopardy. But he did now thanks to Grimes.

"I'm staying at your house until you get out of the hospital and after that if you need me, but Max, you love Goldie. Don't push her away."

He shook his head. "I don't want to talk about it." He quickly changed the subject. "I had a dream that Esther Mason was in my hospital room and was about to smother me with a pillow."

Cordell didn't know what to say. "That's pretty weird."

"One of the state police told me that she provided information about you and me, Josie and Goldie to Grimes."

"Do you want me to take her out for you?"

"Don't even joke about that," Max said. "You got lucky with Grimes, same with Dave. You could have been killed or convicted of a crime."

"But I wasn't," Cordell said, looking worried. "Are you sure you're all right? The nurse told me not to upset you."

"You killed two men and you're acting like…"

"Like life goes on?" his brother demanded. "I almost lost my brother and Josie and my own life. You think I don't know that I had to kill two men?" He waved a hand through the air. "Instead of curling up in a ball, I bought the old Dry Gulch Hotel. I'm going to reopen it."

Max blinked. "That's the dumbest thing I've ever heard."

Cordell laughed. "We deal with what happens to us in different ways, bro. This is my way."

"What does Josie think about this?" he had to ask.

"She thinks the same thing you do, that I'll never make it happen. But that was the old Cordell Lander. I'm going to turn that hotel into a destination resort and pump some life back into this town."

Max shook his head. "Go for it," he said, seeing that there was no dissuading his brother. "Can't wait to see what this new improved Cordell does."

His brother grinned. "I just might surprise you."

"You already have, brother."

THE FIRST CUSTOMER who came through the door of the café sent Goldie's heart hammering and stole her breath until she recognized the rancher. Yet her hands were shaking as she took him a menu and a glass of water.

"Glad to see you're okay," the rancher said. "None the worse for wear."

She couldn't say that, but she smiled and took his order. When she turned it in, she saw Maggie watching her with concern. "I'm fine," she told her.

"Sure you are," the woman said as if trying to sound like she meant it.

A few more people came in, all talking about Big Blue instead of the crazed criminal who had taken her hostage, and Goldie was glad of it.

"Wonder who took it to start with?" a local man said.

"You know it was those folks over in the Rosebud County. They've always been our rivals," another man said.

"I'm wondering more why they brought it back. I heard Josie hired some local kids to scrub the horse down with soap and water. That's the kind of pride I like to see in this town," the woman with them said.

"It's nice to have it back," the men agreed. "I missed it."

That the town could so easily go back to the way it was didn't help with Goldie's unsettled feeling. How could something that frightening and life-threatening happen to you and everything go back to normal so quickly?

She took the table's orders, only screwing up one of them and breaking a couple of glasses and a plate, before Maggie's daughter showed up. "I could really use the work," Lindsey said.

Goldie shot a look into the kitchen, where Maggie was busy at the grill and didn't look up as she did her best to pretend she was innocent. Goldie appreciated the thought. She'd told herself that work was what she needed, but she realized what Maggie had. She wasn't up to this yet. She took off her apron and smiled at Lindsey. "It's all yours. Thanks. And thank your mother."

The teenager smiled and hurried to take care of the couple that came through the door. Goldie wished she was going to the place she had considered home, Max's place. Instead, she headed for the extra bedroom at her cousin Clancy's down the block. As she walked, she found herself looking up the road into town as if expecting something bad to roll down the main drag at any moment.

As a week passed and then another and another, Josie began to wonder if she'd been wrong. Everyone seemed to have gotten over what had happened.

Goldie had been shaky at first when they'd gotten together to share a bottle of wine and talk. But she had bounced back—even when Max hadn't wanted to see her at the hospital or at the house on his return to town.

"It's really over between us, I guess," her friend said one evening at the office. They were sitting on the couch, feet tucked under them, talking about everything that had happened and how it had affected them.

"It's strange how different we all are," Goldie said. "I thought at first I would never get over it, that I would continue to be scared at the café. I actually thought about putting it up for sale."

"You've talked about selling it before," Josie reminded her.

"That's when I thought Max and I would be getting married. I wanted to devote myself to being the perfect wife and figured we'd have kids after that, and I'd be too busy to run the café. I have to accept that it's over between us."

"I'm sorry."

Goldie took a sip of her wine. "I've decided to move on."

"Good for you."

"I told myself the other day that the first man who walked into the café who was under seventy and single, I was going to go out with him."

Josie laughed. "Sounds like a plan."

Goldie laughed with her. "Hope I'm not seventy before it happens." She took another drink. "Can you believe the progress Cordell has made on the hotel?"

Josie couldn't. "He's been working at it constantly for weeks and even hired help. I think he's serious about opening it again."

Goldie looked as skeptical as Josie felt. "He actually thinks that if he builds it, people will come?"

Chuckling, Josie nodded. "He plans to advertise. He was telling me about some ideas he has. They aren't bad, if he can pull them off." While he had stopped by on occasion, he hadn't mentioned going out to dinner again.

"I think he's serious about staying here this time."

"I guess we'll see," Josie said, still feeling that growing darkness hunkered on the horizon as if waiting for something. She had no clarity about what it was or what it meant. Just that it was evil, eviler than Grimes, something she couldn't imagine.

She just hoped it had nothing to do with Cordell. She'd never seen him like this. Every day, she watched the progress on the hotel from her office window, cheering him on and silently willing him to keep going. The whole town was watching the place come back to life and rooting for him, but no one more than Josie. She had a feeling that he needed this as badly as she needed to see him do it.

MAX HAD BEEN glad to get out of the hospital. He kept having bad dreams in which Esther or someone else had tried to kill him. He knew it didn't make any sense. The fear, though, was real. He didn't feel safe.

Back at his house, he wandered through the place, intensely aware of Goldie's missing things. He hadn't realized how much of a home she'd made with a plant here, a candle there, a quilt on the wall behind the couch. The house felt empty and made him sad. He couldn't wait to get back to work so he didn't have to spend much time here.

"You should at least go see her," Cordell said one day when he stopped by.

"You should mind your business," Max had snapped and saw his brother's look. "Sorry."

"Once you get back on your feet, maybe everything will look differently," Cordell had said.

Max knew it wouldn't, but he didn't argue. He'd had enough arguments between his head and his heart over Goldie. Fortunately, he hadn't seen Goldie because he feared his heart would betray his head. Lindsey Dean had been bringing him meals from the café.

He hadn't had to order what he wanted since Goldie knew him so well. Each day, she'd send him something special, making him hurt even worse. Finally, he gave a list of what he wanted to Lindsey—all things completely different from what he normally would have ordered.

From then on, nothing was special about the meals. He could no longer feel Goldie's love and, while that broke his heart, he knew it was the way things had to be. He couldn't offer her the life she deserved. She'd get over him and move on, and he would die a bachelor, old and cranky, just as his brother now predicted.

He listened as Cordell talked about the renovations at the hotel. He'd wondered where his brother had gotten the money. Cordell said he'd been working on several of the ranches when they needed help, although he swore that he still had what he'd saved in the years he'd been gone from Dry Gulch.

"It's going to happen, you know," Cordell said. It took Max a moment to realize what he was talking about. His thoughts wandered more than they used to. "The hotel. It's going to happen. I'm going to call it the Lander Inn and Resort."

"Sounds pretty highfalutin."

"You'll see. I have all kinds of plans. Think I might have a soft opening as early as the spring."

Max envied his brother for taking on such a project, although he had no idea what a soft opening was. "If anyone can do it, it's you," he said truthfully. This Cordell could do anything, he thought. His kid brother had definitely changed, and he wondered how much Josie Brand had a hand in it.

"I'm going back to work next week," Max announced.

"You sure you're ready for that?" Cordell asked, looking concerned.

"Why would you ask? I'm healthy as a horse. Doc told me at my checkup."

"I don't know," his brother admitted. "I just feel like maybe you've lost your drive to be sheriff. If you want to hang up your star, you can go into business with me at the hotel."

Max shook his head. "Nothing's changed," he lied. "So how are things between you and Josie?"

"I'm taking it slow. I need to prove to her the kind of man I am now," Cordell said and grinned. "One of these days, I might even ask her out."

Josie couldn't help her shock when she looked up from her office to see Esther Mason standing in the doorway. Her disgust for the woman must have shown, because Esther bristled and propelled herself forward as if on a mission.

Bracing herself, Josie sighed and leaned back in her chair, ready for the onslaught.

"I just wanted you to know that a lot of lonely women write to prisoners," Esther said. "The whole town wants to make me into the villain. How was I to know that Roger was going to come here and—" She waved a hand through the air before narrowing her eyes at Josie. "You believe what you want, but those boys tried to kill him. That's what brought him here. Wasn't anything I told him."

"I see no reason to debate this, Esther. Roger Grimes is dead. Cordell and I have been cleared in his death. Max is getting better. It's over."

The older woman puffed up like a blowfish. "I know

for a fact that he wasn't the only one writing to someone from around here."

That took Josie by surprise. She had hoped that Esther was the only one who'd had contact with Grimes. "You know that for a fact?"

"Roger told me."

"Did he tell you who?" She could feel her skin crawl, her blood pounding in her ears. Esther was enjoying knowing something Josie didn't. But it quickly became apparent that she didn't know much.

"He wouldn't say, just that I'd been more helpful."

"I'll just bet you were," Josie said, losing patience. "Is that all, Esther?"

The elderly woman looked indignant for a moment. "This is a hateful town. I'm so glad I left it."

Not as glad as the residents, Josie thought, but bit her tongue.

"But you should know. There is someone among you who is deceiving you all." With that, Esther turned and left, slamming the door behind her.

Josie sighed, hoping she was wrong, but worried that she wasn't. If someone in town had been writing to a prisoner and Roger Grimes knew about it, then the two criminals must have known each other. Even been friends?

But other prisoners didn't have any reason to want to hurt anyone in Dry Gulch, she reminded herself as she tried to brush off what Esther had told her. It was just Esther stirring the pot. At the same time, she hated that now she would be unconsciously looking for the letter writer among the town's female residents.

Chapter Eighteen

Cordell grinned when he looked out to see Josie standing on the sidewalk in front of his hotel. She walked by every day, trying to peer into the soaped-over windows, as if wanting to see how the remodel was progressing. Or just maybe, wanting to see him. He could only hope, he told himself, as he went to the front door and threw it open.

Startled, she jumped back and tried to pretend she hadn't been snooping.

He laughed at her embarrassment at being caught. He'd purposely left her alone the past few weeks. He wasn't exactly playing hard to get. More like hoping she'd come to him when she was ready.

Eyeing her now, he couldn't imagine her looking any more beautiful. She'd always taken his breath away. Nor had he ever met a stronger, more determined woman. Her long dark hair was pulled back with a clip that he yearned to open to release her mass of curls. Her lips were freshly glossed, just begging to be kissed.

"Hello, Counselor," he said, trying to rein his bad-boy thoughts in. "Nice of you to stop by."

"I was just on my way to my office," she said. "I didn't mean to distract you from your work."

"Darn, I thought maybe you were wondering when I was finally going to ask you to dinner." He saw her flush. She almost looked nervous, but that was so not like her. "How about this weekend? If you're free." Before she could answer, he rushed on. "I could use a woman's input on the furnishings in the hotel. If you're interested."

JOSIE KNEW HE was toying with her and probably had been for a few weeks now. She eyed him, unable not to notice how good he looked in an old T-shirt under a pair of faded denim bibs. A tool belt hung from his slim hips and he smelled of sawdust and paint. He was tanned from outside work she heard he'd been doing on local ranches to help pay for his endeavor. His arms were more muscled from all that labor plus the work he was putting into the hotel. She often would see lights on at the hotel and knew he'd be working late. His hair was longer again, blonder from the sun. A lock fell over one blue eye as he grinned.

She breathed him in, liking the smell of the sawdust, the paint and the sweat. The man had never looked more male or sexier and he knew it. She swallowed, feeling heat race across her cheeks. "Yes."

His grin broadened. "Yes?"

"Yes, to all of it," she said, meeting his gaze and holding it.

He looked surprised, but equally delighted. "Great. Why don't you come to the hotel Saturday night. Say seven o'clock. I'll be ready for you."

Her heart was already thumping wildly in her ears. "I certainly hope so," she thought but didn't dare say as she nodded, turned on her heel and walked toward her office. She could feel his gaze hot on her backside and felt the exquisite heat shoot straight to her center. No man had ever fired her up like Cordell, but six years ago he'd been more like a teenage boy than the man who'd just asked her out to dinner.

She found herself smiling, anxious for her dinner date with the new owner of the Lander Hotel and Resort.

Dear Angel,

It's a miracle. I got that new lawyer I told you about. Thanks again for sending the money. That really helped. He got me a hearing. I might be getting out of here. I don't understand all the legal stuff. But it seems my public defender really messed up.

I've dreamed of you every night. I just never thought I'd ever get to actually meet you in person. If all goes well, I might be making a trip to Montana. I hope I'm not being too forward since you never thought I'd ever be getting out of here. I never thought so, either.

Write me. Let me know how you feel about this. I'll understand if you don't want to see me. Just know, I'm going to pay you back every dime I owe you. I loved finally hearing your voice when I called you a few weeks ago. Mind if I do it again? Sorry it has to be collect.

Your very happy pen pal,

Shane

"Wow, you look nice," Amy Sue said as Josie came down the stairs at the farmhouse. "I can't remember the last time I saw you in a dress. That's quite the dress. Is that new?"

Josie smoothed the silken fabric down over her hips. "Is it too much?"

"Depends on where you're going and who you're meeting," her sister said.

She knew Amy Sue wasn't going to approve. "I'm having dinner with Cordell at the hotel."

"Is the hotel restaurant even finished?"

"I don't know. He keeps the window covered so it's hard to see inside. Yes, I'm curious. You might as well say it."

Her sister shook her head. "Would it do any good to warn you that he's going to break your heart again?"

"No, it wouldn't," she said, "but thank you for worrying about me. We should talk about your love life instead." Now that Josie thought about it, her sister had been wearing makeup lately and seemed more cheerful. "Is there a man in your life?"

"Maybe, nice you noticed."

"Who is he?" Josie asked, instantly worried. Her sister had never been any better than she herself was when it came to finding a good one. Wasn't that why she'd waited in hopes Cordell would return?

Amy Sue chuckled. "You'll find out soon enough. You'd better get going. You don't want to keep Cordell waiting. You do look beautiful. I like your hair up like that."

"Thank you." She hugged her sister, hoping Amy Sue had found someone. She deserved the best. "I'm staying in town tonight."

"Of course you are," her sister said with a chuckle. "Enjoy yourself."

Josie planned to, but she couldn't help being anxious to see how much Cordell had accomplished at the hotel. It seemed a monumental job and she questioned if he had it in him to see it through.

Just like she questioned if he had what it took to stay in a relationship—let alone stay in Dry Gulch.

CORDELL LET OUT a wolf whistle when he opened the hotel's front door and saw Josie standing there in that dress.

For a moment, he was actually at a loss for words. "You look amazing. Come on in."

He'd set up a table and two chairs in the center of the hotel lobby. He saw Josie's eyes widen at the sight of them. "Aren't these chairs amazing? I love all the curved wood. I had Alice Jones recover them. Do you like the burgundy fabric? It's velvet." He watched her run her hand over the chair seat and back.

"It's beautiful, Cordell. I had no idea these were still in the hotel." She looked around the lobby. "Were these lights here, as well?"

"They were. Just needed to be cleaned up. It was all here just waiting for me to uncover it down in the basement." He couldn't help sounding pleased. Everything he'd discovered confirmed what he already knew. He was supposed to come back here and restore the hotel, restore his life here, hopefully with Josie.

He pulled out the chair for her and she sat. He felt his body respond to the dress she had worn. *Down, boy,* he told himself. He couldn't blow this even though he would have gladly skipped dinner altogether and taken her up to the finished hotel room where he'd been staying.

As he poured them each a glass of wine, he said, "I can't take my eyes off that dress on you."

"Wait until you see it off of me," Josie said and chuckled.

"Don't tease me, woman. I'm not that strong."

At a knock at the front door, he said, "Our dinner has arrived. I hope you're hungry."

"You have no idea," she said and smiled.

JOSIE WOULD HAVE gladly skipped dinner. She took a sip of her wine and looked around the lobby. Cordell had done an amazing job of bringing it back to life.

But it was the change in him that most interested her. She hadn't been able to keep her eyes off him since he'd opened the door. He'd dressed up for their dinner in new jeans and a long-sleeved buttoned-up shirt with a leather jacket.

He came back with a tray full of covered dishes, set it down on a small table to the side and took off the jacket. "Let's finish our wine first, if that's all right with you." He sat down, picked up his glass and held it up. "A toast?" He met her gaze. "I can't tell you how happy I am to be back here. Max is recovering, the hotel is going well and…" His eyes locked with hers. "And you're here in a dress that between you and me, it's enough to make a grown man cry."

They gently clinked glasses. "Can dinner wait? I really want to see what else you have done first."

He cocked his head at her for a moment. "Sure." He put down his glass and rose, helping with her chair, then he led her back to the owner's suite.

She blinked in surprise. "Cordell, this is beautiful. It's so…luxurious," she said as she ran her hand along the rich wallpaper to the king bed with its velvet headboard. "It's like from another time."

"That's the idea," he said, sounding pleased. "It's supposed to be an experience staying here."

She tested the bed with her hand, feeling how soft it was, how inviting. "Is this where you stay?"

He shook his head. "I have one of the unfinished hotel rooms."

"Why aren't you staying here?" she asked, frowning in surprise.

"Come on," he said without answering. "There's something else I want to show you. We're going to have a five-star restaurant. Wait until you see this chef's kitchen."

Josie watched him leave the room, his voice trailing behind him. She almost called him back, thinking she'd been too subtle, but he stopped part of the way and looked back at her.

"I thought maybe…" She'd never been shy or subtle, for that matter. Nor had Cordell ever been slow on the uptake. She nodded as if he'd spoken. Apparently, they weren't taking up where they'd left off—at least not yet.

Disappointed, she took a long breath and let it out, then she followed him into the chef's kitchen, wondering how he was able to afford all of this. It would be months before the hotel was up and running and he couldn't be sure that he could even keep it occupied.

But she knew that wasn't what worried her most. He wanted her as much as she wanted him. What was he waiting on?

"How was your dinner?" Amy Sue asked as Josie came into the farmhouse and dropped her purse unceremoniously onto the table.

"Delicious," she said, feeling guilty because she had barely been able to taste it. "Goldie made us a special meal at Cordell's request."

"Really?" her sister said, studying her. "I thought you were staying in town."

"I changed my mind."

"Hmm."

"What does that *hmm* mean?" Josie demanded, making her sister laugh.

"The dress apparently didn't have the effect you thought it would," Amy Sue said.

"Oh, the dress and me in it had his mouth watering," she snapped as she stormed into the kitchen. "It wasn't that."

Her sister cocked her head at her. "Cordell was the one who said whoa, ponies when it came time for dessert?" She laughed. "Your bad boy isn't bad anymore?"

"Apparently we are taking it slow," Josie said, grabbed a beer from the refrigerator and headed for the porch.

"Want to talk about it?" Amy Sue said after joining her. They both took a drink of their beer and looked out into the night. The velvet sky was alive with stars and just a fingernail slice of moon. A breeze stirred the dried leaves on the aspens. Somewhere in the distance, an owl hooted.

But that darkness was out there, as well. It had been there long enough that she thought maybe it wouldn't come to Dry Gulch. Maybe there would soon be good things on the horizon instead.

"I want Cordell," Josie said after a moment. "I always have."

"You've always taken him anyway you could get him knowing it probably wouldn't last," her sister said without looking at her. "You know what Gram used to say."

"If you say anything about giving away milk—that's so old-fashioned. Times have changed."

"Have they?" Amy Sue said. "Maybe Cordell wants more this time."

She stared at her sister. "What more could he want? I gave him my heart. I would have left here with him, traveled the country with him, gone anywhere he wanted if he had asked me."

"But you never would have married him because you're too sensible," Amy Sue said as Josie started to object. "Have you ever seen yourself married to Cordell Lander, having his children, depending on him instead of yourself?"

She felt tears burn her eyes. She had taken care of not just herself but her grandmother before she died and now her sister. She'd paid off the farm, leased the land to pay for everything else, buried her grandmother and made everyone proud of her. Marrying Cordell had never been in the plan because she'd thought she would just be taking on more than she could handle.

"Can you believe he wouldn't sleep with me after I wore this dress?" Josie asked and laughed. "That's all I wanted."

Her sister laughed. "Sounds like he knew what you were up to, and he wanted more."

She shook her head and took a drink of her beer. In town, she drank wine. Out here, she loved nothing better than a cold beer.

"You know, I'm not always going to be around," Amy Sue said. She shot her sister a concerned look. "I'm not dying or anything. I might want to make a life of my own one of these days. This farm…" she said, looking around. "Grandmother left it to you. But she was wrong about me. I want to farm the land with my husband."

"Husband? This man in your life that you're keeping under your hat, it's that serious?"

"We're just talking, maybe about the future," Amy Sue said and took a sip of beer.

"Sis, you know this farm is as much yours as it is mine."

"Just not legally."

Josie sighed. "That's because of the trust. Nana set it up so it couldn't be changed. But it doesn't matter, does it?"

Amy Sue shook her head. "We're just talking." She quickly changed the subject. "Did he even kiss you?"

Josie shook her head. "I know what Cordell's up to, and it isn't going to work." She swore and her sister laughed.

My Angel,

I can't wait to see Dry Gulch—and you. Thank you for inviting me to come visit. Especially for saying I can stay with you until I get my feet under me again. It won't take me long and I will be forever indebted to you. You've been so generous and sweet.

One of my cellies sold me his motorcycle so I'll have wheels. I just need to pick it up at his sister's house. Thanks, too, for the traveling money.

I still can't believe this is happening. All because of you. You gave me hope when I had none. You definitely are my angel.

Until I see you,

Shane

Chapter Nineteen

When Goldie saw the stranger ride in on the motorcycle, she thought he might be the one—the one she'd been waiting for who would take her away. He pulled up in front of the café and cut his engine. He was dressed in all-black leathers. The only color was the American flag on his helmet.

For a moment, he simply sat there as if admiring the view—the view being Dry Gulch. Goldie couldn't help but stare when he took off his helmet. His long dark hair was pulled back in a low ponytail, which heightened his lean features, the high cheekbones, and when he looked in her direction, his eyes looked dark as midnight.

She felt a shiver she took for desire. This man was nothing like Max Lander, so he was perfect. She heard Maggie hit the bell three times in succession and finally turned.

"Something shiny outside catch your eye?" the older woman asked. "Your order is up."

Goldie grabbed the plates off the pass-through and hurried them over to the waiting table. Out of the corner of her eye, she watched the biker, wondering if he would come in the café. She was sure he was only making a quick stop in town. He looked a little young for her, but maybe that was good.

She realized that what she was really looking for was someone who would make Max jealous—and this biker might be just the ticket. She hoped he was staying in town at least long enough for a meal in her café.

When an SUV pulled up next to the motorcycle and someone got out, Goldie hardly noticed—that wa3s until she saw the biker burst into a smile and walk over to the woman and give her a hug.

For a moment, she was too shocked to take a breath. Amy Sue Brand? The biker was holding her at arm's length. Was Amy Sue actually blushing? Goldie had never seen Josie's younger sister looking like this. Even the way she was dressed—as if she was going on a date. With the biker?

NEWS TRAVELED AT the speed of mouth in Dry Gulch and the town had its share of loudmouths. Josie was having a hard time understanding what Goldie was trying to tell her because she was whispering.

"Your sister just stole my pretend boyfriend," Goldie finally blurted out.

"Have you been drinking?"

"No, I'm down at the café working and this good-look-ing biker pulled in. I was thinking he might want to help me make Max jealous when your sister pulled up. They *know* each other, if you know what I mean."

"I don't."

"They *hugged* and were real friendly."

"I think you're making a bigger deal out of this than—"

"Amy Sue is dressed for a date. She's wearing *makeup*."

Josie spun her chair around to look out the window down the street toward the café. She could see Amy Sue's SUV parked out front. "I don't see a motorcycle."

"That's because she climbed on the back of it—without a

helmet, I might add—and they roared off together," Goldie said. "With her arms around him and her face pressed into his shoulder."

For weeks, Josie been waiting for the darkness on the horizon to either evaporate like a false alarm or descend on the town. She'd been frustrated with her inability to see what it might bode. All she'd felt was that the menacing threat was out there waiting for something.

"You've never seen the man before?" Josie asked.

"No. Why do you sound worried?" Goldie asked, her earlier excitement gone.

She stated the obvious. "This is not like Amy Sue. She hinted there might be a man in her life, but I thought it was Tillis at the grocery store. I saw the two of them laughing together the other day. She put her hand on his shoulder."

"*Tillis?* He laughs with everyone."

"Not me." She could tell that her friend didn't want to touch that remark with a retort. "Let me know when they come back." As she disconnected, she looked down the road out of town, frowning as she felt wisps of the darkness moving in. "Oh, Amy Sue, what have you done?"

CORDELL HAD BEEN mentally kicking himself since the night he and Josie had dinner at the hotel. "She couldn't have made her wishes clearer," he told his brother when he took Max lunch from the café. "I keep thinking about the look in Josie's eyes standing by that king bed in the owner's suite."

They were eating on a picnic table in the grass behind the sheriff's department. "Wait, aren't you the owner?" Max said between bites of his sandwich.

"I'm staying in one of the rooms until…" Cordell shrugged.

Max stopped eating to stare at him. "You're saving that room for when Josie...does what?"

"Realizes she can't live without me and marries me," he said indignantly. "I want a commitment from her. I'm not looking for a roll in the hay."

"Hay, or in your big king bed, either, it appears," his brother mumbled. "When did you become such a romantic?" Max demanded, making it sound like a bad thing.

Cordell bristled. It was one thing for him to call himself a fool, but he resented it when it came from his brother. "I don't want a relationship like you've had with Goldie where neither of us commit for years. If she wants me, then she has to be all in. She has to be my wife."

Max dropped his half-eaten sandwich back on the waxed paper it had been wrapped in as if he'd lost his appetite. "You know why I can't commit to Goldie."

"Roger Grimes is dead. For real this time. Max, we survived it. The worst thing we thought that could possibly happen, happened and we all lived through it. We've had weeks to process what happened down there. Everyone is fine. Grimes is gone for good. It's over. We can finally put the past behind us. No one cares about our childhoods. People are just glad that we're here and life is going on. So tuck your ego into the hip pocket of your jeans and tell Goldie how you feel about her."

His brother shook his head stubbornly. "I'm not like you. It's not that easy for me to brush off everything as if the bad things never happened or couldn't happen again."

Cordell shook his head. "You're scared. I get it. You could have died."

"And left Goldie a widow, left our kids fatherless."

"But you're making a mistake, brother." Cordell rose from the picnic table, wadding up his trash. "Spend your life alone, a miserable old man that no one wants to be around. Your choice, but a woman like Goldie is only going to wait so long before she finds someone else."

MAX BALLED UP his sandwich and threw it in the trash container behind the sheriff's department, his brother's words dying off as he left. He *was* already miserable. Cordell didn't get it. Goldie had been abducted and held at gunpoint. She could have been killed—all because of him and from his past that he'd thought he'd outrun.

Hadn't he always known it would follow him to Dry Gulch, the one place he had felt safe? He no longer felt safe, and worse, he knew that the people of this town weren't safe. Maybe if he left...

"I heard you were back here," said a lilting young female voice.

He turned to see Lindsey Dean standing in the doorway. The sixteen-year-old wore a pair of cutoff jean shorts and a tank top that hugged her ample body, leaving nothing to the imagination. Her long dark hair was pulled into a ponytail to one side. She tilted her head as she grinned at him, her hair swinging.

All he could think about was that if he and Goldie had gotten married when he was twenty, they could have a daughter this age. "You need something, Lindsey?" Max asked. He'd heard she'd been helping out down at the café after the "incident." He hoped this wasn't about Goldie.

She grinned. "I'm selling raffle tickets to raise money for my cheerleading squad so we can go to Billings for the finals."

"Sure," he said. "Just tell Deputy Fletcher I said to buy a half dozen. He can use the money from the swear jar."

Lindsey laughed, her breasts jiggling. What was she

doing not wearing a bra? "I can't imagine you swearing, Sheriff."

He rose from the table, feeling much older than thirty-five. "Lindsey, as sheriff, I want you to go home and put on a bra. And those shorts are way too short and stop flirting with men who are old enough to be your father." Her eyes widened in alarm. She opened her mouth, but nothing came out. "Now get out of here before I call your mother. Come back when you are properly dressed, and I'll be happy to buy some raffle tickets."

And Cordell thought his brother would turn into a miserable old man. Max was already there, he thought with a curse.

JOSIE COULDN'T CONCENTRATE on work. For starters, Cordell was doing some painting on the front of the hotel. He had his shirt off, his skin darkly tanned, his muscles rippling as he worked. She was tempted to close her office blinds, but she was too anxious for her sister to return to her SUV.

When was Amy Sue going to tell her about this man? she wondered. How had she met him? When had she met him? And why had she kept him a secret?

Josie had thought they shared everything.

Worse was the bad feeling that this man was the trouble she'd sensed coming to Dry Gulch. Whatever this new dark threat was, she couldn't shake the fear that it had something to do with her sister and this man.

"Don't let Amy Sue be hurt," she whispered to herself when she heard the throaty roar of a motorcycle and looked up to see her sister hanging on to the back of a man in all-black leather.

The look on Amy Sue's face was enough to bring tears to her eyes. Even from here she could see her sister's wide smile. Her long hair, almost always tamed by a clip, had been unleashed and looked wildly knotted as if she'd been going very fast on the back of that bike.

But it was the look of total abandonment on Amy Sue's face that hit her the hardest. Josie knew that look. Her sister had always been reserved, timid sometimes, rational and reasonable. Amy Sue's expression was wide open with a kind of newfound freedom, and she looked as astonished by that as Josie felt.

She pulled back from the window as Amy Sue threw her arms around the man's neck. An image flew at her, making her start. She wanted to scream *no* and began shaking inside, sick since she'd never felt anything this strongly or ever been this sure.

Amy Sue would soon be fighting for her life at the hands of the man now holding her close.

Chapter Twenty

Cordell wiped sweat off his face as he heard his name being called. He turned, hoping it was Josie, only to find her sister, Amy Sue, peering up at him on the scaffolding where he was standing. There was a man next to her all decked out in black leather.

"I want you to meet someone," Amy Sue said, smiling broadly. She looked excited. In fact, Cordell realized he'd never seen her this excited.

Grabbing his T-shirt from where he'd discarded it on the rail of the scaffolding, he pulled it on, then swung down to the sidewalk.

"Nice bike," Cordell said, nodding to the motorcycle parked in front of the café. He'd heard it roar into town, but he'd been too busy to pay much attention. Now, though, he was curious.

"Thanks, it's actually a friend's. I'm buying it from him."

"This is Shane Wagner," Amy Sue said with a proprietary sound in her voice.

Cordell wiped his hands on a rag next to his paint can and shook the biker's hand. "Cordell Lander." He saw the name recognition in Shane Wagner's eyes for a moment. "Have we met before?"

"I don't think so," the man said quickly, looking over at Amy Sue and smiling at her. "I've never been to Montana before. Amy Sue must have mentioned you."

"It's a huge state with a lot to see," Cordell said. "Are you here on vacation?"

Shane shook his head. "Not really. I'm thinking I would love to make Dry Gulch my home for some time to come," he said, not taking his eyes off Amy Sue.

"That's why we wanted to talk to you," she said quickly. "Shane is looking for a job. I told him that you were going to be opening the hotel and might need some help."

Cordell studied the man. "You ever do any painting, carpentry? I also need help hauling a lot of the old stuff to the dump that I won't be able to use. You have a good strong back?"

Shane chuckled. "I can paint, handle a hammer well enough and I'm strong." He did look strong, as if he worked out on weights.

"I'd ask what brings you to Dry Gulch, but I think I know." He saw Amy Sue's cheeks redden and wondered how these two had met. "I could use the help if you're interested."

"I'm definitely interested," Shane said, his gaze on Amy Sue again.

"Great," Cordell said, hoping this worked out for his sake and Amy Sue's. "You can start in the morning. I'm an early riser, so anytime after seven just come around to the back of the hotel and I'll put you to work. I probably don't pay what you're used to, though." He mentioned a sum and Shane seemed fine with it. "See you in the morning, then."

As he climbed back up on the scaffold anxious to get back to work before his brush dried out, he couldn't help wondering if Josie knew about her sister's apparent boyfriend. Josie had been ignoring him since their dinner. Maybe he'd give her a call later and tell her about his new hire.

JOSIE THOUGHT ABOUT the times when she'd come home late as a teenager and found her grandmother waiting for her. Nana would be sitting on the porch in the dark. Josie remembered the first time she'd rushed up the steps thinking she could get inside before her grandmother caught her—and suddenly sensed her there in the dark waiting.

"You almost gave me a heart attack!" Josie had cried the first time.

"Oh, that is nothing compared to what I am going to give you, Miss Josie."

Now, sitting on the porch, she knew what her grandmother had gone through. It was probably worse for Nana, though, because she had that second sight and knew before anyone else.

"That boy is going to break your heart," her grandmother told her the first time she'd come home from spending the night at a friend's.

She had started to correct the older woman. "I was at Goldie's house. I don't know what boy you're talking about." She'd been young enough that she hadn't bought in to her grandmother's ability to know things she couldn't possibly know.

Nana had looked at her for a few moments. "Cordell is a sweet boy, but he's not right for you. At least not right now. He's going to hurt you, but one day you'll get another chance. You'll just have to decide if you can trust him with your heart again."

"He won't hurt me," Josie had argued. "He loves me. Please don't tell me I can't keep seeing him."

"I wouldn't do that because it wouldn't do any good and we both know it. No," her grandmother said. "You're seeing Doc tomorrow. I want you to know how to protect yourself other than your heart. I can't help you with that." Nana had risen from the chair to pat Josie's cheek. "You're going to be all right, Miss Josie. Remember that and don't close your heart off too much when he breaks it."

Josie wished her grandmother was here now. She would know what to say to Amy Sue. Nana had always worried about Josie's little sister. Had she seen far into the future and known this was coming? What would she have done?

She heard the motorcycle long before she saw it. Her sister's SUV came into view, the cycle some distance behind to avoid the dust. Josie wanted to sit here on the porch and be calm and controlled like her grandmother had always been, but it wasn't her nature.

Josie rose and rushed down the steps, hoping to talk to her sister before the biker arrived. "Amy Sue, we have to talk before he gets here."

Her sister looked startled, and Josie saw the walls go up. "I beg your pardon, Counselor?"

"How did you meet this man?"

Amy Sue looked away. "I don't understand why you're so upset. You've always said that I need to get out more, meet some nice man—"

"Some nice man, yes. Where is he from?"

"Who cares? All over."

"No one is from all over. Where was he born?"

"Is that really relevant?" her sister demanded. "You haven't even met him and you're already sounding like an old mother hen. Shane *is* nice."

"You're avoiding my question," Josie said, digging her heels in. "How did you meet him?"

"This is what I hate, when you go into lawyer mode. I'm not on the witness stand and I'm not going to let you treat me like I am. I've always known that you would be like this. It's why I've never introduced you to anyone I dated."

Josie tried to slow the frantic pounding of her heart. She wasn't handling this well. She needed to calm down, go at this reasonably, or she was going to drive her sister even further into this man's arms—and, ultimately, his control.

"He's dangerous."

Her sister's eyes narrowed. "Have you been reading my letters?"

"Your letters?" The sound of the motorcycle grew louder. He would be here any moment. "What are you planning to do with him?"

"I don't know yet, but in the meantime, he's going to be staying over in the barn. I'm sorry if you have a problem with that."

"You don't know this man."

Her sister shook her head. "I do and don't you try to use that mumbo-jumbo voodoo stuff on me, I don't want to hear it. If you don't like him being here, you can stay at your office."

He roared up in the yard and killed the engine on the motorcycle before dismounting and removing his helmet.

"And buy yourself a helmet," Josie said before she came face-to-face with her worst nightmare.

"His name is Shane Wagner. He's twenty-eight. He did eleven years of a fifteen-year stint in Florida State Prison in Raiford for manslaughter. Driving drunk, he hit a pedestrian and killed the man. Model prisoner." Max looked up at Josie. "What else can I tell you?"

She'd caught him right before he was leaving work for the day and asked for his help.

"What's his rap sheet like?" She saw from the sheriff's expression that he didn't want to say. Josie had already done some digging on her own. What she really wanted was for Max to be aware of the problem. She didn't expect him to be able to stop what was going to happen any more than Josie could herself.

"Fairly minor. Sounds like a troubled kid," the sheriff said. "Arrests for breaking and entering, theft and several assaults, threats against bosses, couldn't hold a job, that sort of thing. Why are you asking about him?"

Had Max really not heard? "Shane Wagner is Amy Sue's boyfriend. She's been writing him while he was in prison and now he's living over the barn out on the farm." It was just a matter of time before the man moved into the house with her sister. "He's done a number on her. I suppose she thinks she's saving him."

"Are you talking about the biker who's working for Cordell at the hotel?"

She nodded. "He's bad news."

Max studied her for a long moment. "I'm sure you tried to talk to your sister about him." He nodded at the face she mugged. "Didn't go well, huh?"

"I've never seen her more serious about anyone."

"You know I can't arrest him until he breaks the law. I checked like you asked. He's not on parole. He's out free and clear. But if you're right about the man and since he's only been out of prison for a short time, I wouldn't be surprised if he went back pretty fast."

"Doesn't it bother you that he was at the same prison as Roger Grimes?"

The sheriff sat back in his chair. "What are you suggesting?"

Max hadn't been the same since what had happened with Roger Grimes and the man Grimes had hired to try to terrorize his stepsons, Josie thought. She blamed it on Max being wounded and almost dying. Something like that could change a person. She had to come to grips with the part she'd played and knew so had Cordell. But the two of them were built differently from Max.

She wondered if it didn't run deeper than Grimes, since Max had made no effort to get Goldie back into his life. In fact, from what Goldie had told her, it was just the opposite. For Max, their love affair was over.

"What if Shane knew Roger Grimes in prison, maybe got information from him, targeted my sister? Roger found out everything he needed to know about this town and the people in it through his pen pal Esther. Doesn't it seem possible that Shane Wagner is doing the same thing?"

"For what purpose? Grimes was looking for Cordell and me. What connection does the biker have to Dry Gulch?"

"I don't know," she admitted. "Maybe only my sister."

"Josie, that prison is huge. The chance the two men even crossed paths is rare," Max said.

She shook her head, unable to put her fears into words. All she knew was that Shane Wagner was going to do something terrible that involved her sister. "The man scares me. He's trouble and I'm afraid he's going to hurt Amy Sue and not just break her heart."

The sheriff sat forward, clearly anxious to go home and put the day behind him—Shane Wagner with it. "My hands are tied until he commits a crime." He got to his feet. "Sorry. I can't believe your sister would be interested in a guy like that. I'm sure it won't last."

"My sister has no idea what kind of man he is."

"But you do," Max said, eyeing her closely. He let out a curse. "If she's as enamored as you say, she won't listen and I'm sure he'll make excuses for his past behavior and swear he's a changed man. That's how Roger Grimes convinced my mother that he was the answer to her prayers." He picked up his Stetson as he rose. "If I were to talk to him, I promise you, it would only make matters worse. Just try not to make it worse. Cordell and I told our mother what Roger was doing to us and she refused to believe it— right up until probably the moment he pushed her down the stairs and killed her."

"Max, that makes me feel so much better," Josie said sarcastically.

Chapter Twenty-One

As she was leaving the sheriff's department, Josie almost collided with Cordell.

"Hey!" he said, grabbing her shoulders to keep her from falling. "I was just thinking about you." She was in no mood, still bristling after their so-called dinner date. "I'm guessing you've met my new employee, Shane."

"I really wish you hadn't hired him," she cried.

He held up both hands. "He's a good worker. What's the problem?"

She sighed and brushed a lock of hair back from her face as she fought tears. "Have a few hours?" She'd been joking, but he immediately took her up on it.

"I have all night. Why don't you come over to the hotel with me. We can talk there. I'll order us something to eat. I bought a bottle of wine with you in mind already."

He'd bought her wine? She eyed him suspiciously. How far was he going to take this game he was playing with her? Right now, she was in no mood for games. But she really needed to talk, and he was offering. "You're on."

They walked the few blocks to the hotel, and he led her inside. She could see that he'd done more work. Once he had rooms available, it appeared he could open. "It looks really good in here."

"Don't sound so surprised. Sit. I'll get the wine."

She took a seat in one of the deep leather chairs he'd added in front of the fireplace. He returned with the wine and two glasses and took a chair across from her.

"Tell me," he said as he poured her a glass and then one for himself.

Josie closed her eyes for a moment as she recalled the moment she came face-to-face with her sister's beau and would-be killer. He was handsome and cocky and so sure of himself that she wanted to scratch his eyes out.

"He's done a number on Amy Sue," she said. "He knows it and I know it, and worse, we both know there is no way to stop him."

"Stop him from what?" Cordell asked.

She looked up at him, took a sip of her wine and put down the glass on the small table next to her chair. "I just talked to your brother. Shane has a long rap sheet. He went to prison for years for manslaughter after running down a pedestrian while driving drunk."

He nodded. "Shane told me."

That surprised her, but it shouldn't have. She let out a laugh. "Of course he did. He seems so transparent. He just wants to put the past behind him and make a new life here with my sister."

"I know that feeling," Cordell said quietly. "It's what my brother and I tried to do."

Josie groaned. "You think I'm judging him too harshly."

"What do you really have against him?"

She met his gaze. "I have this feeling."

"Your second sight." He nodded. "I remember you telling me about it."

"Did I?" It must have been in a weak moment. She didn't tell people because it made them uncomfortable, as if they thought she could read their minds. Or maybe worse, see their futures. Most people didn't want to know what was coming. Josie didn't, either, she thought with a grimace.

"I have this awful feeling that my sister is in danger from this man." She told him how the two had met, about the letters she'd found in her sister's room, how Shane was in the same prison as Roger Grimes and how scared she was that she wasn't going to be able to stop what she feared was going to happen.

"This is one hell of a gift your grandmother gave you, isn't it?" Cordell said when she finished. "What are you going to do?"

Josie shook her head. "I don't know what to do. Amy Sue won't listen to me, and Shane… Anything I say only makes it worse."

"Maybe you could kill him with kindness. Anything else will end up with you in prison."

They shared the wine and Josie stayed as dinner was delivered from the café.

"I have a thought," Cordell said in the middle of their meal. "What do you think he wants from your sister?"

"Isn't it obvious?"

"He could get that somewhere else. If he targeted her as you say, there is something specific he wants that only Amy Sue can provide."

Josie blinked. "The only thing we have of value is the farm. But my grandmother left me in charge of it because she knew I would never part with the place. So it's in a trust. Amy Sue has no claim to it."

"But does Shane know that? I hate to even mention this, but what happens to the farm after you're gone?"

Her blood turned to ice water as she stared at him. "It would go to Amy Sue unless I had an heir."

"Too bad we can't make one quickly enough," Cordell joked. "Josie, in all seriousness, if this vision of yours is true, you're in more danger right now than even your sister."

WHEN JOSIE RETURNED to the farmhouse, she didn't see either Amy Sue or Shane. Cordell was right. Shane wanted something—something more than her sister.

She thought of earlier in town with Cordell. "I was hoping we could go to a movie in Billings some weekend," he had said as he walked her to her car. "Might be just what you need to get your mind off this for at least a night. Also, you'd be completely safe with me."

He'd leaned in then and kissed her. She'd lost herself in that kiss, wanting more, needing more. "A movie?" he asked as he pulled back.

She'd nodded because she'd missed him and the thought of spending time away from Shane and her sister was maybe exactly what she needed. So far, she'd handled it all badly.

"Maybe we could make a weekend of it," Cordell had suggested.

There was nothing she would have loved more. They'd agreed to go the coming weekend, leaving Friday afternoon. She had wondered on the drive to the farmhouse if he was trying to protect her by getting her out of town.

She'd never worried about what the farm was worth since she'd never planned to sell it. But with the changes that had been happening across Montana, the large farm and the buildings would be worth at least a couple of million in today's market.

Too much of an opportunity for a man like Shane Wagner. But first he would have to get rid of Josie. Which she hoped meant her sister was safe until then.

Josie had come back to get her overnight bag and more of her clothing. She was wondering where the two had gotten off to when she heard voices. A few minutes later, the screen door slammed as they entered the house. She tried to still her pounding heart. Now that she had a pretty good idea of what Shane was after, she had to find a way to stop him without him realizing what she was up to.

"There you are," she said as she went downstairs to greet them. Her sister's face was flushed, Shane was holding her hand and both of them looked deliriously happy. For just an instant, Josie wanted to believe that was all that was going on. "What have you two been up to?"

"Shane wanted to see the farm," Amy Sue said. "I was just giving him a tour."

"This is an amazing place you two have here," he said, grinning. "I can see why you love it so much. I can't imagine owning so much land. It must be worth a fortune."

Amy Sue pulled her hand from his and playfully hit him. "He's kidding. We've been talking about farming it and what we would grow."

Josie looked at Shane, not surprised to see a grin on his face, his dark eyes telling her to be afraid.

"I'M WORRIED ABOUT JOSIE," Cordell told his brother later that night. He'd stopped by Max's house to check on him, knowing that he wasn't himself and hadn't been for months now.

He'd brought over a six-pack of his brother's favorite beer, opened one each and told Max what Josie had told him. "I think Shane Wagner's after the farm, but to get it, he'll have to go through Josie."

"You're saying he's going to kill Josie, then Amy Sue,

then sell the farm and abscond with the proceeds. Isn't he employed by you? Is he a good worker?"

Cordell admitted that he was.

"Has he done anything to make you believe this is his plan to murder two people?" Max held up his hands. "I know about Josie's second sight," he said with a sigh. "But like I told her, there is nothing I can do until he breaks the law."

"I feel like we're in the same spot we were with Grimes," Cordell said. "What if the two prisoners did know each other? Is there any way to find out?"

"What would it matter?" his brother asked. "If Shane wanted to know anything about Dry Gulch or everyone else in town, he could have just asked Amy Sue."

"Still, could you call the prison and ask? Maybe they didn't know each other and it's just a coincidence they were both in the same prison."

"Grimes is dead. Can't we just let it go?" Max sighed. "Fine. I'll check. Anything else?"

"I'm worried about you, too," Cordell said. "You're not yourself. What's it going to take to get the old Max back? You know Goldie is miserable without you and you're obviously miserable, too."

"Thanks for the beer," his brother said. "I have an early morning tomorrow."

"Subtle," Cordell said as he got to his feet. "Let me know what you find out."

AFTER ANOTHER ARGUMENT about Shane with her sister, Josie had taken what she'd come to the farmhouse for and gone back into town to stay at her office. She couldn't bear seeing the two of them together, knowing that there was nothing she could do.

She and Amy Sue had always been so close. Now they could barely be civil to each other. She couldn't stand recalling their argument before she'd stormed out.

"You're jealous!" Amy Sue had cried. "This is about Cordell. You're not getting what you want from him, and you can't stand that I have a man and I'm happy."

Josie had groaned. "You do realize how ridiculous that sounds, don't you? I've always wanted you to find someone special and be happy."

"I have, so what is the problem?" her sister demanded.

"The fact that you kept this relationship a secret tells me that you know something isn't quite right."

Amy Sue had shaken her head. "Shane deserves a second chance—just like the one you're giving Cordell—don't you think?"

"It isn't the same and you know it. Sis…" She had reached for her hand, but Amy Sue had pulled back out of her reach. "I've seen things."

With a loud groan, her sister had stepped even farther away. "Oh, I should have known that would be next. You and Grandmother, the predictors of gloom and doom. So what exactly did you see?" When Josie hadn't answered right away, Amy Sue had laughed. "Right, you can't quite see it, but you feel it, right?"

"Yes," Josie had said quietly. "I think he's going to try to kill you."

Amy Sue stepped back some more, shaking her head as tears filled her eyes. The sound of a motorcycle engine filled the air. Shane had left to run an errand and now he was almost back.

"I'm trying to warn you," Josie had cried and again reached for her sister, needing to touch her, needing to get through to her.

Amy Sue had stumbled away from her, headed for the door. "I love him. He loves me. You aren't going to ruin this for us."

Josie had heard the thump of the bike's engine die.

When she'd looked out, she'd seen her sister in Shane Wagner's arms with him looking up at the house over her shoulder. As Josie's gaze had locked with his, he'd smiled up at her. The promise in that smile made Josie fight for breath from the weight on her chest. He was coming for her and couldn't wait.

Now back in her office apartment, she realized that she knew nothing about prison pen pals. She'd assumed that few people wrote letters via postal mail anymore because of the internet. She hadn't realized that some prisoners didn't have access to the web because of their crimes.

What surprised her when she went online was to find that there were programs to help inmates find nonincarcerated pen pals. Just as there were ways for those interested to find prisoners interested in a pen-pal relationship. The letter writers made social connections, relieved loneliness and improved their mental health through the correspondence with the outside world.

She thought of Amy Sue. Had she been lonely? Was that what had led to this?

Pen pals, she learned, were usually strangers whose relationship was based primarily if not solely on their exchange of letters, and some of those relationships lasted for years. Some also led to romantic attractions, with some falling in love.

Josie was aware how intimate a letter could be compared with a text or even a phone call. But surely these nonincarcerated women—since she guessed they made up the larger number of letter writers—should have been warned of the downside of this interaction.

She did find some rules that pen pals were advised to follow. Don't offer legal advice or assistance. Don't share confidential details with others about your pen pal. Amy Sue had definitely followed that one to a T.

Why didn't they also warn people against sharing too much about themselves, including where they lived? At least there were rules for not getting scammed by your prisoner pen pal. A red flag was if the prisoner repeatedly asked for financial help. Josie hated to think how much money her sister had sent Shane, making him think there was more to be had where that came from.

Josie felt sick at the thought of how Shane had taken advantage of her sister. How he was still doing just that—not to mention what his main goal might be. Josie had tried to see, but as her sister had said, she'd only come away with a feeling after that one image of her sister dying on the ground.

She felt helpless, something new to her. Even when Roger Grimes had his arm around her throat and a gun to her head, she'd believed that she could get out of the situation. With her sister, this was even more dangerous because she couldn't do anything until Shane broke the law.

Her cell phone rang. She quickly picked up, although half-afraid it would be bad news.

"I'm looking forward to our trip to Billings this weekend," Cordell said, sounding excited. "Be sure to bring your swimsuit. We're staying at a hotel with a pool." When she didn't respond right away, he said, "Don't try to get out of this, Josie. You can't do anything about your sister, and you need this. Also, it's been a long time since I've seen you in a swimsuit."

He was right about her needing to get away. If Shane was after the land, then he wouldn't do anything to Amy Sue—except scam her more. Since her talk with Cordell about the situation, she'd since gone to the bank and moved as many of the farm's assets into an account that her sister couldn't touch. She hated doing that, but she told herself it was the only way to protect Amy Sue and the farm.

As for her own safety, Josie knew she would be safer away from the farm and Shane this weekend.

"I'm picking you up Friday right after lunch," Cordell said. "Do you still have that black swimsuit with the low neck?"

"You wish. I'll see you Friday after lunch."

MAX HADN'T WANTED to do it. But to pacify his brother, he made the call to the warden at Florida State Prison. He yearned for the day when he never had to hear Grimes's name ever again—let alone say it out loud.

"I have a strange request," the sheriff told the warden when he came on the line. "I need to know if Roger Grimes and a man named Shane Wagner had any contact that you know of while in prison there."

"Any particular reason you're interested?"

"Both of them ended up in Montana."

"I heard about Grimes taking some hostages and getting himself killed along with another former prisoner from here, Dave Peters."

"Montana draws them, I guess," Max said. "I appreciate you doing this."

"I'm familiar with Shane Wagner. Seemed to be a model prisoner, recently released. He already in trouble?"

"Not yet."

"I can do some checking for you. I'll let you know what I find out."

Max thanked him and disconnected. As he did, he saw Goldie crossing the street on the way to the hotel. He hadn't been down there to see how his brother was doing. Truth was, he'd thought Cordell would have lost interest by now. Maybe his brother had changed. Or maybe he'd never really known his brother.

He thought of Cordell stepping up down in Wyoming. His brother had saved them when Max couldn't. Otherwise, they would all be dead.

Not wanting to think about how impotent he still felt, he busied himself with paperwork, but he found himself looking down the street toward the hotel. Goldie didn't look miserable. Every time he'd seen her passing by, she'd been smiling. She looked happy. He told himself it was because she was free of the black cloud he'd been born under. She was better off without him. She definitely deserved someone without so much baggage.

Late in the afternoon, he got a call back from the warden.

"Your instincts were right," the man said. "Grimes and Wagner did know each other. They were set to get out at the same time, but Wagner's release was delayed. I asked around and the guards said that the two of them had their heads together a lot just before Grimes was released. They could have been up to something."

Max felt sick to his stomach. It hadn't been his instincts—it had been those of Josie and Cordell. Grimes had been corresponding with Esther, who was telling him about everyone in town. It might have even been Grimes's idea for Shane to target Amy Sue just as Josie thought, the two of them sharing information as they made their plans.

But other than settling the score with him and Cordell, what had been Grimes's plan? More important, what was Shane's now that Grimes was out of the picture?

He swore, hating that he was going to have to give Josie the news. Worse, what it could mean. How many more parolees were headed up here because of the prisoner pen pals? It probably seemed safe writing to a man behind bars—even one allegedly locked up for life. But what if he got out? Lonely criminals getting letters from equally lonely women who had no idea whom they were corresponding with, both making promises they had no intention of keeping. What could possibly go wrong with that?

After getting the news from Max, Josie couldn't stand another minute in her office. She'd known Grimes and Wagner had to be in on it together once she'd heard they were from the same prison. If Shane Wagner's release hadn't been held up, he would have been here at the same time as Grimes.

She shuddered at the thought of the two of them working together. It was bad enough that Grimes had involved his friend Dave. Would she and Goldie even be here right now if there had been three of them?

Josie hadn't seen Goldie for a few days so she made a point of having lunch at the café before she was to leave with Cordell. The noon rush over, the place was empty except for Goldie, so she took a seat at a corner booth so her friend could join her. Josie knew that Maggie, who was filling in until Ronnie could return, always went out back for a smoke break after the lunch rush.

"How are you doing?" Goldie asked, keeping her voice down even though it was only the two of them in the café. "What's wrong?"

"It's Amy Sue's new boyfriend."

"I saw him. He's adorable. I wanted to ride off into the sunset with him."

Josie leaned toward her friend. "He was in the same prison in Florida as Roger Grimes." Goldie's eyes widened as her expression filled with horror. "They were supposed to get out at the same time. Grimes could have told Shane about Amy Sue since we know they were both involved in some kind of prisoner pen-pal group."

Goldie looked as sick as Josie felt as she leaned back in the booth. "What does this mean?"

"I don't know exactly—just that Shane Wagner could have always had his own plan involving my sister that Grimes didn't even know about. Or they were in it together." She shrugged. "Goldie, he's only pretending to care about Amy Sue. Max thinks he could be after the farm."

"But *you* own the farm."

"Yes, but it would go to Amy Sue if anything happened to me, and I didn't have an heir."

"What are you saying?" Goldie demanded, looking even more stricken.

"He has to get rid of me to get the farm, and if he plans to sell it, which, of course, he does. Amy Sue would have to go, as well."

"Oh, you can't be serious," her friend said, looking around the café as if not sure what to say or do. "Can't you change your beneficiary?"

"My grandmother put the farm in a trust so it stayed in the family. She's the only one who could change it."

"You need to get pregnant and quick," Goldie said, only half joking.

"Then I suspect Shane Wagner wouldn't hesitate to take us both out."

Goldie rubbed a hand over her face. "What are you going to do?"

"I don't know. I've tried to talk to Amy Sue…" She shrugged. "She thinks I'm jealous because she is finally serious about someone. There is no getting through to her."

"Max?"

Josie could hear the pain in her friend's voice, as if even saying his name hurt. "He's the one who just notified me of the connection between Shane Wagner and Roger Grimes. Unfortunately, it's not illegal for the two to have known each other or for them to have been pen pals with women from this area. Max can't do anything until Shane breaks the law."

"You mean kills you."

"Or at least attempts to. But Max would have to be able to prove it and I think Shane is too smart to get caught easily," Josie said. "He has every advantage because he's staying out at the farm and he's working here in town for Cordell."

"But Cordell knows what he's up to?"

"He's watching Shane as much as he can. He's also taking me away for the weekend to Billings. We're leaving soon."

"Josie, that's great. You must be so excited."

"He's been keeping me at arm's length. I'm hoping that's not the case this weekend, but for all I know he might be getting us separate rooms." Goldie lifted an eyebrow. "Apparently he wants more from me."

"Good for him," her friend said. "I made that mistake with Max and look how that turned out."

"I know he loves you," Josie said.

"I thought he did. But now I'm not so sure. I can understand why he broke things off because of Grimes. But once we were both safe…"

Josie shook her head. "I'll never understand the male mind or heart, for that matter."

"You must be so worried about Amy Sue and what this is going to do to her when she finds out the truth," her friend said.

"If she does. Killing me would only be the first step. He'd have to marry her to get the farm, but then he wouldn't need her anymore since I doubt his goal is to become a farmer—no matter what he tells her."

Goldie shook her head. "So your sister was his pen pal and you had no idea?"

Josie shook her head. "I don't think they ever discussed his plans once he was released. She might not have even known he was going to be released. So I'm sure she opened up her heart to him."

"A complete stranger?"

"A criminal behind bars. She would have felt safe."

"Maybe he really does care about her," her friend said. "Maybe there's a happy ending here and we're just over-reacting because he knew Grimes."

Josie glanced out the window to the hotel across the street. Shane Wagner had just come out with a load of what looked like old bedding in his arms. He dumped it into the back of a truck parked at the curb.

As if sensing he was being watched, he looked in the direction of the café and spotted Josie. He grinned and gave her a wink before going back inside.

Chapter Twenty-Two

When Josie unlocked the door to her office and started to step in, she froze. She couldn't tell if it was a scent on the air or something out of place or just her second sight. Yet at once she knew someone had been here. Her mind raced to understand how that was possible. She always kept the office locked. The only other person who had a key was—

Amy Sue.

Her heart lodged in her throat. Whatever Amy Sue had, Shane Wagner now had access to it. Why hadn't she realized that sooner?

Stepping in, she immediately went to her desk to see if anything had been disturbed. The file cabinets were locked with keys that Amy Sue didn't have copies for, so she wasn't worried about them.

Nor did she keep anything confidential dealing with her clients in the desk drawers. But as she sat down, she saw that her top drawer hadn't been closed all the way. She opened it slowly. Nothing seemed out of place.

As she was closing the drawer, though, she saw her notepad lying on her desk and the pen next to it. She had put the pen in the cupholder before she'd gone to the café. She was sure of it. She'd always been a little too fastidious about keeping her items neat.

The notepad still had the information Max had given her about the pen pals and the connection between Grimes and Wagner—but they were in shorthand so whoever had been in here wouldn't have been able to read them.

Josie had learned shorthand from her grandmother, who'd worked as a secretary before marrying and moving to the farm. It had been the way she and Gram could converse without anyone else knowing what was being said. Amy Sue had tried to learn, but didn't have the patience.

As she started to rip the top sheet off the notebook and put it back in its spot, she noticed that someone had doodled on several of the symbols. Her heart was again in her throat, making her jump when her office door swung open.

Amy Sue stopped in the office doorway. "Didn't mean to scare you," she said to her sister, surprised how jumpy Josie was. "You look like you've seen a ghost. You haven't been gone from the farm that long that you don't remember me, have you?"

"Were you in my office earlier?" Josie demanded.

"No," she said, frowning. She'd known her surprise visit probably wasn't going to go well, but she hadn't expected her sister to already attack her. "I haven't been in your office. Did someone move your plant a quarter inch from where you normally keep it, neat freak?"

"Someone was in my office while I was down at the café," her sister said.

"Well, it wasn't me. I just got to town, and I wanted you to be the first to know." She stepped in to her sister's desk and held out her left hand. The diamond caught the light from the window and shone like a star. "Shane and I are engaged!" She couldn't help how excited she was. Not even her sister's weirdness could ruin this for her. "And don't say that it's too quick. I've known him over a year, writing back and forth all these months."

Josie's mouth opened, then closed like a fish out of water.

Amy Sue rushed on, hoping her sister would see how happy she was and not say anything hurtful. "I know you've been skeptical about Shane's intentions. But this should put your mind at ease. We're getting married!" She giggled, wanting Josie to be happy for her as she waited for her reaction.

"You can't marry him."

Amy Sue stared at her as her heart fell and disappointment filled her. "Stop. Just stop!"

"He's after the farm."

She shook her head, tears stinging her eyes as she took a step back while Josie got to her feet and came around the desk toward her. "Of course, I should have known. Shane couldn't possibly want to marry me because he loves me. It's about the farm. Do you hear yourself? The farm's not even in my name!" she cried. "You and Nana saw to that."

"That's why he has to marry you and kill the two of us to get his hands on it."

She blinked at her sister. "Have you lost your mind? Shane's not a murderer! He's made some mistakes but he's not—"

"I'm sorry, but I just found out that Shane and the man who almost killed me, Roger Grimes, knew each other. It's too much of a coincidence that they both had pen pals in this area. Don't you see? They were both planning to get out at the same time, but Shane's paperwork got held up. Shane and Grimes set this whole thing up."

Amy Sue raised her hands to ward off her sister. She couldn't believe this. She'd known Josie wouldn't be happy about the engagement, but she couldn't believe how far she'd go to try to split up her and Shane.

"I refuse to listen to any more of this," she said as she stepped back until she felt the door behind her. "Why do you want to poison this for me? I'm in love for the first time in my life with a man who wants to marry me." She was crying and hating that she couldn't stop. "He loves me, and he wants to make a life with me, have babies, farm... It's the life I've always dreamed of."

"I'm so sorry, but that is never going to happen," Josie said and started to reach for her again, but she waved her off.

"Stay away from me and Shane, you hear me? Stay away from us." With that, she opened the door and fled.

JOSIE'S HEART BROKE as she watched her sister leave in tears. She wished she could take it all back, to pretend to be happy for Amy Sue, but how could she knowing what she did?

Of course Shane wanted to marry her. Now there was nothing stopping him. He would want to move quickly, not waste any time. He had her sister right where he wanted her.

At a knock on her door, Cordell peeked in. "Ready to go?" He seemed to see the expression on her face and came on in. "I know. Shane told me and then Amy Sue came by to show me the ring."

She rose and he held out his arms and she rushed into them. "He had a key to my office. While I was at lunch, he left me a note." She shook her head. "It wasn't anything. Just some doodles so I'd know he'd been here. He wanted me to know that he can get to me anytime he wants."

As he hugged her tighter, she breathed in his scent, never

wanting him to let her go. But he did as he pulled out his phone.

"Which is why we are leaving for the weekend." He began to tap on his cell phone. "I'm having the locks changed on your office and apartment right now. I'll have the locksmith leave the keys with Goldie. You can tell her to guard them with her life."

For the first time today, she felt better. She wasn't alone in this. "I have my bag packed." She motioned to it by the door.

Cordell picked it up, set it on her couch and opened it.

"If you're looking for my black swimming suit—"

"Just checking that Shane didn't put anything in it. Why don't you take a look."

She felt numb at the thought that Shane might have seen her bag, maybe even knew she and Cordell were leaving town for the weekend and put something in there.

At the couch, she went through her bag. She found nothing extra that she could see and checked the side pockets before she replaced the bottle of wine wrapped in a towel that she'd brought and zipped it back up. "Is this going to be my life? Living in fear?"

"No. I promise. I have some ideas I want to run by you, but not right now. Right now, we are going to hit the road. The moment we do, it's our weekend and nothing is going to spoil it."

Josie wished she could believe it, but she smiled and tried. She wanted this weekend with Cordell badly. But that darkness she'd seen at a distance was now in town. She could see it drifting down Main Street, peering into windows, circling back toward her.

"Let's go," she said, knowing that even Cordell's new

pickup couldn't outrun it. Shane would be here when she got back, the darkness growing and getting more menacing.

AMY SUE HAD planned to make something special for Shane for dinner tonight. She had time. Cordell had taken off with Josie, but Shane had wanted to work late to surprise his boss by how much he would have gotten done.

"Let me know when you're on the way. I have a surprise for you," she'd told him when she'd seen him at the hotel. He had to have seen that she was upset and had been crying when she'd stopped by before leaving town. But he hadn't said anything. He knew that her sister was being just awful about the two of them.

"She's not used to you having anyone, right?" he'd said the other night. "She probably liked having you to herself and misses that. You should cut her some slack. I'm sure she just wants the best for you. She probably doesn't think I'm the best partner," he'd said with a self-deprecating grin. "I'll prove to her I'm the right man for you and the right brother-in-law for her. We're going to be the family I've always dreamed of. Trust me, she will come around."

He didn't know Josie, she thought, as she went into the kitchen at the farmhouse to begin dinner but couldn't seem to make herself start. All she could think about was her sister's reaction to the engagement and the awful things she'd said. Josie had her mind made up from the start. Amy Sue couldn't see her changing it no matter what Shane did.

A thought struck her. What if she could prove to her sister that she was wrong? She turned around and left the kitchen to go upstairs to her room. Shane had moved into the farmhouse with her shortly after Josie had decided to stay in her apartment over her office in town. He hadn't brought much to Montana because apparently he didn't have much. She couldn't imagine getting her whole life to fit into a couple of duffel bags she could tie onto the back of a motorcycle.

She'd been amazed when he'd taken a spare pair of jeans, a couple of shirts, two pairs of underwear and a four-pack of socks from the duffel and then put both bags on the high shelf in her closet. The only boots he had were the ones he'd been wearing.

But was that everything?

Amy Sue hated not trusting him, but she had to look. If he was hiding something, she would find it. She stood on tiptoe but still couldn't reach where Shane had stored them. Pulling over a chair, she stood on it and was able to pull down both of Shane's bags. The first one felt empty. It was. She almost didn't check the second one. Of course he didn't have any secrets.

The second one appeared completely empty, as well. She felt small and shameful and blamed her sister for making her have doubts about the man she loved.

But then she felt something thick on the bottom of the second bag. She took the duffel over to the window where more light came through and saw what appeared to be a slit in the fabric of the double bottom. She could feel what felt like folded papers shoved in there.

It took a few minutes, but she was able to work the wad of papers out. Her breath was coming in short gasps as she started to unfold the sheets of what appeared to be copy paper.

She tried to flatten them out on the bed, but the pages had been folded too tightly. Still, a couple of words grabbed her attention. She caught her breath as she realized what she was looking at. This was information about the farm, the kind of information you might get from a real estate agent.

At the sound of a motorcycle roaring into the yard, she hurriedly tried to get the papers folded again. Her hands were shaking too hard to force the thick wad back into the slit in the bottom of the duffel and she was running out of time. Shane had cut the bike's engine. He seemed to be in a hurry. She heard his heavy footfalls on the porch steps, then the porch. The screen door slammed open.

"Amy Sue! You in there cooking already? I've got a surprise."

She tossed the papers into the duffel, zipped it back up and hurriedly tried to return it to the crowded shelf in the closet. But the bag fell to the closet floor.

"Amy Sue?"

Her heart was pounding, her chest hurting with each breath. "I'll be right down!" she called, but he was already heading up the stairs at a run.

She closed the closet door only an instant before he came rushing into the room. Turning, she fought to hide her panic after her discovery, after what her sister had said about Shane killing them both, about him promising her that all he wanted was to farm the place with her.

Fortunately, he didn't seem to notice if she was acting as strangely as she felt. He rushed to her, picked her up and swung her around. "We're getting married!"

"I know," she said when he finally set her down.

"No, silly, we're getting *married*."

She stared at him, trying to tell herself that of course he had an interest in the farm. He had told her that he wanted to work it with her, but that didn't mean he wasn't curious about what it was worth. He'd been excited to find out how many acres there were and talked about what he would grow once it was no longer leased out. The papers meant nothing. She was letting Josie get into her head.

When he set her down, he grinned down at her. He was so handsome and when he looked at her like that, her heart flip-flopped in her chest. He was so sweet. He called her his angel. He said she'd saved him. How could she not love this man?

"I don't want to wait," he said. "We're going to Vegas. We can get a marriage license and get married the same day. There is no required waiting period and there are all these little chapels. They even provide witnesses. All we need is the two of us."

"Shane—"

"I know you'd hoped your sister would come around and we'd get married here. But angel, she doesn't think we're serious, that I'm serious about you. So, let's prove that she's wrong. I can't wait to marry you and make you my wife. It's a two-hour flight to Vegas. I got us two tickets. We fly out of Billings tonight. We're getting married, baby!"

He pulled her into his arms. "Come on, Amy Sue. Let's do this." His enthusiasm was contagious, and the way he was looking at her made it impossible to say no.

She met his eyes and thought about asking about the papers in his bag. She wanted him to tell her that they meant nothing. So why had he hidden them? asked a voice that sounded just like her sister's. But she blocked out anything else Josie had to say, knowing not to spoil this moment or Shane's excitement by bringing up the papers.

They were flying to Vegas to get married. It was romantic and exciting and spontaneous, something Josie could never do. Something Amy Sue would never have done—before Shane.

"Let's do it," she said to him. "Let's go to Vegas and get married."

Chapter Twenty-Three

"Seriously, did you bring the black swimsuit?" Cordell asked after they'd been on the road for miles. He reached for her hand. "I know you're worried. I am, too. But the alternative is what? Kidnapping Amy Sue?"

Josie knew he was right. She'd done her best to convince her sister of the mistake she was making. Amy Sue was an adult. "What if I can't stop this? Short of murdering Shane and going to prison, I don't know what to do."

"Like I said, I have some ideas since he has to get rid of you first," Cordell said with a smile. "I'll tell you all about it at dinner. But know I'm not going to let him hurt you. What I am going to do is try to show you such a good time that you'll quit worrying for forty-eight hours and just enjoy yourself."

She couldn't help but return his smile. "I did bring that black swimsuit."

"Now you're talking," he said as they came over a rise and the Magic City, as Billings was called, came into view. "What do you say about the two of us going for a swim before dinner?"

Josie tried to relax. "You're just determined to get me in that swimsuit, aren't you?"

He grinned. "I'm just as determined to get you out of it later."

"What changed your mind?" she asked as he drove into the largest city in Montana.

"Changed my mind about what?"

"You and me."

He shot her a look. "Nothing has ever changed my mind about you and me."

"But the other night before dinner at the hotel when you showed me the owner's suite…"

He nodded, his eyes back on the road. "Make no mistake, I want you, but it's true I want you for more than one night or even a weekend." He braked for a red light and looked over at her. "I'm not like my brother. I know what I want and yes, I'd like to nail it down with a commitment."

She started to say something, but he stopped her.

"I can understand that you don't trust me completely. I left to make something of myself. For six years, I worked construction jobs. I saved every penny I could. I had plans for when I came back to Dry Gulch."

"The hotel," she said in surprise.

He grinned over at her. "I've always wanted to bring it back to life."

The light changed and he pulled away. "I know I have to prove myself to you. That's fine. I can do that. But I'm not like Goldie. I don't want to wait years, just hoping you love me as much as I love you."

She wasn't sure what to say to that. He'd said he loved her, but she'd already known that. "I think that sounds very reasonable."

He grinned over at her. "I'm glad you agree."

CORDELL SAW JOSIE'S expression when they checked into the hotel, and he'd reserved two separate rooms—though connected.

"What kind of commitment is it going to take?" she asked in the elevator as they rode up to their rooms.

"Aren't you a lawyer?" he asked.

"You need something legally binding?" she asked, looking over at him to see if he was serious.

"I'm sure we can pound out the details over a drink later," he said without meeting her gaze.

As the elevator door opened, he handed her the key to her room. "Let me know if you need anything. Just knock on the door between the rooms when you're ready to go to the pool. We can go together."

She took the key, her mind on what he'd said earlier. Was he talking marriage before they slept together again? It wasn't like they hadn't already had sex when they were younger. They hadn't been able to keep their hands off each other. They'd made love on a blanket in the woods, in the grass down by the river, on a towel on the dock at the lake—everywhere but in a bed. Even on the tailgate of his pickup truck.

What he was suggesting surprised her. It was as if her bad boy had grown up and wanted everything that came with it.

Opening her bag, she pulled out the black swimsuit. It had been six years since she'd worn it. Josie remembered the last time as she pulled it on again. She shivered at the memory since it was also the last time she saw Cordell for six long years.

She felt sick at the thought that he might disappear again after this weekend. Wasn't that her fear? Did she trust that he was truly back?

Her skin felt prickled at memory of Cordell's breath on her neck as he came up behind her at their swimming hole.

His fingertips brushed across her shoulder and down to the hollow between her breasts.

She straightened, but the memory stayed with her. It had been too long since she'd felt his touch on her bare skin. She ached for it, just as she ached for him. But how far would she go to get what she wanted?

Or more to the point, how far would he go?

SHANE WAS LIKE a kid on the plane. Amy Sue traded places with him so he could sit by the window after he told her he'd never flown before. She loved seeing how happy and excited he was.

She just wished she could feel the same. As hard as she tried to push what she'd found hidden in his duffel out of her thoughts, she couldn't. Just as she couldn't forget what Josie had told her about Shane and Roger Grimes having known each other. They would have gotten out of the prison at the same time except for that paperwork that kept Shane in longer.

Amy Sue remembered his writing her about that. He'd sounded as if he was surprised to be getting out when he did. But he must have known for some time that he was being released. He'd kept that from her and had only recently let it slip.

"I didn't want to get my hopes up or yours, either," he'd said when she'd questioned him about it.

At the time, she'd accepted his answer as being responsible. She would have been disappointed had he not gotten out.

"Look," Shane said, drawing her over to the window. "It's Vegas."

She didn't have to ask. Clearly he'd never been there. She watched him take in all the large buildings with a kind of awe. Again, she heard her sister's voice. *Does this look like a man who would be happy farming outside of Dry Gulch, Montana?*

Shane had to put a couple of quarters in the slot machines at the airport before they caught a taxi. He instructed their driver to take them to the Regional Justice Center downtown, where they would get their marriage license.

"Don't you want to go to the hotel first so we can get rid of our bags?" she whispered to Shane, who shook his head.

"We'll go to the hotel after we get our license. We're getting married today!"

She couldn't understand the rush. He'd already told her that the Clark County Marriage License Bureau was open from eight in the morning to midnight 365 days a year. They had the whole weekend since he said they wouldn't be flying back until late Sunday.

He was definitely enamored with Vegas and the bright city lights, she thought, amused and also worried as he took in the city from the taxi window. Clearly, there was so much he hadn't experienced. From his letters, she'd gotten the impression that he'd had a rough life, no money, not much hope, and that he'd spent much of his youth behind bars.

She tried to see it all through his eyes but as they passed one gaudy wedding chapel after another, this all felt too rushed and not what she'd ever pictured. She'd never thought she'd ever get married without her sister by her side.

DOWN AT THE POOL, Josie removed her cover and dropped it and her towel on a chair. There had been a couple in the hot tub, but they were leaving as she and Cordell came in.

She could feel his gaze on her as she turned, walked to the edge of the water and dived in.

By the time she surfaced, he was right beside her. His hands cupped her waist as he drew her to him and kissed her. They floated together, barely moving more than it took to keep them afloat. He pulled her closer with one arm and cupped her cheek.

"I've loved you since the first time I laid eyes on you in sixth grade," he whispered as he brushed over her lower lip with the rough paid of his thumb.

"As I remember, you were still eating glue like the elementary schoolboys back then," she joked even as his touch sent a tremor through her.

"Oh, so you did notice me, huh?" His chuckle was low, seductive. He dropped his hand, those fingertips grazing the top of her breasts. Her nipples were already taut and aching. "I do love this swimsuit," he said as one finger dipped under the fabric to rub her nipple.

She arched against him, her body crying out for this man whom she'd loved as far back as she could remember, whom she would always love. She cupped the back of his head and drew him into a kiss, her tongue teasing his. She felt his own need growing against hers. If they weren't careful, they would be making love right here in this pool like they would have done when they were teens.

Cordell pulled her down under the water before breaking off the kiss. His hands on her waist, he lifted her and surfaced beside her again—just not as close.

"I hope there is no more question about whether or not I want you," he said as if seeing that she was shaken as badly as he was by their intimacy.

She couldn't speak. Her body vibrated with a primitive need that she knew only he could fulfill.

"We'd better get ready for dinner," he said as he quickly kissed her, then turned and swam toward the edge of the pool.

SHANE HAD GOTTEN them a beautiful room with a view of the Strip. The moment they entered, he threw himself on the bed, bouncing and laughing. "This is the life!" His gaze met hers. "Come on."

She knew what he wanted. A quickie before they got dressed to go to the wedding chapel he'd reserved. "Not until you make an honest woman out of me," she said as she grabbed the dress she was going to wear and headed for the bathroom. She could hear him chuckle before ordering champagne from room service. She wondered if he'd used her credit card to pay for all of this, then hated herself for thinking it.

Leaning against the glass shower wall, she tried to catch her breath. This was happening too fast; she wasn't getting time to think. Back at the farmhouse before the flight, she'd seen him take down his two duffel bags. There wasn't any way he hadn't noticed that the copies he'd made about the farm weren't where he'd hidden them. She'd watched him out of the corner of her eye, expecting some kind of response.

But there'd been none as he'd turned and began putting clothing into the bag. The other one he rolled up and pushed into the first bag.

"You're taking both bags?" she'd asked.

He'd hesitated but just for a moment before he'd turned to look at her. "You caught me. I'm hoping I can pick up some new duds in Vegas, dress a little better for my soon-to-be wife." His smile hadn't reached his eyes.

"There is nothing wrong with the way you dress," she'd

said and had to bite her tongue to keep from adding, "After all, you're going to be a farmer soon."

"Hey," he now called from the other room. "We need to get going."

With trembling fingers, she pulled on the dress. It was one she'd been saving for a special occasion, never dreaming she would be getting married in it. She looked at herself in the mirror. *Are you really going to do this?*

She closed her eyes for a moment, remembering the day she saw him waiting by his motorcycle. She could still recall that well of emotion she felt when he'd looked at her. She'd gotten to know this man from his letters. He was sweet and thoughtful, and he'd come all the way to Montana for the dream the two of them had of running the farm together.

Opening her eyes, she took a breath and let it out before she opened the door and plastered a smile on her face. "Let's get married!"

Shane took her in with his eyes, looking as if he'd never seen anyone more beautiful. "My bride," he said and pulled her into his arms for a quick kiss. "Come on. You don't want to be late for your own wedding."

Josie's body felt alive even after the shower and getting dressed for dinner. Cordell had told her that he'd asked around for the most romantic place to have dinner in town. He was definitely pulling out all the stops, she thought.

The restaurant exceeded its reputation. It was elegant, small, private and very romantic. But she would have found having a hot dog from a vendor on the street romantic as long as she was with this man. He wore new jeans, a white shirt and a sports jacket and boots. He'd never looked more handsome.

After their almost lovemaking in the pool, she was ready to sign on the dotted line. Cordell didn't have to prove himself. She saw the man he was. She felt him in her heart. He'd come home to her. He was all she'd ever wanted.

A part of her wanted to argue about how she could agree to marry him, though, when her sister was in this relationship with Shane.

"Nope, not tonight," Cordell said as if seeing that she was worrying about her sister. "Tonight, it is just you and me."

She smiled at him and nodded. "Just you and me," she said, looking at him in the candlelight. "Thank you for this."

"My pleasure. Did you enjoy the swim?" That mischief she'd loved so much was right there along with that dimple.

"Oh, I did," she said with a chuckle. "If I didn't know better, I'd think you were trying to seduce me."

He gave her his best innocent look. "On the contrary. I've never wanted to make you do anything you don't want to do."

"This commitment. Does it have to be written in blood?" She saw his expression and realized the joke hadn't come off as well as she'd hoped. "Sorry."

"No, *I* am. I don't want you to feel pressured."

"I don't," she assured him as the waiter approached their table. They ordered drinks and appetizers. She asked for a pen and paper, avoiding Cordell's questioning look. The drinks arrived quickly—along with a pen and paper.

She took a sip of her drink, looking at him over the rim of her glass before she put down her drink, picked up the pen and began to write.

The next time she looked up, Cordell appeared amused. With a flourish, she signed what she'd written and added the date, time and place. Then, taking her time, she folded the paper and put it on the table next to her before picking up her drink again.

"You aren't going to let me read it?" he asked, studying her.

"Let's see how the night goes," she said and took a sip of her drink.

Cordell chuckled and raised his glass to hers. "To the perfect evening." They clinked glasses.

Chapter Twenty-Four

A taxi took Shane and Amy Sue to the wedding chapel. It wasn't as corny as some she'd seen on the drive from the airport, but she couldn't help feeling that Shane had skimped on this part. Or maybe it was the only one available at such short notice.

It smelled inside like an antiques store. She realized that it was probably the heavy old velvet drapes that lined the walls. "Wagner wedding?" an elderly woman asked, appearing from off to the right.

"That's us," Shane said. He seemed even more anxious than he had earlier at the license bureau. "You have witnesses?" he asked, looking around.

"They're already in the chapel." She motioned him to follow her, telling Amy Sue that she could wait there. They disappeared through the drapes. She could hear the woman trying to upsell Shane, offering other services that cost more money. Shane kept saying no and finally lost his temper.

"We just want to get married," he snapped. "Quick and simple. Husband and wife. Can you do that?"

The woman made a rude sound, then told him how much it would cost—more than what she'd apparently told him over the phone when he'd made the reservation. "That's criminal, you know that?"

Amy Sue would have found that funny, if she wasn't so nervous. She heard Shane slam down the money. When he came through the curtain, his face was twisted into a look she had never seen on him before. She must have showed surprise, because he quickly changed his expression.

"Time to go on back to the chapel." He took her arm and kind of pushed her forward as if he wanted to get this over with as quickly as possible.

Amy Sue couldn't blame him. The smell of the place was making her nauseous and the voice in her heard telling her to run was no longer Josie's. It was her own.

The chapel appeared before them. As they moved forward, a white-haired man with a limp motioned them to come closer. Out of the corner of her eye, Amy Sue saw the witnesses. They looked like two people who'd been kidnapped from a rest home.

Swallowing around the lump in her throat, she turned to Shane and whispered, "I need just a minute."

"What?" he snapped, clearly irritated.

"Just a moment," she told the man who was to officiate their marriage as she walked back the way they'd come, Shane going with her.

"Amy Sue, come on, this is—"

"I need to ask you something. It's important and I need you to tell me the truth. Did you know Roger Grimes?"

Shane frowned. *"What?"*

"You heard me. Tell me the truth."

He looked her in the eye. She saw him visibly trying to rein in his temper. "I have no idea what you're talking about. I've never heard that name in my life."

She nodded. That was exactly what she had needed to

hear. He didn't ask who Roger Grimes was or why she needed to know because he knew the answers to both. He had lied through his teeth.

"We need to get on with the ceremony," the older man called. "We have another one coming up next. I also have some paperwork for you to sign."

"Go sign, I'll be right there. I just need to catch my breath."

Shane studied her for a moment, clearly afraid to leave her.

"I'm sorry. I always thought Josie would officiate my wedding. This is a little overwhelming, but I'm going to be fine." She smiled and touched his arm. "Please, just give me a moment."

He relented and the instant he turned his back, she ran to the exit, disappeared through the velvet drapes and out the door. She didn't know how far she'd run, winding her way through the streets until she saw a bar and ducked into it, then into the ladies' room, where there was less noise. Once inside a stall and the door closed, she pulled out her phone and called for an Uber. Two minutes. Driver's name was Kevin.

Her grandmother would have said she was shaking like an aspen leaf in a Montana gale. All she knew was that her heart was threatening to burst from her chest. Back in the bar, she waited by the door. The moment Kevin drove up, she ran out, jumped in and asked him to take her to the airport. She would take any flight she could get out of Vegas as quickly as possible.

As it was, there was one leaving in forty-five minutes for Bozeman, Montana. She booked the flight, paying with her credit card. Once the charge went through, she took a seat and contacted her credit card company to let them know that after the flight, she needed to cancel it. Then she contacted her bank to freeze her account.

She hadn't realized that she'd been crying until she sat down in her seat on the plane and the lady next to her handed her a tissue. "Thank you, but I don't want to talk about it," she said to the woman.

"Oh, honey, you don't have to. I know. We've all been there. You're much better without whoever he or she was."

THE DINNER WAS the loveliest one Josie had ever had and the most enjoyable. Cordell never mentioned the folded sheet of paper on the table next to her plate the rest of the night. They talked about the hotel, the remodel and his plans for making Dry Gulch a destination resort.

While she might be skeptical about what Dry Gulch had to offer, she had complete faith in Cordell Lander. She loved seeing his dreams come to life. Everyone in town was excited about him restoring the hotel. It had been abandoned for far too long, making it look like Dry Gulch was a dead end.

The truth was that the town had been dying. Maybe restoring the hotel would give the town a boost, she thought. At least it had already had a positive effect on the town's people. She saw some of the residents fixing up their places, putting on a new coat of paint, hauling away junk or making a pretty wreath for their front door.

Goldie had commented on how she'd heard people saying they hoped Cordell finished the job. "They're rooting for him," she'd said. "Though most of them think he's wasting his time."

She and Cordell talked about her pro bono work. He'd asked about Big Blue and how she'd gotten it replaced without anyone knowing where it came from.

"My secret," she said. "Everyone in town is just glad to have the horse back where it belongs. I'm sure there are some people who are suspicious of the coincidence of Big Blue turning up at the same time bad-boy Cordell Lander returned, but once they saw you unloading lumber from the back of that trailer you hauled to town, I think they changed their minds."

He grinned. "Thanks. You've always gotten me out of trouble."

"I could say the same about you." They'd never talked about that day with Roger Grimes. "You saved my life that day."

"Doesn't count. I was the one who put you in jeopardy to begin with."

"We worked pretty well as a team, though, didn't we?" she said and he nodded solemnly. Both of them were putting the incident behind them, but it wasn't easy. Their brush with death would always be with them, just as the memory of what they'd had to do. The one thing they didn't talk about was Shane Wagner, purposely staying clear of that topic.

After dinner, Cordell asked her if she would like to go to a movie or go back to the hotel and swim. "Or we can go to a movie Saturday night. Whatever you would like to do."

"I'd like to go back to the hotel." If he'd noticed that she'd picked up the paper she'd written on earlier and put it in her purse, he hadn't commented.

"You can come over to my room and we can watch a movie if you like," he suggested when they reached the hotel.

"Sounds great. I brought a bottle of wine. I'll get it out of my bag, change into something more comfortable and come right over."

She put on a T-shirt and shorts, grabbed the bottle of wine and tapped at the door. He opened their adjoining door and took the bottle of wine from her.

"I forgot something," she said and rushed back to her room to get the paper she'd written on earlier.

Cordell was busy getting a couple of glasses ready for the wine. He was about to open the wine when he stopped. "Josie, the seal is broken on this bottle. Did you already open it?"

She shook her head and stepped closer.

"There's something floating down in the bottom of the wine bottle," Cordell said. "This was in your bag at the office, right?"

She felt goose bumps ripple over her flesh. "Shane. You think he put something in it."

"I think we should wrap it up. Max can have the lab run tests on it. Shane's fingerprints might even still be on the bottle."

Josie sat down on the edge of the bed. "We've avoided mentioning him all night, but he's been there the whole time. I need to call Amy Sue to make sure she's all right." The call went straight to voicemail. She left a message and started to put away her phone when she saw a message from Goldie.

"This wasn't what either of us hoped for," Cordell was saying.

"I need to check this." Goldie wouldn't have reached out unless it was important. Her heart sank as she read the words. "Shane and Goldie have eloped to Vegas!"

She had to sit down, but as she did, she realized she was still holding the folded sheet of paper. "This is for you."

He took it but didn't unfold it. "How about I hang on to

this for another time? I'm going to call Max. We might be able to drop off this bottle with the state police lab here in Billings."

AMY SUE WOULDN'T have been surprised to find the farm-house burned to the ground when she finally reached home. She burst out crying when she saw that everything looked exactly the same—except that the motorcycle was no longer parked out front.

She'd been afraid he would be here waiting for her. When she'd walked out of the chapel, he might have thought he still had a chance. But once she cut off his money, he'd obviously gotten the message. At least she hoped that was true.

Turning her phone back on, she listened to a series of messages pleading with her to tell him what was wrong. Then the messages got angrier and meaner. She didn't have the heart to hear any more and deleted all of them.

She saw that her sister had called numerous times, but only left one message. *I'm worried about you. Please just let me know that you're all right.*

Inside the house, she looked around, surprised how empty and cold it felt. Upstairs, her room looked exactly as she'd left it. She'd thought Shane might have returned to leave her something disgusting to remember him by. But if he'd been here, he hadn't bothered to leave a note. Why would he? There really wasn't anything he could say.

At the sound of a vehicle, she looked out to see the sheriff drive up in his patrol SUV. Her heart dropped as she watched him climb out, looking like a man bringing bad news. Suddenly everything her sister had tried to warn her about came rushing back. What if Shane had killed Josie?

Amy Sue raced down the stairs and had just pushed out the door onto the porch when Max reached the steps. "Is it Josie?"

He looked surprised, then said quickly, "She's all right. She didn't drink any of the wine Shane had tampered with. It was poisoned, though. Lab said rat poison. Probably got his hands on it out here on the farm."

Rat poison? Josie's wine? She dropped into a porch chair and put her head in her hands as the sheriff told her how Cordell had noticed that the bottle had been tampered with and had called him and Max had instructed him to take it to the crime lab.

She felt all the pieces drop, one after another, as she recalled Shane mentioning something about Cordell taking Josie to Billings for the weekend. Josie had thought someone had gotten into her office. Amy Sue remembered seeing her sister's overnight bag by the door when she'd stopped by. Shane must have had her keys copied the time he used her car.

"We have a BOLO out on Shane," Max continued. "I'd advise you not to have any contact with him. If you hear from him, let me know."

She raised her head, nodded and said, "I don't think I'll be hearing from him."

"I'm sorry, Amy Sue. Will you be all right out here by yourself?"

"I'll be fine, Sheriff." But she could tell that he didn't like leaving her alone.

"I heard around town that Shane was taking you to Vegas to get married." He looked down at his boots before looking up at her. "Did you—"

"No. There is nothing legally binding between us, if that's what you're asking. I didn't go through with it. I've already canceled my credit cards and frozen my bank account."

He nodded, looking relieved, but also embarrassed for her. "Call me if you need anything."

"Thanks." She looked down and realized she was still wearing the ring Shane had given her that she was pretty sure she'd paid for. She slipped it off her finger, tempted to throw it as far as she could. Instead, she slipped it in her pocket. Their grandmother had taught them not to waste money.

She watched Max drive away before she pulled out her phone and called her sister.

AFTER CUTTING THEIR trip short, Cordell had dropped Josie off at her office. As she was unlocking the door, she'd seen Clancy Roberts, who asked if she knew that Amy Sue had gone to Vegas to get married.

"She's not back?" Josie asked.

"Not that I know of," Clancy said, "but someone thought they saw Shane on his bike headed south."

As her phone rang, Josie excused herself and opened her office door, stepping inside before she checked the call. Seeing it was her sister, she quickly picked up. "Amy Sue, are you all right?"

"I'm fine. I'm home. Alone."

She burst into tears at the sound of her sister's voice, her relief overwhelming her. She'd been so worried about Amy Sue, especially after realizing that Shane had tampered with the wine. "Are you...married?"

"No. I couldn't go through with it even before I realized he was lying. If I ever get married, I want my sister to officiate, not some old man in a dingy wedding chapel in Las Vegas without you there."

"I can't tell you how happy I am to hear you say that," Josie said as she dried her eyes. "I've been so worried about you."

"You were right about everything."

"I wish I wasn't," Josie said and realized that darkness she'd felt suffocating her and the town had lifted. Shane was gone. Her sister was safe. She was safe. "Do you want me to come out to the farmhouse?"

She feared her sister would say no after the awful arguments they'd had. "Could you pick up ice cream?"

Chapter Twenty-Five

It felt as if there was something in the air making the people of Dry Gulch, Montana, happier than Josie had ever
seen them. Or maybe it was just her own feelings of relief
since she no longer saw dark clouds on the horizon. She
felt as if she could breathe again.

Her sister had bounced back from her bad romance
quicker than Josie had thought she would. The day Josie
had gone out to the farmhouse with several quarts of their
favorite ice cream and a six-pack of beer, they'd built a fire
in the pit out back and talked. After a couple of beers each,
Amy Sue had burned Shane's letters.

It was as if the fire had released the spell the man had
placed on her.

"You saw him coming after me, didn't you?" Amy Sue
said quietly as the fire popped and sparks rose, glowing in
the darkness overhead before burning out.

"I saw someone coming who was more dangerous than
Roger Grimes," she said, staring into the flames.

"I've always made fun of your…gift, as Nana used to
call it. I was jealous that you had one more thing to share
with our grandmother that I didn't."

"It's not a gift," Josie said. "It's a curse. I hate it. I would love to wake up in the morning and not see anything, be totally oblivious to anything bad coming. That would be a gift. What makes it worse is that I can't see as clearly as our grandmother could see things. All I usually see is darkness closing in until I come face-to-face with it."

"I'm sorry I've given you such a hard time about it," her sister said.

Josie had smiled over at her and helped them both to another beer before throwing more wood on the fire. They were silent for a long time, listening to the music of the warm night.

"I loved the idea of Shane Wagner," her sister said after a while. She had leaned back to stare up at the stars. "I hate that he played on my vulnerabilities to work his way into my heart. He knew exactly what to say and do to win me over."

"He was a born con artist," Josie said. "He would have fooled anyone."

Her sister laughed. "Not you." She pushed herself up on one elbow. "Did I ruin your weekend with Cordell? If so, I'm sorry."

"No, it actually brought us closer together. Cordell's been trying to prove to me that he's a changed man. I saw that changed man and I like what I see."

Amy Sue laughed. "You are always so cautious."

Josie laughed with her. "I haven't always been. I fell for Cordell when we were teens because he was Dry Gulch's bad boy. It's just been hard to wrap my mind around the change in him."

"You liked him as the bad boy and you weren't sure about your feelings for the changed Cordell," her sister said. "I can see that. But I suspect that bad boy is still in him." She chuckled. "You just have to bring it out."

Josie had found herself smiling as she reached for her sister's hand and squeezed it. "I never want anything or anyone to come between you and me again."

"I don't think you need to worry about it. I've given up on finding love— Why are you laughing?"

"Now that you say you've stopped looking, I wouldn't be surprised if it snuck up on you when you least expect it."

THE UPCOMING GRAND OPENING of the new and improved Dry Gulch Hotel was the talk of the town. Max couldn't believe all the work his brother had done to bring the hotel back to its earlier glory. At one time, the town had sported a hot mineral swimming pool behind the hotel that had brought in people from around the world. If Cordell had his way, it would again.

While his gunshot wound had healed, he often felt a twinge for no apparent reason, making it a constant reminder. But today, he tried not to think about anything but his brother's success. The town had taken pride in what Cordell had done as if they'd swung the hammer and wielded the paintbrushes.

Max had noticed more people freshening up their property. At first people had been skeptical about Cordell reopening the hotel. But not anymore. Everyone seemed excited, as if Dry Gulch was coming back to life. As usual, Cordell had started something and this time hopefully it wouldn't land him in jail.

"Only you get the grand tour before the grand opening," his brother said as he showed him around. Cordell had purchased acreage behind the structure for the second phase of his resort. "Guests will have the full Montana experience, from horseback riding into the hills to sleeping in fancy tents or even staying in tree houses. I have an entire section for kids planned, including several swimming pools."

Max could only shake his head. "You really think enough people will come to Dry Gulch?"

Cordell laughed. "We're already booked through next summer. Hot springs are really popular, especially where the whole family can come."

He shook his head. "I'm really proud of you."

His brother shrugged. "It's always been something I've dreamed of doing. Dry Gulch is home. I'm anxious to start a family and settle down."

Max thought of the family he'd dreamed of starting here and felt the pinch of pain that came with that dream's loss. "Good for you, but shouldn't you get started on that? What's going on with you and Josie?"

Cordell got a twinkle in his eye. "I think I'm making progress. She's coming to the grand opening with me." He reached into his pocket, looked around to make sure it was just the two of them and pulled out a velvet box. As he flipped it open, Max pretended to be blinded by the diamond ring inside.

"When are you going to pop the question?"

"After the grand opening. I want you to be my best man. Is that going to be a problem since Goldie will be Josie's maid of honor?"

He held up his hands. "Slow down. Josie hasn't even said yes yet. Let's wait and see before you start planning the seating at the reception."

CORDELL FELT AS if he were floating. This grand opening was really just a party for the town. The hotel wouldn't be open for guests until spring, when more of the amenities would be available. There was still a ton of work to be done, but he had faith that it would be finished before the first guests arrived.

Tonight was a celebration he wanted for the town. He'd made a point of not allowing anyone inside the hotel until it was done, except for Josie and his brother. He knew people couldn't wait to see what he'd done. He just hoped they liked it. Goldie was catering the event. He'd let her hire whatever people she needed.

As he dressed, he saw the folded sheet of paper from his dinner with Josie in Billings. He hadn't opened it and read what she'd written. Oh, he'd been tempted more times than he wanted to admit. But he'd told her he would wait, and he had.

Cordell glanced at the time. Josie would be here soon. He felt his excitement rise. If all went as planned, he and Josie would be planning their wedding after tonight. He picked up the sheet of paper and folded it into his pocket, patting it for luck.

At the sound of the back door buzzer, he hurried down to let Goldie and her crew in with the food and drinks.

"You look so handsome," she said, her eyes flooding with tears. "I'm so proud of you."

He hugged her, thinking how much he wished she was his sister-in-law. He had learned not to mention Goldie to his brother. But he still couldn't understand what had happened. Or maybe Max had never planned to marry her. Cordell feared it had something to do with their mother, Roger Grimes and his brother's fears that their earlier life had twisted them in ways that they might not even know yet.

But that was his brother's problem—not his. Cordell refused to let the past define him. He glanced around the hotel. Tonight was his night. He touched the tiny velvet box in his jacket pocket. Nothing could ruin this night for him.

ALL DRESSED AND ready for the opening, Josie stopped at her apartment door, hesitating. She awakened this morning with a bad feeling. Of course, she couldn't see what it was, but it made her stop now and call to check on her sister.

Amy Sue had a date tonight to the grand opening with local plumber Rick Baker. He was picking her up at the farmhouse soon. Everyone had been looking forward to this night for some time now. She knew how important it was to the town, but so much so for Cordell. It angered her that something might go wrong tonight.

What she'd told Amy Sue that night under the stars had never been truer. Her second sight was a curse, one she would give anything not to have. Why couldn't it have been more like her grandmother's where she could more clearly interpret what was coming?

"All set," Amy Sue said when she answered. "Oh, there's Bob now. Got to go. See you there."

Josie started to put her phone away, but on impulse called the sheriff's department. Max had been working long hours. It didn't take a psych degree to know that he was hiding from his true feelings and avoiding Goldie. But he wouldn't be able to tonight.

"You're going to the opening, right?" she asked the moment he answered.

"Yes, I plan to make an appearance."

She sighed, knowing what they meant. He'd show up and leave as quickly as he could. "Goldie is catering the event, so she'll be busy. You should be safe."

"Josie—"

"That isn't why I called. Has Shane Wagner been picked up yet?" She heard the answer in the silence that followed.

"There was a sighting in Idaho, but to answer your question, no."

"Tell me he isn't going to show up tonight at the hotel."

"Josie, unlike you, I can't see past the nose on my face what is going to happen."

"I can't see much, either, but I have this bad feeling that whatever it is, it will happen tonight."

"Rance and I will be at the opening," Max said. "If Shane shows up, we'll handle it."

"Thank you." She disconnected, feeling a little better. All she could do was warn Max. Still she had no idea what was coming. It might not even be Shane she had to worry about.

Josie glanced at the time. She'd promised Cordell she wouldn't be late. She reached for her wrap and headed for the door. She wanted this night to be everything he'd dreamed possible. He deserved this. She hated that something might spoil it for him.

The hotel was aglow, the light shining through the large front windows to paint the sidewalk in gold. Music spilled into the streets as the front door opened and closed, guests moving into the large lobby. Dry Gulch hadn't seen anything like this in years.

Josie felt the excitement and tried to relax as she heard laughter. She let herself in the back way. Goldie was catering the event. She wanted to say hello and make sure that her friend wouldn't be stuck in the kitchen all night. She'd offered to help but Goldie wouldn't hear of it.

But as Josie walked into the huge commercial kitchen, she was surprised to find it empty. She saw trays of food on the counters, but no one was around. Maybe they were already out in the lobby offering the guests appetizers, she told herself.

Leaving the kitchen, she went through the large restaurant area with its white tablecloths and beautiful dishes. She was in awe of the job Cordell had done.

But before she could reach the doors that opened out onto a hallway to the lobby, she heard a sound behind her. She turned, expecting to see Goldie or one of her helpers.

Shane was on her before she could run, let alone scream. Not that anyone would have heard anyway with the noise and music coming from the lobby. His hand clamped over her mouth as he lifted her off her feet. "You should have stayed out of my business," he whispered in her ear as he carried her toward the back stairs.

She struggled, kicking and clawing at him, but he only chuckled as he dragged her up the stairs. The music wasn't as loud in the stairwell. Not that she could have screamed loud enough even if he wasn't covering her mouth.

"Time to make your spectacular entrance into the party," he whispered as he pushed open the first-floor door and Josie found herself on the balcony overlooking the lobby. The room roared with voices and laughter and music. No one looked up as he carried her over to the railing. With his arm still around her waist, he swung her legs over the railing so she was dangling from the second floor facing the party. He took his hand off her mouth to pull the gun from his jacket pocket.

The first shot fired at the ceiling had little effect. The second caused some people to look around. The third report of the gun stopped the party as people began to gaze up to see Josie being dangled over the railing. There were screams and shouts. The music died and Josie saw Cordell headed for the stairs.

"Looks like your boyfriend wants to join the party," Shane said. "And your sister, too. Hey, Amy Sue, didn't really appreciate being stood up at the altar in Vegas."

Josie saw Max and Rance, both trying to work their way through the crowd, their weapons drawn. If they shot Shane, he would drop her. That's if he didn't shoot her—after he shot her sister.

"Shane!" Cordell called as he started up the staircase. "You don't want to do that."

"Oh, you have no idea how badly I want to drop her. I'd like to drop her sister, as well. You need to stay back, Cordell. I can barely hold on to her now."

"Do what he says, Cordell. Please," she called to him.

But he hardly seemed to hear her. "It doesn't have to end like this," he said, still moving toward them.

She saw Amy Sue come running up the stairs, but Cordell held her back with an arm.

"Nice party, sorry to ruin it," Shane said, and Josie felt his hold on her loosen. Below her, Max and Rance had men moving the table and chairs that had been set up in the lobby out of the way. Shane wouldn't be able to see what they were doing, but they were making a place for her to fall, she thought with a wave of terror. She heard dishes crash to the floor as they pulled several tablecloths from the tables, and now a half-dozen men were holding them directly under her.

Josie could feel Shane about to let her go so he could turn the gun on Cordell and her sister. She saw it as clearly as she'd ever seen anything. Her sister lying on the floor bleeding with Shane standing over her.

She nodded to Max and sank her fingernails into Shane's hand around her waist. He let go immediately and she felt herself falling as gunshots rang out over the screams.

Then the back of her head connected with the balcony floor's edge and everything went black.

Chapter Twenty-Six

Cordell knelt down beside Josie on the hotel's lobby floor. He was still in shock. When Shane had let go of Josie and she'd fallen, Cordell had rushed the man. But Max and Rance had already opened fire on Shane, killing him before he could get another shot off—or Cordell could reach the man.

"Josie?" He could hear his brother and the deputy clearing the guests out of the hotel, but all he cared about was Josie being all right. "Open your eyes, Josie. Tell me you're still with me." Her fall had been broken by the men below holding tablecloths. Still, she'd hit her head on the way down, Cordell had been told.

Doc had been in the group attending the grand opening and he'd gotten to her quickly to assess the bump on the back of her head. He said he didn't think it was life-threatening, but he'd called an ambulance. The coroner had been summoned for Shane.

"Josie, please," Cordell said, brushing a lock of hair back from her face, his heart threatening to burst from his chest as he saw her eyes flutter, then open. "Josie. Oh, darling." He couldn't tell how badly she was hurt as she started to sit up. "Maybe you should lie there for a moment and make sure nothing is broken."

Still, she was determined to sit up so he helped her. She seemed to look around, though, as if she didn't know where she was. Worse, when her gaze focused on him, she looked confused, almost as if she didn't recognize him.

"Josie?" he said on a frightened breath. "Tell me you know who I am."

A smile curved her lips even as her eyes closed for a moment. "You're the man I'm going to marry."

He laughed nervously. "Is that right? Do you know my name?"

"Cordell Lander," she said and glanced around. The lobby was a mess with balloons and confetti all over the floor. "What did I miss?"

"Besides the stairs from the second-floor balcony, hardly anything. So you're really going to marry me?"

She seemed to see the paper she'd written on at their dinner in Billings. She pulled it from his pocket. "It's legally binding," she said to him. "Haven't you looked at it?"

He shook his head. "I won't believe it until I see a wedding ring on the finger of your left hand." He heard the ambulance pull up outside. "But until then…" He reached into his pocket and took out the small velvet box and opened it. "This will have to do."

Josie smiled and held out her hand, her gaze on his as he slipped the engagement ring on her finger. She looked down at it and her eyes filled with tears. "It's beautiful, Cordell."

"Like you," he said and kissed her. Behind him, he heard the EMTs come in with a stretcher. "Let's make sure you're not just saying this because of that bump on your head," he said and moved out of the way for the EMTs.

JOSIE DIDN'T REMEMBER the ambulance ride to the hospital, but she was told that Cordell held her hand the whole way. Now at the hospital after seeing the doctor and finding out that she had a concussion, she kept asking Cordell questions about what had happened.

"Goldie?" she asked. "I remember looking for her."

"Shane had locked her and the servers in the walk-in cooler," Cordell told her. "They're all fine."

"Amy Sue?"

"She's fine, too. Worried about you, but so is everyone," he said.

"Shane?"

"Dead. Max said you gave him a signal right before you fell. He and Rance were ready. As soon as they got a clear shot, they took it. Which was good because I was rushing Shane when he turned his gun on me and Amy Sue. He never got the chance to pull the trigger."

Josie shook her head. "I'm so sorry he ruined your grand opening."

Cordell laughed. "Other than Shane, no one got killed. You got hurt, but the doctor said you're going to be fine. I'm just thankful for the party since it brought Shane out in the open. Everyone pulled together and saved the night."

She couldn't help but smile at him. "You really are so resilient. I love that about you."

"I'll have a genuine grand opening come this spring when the hotel is about to open for real. This was just a preview."

Josie closed her eyes, thinking she hoped it wasn't a preview of more trouble. She tried to see into the future but realized with a start that she didn't sense anything. There was nothing but a blank wall. She opened her eyes and looked at Cordell. Maybe she was hurt worse than she thought.

"The bump on my head… I can't see…"

"What? You can't see?" He started to ring for a nurse, but she stopped him.

"No," she assured him. She no longer had the gift. She could feel it. It was just…gone. "I'm fine. Actually, I've never been better." She let out a laugh when she saw him giving her a side-eye look.

She'd always said it was a curse and wished she'd never had it. Well, now it appeared to be gone. She would be surprised like everyone else when something bad happened. She was free from knowing just enough to be dangerous.

"I see a very happy future for you and me," she told him. "In fact, let's get married as soon as we can throw a wedding together. I'd suggesting eloping, but the town would never forgive us."

Cordell grinned, exposing that wonderful dimple. "You mean it?"

She nodded and reached for him, pulling him to her for a kiss. She'd never felt so free or so alive. "I also think we shouldn't waste any more time. Let's start our family right away." She grinned back at him. "Maybe you should lock my hospital room door?"

"You are so bad," Cordell said with a laugh as he hurried to do just that. "Everyone in town is going to say that I corrupted you."

"Only you and I know the real truth," Josie said, thinking about the day their first child would ask where she or he was conceived.

"In love," she would say. "You were conceived in love in Dry Gulch, Montana."

* * * * *

WITNESS TO MURDER

DEBRA WEBB

Chapter One

Chicago
Saturday, August 9
Chicago Chop House
La Salle Drive, 11:30 p.m.

Leah Gerard had waited, seated at an elegantly set table in a barely lit, well-appointed dining room, for more than thirty minutes.

Many things could be done in half an hour. She could have a leisurely lunch in that same amount of time. Or she might read a couple of chapters in her current favorite book. For that matter, she could vacuum her entire apartment or have her biannual dental cleaning.

But she was doing none of those. Leah had waited thirty-three minutes, now, for her date to finish up his business meeting. And it was nearly midnight. This was not the way a first date should go.

She rolled her eyes. Honestly, if her best friend hadn't been on her back for weeks now about Leah jump-starting her social life, she would not have bothered with this date thing. Who had time for a social life when her final semester of graduate school started in just over a week? She needed every minute that she wasn't working to get a head start on the required reading. This was, admittedly, something she should have started weeks ago, but she'd taken every extra shift at work possible to build up her savings.

Between her share of rent and food, she barely scraped by. Once the semester began, she would be forced to drop back to part-time at the library. Until then, every paid hour counted. As much as she wanted to maintain her grade point average, she also wanted to eat and have a roof over her head.

She braced her elbows on the table, rested her chin in her hands and sighed. What the heck was she even doing here?

"Good question," she muttered with mounting disgust—mostly at herself.

The dining room part of the restaurant was barely lit because the place was no longer open. The Chop House had closed at ten. Cleanup had been done, and the staff had departed. Raymond, her date, had promised he would be ready to go at eleven. He'd asked Leah to meet him here so they could go straight to a nearby after-dark art exhibit that was supposedly all the rage. The gallery was only a few blocks away from the restaurant and the opening began at midnight, so they would have time for a drink before things got started.

Leah checked the time on her phone and shook her head. That would not be happening at this point. Oh well. Raymond Douglas was supposed to be a real catch. She'd met him only once and he had seemed very nice. He was certainly handsome. And he was a rising star in the culinary world. In fact, he owned 10 percent of this exclusive downtown restaurant, as well as a few others. He'd met with the other investors right here tonight and stayed after closing to work out a number of issues with management. Except, apparently, things had not gone well, or surely he would have been finished by now.

With another quick check of her cell phone, she confirmed that he had not sent a text to explain why he was running behind or how much longer he would be. She'd done exactly as he'd said she should—she'd arrived at eleven. The last of the staff had been leaving, and no one had questioned her coming in as they hurriedly departed. She assumed Raymond had informed them that he was expecting a guest. Either that, or the crew had been too tired or so happy to be off work—maybe both—that they just hadn't noticed her at all.

Leah checked the time once more: 11:40. This was inching toward ridiculous. As patient as she wanted to be, the last of that patience was swiftly running out. Five more minutes, she decided. She could give him that much time. Isla Morris, her roommate and best friend, had reminded her that Raymond was no one to blow off. Leah had googled him. She had a feeling he was more playboy than she was interested in. Frankly, she was stunned he'd called her. The one night they had run into each other was when Isla and two of their friends had taken Leah to their favorite dance club for her birthday just two weeks ago. Isla had told Leah that she had worked at the Chop House through her undergraduate premed years, which was how she'd gotten to know the guy. After the chance encounter on Leah's birthday, Raymond had called Isla and asked for Leah's contact information. And here she was.

So far the night wasn't exactly social media post worthy. Not that she posted that often. She was too busy, and frankly, she just wasn't that into online social stuff.

Next year, she told herself, life would be different. She would be finished with school, would find a great job and

life would start to shape itself into a good, financially se-
cure future.

Leah occupied herself with surveying the dimly lit dining room. Most of the lights were out, but the room wasn't
completely dark. There was just enough light to give anyone who walked by on the sidewalk a glimpse of high-class
dining. The tables were all dressed in fresh white linens.
Crystal and silver flanked elegant white plates. All was
set for lunch tomorrow. Stylish, modern chandeliers hung
from the towering ceiling like icicles. Sleek black marble
floors were the perfect backdrop to all the white and silver. The floor-to-ceiling windows framed the vast room
like a stage for passersby to admire. It was all very chic.

Enough waiting. Leah scooted her chair back and stood.
With a big breath, she walked across the room, weaving
through the sea of tables. A thump startled her to a stop.
Was that a door? Was he leaving the office finally? Should
she go back to the table?

Another thump…then a series of dings like hanging
stainless steel pots swaying together.

Leah moved closer to the swinging door that led into
the kitchen area. The echo of footsteps had her expecting
Raymond to walk through the door before she reached it.

But he didn't.

What was he doing in there?

She stepped closer to the door, stood on tiptoes to see
through the octagon-shaped window that allowed for viewing comings and goings. Her gaze first settled on the rows
of pots and pans hanging from overhead hooks. A long
stainless steel table that gleamed from its recent cleaning
sat beneath them. Then…

She froze.

Blond hair…black suit jacket… Leah blinked. Raymond

lay supine on the floor. The stainless steel table blocked her view of the lower half of his body. But his upper half was right there in full view. Blue shirt…darker blue tie. Her gaze settled on his face. His eyes were open. Blood made a path down his forehead.

The air stopped flowing into her lungs.

Leah blinked again to give her brain a moment to make sense of or refute what her eyes saw. Her lips parted, and a scream swelled in her throat.

Then he moved.

The scream deflated.

His upper body slid fully behind the table, out of her view, as if someone had grabbed him by the legs and pulled him away.

A smear of blood on the gray flooring was left in his wake.

Leah cupped her hand over her mouth to hold back the new scream that burgeoned.

Footsteps and another thump echoed.

Abject fear sent adrenaline rushing through her veins. *Run.*

Leah turned around to run and stalled once more. *Don't make a sound.*

She forced herself to move more slowly and silently as she wove her way through the tables and toward the entrance. Her heart pounded harder with each step. Her body weak with relief, she pushed against the doors. They didn't move.

The heavy wooden set of French doors were locked.

Ice formed inside her. *What now? What now?*

She eased away from the door and the hostess station. Head spinning, she hunkered down behind a table. There had to be an emergency exit somewhere…

Think!

In the corridor where the bathrooms were located, maybe.

Or was it?

She'd never been here before, but she had gone to the ladies' room when she first arrived to check her hair and makeup. She closed her eyes and called to mind that short corridor. There had been an emergency exit there…right? *Yes.*

But that corridor was on the other side of the dining room. As she stared across the expanse now, it seemed miles away.

Another indistinct sound came from the kitchen.

Didn't matter how far to the exit…she had to get out of here.

Heart thumping wildly, she got on all fours, tugged up the skirt of the black cocktail dress she'd chosen for this date and then crawled along the floor. She couldn't risk standing up again. If whoever was back there glanced through that kitchen-door window, he would see her. She remained on all fours, rushing around and between the tables as quickly as the building terror would allow. When she reached the corridor, she almost cried out with relief.

Once she was in the short hallway, she dared to stand.

Even before she reached the emergency exit she saw the sign. Opening the door would trigger an alarm, which the killer would hear. He would know someone was here…a potential witness.

Defeat sucked the wind out of her.

Desperate, she eased into the ladies' room. She wished there was a lock on the main door, but there was not. She hurried into one of the stalls and locked the door, for all the good that would do if someone wanted to get in. It was meager protection, but it was the best she could do. Leah drew in a steadying breath and used her cell phone to call 9-1-1.

As soon as the dispatcher was done reciting her spiel, Leah whispered, "My name is Leah Gerard. I'm at the Chop House on La Salle Drive. Someone murdered Raymond Douglas. Whoever killed him is still in the restaurant. Please…help me." A keening sound rose from the depths of her soul.

"Are you safe?" the dispatcher asked calmly.

Leah forced her mind to focus. "I… I don't know. I'm in the ladies' room, locked in a stall. I don't think he knows I'm here." She listened intently for sound beyond the room. Nothing. "Please hurry."

"Did you see or hear a weapon?"

"No," Leah murmured.

"Are you armed, Ms. Gerard?"

"No. Please. Hurry."

The dispatcher assured Leah a unit was already en route to her location. She was to stay in place and on the line until help arrived.

Then Leah did the only thing she could… She waited.

Sunday, August 10, 2:00 a.m.

FOUR UNIFORMED POLICE officers had arrived. One had stayed with Leah, taking her statement, and three had searched the entire restaurant. They had combed through the alley behind it…the dumpsters. They had scrutinized all vehicles parked in the area. Neighboring businesses had been checked, but all were closed for the night, with no signs of breaking and entering or other foul play. There was no one else on or around the property except Leah and the police.

Presumably, whoever had…*hurt* Raymond had also taken him away, completely disappearing by the time the police arrived.

Harold Manafort, the restaurant manager, had been called.

The good news was, they had not found a body.

There was no blood anywhere.

There were no signs of foul play whatsoever.

Nothing.

The bad news was that Leah looked like a fool.

She sat at a table now, only a few yards from the corridor where she'd hidden in that ladies' room for what had felt like an hour but was likely only fifteen or twenty minutes. Detective Anthony Lambert sat at the table with her, a pen poised above his notepad. He scribbled and turned pages and scribbled some more as she told her story for the second time.

She'd told it first to the female police officer who had come into the ladies' room looking for Leah after the four had forcibly entered the building. Her three fellow officers had spread out and begun the search that proved futile.

Eventually, a detective, the one now seated at the table with Leah, had arrived, and she'd repeated her story. He'd asked a few questions, and then he'd spoken with the uniformed officers and gone through the restaurant and the alley with them. A moment ago he had returned to her table and started to ask more questions. Throughout it all, the female officer, whose name Leah still could not remember, held vigil nearby. Leah wasn't sure whether they feared she would take off—obviously she could get out, now that the front entrance had been breached—or that she would call someone on her cell. She was surprised they hadn't asked for it yet. After all, she was no doubt considered suspicious at this point, seeing as how no body or blood had been found in the place where she'd insisted on having seen both.

"So," Lambert said, drawing her attention back to him, "you sat out here alone in the near darkness for forty-five minutes, waiting for your date." He leaned forward and peered at his notebook. "One Raymond Douglas."

It sounded particularly sad when he said it aloud that way. Who waited that long in a dark restaurant for a man she didn't even know—had only met briefly that one time? "Yes. He'd asked me to wait in the dining room for him and I did."

Desperate. Besides suspicious, the detective likely now believed her to be desperate.

Lambert studied her over the bifocals he'd settled into place on the bridge of his wide nose. He was not a large man. Average height, slim build. Yet it was obvious he spent some time in the gym. His arm muscles bunched and flexed against the sleeves of his shirt. He'd long ago removed the suit jacket and hung it on the back of the chair next to him.

He had keen, probing eyes. He seemed alert, ready to dive across the table and kick some butt if necessary. Not at all the cliché detective so often depicted on television. If not for his gray hair, she would never have believed the man was fifty-eight. She wouldn't have known his age had he not said something to one of the uniformed officers about being too old at fifty-eight for these sorts of calls. At this point, Leah was feeling far older than her twenty-eight years as well.

"He'd never asked you out before," Lambert said. Not

really a reasonable question, because she'd explained the extent of her knowledge of Raymond Douglas already. But she'd watched enough crime dramas on television to recognize the drill. He was fishing around to see if her story would change.

"We didn't know each other before two weeks ago."

He flipped back a page and appeared to verify that his notes were correct, or maybe he was simply buying time. He looked up. "Do you understand the ramifications of making a false statement to the police?"

Leah's jaw dropped. "What?" Was he seriously asking that question? She really had not expected him to go in that direction. What kind of person did he think she was?

"We found no body. No blood. No *nothing* to suggest what you say you saw happen actually happened."

Anger flared in her belly. "I know what I saw."

"Perhaps you fell asleep while you were waiting and dreamed it." He shrugged. "It's happened to me. I fell asleep once and dreamed my wife left me. Only difference is, three days later she did."

"I did not fall asleep," Leah said, unable to keep the bitter edge out of her voice. This was bordering on ridiculous.

"Mr. Manafort said Raymond Douglas told him and the investors who came to last night's meeting that he was leaving immediately after that meeting for a long-awaited vacation."

The statement took Leah aback. "Why would he ask me to wait here for him if he was going on vacation right after his meeting?" It made no sense. This had to be a mistake.

"That's a very good question," Lambert agreed. "My first inclination is to not believe he asked you to wait."

"You think I'm lying?" A glimmer of outrage flashed

through her. "Why in the world would I do that?" This was insane!

She was a full-time student who worked every minute she wasn't glued to a book or a laptop. There was no time in her schedule for games like this. There was, frankly, no time for anything. The idea of how many hours she had just wasted made her all the more furious.

So much for putting herself out there, as her roommate had insisted.

Lambert studied her for a long, uncomfortable moment. "I'm not sure why you would do this," he admitted, "but I will certainly find out. So if you're not being completely honest with me, you need to do so right now."

He actually thought she was making up the story. "I am telling you that Raymond Douglas was here and someone killed him…or at least hurt him. I saw him—his body—being dragged across that kitchen floor, and I saw blood."

This was unbelievable. Frustration joined the mix of anger and outrage.

"I've interviewed by phone three of the five employees who closed up the restaurant tonight," Lambert said. "They all confirmed that Mr. Douglas was fine and intended to leave shortly after they left. In fact, one saw him at the rear exit just before she left the kitchen."

"Wait…what?" How could that be? Those people had let her inside. Why would they leave her in an empty restaurant? Wouldn't they have been suspicious? "That makes no sense at all. Why wouldn't at least one among them have demanded to know why I came into the restaurant? Why would they have allowed me to come inside if no one else was around?"

"That's a question for the manager to pose to his employees." Lambert closed his notepad with a distinct snap.

"Since you are not an employee of this establishment, and none of the people to whom I spoke who *are* employees had any idea why you came inside as they were leaving, I can only say that your story feels off somehow. Why would you not ask after Mr. Douglas as the others filed out and you entered? Why would you sit in the dark—basically— for forty-five minutes? You're a bright woman. It seems illogical to me that you would do this."

The idea that he was making far too much sense rattled her.

"I... I don't know what else to say. He asked me out on a date, and I followed his instructions on where and when to meet him. The delay was annoying, but I wanted to be patient." She shrugged. "To tell you the truth, it's been a while since I've been on a date, period, much less basically a blind date. I guess I thought I was giving him the benefit of any doubt."

Again, Lambert considered her for several seconds. "I also called Mr. Douglas's assistant, who confirmed he was scheduled on the red-eye to Los Angeles. We're still attempting to verify that he boarded the plane, but the vacation appears to be legitimate. It's your date we can't seem to verify."

This couldn't be. Why would Raymond ask her out and then do this?

It made no sense. They had talked an hour before she came to the restaurant. Maybe he was scheduled for a vacation starting tomorrow. Who knew? Today, actually, since it was well after midnight. Whatever his plans for today, Raymond Douglas had scheduled a date with her for last night. Her friend Isla could verify this.

"I can't tell you about the plans he'd had for today or any other upcoming days," Leah said, her patience thinning, "but I know his plans for last night. As I've told you twice already, you can verify this with my friend, Isla. Raymond and I were going to an exhibit—"

"So you say," he interrupted. "Your friend has not returned my call. In any event, we will locate Mr. Douglas, and I hope that he is alive and well. Either way, I will be speaking with you again, Ms. Gerard. You are free to go for now. I'll be in contact as soon as I confirm our missing *victim's* whereabouts. Then we'll go from there."

This was so wrong. Leah pushed back her chair and stood. She swayed just a bit. She was tired and totally at the end of her emotional rope. All that aside, she was not some prankster or criminal or whatever this detective thought she was.

"I know what I saw, Detective," she repeated. "Apparently, I can't make you believe me—but when he doesn't show up you'll know I was right."

"If," he said, waylaying her plan of turning her back to him and marching angrily away, "he doesn't show up, I'm afraid your problems will be just beginning, Ms. Gerard."

"Why is that?" What the heck was he insinuating?

"If Mr. Douglas is truly missing and you were the last person in the vicinity of where he was last seen, then that would make you our prime suspect—wouldn't you agree?"

Oh. My. God. This could not be happening. "If I had something to do with his disappearance—injury and probably murder, because I know what I saw—why would I call the police? More importantly," she added, "why would I stay here and wait for them to arrive?"

"Stranger things have happened, Ms. Gerard, believe me. For now, don't leave the city. We will be talking again." He rose from his chair. "Since you walked here, Officer

Clayton will take you home." He nodded to the female officer standing by.

Leah almost said she would prefer to walk back home as well, but given the circumstances, she would gladly accept a ride.

No matter what this detective believed, Raymond Douglas was likely dead. Leah firmly believed that someone had murdered him right here in this restaurant.

Surely the police would figure that out when they didn't find him. Knots tied in her belly. But then, Lambert was right: she was the only person left in this restaurant when he vanished.

"This way, Ms. Gerard," Officer Clayton said, breaking into her new nightmare.

Leah followed the other woman, unsure of what else to do. There was one other thing she suddenly understood with utter clarity.

Once the police involvement in whatever happened here tonight got out, the killer—and there was a killer, or kidnapper, or *whatever* out there somewhere—would know someone else besides him and Raymond had been in the restaurant.

How long would it take that person to find Leah?

Chapter Two

Monday, August 11
Gerard/Morris Apartment
Chestnut Street, 9:30 a.m.

Leah parted the slats of the blinds and peeked out the window. Her heart sank. The car was still there. Fear crept up her spine, making her shiver.

That car had been there all night. Two-door sedan, black. She couldn't determine the make. Nothing sporty or particularly sleek. Generic…nondescript.

The first time she had spotted the vehicle was late yesterday, just before dark. After getting home from the nightmare would-be blind date, she had gone straight to bed. Ended up sleeping a good portion of the day away. She hadn't even bothered to call Isla and tell her what happened. Surely the detective had gotten in touch with her by now. Frankly, she was surprised her friend hadn't called her and asked what the heck happened.

Didn't matter. Isla would be home tonight anyway. Leah could tell her everything then. This was not the kind of conversation to have over the phone. It was too bizarre… too personal.

She cradled her mug of coffee, wished the caffeine would kick in. This was her second cup, and she really, really needed the boost. Detective Lambert would be here at ten. She'd spent hours last night searching for news about Raymond, but she'd found nothing. No mention of him at all, actually. Not a single word about an incident at the Chop House. Did that mean Raymond really was on vacation? She supposed she would find out when the detective arrived. More knots twisted in her belly. On some level, she understood that somehow this was not going to turn out well. The whole situation was far too strange. As much as she wanted to believe there would be a logical—if not reasonable—explanation, she didn't believe that to be true.

She'd already missed a shift at the library, and she'd had no choice but to call out today as well. So much for adding to her savings. But work was the furthest thing from her mind just now. She wanted—no, she *needed* to understand what had happened in that restaurant kitchen. To the man she'd gone there to meet. The idea that she had fallen asleep and somehow dreamed the whole incident was absolutely ludicrous.

The buzzer sounded, warning her that she had a caller at the entrance to the building. Bracing herself, she crossed to the door and picked up the handset of the intercom mounted on the wall.

"Yes?"

"Detective Lambert here for our appointment, Ms. Gerard."

"Come on up." She pressed the button that would release the door lock for the detective. She desperately wished to never see him again, but there was no hope for that until this thing was figured out. Her head still swam with uncertainty each time she replayed the events of last night.

A tiny part of her had even started to wonder if she was losing her mind.

No, she saw what she saw. This detective needed to figure out what had happened. That was his job.

Maybe, if she was really lucky, he had news that would clear up this terrible mess. Doubtful, but she could hope. Leah hung up the handset and readied to open the door. Depending on whether he took the elevator or the stairs, he'd be here fairly quickly. The apartment she and Isla shared was on the second floor. It wasn't very large, but it was affordable for two students juggling jobs and student loans to get their educations. She and Isla were the same age, but unlike Leah, her roommate hadn't taken a break before continuing her education. By this time next year, Isla would be moving on from medical school to an internship while Leah would be hoping to land a position teaching English literature at a university. She should have completed her undergrad degree and this master's years ago, but a bad decision she never again wanted to think about had gotten in the way.

A knock on the door made her jump, even though she'd known it was coming.

She checked the view finder. Detective Lambert, shoulders squared and eyes narrowed, stared back at her. She opened the door and propped a smile into place. "Please, come in."

"Thank you for seeing me on such short notice," he said. He stepped inside and surveyed the space.

Leah closed and locked the door. She always did so without thinking, but with the possibility that someone was watching her apartment, she was uncomfortable even with it locked. For a moment she wondered how the detective was sizing up her place. Small, but nice—*nice* meaning well maintained and in a good location. There wasn't much on the walls as far as photos or decor of any sort. Who had the time? The furnishings were a mishmash of what she and Isla had each owned before Leah had moved in. Since their styles were completely different, there was no true theme to the decor. Just a mix of Isla's ultramodern pieces and Leah's slightly more traditional stuff. Actually, the place had looked better—cleaner design-wise—before Leah added her things. The apartment had been Isla's for several years when she and Leah met and became roommates.

She gestured to the living room area. "Have a seat."

Though the detective crossed the room and paused at the sofa, he waited until she settled there to lower into one of the chairs. He chose the traditional overstuffed, upholstered one that belonged to Leah instead of Isla's modular leather-and-chrome one. The sofa and chairs were clustered near the one double window in the room. In Leah's opinion, that rather large window was one of the most important features of the space. She loved that she could watch the people on the sidewalks and the comings and goings on the street whenever she wanted, since they lived in such a vibrant neighborhood.

She really enjoyed living in this city. Hadn't regretted her move here five years ago for a single moment. Well, at least until Saturday night. She had to admit a brief bout with regret after that disturbing event.

"Did you find him?" she asked the man watching her intently. Perhaps that explained the unexpected meeting. She braced herself for bad news.

"Well—" he crossed one leg over the other, settling his ankle atop his knee "—that depends on how you define the word. We did find evidence that he had a vacation planned. At some point before the scheduled flight, he changed it to Sunday afternoon rather than the middle of the night on Saturday, which, for what it's worth, lends some credibility to your story of a date. We also learned that he did not make the flight. His assistant has not heard from him. He has not checked in to the hotel in Los Angeles, and he is not at home. Based on a search of his residence, he had packed for the trip, but his suitcase still sits on the bed."

Regret and dread funneled through her. She had sincerely hoped he would be found on vacation in Los Angeles and would admit that he'd decided to stand her up but hadn't possessed the guts to even send a text. Although she had known better, she had still, deep down, hoped she'd imagined or dreamed the whole thing.

"He *is* missing, then." Of course he was. She had seen him dragged across the floor, blood leaking from his head. He was missing and injured…possibly dead.

"Yes. Raymond Douglas is officially missing. Since there has been no ransom demand, it's unlikely that he's still alive—based on what you allegedly witnessed. Whatever the case, be aware," he warned, "that this information has not been released. The few details we have are not to be shared under any circumstances. I tell you this only because I need your full cooperation."

His last statement hit her the wrong way. "Are you suggesting I haven't been cooperating? For God's sake, I've done everything you asked me to do. I've answered all your questions." *Suffered being made to feel like a fool*, she kept to herself.

He studied her for another long moment. "Tell me about your relationship with Chris Painter," he said, rather than answer her question.

The unexpected change in direction of the discussion was like a dash of cold water in her face. Where the hell had that come from? "What does a personal relationship I had over nine years ago have to do with what happened to Raymond?"

"Maybe nothing," he returned with a half shrug. "But indulging my curiosity is part of cooperating, to my way of thinking."

Her pulse revved up. He was serious. Clearly, he'd been digging around in her past. She shouldn't be surprised, but somehow she was. "What is it that you want to know?"

"The two of you had a bad breakup, and then Painter disappeared," Lambert said. "No one heard from him again. Still haven't, according to the detective I spoke with from your hometown."

A twisted combination of fear and anger swelled inside her. "If you spoke with Detective Hawkins," she began, choosing her words carefully, "then you know that Chris was a drug dealer. A thug. He was in and out of jail, and he made a lot of enemies. When he disappeared, most people believed he crossed the wrong guy and was taken out of play. I was eighteen, naive and wild about a very bad man. My parents tried to tell me that he was serious trouble, but I wouldn't listen. I was convinced I was in love, but I was wrong. That is all I know about the disappearance of Chris Painter."

Humiliation joined the other emotions swarming inside her. As a teenager, she had made a terrible mistake. She'd hurt and disappointed her parents, and she'd been dragged into a long and painful criminal investigation because she had been an immature and foolish girl who acted on impulse and emotion rather than logic and intelligence. Her senior year of high school was not her best by any stretch of the imagination. For the entire rest of her academic days, from kindergarten on, she had been a model student—one who made the very best grades and good choices. But it was that one lone, final year of high school—actually, the last few weeks—for which everyone in her small home-town would remember her. How sad was that?

Lambert nodded. "That's basically what Detective Hawkins said," he admitted. "But you can see how learn-ing this information would give me pause under the cir-cumstances."

She nodded, uncertain of her voice at the moment.

"The circumstances are oddly similar. Don't you agree?"

"Actually, I don't." She managed a tight swallow to dampen her dry throat. "I did not see whatever happened to Chris occur, and it was fairly clear to all who knew him why he vanished. At least, as clear as an unsolved disap-pearance can be. But this is not the same at all."

When he made no comment, she kept going. "Obvi-ously, you don't believe me when I say I saw Raymond on that floor. His eyes were open and unblinking. Blood was leaking down the side of his head." She gestured to her left temple. "From where I was standing, he looked dead or… maybe unconscious."

Lambert took a long, deep breath, then released it. "I'm supposed to believe that in the twenty-odd minutes be-tween the time you witnessed his body on the floor and being moved until the first on the scene arrived, someone removed the body from the building and cleaned up any evidence a crime had taken place in that kitchen?"

His doubts were undeniably justified…but she was tell-ing the truth. "It's the *only* explanation because I know what I saw."

Lambert uncrossed his legs and leaned forward, braced his forearms on his knees. "Did you know that Mr. Douglas carried a ten-million-dollar life insurance policy?"

Leah made a face. "Why would I know that? We'd only ever met once." She shook her head. "I can't believe this."

The detective turned up his hands. "It was necessary to ask. Just another worrisome detail to clear up."

"Then the beneficiary on the policy should give you a starting place on who might have reason to want him dead," she suggested. This man was a seasoned detective. She had done a little research on him too. He was good. His name or face was, it seemed, always in the news for solving some case or another. Unquestionably, he was well-versed in how to conduct a criminal investigation. She suspected he only wanted her reaction to the question. Evidently, unsettling the witness was part of his strategy.

"His ex-wife is one of the beneficiaries," Lambert said. "But she has an airtight alibi—she and her two teenage children spent the weekend with her mother."

Leah lifted her chin in defiance of the statement. "Maybe she hired someone to do it. Based on how quickly everything happened that night, it certainly gave the appearance of a professional job. A well-planned one, obviously." As soon as the words were out of her mouth, she wished she could take them back. Knowledge of that sort of thing was not a good look on a suspect. But she was only guilty of watching too much crime TV. And, admittedly, mystery novels were her favorite.

He nodded. "It does."

To her surprise, it practically sounded like he believed her. Leah had told herself not to forget to ask this next question, but she almost had. "What about cameras? Were there no cameras in the alley, or anywhere around the building, that showed the comings and goings at the rear exit of the restaurant?" She found it difficult to believe there weren't, but there had been no mention so far.

"Only one, and it wasn't working at the time."

She should have seen that one coming. "So, what now? Do you have other suspects, or are you determined to try and pin this on me, because I can tell you—" her voice rose with each word "—I did not have anything to do with this. I didn't even know the man."

"Well." He stood. "I'm sure I will have more questions."

Leah stood, too, her knees a little weak. Why couldn't he just give her an answer? Was she still a suspect, given what he'd learned about the insurance policy?

"Did you speak to Isla?"

"Unfortunately, I have not been able to reach her."

Frustration wove its way through Leah, but she wasn't surprised. When Isla was at work at the ER, she often-times left her cell phone in her locker. If she was in class, she had no doubt turned it off. Still, she usually returned calls. A new thread of uneasiness trickled through Leah.

"I hope you will contact me if you recall anything else I might need to know."

She followed him to the door, the urge to shake him and somehow make him understand that she was innocent in this a pulsing urge in her body.

Lambert hesitated at the door. "Was there anything else you wanted to tell me?"

She thought of the car. "Yes." She moistened her lips. "There's been a black sedan across the street since last night. There's a man—I think it's a man—inside. I feel like he might be watching me." She shrugged. "I can't help wondering if perhaps I'm in danger."

Concern or something like it materialized in his expression. "Show me the car you mean."

She led the way back to the window and surveyed the street. Frustration sagged her shoulders. The car was gone. "I guess he left."

"Perhaps it was one of ours," he suggested. "We had some-one keeping an eye on your apartment the first eight or so hours after you left the restaurant, but not since. It's not impossible there was a miscommunication on the time frame. Still, if you notice anything that makes you feel threatened, call me." He hesitated. "You make a good point about the wife maybe hiring someone to get rid of her husband."

Hope dared to sprout. "Yes," she said with a nod. "It happens in the movies all the time."

"Maybe she hired you to play the part of witness to his murder."

Her jaw dropped, but any potential rebuttal flew out of her head.

With that blatant accusation, he walked away. This time when he reached the door, he opened it and left, calling out a *good day* over his shoulder.

She hurried across the room, locked the door and sagged against it. She was in serious trouble here. Somehow she had believed this would sort itself out, but that wasn't happening. At this point, she would be a real fool not to recognize it was only getting worse. What she needed was an attorney. No, Leah decided… What she needed was someone who could help her figure this out. Maybe even help her find the person responsible for this nightmare.

A private investigator. A good one. A really, really good one.

The Colby Agency, 2:00 p.m.

"Ms. Gerard."

Leah jerked to attention. She'd been a million miles away. "Yes." She stood and produced a smile for the young woman who had called her name. Blond hair, blue eyes, very well put together. Professional pale blue suit.

"I'm Jamie Colby." She extended her hand.

Leah shook her hand, then suffered a fleeting doubt considering how very young the woman appeared to be. Maybe she was an assistant? "Thank you for making time to see me." Leah was so, so grateful to be able to get an appointment today—even if only with an assistant.

"Of course." Jamie gestured to the corridor beyond the lobby. "Walk with me to my office, and we'll figure this out."

Leah strode alongside the other woman as she led the way down a carpeted corridor flanked by doors on either side. The decor was surprisingly elegant—more so than Leah had expected, even though the agency was listed as the top in the business. Somehow the idea of a PI always made her think of shabby offices on the seedy side of town. This was a seriously upscale area and a prestigious building.

Jamie's office was spacious and filled with light. A large window looked out over the street. Maybe not an assistant. The realization that her last name was Colby struck Leah just then. Probably...definitely not an assistant.

After the offer of refreshments, they settled at a small conference table on one side of the well-appointed room.

"You mentioned the Douglas case," Jamie said, kicking off the meeting. "I reached out to my contact at Chicago PD and learned that Detective Anthony Lambert has that one. He has a very good reputation and will go to great lengths to solve the matter."

Leah nodded. "I read about him on the internet. The trouble is, he's so focused on me it feels like he isn't looking at anyone else."

"You are listed as a person of interest," Jamie agreed. "But that's not unusual. Oftentimes an investigation will include a good many persons of interest, and that list will get whittled down as the investigator moves forward, gathering information and evidence." She smiled reassuringly. "It's not personal, just part of the process. So, why don't you walk me through how you're involved?"

Leah didn't hesitate. She launched into the unnerving story, taking care not to leave out a single detail. If this agency was going to help her, she had to ensure they knew everything. It certainly sounded as if they had all the right contacts. Just further proof of the caliber of investigators on staff. In light of Lambert's visit that morning, Leah went ahead and shared the details about Chris Painter. Though her distant past couldn't possibly have anything to do with this case, Lambert seemed to think otherwise or wanted to give that impression. She was here for help. No one could help her without all the necessary details—even the ugly ones that seemed irrelevant.

"I appreciate your thoroughness," Jamie said. "Based on the situation as we know it at this time, I feel that investigator Owen Walker would be an excellent fit for your case. I've spoken with him at length, so he's aware of the situation. I'd like to introduce you and let the two of you talk, if you're ready to move forward."

Leah nodded. "Yes, please."

She had been informed of the retainer fee and costs during her initial call. As much as Leah hated to part with any of her savings, she had a feeling this was necessary to her survival of whatever was coming. If she'd had any doubts, seeing that black sedan parked outside her building again when she left for this appointment had sealed her decision.

Jamie used the phone on her desk to summon the investigator. Half a minute later the door opened, and he joined the meeting.

Owen Walker was a very attractive man. Tall, broad

shouldered. Maybe thirty-two or thirty-three. Isla would swoon. Leah couldn't deny a bit of a swoony reaction herself. She could see him on the cover of a fashion magazine or leading the cast in a television series. Not to mention on a romance novel.

She just hoped his skills were as impressive. The last thing she needed was eye candy.

He introduced himself, shook her hand, but he didn't take a seat. "I prefer to kick off a relationship with a new client in a less formal setting," he explained.

Nice voice too. Deep, smooth. A charmer. Her failed blind date had been a charmer. Oh God…maybe this had been a mistake.

"There's a coffee shop," he went on. "Just down the block."

Leah pushed to her feet. "Sounds good." She turned to Jamie, who had risen from her seat as well. "Thank you for your time, Jamie." She prayed it wasn't going to be a waste of her own.

"Thank you." She gave Leah a nod. "You can stop worrying now. You're in very good hands."

Leah hoped, hoped, hoped that was true. She had never done anything like this, and she wasn't sure how it worked. She glanced at the man assigned to her case. This was the Colby Agency. The agency had a fantastic reputation. She had to believe this man would be of the highest caliber available in the field. She drew in a deep breath. At least she'd gotten the ball rolling. This thing was getting far too complicated and more than a little scary.

Doing something was better than doing nothing.

As they rode the elevator down to the main lobby, he asked, "How long have you been in Chicago?"

"I moved here five years ago." For four years after the

Chris disaster, she had drifted around, never feeling completely comfortable anywhere she landed—from Peoria, where she'd grown up, to Springfield and then up to Rockford and a few places in between, eventually landing in Chicago. Even though she'd spent the first two years in the Windy City juggling school and keeping a low-rent roof over her head, this felt like home for the first time since she'd left Peoria. Maybe it was more about finding her good friend Isla two years after settling in Chicago. "I can't see myself ever leaving."

"It's a dynamic city, for sure," he agreed.

When the elevator stopped, they crossed the grand lobby and exited the building. The afternoon sun had cranked up. This summer had been one for the books so far. Leah was ready for fall.

"What about you?" she asked.

"I'm a transplant. Moved from Miami ten years ago."

"Talk about a climate change."

"A bit different, yes."

He smiled, and it only confirmed her idea that he could certainly grace the covers of magazines and books. Wow.

But could he solve this case?

Deep in her shoulder bag, her phone clanged its vintage ringtone. Even though she'd lowered the volume, it still sounded too loud in the moment.

"Excuse me." With her mother's health deteriorating these days, she was careful never to ignore her phone. She checked the screen. Didn't recognize the number. She frowned, then glanced at the man beside her. "I should probably get this."

He nodded and she tapped the screen. "Hello?"

"Leah, it's Roger Bolling."

The building manager. Her instincts sharpened. "Hey, Roger. Is everything all right?"

"Not really. There was an explosion at your door."

Leah stalled. "What?" She couldn't have heard him right.

"Some guy made a flower delivery. Since you weren't home, he left it outside your door. Five minutes after the guy exited the building, there was an explosion. Blew the door off its hinges and started a fire. Luckily, I was here and got it put out before there was much damage. The fire department is here. Cops too."

"Oh my God, was anyone hurt?"

"No, no. That's the upside. But, as I said, the police are here, and they want to talk to you."

What in the world? Emotions twisted inside her. "I'll be there in fifteen minutes."

Chapter Three

Gerard/Morris Apartment
Chestnut Street, 5:00 p.m.

The wall around the hole that had once been the door to her apartment was blackened by the fire the explosion had caused. The door itself had splintered into numerous pieces and was scattered all over the living area inside the apartment. The odor of smoke lingered in the air, even though the flames had been extinguished almost immediately, before Leah even got the call.

Detective Lambert was already at the scene when they arrived. There were several other uniformed police officers and at least two more in plain clothes like Lambert. The fire department was just preparing to leave, except for the fire marshal; he and Lambert were in deep conversation.

Leah felt numb. This couldn't be happening…and yet, it was.

"Were you expecting flowers from anyone?" her newly hired PI asked.

Leah laughed despite the fact that she felt more like crying. "No. I haven't been sent flowers…" She laughed again, a sad self-deprecating sound, and shook her head. "Ever."

He gave a nod. "I'll talk to Detective Lambert and see what they've learned."

Leah stood several yards away from her apartment, behind a ribbon of yellow crime scene tape. She sagged against the wall. The whole building had been evacuated, and residents were only now being allowed back inside. The neighbors who lived nearest to her eyed her suspiciously as the ribbon was moved aside for each one to pass through. She was the only one who wouldn't be moving beyond this point. The hole that had been her door was draped with two more ribbons of yellow crime scene tape. The ribbon hung like an X over the opening.

She had called Isla and left a message warning her about the explosion. Leah already knew exactly what her friend and roommate would say when she called back: Isla would insist she cared nothing about the personal items they might have lost. She only cared that Leah was safe and unharmed. And she was—physically, anyway. Her mind, however, was reeling. Her emotions were a shipwreck. How on earth had this happened? First the blind date from Hades, and now this!

Who sent a bomb hidden in flowers? There was something so very sadistic about the idea.

Her arms tightened around her torso. How was she supposed to react to all this? To feel? The one thing she sensed with certainty was that she had to find out why this was happening. And where the apparent danger was coming from.

Danger. Why in the world would she be in danger? She had nothing and knew nothing that was overly important or represented a threat to anyone. It was sad to say, but basically she was a nobody.

This could not be her life!

But then again, it wasn't like it hadn't happened before.

She closed her eyes and blocked the memories from nine plus years ago. That had been another life. This one was calm and sedate…boring, even. How could she possibly be relevant enough to anyone or anything to be in danger?

Yet somehow she felt exactly like one of the informants in a crime movie, where the bad guys were doing everything possible to stop her and the good guys weren't sure they could trust her.

It was the most bizarre situation. Leah had done nothing wrong. She'd agreed to a date. A sort of odd one, to be sure—to meet someone at half an hour before midnight and wait in a closed, dimly lit dining room while he handled a bit of business. In hindsight, the whole plan was the very picture of a scene from a gangster novel. Why had she not considered the oddity of it all before agreeing? Was she that desperate?

No, Isla had been that desperate for her. Leah had never been the pushy type. Nevertheless, she appeared to be drawn to that very personality type. She was the one who went along. Her life was busy enough without shoehorning social activities into it. But her friends—Isla, in particular—had insisted she needed to get out more. One thing was certain: This was the last time she would agree to a blind date. Ever.

The next time she agreed to spend time with a potential boyfriend—assuming she wasn't dead or in prison after this—she would set the terms. And she would do her homework. Her frustration wasn't aimed at Raymond— not really. He had seemed like a perfectly nice guy. It was difficult to hold a grudge against a man who could very well have been murdered.

Don't even go there, Leah. At this point, she had no

idea what had happened to him. Kidnapped? Murdered? She shuddered.

As if her thoughts had summoned the two of them, Owen Walker and Detective Lambert started toward her. Her anxiety crept up a notch.

Just stay calm and tell the truth.

But that was what she had been doing, and look where that had gotten her. She stared at the hole of a door to her apartment, and her shoulders slumped.

Whatever else happened, and whatever it meant, the truth was all she had. The many and varied possible unknowns made her feel cold and alone. Who would do this to her? When she and Owen had arrived at her building, she'd been fairly certain she spotted the black sedan. With all the worries about the explosion, she hadn't mentioned it. There was no time to agonize over whether she was being paranoid.

There were bigger issues.

Who would send her flowers? More importantly, who would send her flowers with a bomb inside? This truly was so far over-the-top that she couldn't even see it, much less begin to understand it.

But it was happening…*to her.*

"Mr. Walker tells me you have no idea who would have sent you flowers," Lambert said as he came to a stop next to her.

"None." She shrugged. "I mean, I never get flowers." Never had, but there was no need to repeat that sad fact. Owen had likely already told the detective as much.

"The building has security cameras," Lambert said. "We were able to see the delivery person stopping the van on the street and bringing the flowers inside, then him exiting the building. Unfortunately, he wore a baseball cap with the bill pulled low, shadowing his face. He seemed quite aware of the security cameras. There were no markings on the van, on his clothing. He may have been a hired driver and had no idea there was a bomb."

Just like last night…except this time the results of the incident were undeniable.

"What do I do now?" She glanced once more at what remained of her apartment. "I understand I can't stay here, but how in the world will you figure out who is doing this and why? It all started with what happened at the restaurant, and I am quite honestly completely at a loss as to what to expect next." She hated that she sounded as if she was at the end of her rope, and she hated even worse that tears were burning her eyes. If she cried now, she would just crumple into a heap on the floor.

Keep it together, Leah.

"These things take time," Lambert said. "Fortunately, the quick reaction time of the building manager, Mr. Bolling, prevented any real damage beyond the door. Even so, you and your roommate cannot go into the apartment until the forensic work is done. I'm sure Mr. Bolling will have the door repaired as quickly as possible. But for now, if there are items you need from your room, one of my officers can pack a few things for you."

Leah nodded. "That would be very helpful. Thank you."

She'd wanted to complain. To demand why she was being cast out of her home because someone else had decided to do a bad thing. But it wouldn't change the situation. There were rules, and she had to obey. This whole episode—the past thirty-odd hours—had been mind-boggling. She kept expecting to wake up and realize it was just a bad dream.

Detective Lambert went to one of the uniformed officers and spoke quietly to her before returning to his conversation with the fire marshal. Then Officer Brant—a woman, thankfully—took notes on her cell phone of what items Leah needed and where they could be found in her bedroom. Once Leah had told her everything she could think of, Brant moved the crime scene tape aside and disappeared into the apartment.

"I've spoken with Victoria," Owen said. "I'm to take you to one of our safe houses until we figure this out—if that's okay with you."

A safe house. Dear God, she really *was* in a movie… only this one was far too real.

Leah attempted to work up a smile, but the effort felt entirely miserable. "Thank you. I am so grateful I found the Colby Agency and had the good sense to make that call. Jamie was incredibly helpful."

"She's pretty amazing," Owen agreed. "She's Victoria's granddaughter. You may or may not have read the About section on the website, but Victoria is the one who calls the shots."

"I did, and I also read several articles about Victoria. Her life story is astonishing." Leah wondered how a person—a mother whose son was abducted when he was seven years old, then suddenly returned twenty years later with the single goal of killing her—could survive such an ordeal. She couldn't imagine the strength and fortitude Victoria must possess.

"Then you appreciate that one of her top priorities is protecting those who need it most. We will keep you safe, Leah, until this is done."

She smiled, and this time it was real. "Well, maybe I'll actually sleep tonight. Between worrying about what happened to Raymond Douglas and the person in the black car watching my apartment, I barely slept at all last night."

"There's been someone watching your apartment?" Concern flashed in the investigator's eyes.

"I first noticed it late yesterday, and it was here this morning. When I told Detective Lambert about it—during his visit this morning—we checked, and the car was gone. But I think I saw it when we arrived here a little while ago."

His jaw tightened. "We'll have a look when we leave, after the officer returns with your bag."

Thankfully, the officer ducked under the yellow tape just then, Leah's overnight bag in hand, and made her way toward them.

"Found everything you asked for," Brant said. "You gave very good directions on where to find what you wanted. I wish my bedroom was so orderly."

"I'm a little obsessed with organization," Leah admitted. Disorganization was a pet peeve of hers. The first thing she and Isla had agreed upon when she had asked Leah to share the apartment was the necessity of organization. They were both a little overenthusiastic when it came to everything being in its place. But living in such a small place essentially demanded it.

"Nothing wrong with that," Brant said with a smile.

When the officer had gone on her way, Owen said, "I'll check with Lambert and make sure we're clear to go."

While he walked to the other end of the corridor where Lambert and the fire marshal remained in deep conversation, Leah remembered that she'd forgotten her cell phone charging cord. Oh well, she'd just have to pick one up on the way to the safe house. She wasn't asking the officer to go back into the apartment.

A safe house. She would be staying in a safe house. How in the world had this happened? Didn't matter how many times she asked that question, the answer was always the same: she had no idea.

When Owen returned , he nodded. "We can leave now."

As grateful as she was to be leaving, the lingering smell of smoke and the realization of what had happened were ramping up her anxiety. She couldn't help feeling just a little terrified at the prospect of what might happen next. She'd seen lots of safe houses in the movies and in television shows, but she'd never expected to be staying in one herself. How long would she be expected to stay there? Would there be additional costs? Her budget couldn't take many more surprises.

Outside, she scanned the street for the black sedan. Like before, when she wanted to show someone she wasn't imagining things, it was nowhere to be seen. But it had been there when they arrived, she was certain of it.

"I saw it," she said, suddenly feeling defensive. She realized how she sounded but, damn it, this was ridiculous.

"I'm sure you did," Owen said. "Unless the driver already saw what he needed to see or found what he needed to find, the one thing you can count on is that he or she will be back. We will catch him."

His words relaxed her just a little. Her shoulders loosened, and drawing in a breath came easier. "I like that plan."

He opened the passenger-side door of his sporty silver car and waited for her to settle in. Once he'd closed the door, he moved around to the driver's side and slid behind the wheel.

"Where is the safe house?" She sank deeply into the luxurious leather seats and relaxed a bit more.

"This one's on Elm Street. It's great. You'll see."

Colby Agency Safe House
East Elm Street, 6:50 p.m.

HE WASN'T WRONG when he said it was great.

Leah wasn't sure how she would prevent her jaw from perpetually dropping. The safe house was an 1879 brownstone in the fabled historic area of East Elm. The place was truly gorgeous.

Just walking up the steps was awe inspiring. The architecture was splendid. Inside, things only got better. The ceilings soared, and the historic details had been carefully maintained while, at the same time, modernizing as needed. The windows were large and allowed a tremendous amount of natural light to flood into the rooms. Beautifully maintained hardwoods and a staircase that made you want to climb up to the next floor, your fingers trailing the intricately carved railing as you went. There were fireplaces in every room, her host explained. All restored so meticulously. The pièce de résistance was an intimate courtyard in the back that was completely self-contained with trees and shrubs, making it at once welcoming and utterly private. It was like being in a natural refuge miles from the city, and yet it was right here in the heart of Chicago.

"Wow, this is incredible. Like a vacation in a perfectly splendid VRBO."

"The agency has safe houses all over. Some in town, some miles away. This one allows us to be close to the ongoing investigation and yet securely away from any trouble. Your privacy and security are our top priority."

"And I appreciate it more than you can possibly know." Well, if this investigation was going to test her sanity and her safety as well as decimate her finances, at least she would be living in luxury.

"I'll take your bag to your room, and then we can see what's in the kitchen."

He'd insisted on carrying her bag from her building to the car and then into the brownstone. She imagined he was a real gentleman even when he wasn't on the job. Owen Walker gave every impression of being a really nice man.

"Should I come along?"

He smiled and indicated that she should go first. "Of course. You can pick your room instead of me selecting it for you, if you'd like."

"I imagine all the rooms are lovely," she said as they climbed the stairs.

"They are. You'll only need to decide if you want a street view or a lake view."

"I think I'll go with the lake view." Maybe the water would calm her nerves. She could use a little serenity right now.

"Very good choice." He flashed her another one of those smiles that made her smile back without thinking.

A new worry nudged her. This part of her current reality was suddenly feeling far too good to be true. When would the other shoe drop? She banished the thought. Clearing those haunting *what-if*s from her head was the only way to hang on to some semblance of peace of mind.

The room with the best lake view was on the third floor, according to her host. The large window turned out to be French doors that opened onto a small balcony. And like he said, the view from that balcony was utterly breathtaking.

"What about you?" She turned to her host. "Where will you be sleeping?"

The notion that she would love to hear him say "with you" flashed through her sleep-deprived mind.

Not smart, Leah.

"I'll be on the second floor, just below you. No one is getting to you without going through me first."

If he'd meant to make her feel safe, he'd done a fantastic job. "That definitely makes me feel better."

He deposited her bag onto the four-poster bed. "Now, let's see what we can scrounge up for dinner."

She didn't mention that ramen noodles were a mainstay at her place. Owen didn't look like an instant-meal kind of guy.

Leah loved how the staircase spiraled through the brownstone from the first floor to the top. She could glance over the railing and see all the way to the entry hall. It was so lovely. It really was like taking a vacation without ever leaving the city. Isla would be jealous. They often talked about getaways in some beautiful European city. Isla was likely the one who would eventually be able to afford an international vacation.

But this was pretty close...sort of.

The kitchen appeared to have original cabinetry—or at least something similar. But after opening a few doors and a few drawers, Leah recognized they were new, state of the art. The appliances were as well, but somehow the designer had found a way to bring it all together, as if every aspect was original and belonged exactly where it was, even though the house was more than a century old. There was even a hidden microwave and pantry. An island that looked like an old butcher's table from a shop that once sold select meats hand-carved right in front of the customer stood in the middle of the generous room. Though the island looked vintage, it was complete with at least one electrical outlet and a beautiful light fixture hanging above it.

"As you can see—" Owen pointed to the interior of the

massive fridge "—the menu is quite extensive. We can throw together any number of entrees."

He was right about that. Someone had stocked the fridge with a wide variety of goodies. She spotted the ready-to-bake pizza from her favorite local artisan shop. The pizzas were prepared fresh every day.

"Someone must have known I love Giovanni's pizza." She didn't even care if it was veggie or meat lovers; the crust was to die for. Everything else was just icing on the cake.

"Pizza it is, then." He reached for the package.

She scanned the contents of the fridge once more. "I can put together a salad."

"Perfect." Another heart-stopping smile flashed at her.

As he headed for the range, another worry poked into her head. This spending 24/7 together might not be as simple as she'd first thought. At least not until she got her mind off his smile and his...other assets. The primary problem was, she'd been dateless for far too long.

Salad, she told herself. *Focus on prepping the salad.*

She moved the ingredients to the island and then searched for bowls. "There is a variety of dressings. Which would you prefer?" Small talk was good. Kept her from overthinking.

"Surprise me." He glanced over his shoulder. "Truth is, I like them all."

Handsome and easy to please. "You got it."

The next few minutes were filled with sounds of the flames in the gas oven roaring to life and the chopping or tearing of veggies until the two bowls she had selected were brimming with lush salad. She took two plates to the dining table, then the necessary silverware and the bowls of salad.

"Wine?" she asked as she reentered the kitchen.

He pointed to the end of the kitchen where the back door was located. "The wine cabinet and fridge are in those cabinets."

The doors that she had thought belonged to the pantry actually opened to a sort of wine bar. The overhead criss-cross shelves held a wide selection to choose from. Below were two counter-height wine fridges that were also well stocked. Since the pizza had a little bit of everything in the way of toppings, she selected a prosecco. With the bottle tucked under one arm, she claimed a couple of wineglasses and carried everything to the dining table.

By the time she had located the linen napkins and arranged the settings, Owen arrived with the pizza.

They settled around the table, and he served the pizza and poured the wine. For a few minutes they enjoyed the meal. Leah hadn't realized she was ravenous until she smelled the pizza baking. She had missed lunch entirely. Breakfast had been a protein bar nearing its expiration date.

It was possible she would be embarrassing herself in the next few minutes because she was starving. Just as she had anticipated, the pizza was amazing. She'd done pretty well with the salad too.

After they'd eaten for a while, he said, "Tell me about the boyfriend who disappeared when you were eighteen."

Leah dabbed her lips with the napkin. She'd expected the subject to come up eventually. "Like I told Detective Lambert—"

He held up a hand. "Don't tell me what you told Lambert. Tell me how it was for you. The facts are one thing, the impact another."

Her face flushed a little. She hadn't expected him to pinpoint the difference so precisely. "All right. I was young. My parents were intensely strict. Religious, but not overly so. Just strict. They wanted their only child—me—to make good choices. To grow up and do important things. Their way of making sure that happened was keeping me under their thumb."

"To protect you." He sipped his wine, his blue eyes watching her intently.

He had the bluest eyes. "Yes."

A moment passed, and then she went on. "I was at the Stop-N-Go, grabbing a soft drink after school. I was two weeks away from graduating, and I could not wait to get out of Peoria. I was humming with the need to be on my own—to be free! Chris came in to pay for gas, and I was infatuated instantly. The way he talked…the way he walked… everything about him screamed *wicked*, and he was very handsome. I was a kid, and that was all I saw. He must have noticed me gawking, because he started flirting. The next thing I knew, I was giving him my cell number and that was that. I was hooked." She shook her head. "I had no idea what he really was. My parents tried to tell me, but I wouldn't listen. He was all I thought about. I spent that entire summer hanging on his every word and deed. My poor parents were both horrified and terrified."

"How did the summer end?"

He asked the question so quietly, but there would be nothing quiet about the answer. The noise and the trauma that answer contained was deeply disturbing. It was the nightmare her parents had worried about.

"Everyone who knew my family understood what my parents were going through in an effort to keep their good girl from going bad. So when Chris disappeared, the community thought my father had killed him. And not a single one blamed him." She shook her head, bit her bottom lip in an effort to stem the tears that rose instantly. "My father was the kindest, gentlest man you would ever meet. The idea that he would harm another soul was ludicrous, and yet, even the police were certain he'd killed Chris and buried him somewhere. The investigation was sheer misery. The way this one detective—not Hawkins, but the one before him—grilled and pushed my father…it was awful."

"But the case was never solved."

Another shake of her head. "Hawkins dug up enough details about Chris's *colleagues* in the drug business to take the heat off my father, but the damage was done. Not to his reputation, mind you. To his health. He suffered a fatal heart attack." She fell silent for a long moment, let the hurt trudge through her. "It was my fault. My mother insisted that was not the case, that heart problems ran in his family, but she knew." Leah nodded, losing the battle with the tears. "I could see it in her eyes no matter what her words said. I killed him."

"I'm certain that was a very difficult time for you and your mother."

"Yeah, well, stupid is as stupid does, and I was stupid. I spent the next four years drifting around trying to find myself, but what I was really looking for was forgiveness… peace. Something along those lines. Sadly, there was no finding it anywhere but in here." She pressed her hand to her chest. "I can't say that I've completely forgiven myself, but I've learned to live with it, and I've taken care of my mother the way my father would have wanted."

As her mother's health had deteriorated in recent years, Leah had made sure she was in the right assisted-living facility and saw the best doctors. Every single dime in the trust her father had left her had gone to making sure her mother was comfortable and as happy as she could be without him. Her mother wasn't pleased with the decision

Leah had made, but she had relented when it became clear her daughter wasn't changing her mind. She would be fine. She would be an English professor the way her father was, and she would be a good person. She didn't need the money her father had so carefully saved. She didn't deserve it.

When she was young, Leah and her father would read endlessly and dissect the great classic novels together. To this day, she cherished those memories. If only she hadn't made the mistake of her life. No amount of wishing and using her trust to take care of her mother could fix what she had done.

She could only do her best at being the person her father had believed she could be. It was her singular goal now—besides taking care of her mother. She would be the person he had hoped she would be.

And maybe, just maybe, one day she would be able to forgive herself.

"Tell me about your friend Isla," Owen said then, dragging her from the painful thoughts.

"She's wonderful." A smile tilted Leah's lips, and the tears receded. "She's like the sister I never had. She would do anything for me, and I would do the same for her." She laughed sofly. "Sometimes I can't believe how lucky I was to find a friend like Isla. We really are like sisters."

"The two of you know each other's histories. Like what happened when you were eighteen?"

"We know everything about each other." Leah nodded. She and Isla had no secrets.

"She is the one who introduced you to Raymond Douglas."

"She is. She hadn't seen him in a while, but she had a friend, Maya Ortiz, who served as a sous-chef at the Chop House back in the spring. Maya said Raymond was recently divorced and back in the field. She, Maya and I were at one of our favorite clubs one night a couple of weeks ago and ran into Raymond. I thought for sure Isla was interested in him, but that wasn't the case. She felt he and I would make a good match and…" Leah shrugged. "You know the rest."

"Have you seen Isla or spoken to her since the incident in the restaurant?"

Incident. That was a good way to put it. It was a murder, in Leah's opinion—kidnapping, at the very least—but they had no body, no murder weapon and no evidence of any crime at this point.

She thought about his question. Glanced at the clock on the wall. It was 8:15 p.m., and Isla hadn't called her back about the explosion. "No," she said, frowning.

What could have prevented her friend from calling after receiving the message about the explosion in their apartment and Raymond's disappearance? Until right this moment, Leah had assumed her friend had been busy…but they were beyond that now. This wasn't right. Isla never went this long without letting Leah know what was going on.

"I would have expected her to call by now, but I'm sure something came up and she'll call as soon as she can."

"Have you considered," he ventured, "that Isla could be involved in what happened? Maybe the flowers were for her…rather than for you."

Leah blinked. Made a face. No…that wasn't possible. She and Isla talked about everything. She would never hide anything like that from Leah, and she certainly would not leave her to deal with all this alone. It had to be something major to keep her away…something at work, Leah decided.

"No." She gave her head a hard shake. "Isla wouldn't… That's impossible. We tell each other everything." No way. The very notion was impossible.

Wasn't it?

Chapter Four

Leah stood on the small balcony, enjoying the pleasant view and the morning air. She could stand here for hours. Maybe that would help her mind relax and stop spinning.

Isla still hadn't called, and Leah had left her another voicemail.

Something was wrong. Very wrong. She and Isla hadn't been out of contact for this long since their friendship began three years ago.

Isla was in the final weeks of her first year of medical school and working part-time at the Northwestern Memorial ER. Leah had just gotten the job at the library. Her first two years in Chicago, she'd been thankful for her job as a barista at a corner coffee shop near her very modest studio. Another one of Isla's friends had frequented that same library for the workshops. Often, that friend would drag Isla along with her and the two would go for a drink or dinner afterward. On one of those occasions, Isla had invited Leah to join the two of them. She and Isla had become close friends very quickly. The instant Isla found out where Leah lived, she insisted on having her move in with her. It was true that the other neighborhood wasn't the best, but Leah hadn't minded. She was spending all her time at work or at school, so she never really had time to notice. Still, the prospect of moving into Isla's much nicer apartment in such a great neighborhood had been an offer too good to turn down.

From that point forward, they shared everything.

Isla wouldn't just vanish without saying anything unless something was very wrong.

She certainly wouldn't have anything to do with whatever happened to Raymond. Isla was going to be a doctor. She was in her final year of med school, for God's sake. Why would she throw it all away at this stage, when she was so near the finish line?

The concept made no sense at all.

Leah exhaled a big breath and did what she had to do. She couldn't put off any longer going downstairs and facing whatever music fate planned to play for her today. Somehow she would get through it.

She checked her phone once more in the hope that she'd somehow missed the alert indicating Isla had sent a text message or left a voicemail. Nothing from her friend. Nothing from anyone, not even Detective Lambert—the latter actually being a relief. Leah exhaled a big breath and tucked her phone into the back pocket of her jeans. Thankfully, there were extra charging bases and cords here, so she was able to plug up her phone last night without the added trouble of stopping for a new accessory. This safe house came with everything, apparently.

She closed the French doors and walked through the bedroom. The bed had been so comfortable, and still she'd hardly slept. How could she, with all the questions and worries whirling in her head? How had her life become this series of out-of-control elements so quickly?

She glanced at herself in the mirror as she passed the dresser. An elastic she'd forgotten about had been hiding in the bottom of her purse, so it was a ponytail day. She'd tucked her plain white T-shirt into her jeans and donned her favorite sneakers. After all that had happened, she decided casual was the theme until this was done. Worrying about fashion or makeup or any of those usual everyday issues was out the window.

This was way bigger than all those petty concerns.

Her fingers slipped along the sleek railing as she descended the stairs. Such a beautiful old house. She would love to own a brownstone or greystone one of these days—a pipe dream, of course. Her father would say the architecture was befitting an English lit professor. A smile tugged at her lips for a moment before the memory of that devastating loss intruded.

She would get through this, and she would make her father proud. Coming this far had been much too hard to allow anything to get in her way now.

Funny, she mused, if she'd just kept her head down and focused on work and her education, she wouldn't be in this predicament. Evidently, her ability to choose relationship material—or even date material—was seriously lacking.

But then, she hadn't actually done the choosing, had she? She'd allowed her friends to talk her into this one.

Still, it was her decision, ultimately. There was no one to blame except herself.

Isla would never have suggested Raymond Douglas if she'd suspected for a moment he was involved with bad people. She hadn't seen him in ages herself. Perhaps he had changed since she'd known him before. Maybe the trouble that had found him in that restaurant kitchen was part of the reason he was now divorced.

People changed, and sometimes not for the better.

When she was at the bottom of the stairs, the smell of freshly brewed coffee drew her to the kitchen. But it was the basket of muffins and scones on the island that had her mouth really watering.

"Good morning." Owen lifted his mug of coffee in a salute. "I hope you slept well."

"Good morning." Leah picked up a scone and bit into it. Warm, fruity—orange and cranberry—and so, so good. She chewed, moaned. "Did you bake these?" She licked her lips. "If you did, I might just have to keep you forever."

He chuckled. Shook his head.

It was at that exact moment she realized how her comment sounded. "I mean, they're just so good." She took another bite to prevent having to say more and putting her foot further into her mouth.

"I laugh," he explained, "because the idea that I baked anything other than ready-made pizza is funnier than you know. I'm great with simple stuff, but not so much with real baking—or cooking, for that matter. I had the basket delivered by a favorite bakery of mine."

She relaxed, grateful that he wasn't completely perfect. "This scone is to die for."

He smiled. "I'm glad. I wasn't sure if you were a protein-only breakfast person. Or maybe all egg whites and guacamole toast or something like that."

Leah was the one laughing now. "Hardly. That would be Isla. She is the clean eater. I just eat what I like, even if it isn't good for me."

The mention of her friend's name turned the delicious bite of scone to sand in her mouth.

"I take it she hasn't contacted you."

Leah shook her head. "I'm really worried at this point. This is not like her at all."

"Have you met her family? Do they live in the area?"

"Arlington Heights. And yes, I've been to dinner with her mother many times. Her father was never in the picture. She does have a brother, but he lives in New York. I could call him to see if he's heard from her. He's much older than Isla, so they aren't really close."

Owen considered the information, then suggested, "I think a cold call to the mother would be the most helpful route."

"I was thinking the same thing." Leah abandoned the remainder of her scone to make herself a cup of coffee. She added a little cream and savored the smooth taste. Then she returned to the island and finished off the scone. When she'd devoured the last crumb, she realized he was watching her. She swallowed, grabbed her cup with both hands and took a sip.

"Before we get going this morning," he said, "I wanted to explain that your participation in the investigation is optional—entirely up to you. If you'd like, you can stay here. Catch up on your reading or just relax. It's not necessary for you to be involved in the legwork."

She hesitated a moment before responding. The option of just relaxing was appealing, no question, but she couldn't do it. She had to be part of this. This was her life. Her friend could be in trouble. She couldn't sit around and just wait to see what happened. Not as long as she had a choice, anyway.

"I would prefer to be involved." She really hoped he

wasn't going to be disappointed by her answer. She needed to do this.

His lips quirked in a small smile. "I expected as much, but I had to make the offer."

Relief rushed through her. "Since I'm going to be working rather than relaxing, I think I need another scone for fuel." She shot him a look. "Don't judge."

He gave another deep chuckle. "I had two of those large muffins myself. Fuel is a good thing. And for the record, I never judge."

Handsome and kind too. Sigh. Why was it she'd never run into a guy like him before?

A mental eye roll followed the thought. Because she'd kept her head down and her attention on work since pulling her act together five years ago. Prior to that, her decisions had been a little hit or miss, as far as making good ones was concerned. In truth, she was really rusty in the dating field. Her instincts weren't so keen.

Rather than continue to berate herself, Leah concentrated on her coffee, nibbled on that second scone. Then she shared some additional information she'd remembered while she lay *not* sleeping last night. "Isla told me that Raymond has a mother in an assisted-living facility, and she wondered sometimes if the reason he was divorced was because he spent too much time catering to her. Apparently, there was some discontent related to the mother in his marriage. We could talk to his mother, if you think it might be helpful."

"According to the extensive background search done by the agency—I received a copy of it early this morning—his mother has advanced Alzheimer's. She's in a very upscale facility, and I have my doubts as to whether we would be allowed a visit, or if she would be able to help if we were."

Well, there went that theory.

Again, Leah considered how much she appreciated having the Colby Agency on her side. She had a feeling that finding her friend, the real story about Raymond and her way out of this depended on the man watching her right now.

Morris Residence
Patton Avenue
Arlington Heights, 10:00 a.m.

OWEN PARKED AT the curb in front of the Morris home. The house was small, more a cottage, with an equally small yard filled with blooming shrubs and flowers.

"Her car is home," Leah said.

Owen watched the woman in the passenger seat for a few seconds. Leah Gerard was worried. Understandably so. Her life had been turned upside down with this business. He'd done his research, and Raymond Douglas wasn't quite the upstanding businessman Leah had been led to believe. He'd spent some time as a chef but then realized there was far more money to be made in investments. With that in mind, he'd used his knowledge of Chicago's culinary world to get in on the best and biggest options. In the past five years, his financial worth had skyrocketed. The agency was looking into the possibility of such a huge change in status when his only assets were in the restaurant business. Owen wasn't convinced his new net worth matched his investments.

As well, Leah's friend Isla had a vaguely troubling background as well. Five years ago, there was a brief stint in a private mental hospital. A few months later, a disappearance that was reported to the police and then, only a week later, withdrawn and the case closed. Both parties hid these discrepancies well, but a solid background check and a little extra digging told the tale. Douglas's history showed indications of being a possible scam artist. Morris's reflected a brief period of instability and then nothing but smooth sailing. The real question for Owen was, how did whatever was going on with those two affect or involve Leah—or each other, for that matter?

There were some aspects of the situation that Leah needed to see and learn for herself. It would make accepting how badly she had been fooled somewhat easier. For her sake, he wished there would be better news, that perhaps things weren't as bad as they looked, but he doubted that would prove the case.

Owen had shared the information with Detective Lambert on a phone call that morning. Lambert had been on the right track, but his resources weren't what the Colby Agency's were. He was grateful for the assist. In Owen's opinion, the sooner Leah was cleared of any wrongdoing, the better.

His read on Leah Gerard assured him she was telling the truth about Isla Morris and Raymond Douglas to the best of her knowledge. Not that she was naive; she simply took people at face value until she saw otherwise. There was nothing wrong with that approach, except it did make her susceptible to particularly cunning people. He had a feeling Douglas was a very experienced player. Morris perhaps more so, in hiding secrets. There was no solid proof of wrongdoing in their known histories, but there were all the earmarks that Owen had instantly recognized: A lack of true friends. Lots of acquaintances but few who were really close. Little or no acknowledged family. In Douglas's case, there was undocumented work and discrepancies in school history.

"Did I pass?"

He frowned, zeroed in on the woman in the passenger seat. She stared at him expectantly. "Pass what?"

It was always easier to mine for more information with a question rather than an answer. Just a little technique he'd picked up during his tenure at the Colby Agency.

"I don't know." She stared out the windshield then. "The way you were staring at me just now made me wonder if you were trying to decide if you trusted me."

"Why wouldn't I?"

"I don't think Detective Lambert believes my story." After a five-second lapse, she turned back to Owen. "Maybe you don't, either, but you just haven't told me."

"Well—" he shut off the engine "—I have found no reason not to believe your story."

"So you've looked," she countered. "Into my background."

"I have. It's necessary to find and consider all that the police will be studying." He offered a reassuring smile. "But don't worry, you have a very good record, save for that brief period related to Painter. Even then, it was only your involvement with bad characters that reflected poorly on you. So you can rest easy. There is no evidence whatsoever that you are not the person you purport to be."

"But I was a terrible person." She looked him directly in the eyes. "I caused my father's death, and that was very bad."

"We all have our own way of looking at ourselves, our individual scale of standards. Some of us set unreasonable expectations for what we can do or did. Some too easily accept blame for the actions of others. It's part of what makes us who we are. You, Leah Gerard, are a good person who made a foolish mistake at a very young age. What you have now is a big problem looming over you like a dark cloud. We're going to alleviate that problem, and we're going to start right now."

She nodded, her eyes a little bright, and reached for the door.

They walked side by side to the front door of the small cottage. Since there was no doorbell, Owen knocked. Two more knocks were required before a voice called out, "Coming."

Leah's relief was palpable. Owen flashed her a smile to reassure her. All they had to do was ask the right questions of the right people, and they would find the answers they needed. That was always the most direct route to resolving a case.

The door opened and a petite woman with gray hair and keen brown eyes looked from Owen to Leah. "Leah! How nice to see you." She instantly drew Leah in for a hug. "You should have called." She patted her loose shoulder-length hair. "I would have prepared myself for visitors."

"You look wonderful as always," Leah insisted. She glanced from Mrs. Morris to Owen and back. "This is my friend Owen, and we're looking for Isla. Have you spoken to her since Saturday?"

A frown marred the older woman's features. "I haven't, and I've been worried." She offered a smile for Owen before shifting her attention back to Leah. "Please, come in. Would you care for some coffee or tea?"

"No thank you," Leah said.

"None for me, thank you," Owen echoed.

Mrs. Morris ushered them inside, closed the door and then took a seat. The door opened right into the small living room. It was a cozy space with lots of clutter—"collections," the lady of the house would likely call them. Bells, little statues of animals.

"Sit wherever you'd like," she insisted.

Owen chose a side chair while Leah settled on the sofa with her friend's mother. His goal during this visit was to watch the older woman closely for any tell that she might be holding back or not speaking the whole truth.

"I'm so worried about her," Leah said. "She never ignores my calls or texts. Do you think something happened with her work at the hospital?"

According to Leah, Isla worked part-time at Northwestern Memorial ER. The background search confirmed as such. She'd moved to that job four years ago, leaving Mount Sinai. It was possible she'd had to work double shifts, but this was well beyond those hours. Only a crisis would keep her there for going on seventy-two hours. The hospital was on his list of places to potentially visit today.

"She hasn't called me back either," Mrs. Morris said, her face pained. "She's supposed to have lunch with me today, but I haven't heard from her."

Leah looked to Owen. "This isn't like Isla at all."

"It is not," Mrs. Morris confirmed. "She is always on time. Never misses an appointment. Really, I'm not just saying that because she's my daughter. This truly is most unusual."

Owen pulled out his cell phone and showed her a picture of Raymond Douglas. "Have you ever seen this man?"

Mrs. Morris took the phone and studied the image. "I don't think so." She frowned, shook her head slowly. "Is he a friend of Isla's?" She passed the phone back to him.

If she recognized Douglas, she hid it well. Owen deferred to Leah for the answer to the woman's question.

"Isla told me she and Raymond—that's the man in the photo—have been friends for years," Leah explained. "She orchestrated a blind date for me with him."

Mrs. Morris's brow furrowed in concentration, as if she were trying to recall the name. "Perhaps he's someone she knows from the hospital or school."

"Perhaps," Leah agreed.

She knew this was not the case, but Owen understood there was no reason to upset Isla's mother further. Owen inquired, "Mrs. Morris, did Isla mention any trips she intended to take or issues she needed to resolve?"

Mrs. Morris searched Owen's face for a long moment, her own clouding with increased worry. "Are you suggesting my daughter is missing or is in some sort of trouble?"

He considered how to answer for a moment. Leah's eyes had widened with uncertainty. She didn't want to upset her friend's mother, which was understandable. But this woman—this mother—was not naive. She knew something was not as it should be.

"There was an incident late Saturday night at the restaurant where Leah was to meet Raymond Douglas for the date Isla had arranged. No one has seen Raymond or Isla since—at least, no one we've found."

"Oh no." Mrs. Morris pressed a hand to her chest. "Should we call the police?"

"The police are already involved with the Douglas case," Owen explained. "We're only just learning that Isla hasn't been returning calls either." He leaned forward, braced his elbows on his spread knees. "So you can see how it's very important that you let Leah know if you hear from Isla or if you have any idea where she might go to get away from the stress of school or work or a boyfriend. The sooner we can confirm her safety and her whereabouts, the better for all concerned."

Mrs. Morris blinked several times, the emotion in her eyes visibly threatening her control. "I will certainly let you know," she said to Leah. "I know Isla adores you, and whatever is going on, she would want you to know."

"I would really appreciate it," Leah told her.

The older woman drew in a big breath. "Some years back, I bought a lake house," she said, this time to Owen. "I haven't been there in a very long time. I actually bought it because the man I was dating at the time loved going to the lake. Ridiculously, I thought we had a future together. Anyway, Isla goes there occasionally." She turned to Leah. "Isla mentioned the two of you going several times. She always enjoyed telling me about your adventures. She said you were too afraid to swim in the lake. That you preferred soaking up the sun on the dock."

Leah's tight smile and vague nod warned there was something off with the story.

"Why don't you give me the address," Owen said, drawing Mrs. Morris's attention to himself. "Leah and I will go out there and see if Isla is perhaps taking a break from the world. She's done that before, I believe."

"She has," the woman agreed. "She went through a little breakdown during her final year of premed. It happens, you know. These high-achieving kids go off to college and overextend themselves on all fronts. The next thing you know, they're breaking down or turning to drugs. I'm just thankful Isla didn't end up involved with the drugs."

"I understand." He gave Mrs. Morris a knowing nod. "We'll find her, see that she's safe."

"I would appreciate it so much," Mrs. Morris said, gratitude in her eyes and her smile. "Remember," she said to Leah, "the spare key is under the fairy."

Mrs. Morris reminded Leah of the address for the Fox Lake home. She went on and on about the amenities and the lovely views. Leah nodded and made agreeable sounds, when it was obvious she had no idea where this retreat was located, much less what it offered.

But they were about to find out.

Leah hugged Isla's mother and promised to keep her apprised. Mrs. Morris promised the same. By the time Owen and Leah were back in the car, she was shaking.

"I have no idea about this lake house." She turned to Owen. "I have never been there with Isla. She has never mentioned that her mother had one. It's true I'm not big on swimming in anything other than pools where I can see the bottom, but I have never been to that lake house. And Isla never told me about any sort of breakdown."

And there it was, the first crack in the beloved, seemingly steadfast friendship. One of the two had not been sharing *everything*.

"Maybe Isla was taking a friend with whom she had a physical relationship to the lake house," Owen suggested. "She may have told her mother it was you to avoid questions." He wasn't buying that story just yet, but if it made Leah feel better in the short term, that was the immediate objective. He started the car and pulled away from the curb.

"That's possible," Leah agreed after pondering the suggestion. "Her mother was always after her about the future and starting a family. She didn't want Isla to wait until it was too late. You know the routine. 'Get married and make me some grandbabies.'" Leah laughed but the sound held no humor; it was more sad than anything. "Isla does not want children. She's all about her career. I'm not sure how she'll ever break it to her mother."

For Leah's sake, he hoped that was her friend's only dreaded secret. Though Owen now suspected it was just the tip of the iceberg.

Chapter Five

Morris Lake House
Fox Lake, 12:50 p.m.

Owen brought the car to a stop in the small area of gravel just off the narrow road provided for parking at the rear of the house. Leah was awed by the view, for sure. The house was perched so close to the shore that it looked as if it might slide off into the water at any second. It was breathtakingly beautiful. Very private, with a wooded area separating it from the nearest neighbor.

Aside from the one Owen had just parked, there was no vehicle there. If Isla was here, someone had dropped her off or she had walked. Leah was confident that was not the case. This place was nearly an hour's drive from the city.

As they climbed out of the vehicle, Leah couldn't ignore the very bad feeling mounting inside her. Something about this situation was very, very wrong.

"I have never been here," she said to the man standing next to her. "I can't imagine why Isla told her mother I came here with her—unless it's…it's like you said and she was covering for who she was really bringing." She shook her head. "But that's so un-Isla-like. She always seems in charge and straightforward." Leah moved her head side to side in dismay. "She's the most independent and put-to-gether person I've ever known. I just can't see her sneaking around. I don't even see a reason for her to have told her mother about coming here, much less making up who came with her."

"I'll look for that key," he said, rather than comment on her assessment.

She got it. He didn't know Isla. What could he say?

While he located the fairy statue and the key hidden beneath it, she took in more of that amazing view. After a moment, she started helping with his search. It took a minute. The shrubs next to the less-than-two-feet-tall statue had grown so that it was very nearly concealed. A good thing, Leah supposed, to prevent anyone from noticing it and looking under it.

On the stoop, Owen knocked several times, but there was no answer. Finally, he inserted the key and unlocked the door. Leah held her breath as they dared to cross the threshold. Inside was bright, even though the lights were off. The abundance of windows across the lake side of the house ensured good lighting. The air was stuffy and a little too warm. The air-conditioning was either off or set high enough that it hadn't kicked on. Leah's nose wrinkled. There was an underlying unpleasant odor. Maybe from being closed up for a while.

As with many homes on the water, the front of the house faced the lake. With that in mind, the entrance door, which was actually at the back of the house next to the small parking area, led into a little mudroom and then the kitchen. The kitchen was the usual cottage-style and wide open to the rest of the central part of the one-story house. Without the interruption of walls, it flowed straight into the living area, where several conversation groupings were scattered around those large front windows. One grouping included a television while the rest came with only the view—which was more than sufficiently inspiring. A bookcase stuffed with books and comfortable seating made the space even more inviting.

"Isla?" It seemed obvious enough that she wasn't in the house, but Leah felt compelled to call out her name.

The house was strangely quiet. And so still—eerily so, like the water beyond all those windows.

Leah turned to the professional in matters such as this one. "Should we search the rest of the house?" She wasn't sure of the protocol in these situations. Her instinct was to tear through the house calling her friend's name.

"We're here," he said. "The owner gave us permission to be here. We might as well see if there are any indications Isla or anyone else has been in the house at some point during the last three or four days."

A perfectly logical analysis. "I'll take the bedrooms."

Leah turned down a short hall to the left. There were four doors: two on her right—the lake side—one at the end and one on the left. The door on the left was a bathroom. Neat and airy, very beachy looking. Typical vintage tile and fixtures. A surprisingly large shower for a house of this age. The inside of the toilet bowl had a dark line of old mold or mineral deposits circling it, suggesting it hadn't been flushed in a while.

The two doors across the hall led to smallish bedrooms furnished with double beds and a single dresser each. The focal point in both rooms was the window looking out over the lake. No indications that anyone had been in either of the two rooms in the past few weeks. Nothing unexpected in the tiny closets. Each of the dressers sported a fine layer of undisturbed dust.

The more Leah looked, the more worried she grew. *Where are you, Isla?*

The door at the end of the short hall would likely lead to the larger bedroom. So far, the trip all this way had been a waste of time. But at least it got her out of the city and away from the horrors of the past few days.

Leah drew her hand back when she would have opened the final door. On some level, she suddenly wished she had worn gloves. She had never been to this house, no matter what Isla had told her mother. Today was her first time here. Now her prints would be all over the place as if Isla had been telling the truth.

She closed her eyes and shook her head. This whole thing was making her paranoid.

Whatever Isla's reason for telling her mother that story, it was not related to the missing Raymond Douglas or anything else untoward.

With renewed determination, Leah grasped the knob and gave it a twist. The door opened. Instantly, an overwhelming, sickening metallic odor hit her in the face. The space was nearly pitch black. A frown tugged at her lips. Why so dark?

She felt along the wall next to the doorframe and flipped the switch. Then her hand went over her nose and mouth to ward off the stench. Directly in front of her was the bed, larger than the others. But unlike the others, the covers were tousled. There were handcuffs on the headboard and footboard. Also unlike the others, the windows were covered, blocking that fabulous view of the lake.

"What the…?" She stepped fully into the room, surveyed more closely the windows that extended half the width of the room and then stretched around the corner and ran down half the length of the other side of the room as well. The interior shutters were all closed.

She shivered. But it was the smell that unsettled her the most. What was that unbearable odor?

A step, then another took her beyond the bed that stood in the center of the room. On the other side was a large circle of something rusty and thick-looking.

Blood.

Leah's first thought was to scream, but the sound wouldn't emerge from her throat.

She backed out of the room and turned, bumping square into Owen.

"Nothing anywhere in the main living area or in the laundry room," he told her. "That smell—" He took in her expression, then frowned. "What's wrong?"

"The bedroom," she said, her voice scarcely a whisper. Then she hitched her thumb toward the room behind her. "There's blood. A lot of blood."

"Stay here." He ushered her aside and disappeared through the door Leah had left standing open.

She pressed her hands to her face and struggled to hold back tears. That couldn't be Isla's blood. No. Her friend could not be hurt…or dead. Images of Raymond being dragged across that kitchen floor…blood trickling down the side of his head…flashed erratically in her head.

What if the blood belonged to Raymond? What if he had been brought here from the restaurant? But why here? Did he and Isla know each other that well? Why hadn't she told Leah? It made no sense.

Was he the one who would come here with Isla? That would explain the visits she'd claimed to her mother were with Leah.

But why? It just didn't feel reasonable.

If Isla were involved with Raymond, why on earth would she try to set Leah up with him? The idea was ridiculous.

Stop, just stop. Whatever had happened…it wasn't good.

Had someone been held against their will and then died here? Or were the handcuffs part of a sex game? The blood might have been from a situation that got out of control… Was that why Isla was not returning calls? Was she in hiding? Injured?

Oh God.

Just calm down.

There was no body. There was only blood. This didn't mean anyone was dead.

The sound of Owen's voice snapped her out of the troubling thoughts. She heard him say the detective's name. He was calling the police.

This was bad.

She steadied herself. Of course he was calling the police. Someone had been gravely injured in this house. Someone…not Isla. *Please not Isla.*

Even if it was an accident, something had happened here. The police had to be called.

When Owen finished his call, he came out into the hall. "Detective Lambert is sending a forensic team to investigate. We're to wait outside until he arrives. If the team gets here first, they will come inside and start processing the scene."

The scene. This was a crime scene.

Just like the restaurant had been a crime scene, only no one had believed her. Like her and Isla's apartment. Dear God, what was happening?

She cleared her throat, braced herself for the answer to

the question she was about to ask. "Is that enough blood to suggest whoever lost it died from his or her injury?"

"It's a lot of blood, Leah." He spoke softly, kindly, as if he knew the answer already and wanted to keep her calm. "Let's just wait to see what the forensic team has to say before we jump to any conclusions."

Her stomach lurched. "I need to…to go outside."

She hurried through the house until she was out the back door. Her stomach churned with the need to evacuate its contents. *Deep breath.* Two, three more deep breaths later, and the nausea settled down.

For a while she paced. There were so many things she wanted to ask, but who would have the answers? Not her top-notch private investigator, not Isla's mother and certainly not Detective Lambert. How could they? No one was here. Neither Isla nor Raymond were at the places they lived or worked. Isla's mother had not heard from her.

This was…unbelievable. Beyond bizarre.

Owen sat down on the bench that stood next to the back door. Above his head was a sign that said *Welcome. To what?* Leah mused. *Hell?* She collapsed next to him.

"Isla would have called already if she was okay." Her gaze collided with his. "She's not, and I'm terrified that the blood in there confirms it."

"I want you to think carefully, Leah," Owen said with infinite calmness and a sense of reassurance she wanted desperately to latch on to. "When was the last time you were in contact with Isla?"

Leah closed her eyes and ordered her mind to stop twisting with scary thoughts. "We were both home most of the day Saturday. We were just relaxing and reading. Later that evening—about seven, I think—she left for work. I dressed for the date that will go down in infamy as the world's absolute worst blind date."

He smiled sadly. "You haven't heard from her since around seven on Saturday evening."

Leah nodded. Three days, basically. There was no denying it now. Even without the blood, Isla would never be out of contact for that length of time. Especially with her mother. Isla often said that she was all her mother had since her brother never seemed to have time for either of them.

She and Isla were both the single support systems for their mothers. Not that Isla's mother wasn't able to take care of herself like Leah's mother, but when she needed something, Isla was her go-to person. Just as Leah had been for her mother since her father died.

That familiar old pain arced through her, amplified by the dread knotting in her gut. Who would want to hurt Isla?

Why? She was such a good person.

"When Detective Lambert arrives," Owen said, interrupting her troubling thoughts, "he'll have a lot of questions. I want you to take your time and think carefully before you answer. If during his questioning I interrupt whatever you're about to say, stop immediately and say nothing more. All right?"

She nodded but didn't really comprehend why it was necessary to be so careful. "I don't understand. Is there some reason I should be worried about what he might think of what I say?"

Of course there was. Leah didn't want to believe it, but this was bad, and somehow she was connected to it.

"Sometimes our words can be misconstrued or taken out of context—especially when we're emotional," Owen explained. "It's obvious to me that someone is setting you up. We just need to proceed with caution until Lambert understands that as well."

The bottom dropped out of her stomach right after the words *someone is setting you up*. Who would do that? She had friends. But only one close friend, and that was Isla. There was no way Isla would be setting her up. Besides, Leah had no real money or other marketable assets that anyone might want. She had a job, but she barely made enough to keep her head above water. She owned nothing except a few odd pieces of furniture, and she had no social life. She'd just appropriated the better part of her savings to figure out this insane mess.

"Why?" She searched his eyes in hopes of finding the answer there. "Why would anyone pick me for this, whatever it is?"

"Two reasons, as far as I can see," he said. "You have a record—however distant—of being involved with unsavory types."

Leah groaned. "I'm a model human for most of my life, and no one notices. I screw up once and get involved with a thug, and I'm a suspected criminal forevermore."

Owen shrugged. "Look at it like getting hacked on social media. It's the people who would never dream of or even know how to hack an account who get hacked. It's the same people who want to believe the best in everyone they meet. Those who trust maybe more than they should. Sometimes we just don't see what's right in front of us."

"You believe this comes down to Isla." He didn't have to say it outright. She got it. At this point, even she was admittedly having difficulty denying the possibility. But why would her friend do all this? What did she have to gain?

"It's the most logical possibility, given what we know at this time," he confirmed. "But remember, we're going on only a small amount of knowledge. There is still a lot we haven't figured out. Many things can happen in seventy-two hours. We are only aware of a few of those events. This entire situation could change direction at any moment."

He didn't say change for the worse, but she understood that was what he meant.

This could get exponentially worse.

JUST OVER AN hour later, a dark sedan arrived at the lake house. Not the black car that had been following her; Leah hadn't seen it since arriving at the safe house. Owen had made sure the driver was unable to follow. The man had evasive driving tactics down to a science.

While she watched, Detective Lambert emerged from the sedan. Before he'd closed the door, a white van sporting the Chicago PD logo arrived, and an official police cruiser as well. Leah wondered if this location was still in Lambert's jurisdiction. Maybe it didn't matter, since the situation was related to his ongoing case. Or so it would seem.

"Ms. Gerard," he said as he approached her, "this isn't an address I had associated with you."

"This lake house belongs to Isla's family."

"You've been here before," Lambert suggested. A reasonable assumption.

Before Leah could answer, Owen explained, "We visited Mrs. Morris this morning to see if she has heard from her daughter. She has not. She suggested we look here. She gave us the location of the house and the key to go inside. As soon as we discovered the blood, we called you and came outside."

"Had you been here before?" Lambert asked Leah again.

"No." She shook her head. "Mrs. Morris seems to think I have. She said Isla told her on several occasions that she was coming to the lake house with me, but that isn't true. I've never been here before today."

"We suspect," Owen said, "that Isla was giving her mother Leah's name to conceal the identity of the person she was actually bringing here."

"Any motive you're aware of that would prompt her to take such a step?"

"We have found no motive as of yet," Owen admitted.

"How long will it take," Leah asked, "to figure out whose blood that is?" Her heart squeezed. Someone would have to talk to Mrs. Morris. She needed to be aware of what was happening. What a nightmare this would be for her until she knew what had actually happened.

"It's difficult to say," Lambert conceded. "We'll need to find out her blood type, as well as that of Raymond Douglas, and then we'll do DNA testing using Isla's mother and, I suppose, one of Douglas's children, assuming all involved will cooperate. If not, we have other ways. Hair from a brush or comb they used. A toothbrush."

The worry would eat Leah alive before then. "Can your forensic people determine how long the blood has been in that room?"

She had seen both Isla and Raymond on Saturday evening.

"That, we can do, and fairly quickly." Lambert hitched his head toward the house. "I should get inside and see what we have." He hesitated. "If you would wait here, I'm sure I will have more questions."

Oh yeah. Leah was confident he would have plenty more questions. Questions she could not answer.

As she and Owen sat in the quiet of the outdoors for a few moments, she thought about what she had seen in that room besides the blood. Handcuffs. Someone had presumably kept Isla or Raymond against their will. Or it was a part of some sex game gone wrong.

Either possibility made her feel sick. Worse, it was possible he or she had been tortured—she thought of the blood—and killed.

Leah wished there was a way to protect Isla's mother from all this until they knew more. She would be devastated. And then, if the blood turned out to be Raymond's...

Then what? Isla was still missing. Something had happened to her, whether it was in this house or elsewhere. She was missing. The police needed to be looking for her. Yet somehow, this all felt as if it were moving in slow motion. Yes, the detective was here, but nothing seemed to be getting done. No answers appeared to have been found.

The weight of it all settled on Leah's shoulders, and she desperately wished she could shake it off. But that was impossible.

Owen leaned forward, braced his forearms on his knees and turned his face to hers. "Isla set you up on a blind date with Raymond Douglas. When Douglas disappeared, Isla disappeared. If one of the two set this up, Leah—and I can't see any way around that possibility—they set you up to take the fall for whatever the finale is to be. But the real questions are, which one and for what reason?"

"I can give you a reason—five million of them, as a matter of fact."

Leah and Owen turned to the detective who had just walked out the back door.

"What?" Leah demanded.

Owen put his hand on her arm and said to the detective, "We're listening."

"The ex-wife, Louise, is the one who first told me about the insurance policy. When I spoke with the insurance company, I learned there was not one but two beneficiaries—who would receive five million each."

Leah remembered him saying there was an insurance policy, but he'd only mentioned the ex-wife.

"The sole beneficiary was Louise until just a few months ago. Douglas changed his policy at that time. Half of the proceeds go to his ex-wife, and the other half goes to you, Leah."

"What?" She shook her head. "No." That was absurd. She shook her head again. "Why would he leave me anything? We hardly know each other. We'd never even met before two weeks ago."

"That, Ms. Gerard, is the five-million-dollar question," Lambert said.

No, no, no. This simply could not be right. It was completely ridiculous. Outrageous.

This situation grew more inexplicable by the day. It was as if, once the momentum started, there was no stopping it. The absurdities just kept piling up.

Leah turned to Owen. "I do not know Raymond Douglas. Not like that. There is no way he would want to leave me anything. This is all wrong."

But how would she make anyone believe her?

Chapter Six

Owen spotted the black sedan in his rearview mirror less than a minute after they drove away from the lake house. He glanced at his passenger. She stared out her window, arms crossed protectively over her chest.

This day had been particularly tough for her. She had every reason to fear that her friend was gravely injured or perhaps dead. The situation with the missing date, Raymond Douglas, had grown exponentially more complicated with the insurance-beneficiary revelation. At this point, all Leah had was her word that she did not know Douglas other than as a potential blind date. Isla was not here to confirm, and the other friend, Maya Ortiz, who had been with Leah and Isla the night Leah briefly met Douglas, was no help.

According to Lambert, Ortiz had no idea if Leah and Douglas had dated once or a dozen times since that accidental encounter. She claimed to have been preoccupied that night with watching an ex-boyfriend she had spotted in the crowd at the club. If there were other newly discovered details, Lambert wasn't sharing. Owen was surprised the detective had revealed as much as he had.

As if all the questions and the troubling lack of any ability to confirm her statements wasn't bad enough, Leah was faced with yet another blow: Lambert asked for permission to search the apartment she and Isla shared. Owen had recommended she agree to the search. With the discovery at the lake house, obtaining a search warrant for the apartment was a mere formality—no judge would deny the request. Leah's cooperation was necessary to prevent any additional suspicion being cast her way. She had nothing to hide, and Lambert needed to see that.

The problem was, her innocence didn't mean someone hadn't planted something to make her look guilty, which was why the two of them were going straight to the apartment right now to look around. Bolling, the building manager, had confirmed that the police had released the apartment and the repairs had been started. Owen and Leah could go into the apartment, but there was still work to be done before she could move back in. Bolling would provide them access.

Owen checked the rearview mirror once more. The sedan was still behind them.

He might as well wait until they were in the city to bother with losing him. If he could somehow manage to get the license plate number, that might prove useful in identifying the driver.

"He's following us again," Leah said, sitting up straighter. She'd obviously spotted the tail in her side mirror.

"He is," Owen confirmed. "Unless he makes an aggressive move, we'll just pretend we don't notice until we're in the city. Losing him will be simpler, and arriving at our destination before he finds us again will be far more likely."

"Okay." She relaxed into her seat, but her attention remained on the mirror.

Rather than allow her to fixate on that troubling detail, Owen opted for making conversation. "Tell me about when you met Isla."

Leah glanced at him. Her brown eyes reflected the increasing worry haunting her. She had beautiful eyes—deep brown, and such a generous oval shape. She was a very attractive woman. Her quiet nature made him curious, knowing her history as he did. Those painful years after the Chris Painter situation had changed her, it seemed. He wondered if she would ever allow her adventurous spirit to slip past all those tight restraints put into place in an attempt at self-preservation. It was a shame that a single incident stole so much of what made her who she was. Maturity and wisdom were always valuable, but one's true spirit should always have a place inside the normal course of development.

"She had just finished her first year of medical school, and I was deep into my undergrad work." She stared forward. "I felt so far behind before I even started. Most people start college right after high school. Here I was, more than four years later." She sighed. "Once I arrived in Chicago, the first order of business was to find a place to live, and truthfully, I was drowning in uncertainty. The only good thing was that my student loan had come through, so I was okay with the education costs. I had decided I might just survive. The first couple of years, I managed by the skin of my teeth and the bit of extra allowance in my student loans. Eventually, I landed the position at the library, and I was in heaven. Isla and one of her friends were there one night for a workshop, and that was the beginning."

"You said Isla was already in the apartment you share now."

"Yes, she'd been there awhile. Later, I learned she hadn't

really needed a roommate, but she wanted to help me and decided to make the offer." She fell silent a moment. "Not long after I moved in, Maya—Isla's friend, and mine, too, eventually—made some remark about Isla always taking on projects. I was offended at first, but in time we worked it out."

"This Maya," he glanced at Leah, "never apologized or elaborated?"

"No." She laughed dryly. "Maya does not apologize for anything. She has a rich daddy and an even richer new boyfriend. She has her master's in journalism. She works for one of the major networks now. She is utterly unrepentant. But she is Isla's friend, so I have to like her."

"You and Isla became friends quickly." From all Leah had said so far, their relationship evolved swiftly and deeply.

"Over the fall," Leah explained. "By Christmas, I was moving in, and we were like sisters."

"What about Isla's dating habits? Does she date frequently? Different people, or was there anyone who lasted longer than the others? Maybe someone who left her upset?"

"Unlike me," Leah said, "Isla is very social. That said, she's as happy with a group of girlfriends as she is with a guy. In the time I've known her, she has not dated anyone seriously or for any length of time. There were a few who got past the third date but none who lasted more than a month or so. She is thoroughly focused on the future. I mean, totally dedicated to a singular goal. She has this plan and is determined that nothing will stop her or get in the way. I've tried really hard to do the same. She's helped me a lot with moving forward and not looking back."

"The man, Chris Painter ..." Owen braked for a traffic light and spent a moment studying her. "Were you in love with him?"

Though she had been young, her heart could still be broken. Sometimes an old wound like that one was difficult to heal.

She leaned against the headrest. "I was as in love with him as a naive eighteen-year-old, incredibly overprotected girl could be. I was devastated when he just vanished. I searched for him. Confronted his friends and a few of his enemies. Had the bejesus scared out of me more than once and ended up in the ER with a black eye, busted lip and fractured rib." She met his gaze. "There are some bears one shouldn't poke."

He could see the fearless girl-woman storming into the presence of dangerous thugs and demanding answers. She was lucky she hadn't gotten herself killed.

"At that point I stopped trying to force the truth out of the people he'd surrounded himself with. I went home with my tail between my legs and told myself falling for a guy like Chris would never happen again. And it hasn't. But it took time and distance to put it behind me. I changed myself and my life over and over until I realized that it wasn't my physical being that needed to change—it was my mental self. My attitude and personal boundaries. I'm still a work in progress."

"I think you're doing great." He checked the rearview mirror once more. Their tail kept his distance but remained vigilant.

"Well…" She drew in a big breath and released it slowly. "If I don't end up charged with murder, maybe I'll be able to keep moving forward." She fell silent for a time. "But I have to tell you, Owen, I'm worried. The trouble just keeps stacking up, and every time something new is discovered, it points to me."

"That is the way a good setup works," he told her with a sidelong look to punctuate it. "Which is why I believe whatever we're wading into was well planned, perhaps for a considerable period of time."

"But how do I prove my innocence when I have no *proof*? No one besides Isla and Raymond know when I first met him. No one but those two know Saturday night was our first and only date—not that it was an actual date. And until Mrs. Morris told me that Isla claimed I went to the lake house with her occasionally, I was certain she was as much a victim as me—maybe more so since she's missing. But now I don't know. Nothing we learn makes sense. Nothing Lambert throws our way makes sense—like that insurance policy."

"We will find the right answers," he promised. "I'm very good at my work, Leah. You can count on that."

She turned toward him fully, her expression steeped in concern. "I am counting on that. I mean, *really* counting on it."

Gerard/Morris Apartment
Chestnut Street, 5:15 p.m.

"KEEP YOUR ATTENTION FORWARD," Owen said when he shut off the engine. "Don't look at him. Just ignore him completely. We'll go inside and have a look around. Then when we head for the safe house, we'll lose him."

Leah nodded. When they'd reached Chicago proper, Owen decided to let the guy in the sedan follow them to the apartment. It wasn't like he didn't already know where it was. Brilliantly, Owen had called a fellow Colby investigator and asked him to do a drive-by and snag the guy's license plate number. Leah was impressed with the idea. The sooner they found out who the guy was, the better. She assumed he was a hired spy or maybe even an assassin working for the bad guys. The problem was, who were the bad guys? And why was Leah their target? Or at least one of their targets, it seemed.

Was the bad guy the person who'd dragged Raymond out of the kitchen, dead or unconscious? Or the best friend she had come to think of as a sister?

The mere thought had more of those knots twisting in Leah's belly.

She and Owen opened their doors and exited the car. Leah fixated on the sweltering heat and the drooping flowers in the pots on the steps that led to the entrance of her building. This really had been a very hot summer. Sadly, it just wasn't getting any better. All sorts of little fires were cropping up around her as her life fell apart one piece at a time.

She entered the code and Owen opened the main entrance door. They walked together to the stairs and climbed up to the second floor. Thinking back on their conversation in the car, she was surprised at how easy talking to him was. Usually, she had a difficult time discussing personal relationships or details with others—especially strangers. And he was a stranger. No matter that he was so comfortable to be around…to talk to. Honestly, he didn't feel like a stranger at all. He somehow made sharing comfortable. Then again, she supposed it was part of his job to know how to mine cooperation from a subject. But the way their conversations developed, they never felt anything but completely natural and well-intentioned.

Bolling waited outside the apartment. The repair work

was moving along. A door had been framed in, but the drywall around it had not been finished, and there was still the painting and necessary trim work. She was actually surprised it had happened so quickly.

The manager unlocked the door and passed the key to Leah. "This is the key you'll need when the repairs are completed. Shouldn't take more than another day."

That really was fast. "Thank you."

Bolling nodded and headed back downstairs.

Walking into her apartment now, knowing all that she knew, felt strange. It no longer felt like home. And certainly no longer felt safe.

Where was Isla? Had she been injured? What in the world had happened to Raymond, and what did any of it have to do with Leah?

The most damning and startling piece of this puzzle was the fact that she had been named a beneficiary on his life insurance policy. The idea was ludicrous, irrational. Totally out of left field.

How could she be a beneficiary of his when she hardly knew the man?

"Let's start in this main room," Owen suggested. "We touch everything. No matter how small or seemingly insignificant. Whatever is here, we want to see it and feel it, as well as recognize its reason for being in this space. A piece of the puzzle could be hiding in plain sight…anywhere in this apartment."

He was right. *Deep breath.* "Okay."

They started at the door. Checked every piece of furniture. Inside and under the drawers. Behind doors on the lower portion of the one large bookcase and inside every single book that lined its open shelves. Every item discovered was picked up and examined. Leah found a couple of appointment cards she'd forgotten about entirely. One was from the dentist's office for her annual cleaning. The other was for a meeting with her mother's doctor.

When they had handled every item in the main living area, they moved on to the bedrooms. There were only two, and each had its own bath.

"I'll take your room," Owen said. "You take Isla's. It's important to determine if anything looks out of place. I wouldn't know, because I've never met Isla or been in her room. As for your room, I'm sure you would have noticed anything out of place already. I'll just be a fresh second look."

Made sense, even though Leah was embarrassed at the idea of him going through her things. "Sounds good." He was right about her needing to be the one who went through Isla's things.

In Isla's private space, Leah first got down onto all fours and looked under the bed, the night table and the dresser. All stood on legs that left about fifteen inches of space beneath them. Prime territory for storage, particularly under the bed. Nothing but a few dust bunnies. Isla wasn't one to hoard, even a little bit. Then Leah moved on to the window. She checked the drapes and the chair and the table that sat in front of it. Isla's desk was on that same wall. Leah surveyed the cluttered desktop and awakened her friend's computer in hopes of perusing her email and having a quick look at her search history.

The computer required a password.

Leah wasn't even going to attempt figuring it out. Instead, she surveyed the notepad and two sticky notes posted on the sleek wood surface. One was a list of personal items she needed. The other sticky note reminded Isla to talk to her boss about a raise.

"You go, Isla," Leah murmured.

Leah moved on, checking the drawers in Isla's dresser. Nothing unexpected or seemingly out of place so far.

Next, she checked the closet. Lots and lots of clothes. Isla really was a clotheshorse, but she shopped smartly, never paying full price for anything, she often bragged.

Even after a thorough second look of the room, Leah found nothing that didn't belong.

She walked out of the room just as Owen exited hers.

"Anything?" she asked. "I found nothing in Isla's room."

"Is this yours?" He opened his hand, revealing a black cell phone. Smaller than the one she carried.

"No." She pulled her phone from her pants pockets. "This is my phone."

"This one," he said, "was tucked into your lingerie drawer."

The idea that he had touched her *lingerie*, as he'd put it, made her heart thump hard against her sternum. She hadn't even considered he would have to filter through her most intimate apparel. Ridiculous. Of course, searching each drawer was necessary.

She shook her head, not daring to touch the phone. If she didn't touch it, her prints wouldn't be on it. "I've never seen it before."

"The battery is dead. We should charge it up and see what we find."

"I agree." She folded her arms over her chest and suppressed a shiver. The idea of what else they might find was terrifying.

Owen had been so smart and definitely one step ahead to suggest they come here and have a look. If not, Lambert would have found that phone and assumed it was hers. How had it gotten into her room? Given all that had happened, she could just imagine what kind of incriminating "evidence" was on it.

Owen slid the phone into his back pocket. "If you need to get anything else while we're here, you should pack it up—and have a look around just in case. Then we'll get going."

She nodded and went into her room. Leah tried to center on what she might need and not think about what he'd found, but it wasn't easy. She grabbed a dressier shirt in case she needed something more than the T-shirts she had taken to the safe house. Then she remembered she had forgotten lotion, so she picked that up too. And a nightshirt; she'd completely forgotten to take anything for sleeping. With a final quick look around to ensure nothing was missing or there that shouldn't be, she decided she was done. Her overnight bag was already at the safe house, so she opted to just carry the three items.

She went to the living room, where Owen waited.

"Got everything you need?"

"I think so."

He grinned. "Now to ghost our nosy friend."

That made her smile. The guy in the black car wouldn't be happy, she imagined.

But when Owen opened the door for her, her smile died.

Detective Lambert and his forensic team were standing in the corridor.

"What a surprise," the detective said. "Did you find whatever you were looking for?"

Leah held her breath…didn't dare speak.

"Just dropped by for a few items she needed," Owen said with a gesture toward the items she clutched.

Good grief. She'd completely forgotten she was holding anything. The craziness was getting to her, making her paranoid.

"I needed a few more things," she said, her voice a little high, a little shaky.

Lambert nodded. "Well, if you're quite finished, we'll get started on our search."

"Of course." Leah slipped past him, her heart pounding way too fast.

What if he spotted the bulge of that cell phone in Owen's pocket? What if he decided it was necessary to pat them down like the police often did to suspects in the movies? The phone would only make her look guiltier.

Worry twisted like razors inside her.

Owen joined her in the corridor, and they walked casually toward the stairwell. He set the pace. Slow and steady. She forced her respiration to slow and followed his example. No one hurried after them, demanding to check their pockets. But she didn't relax until they were out of the building and in his car.

Once they were driving away, he said, "I have to make a quick stop before I lose this guy."

She frowned. "Where?"

"Anywhere." He shot her a grin. "Just long enough to make sure our shadow didn't put a tracking device on the car."

She hadn't even considered the person watching her— following them—might do something so obviously smart in a situation like this. Good thing she had this man on her side.

Her gaze lingered on Owen's profile. *A really good thing.*

Chapter Seven

There had been no tracking device on the car.

Losing their tail had been fairly easy, or maybe he just hadn't tried so hard to keep up with them. Either way, Leah had watched Owen expertly outmaneuver him. They made it back to the safe house without the trouble following them.

Now, seated on a stool at the kitchen island, Leah watched as Owen plugged up the phone he had found in her underwear drawer. Heat climbed up her throat and rested on her cheeks each time she thought of him touching her underthings. Thankfully, she had packed most of her favorites when preparing to come here, leaving the less-worn pairs in the drawer. Who wanted such a handsome guy—any guy, really—discovering she preferred comfortable panties?

She shook herself mentally. What was she thinking? Someone had, in some way, disappeared at least two people she knew, and that same person seemed to want to pin the blame on her. This was not the time to be wondering what this man thought of her underwear.

"Here we go."

The screen of the phone lit up.

Leah held her breath. Maybe now they would find some answers or at least a clue of some sort as to what the heck was going on. Her pulse gained an extra beat every second or so as she watched him scroll, pausing now and then perhaps to read. The furrowing of his brow and the stony set of his jaw made her stomach sink.

Finally, he stopped and looked up at her. "I need you to scan the call list and see if you recognize any of the numbers. Then go to the text messages and read those to see if any of it is familiar to you or if you recognize the way the messages are worded. We all have our favorite buzzwords and sentence structures."

Cold leeched from her limbs. "Okay." She held out her hand, and he placed the seemingly harmless device on her palm.

Leah swallowed around the lump swelling in her throat and concentrated on the small screen. The one currently displayed was the log of recent calls. There were no names, just phone numbers and the word *Him*. The call log ended on Saturday night and only went back five days. From late on Monday of last week until this past Saturday—the night Raymond disappeared. Isla, too, apparently.

There were nine calls, one each day until Saturday, and then there were four. All to or from the same number.

Raymond's.

Fear trickled through her chest. Ordinarily, she wouldn't have remembered a phone number so easily, except his last four digits were 1001. It had to be his. But just in case she was wrong, she reached for her cell phone and checked the call log for the one time she had spoken to him. There it was: 312-555-1001.

"The person using this phone was talking to Raymond." She looked up at Owen. "It wasn't me. I swear."

He nodded once. "Read the text messages."

The urge to throw the phone across the room and run was nearly overwhelming. She did not want to read those messages. It didn't matter that they had absolutely not come from her or been sent to her. This was not right.

Deep breath. She forced her fingers to work, tapping and swiping as needed until the Messages app opened. There was only one listing. She tapped on *Him*. The next screen opened to a long thread of message exchanges.

Are you ready for our big night???

That one was from whoever *Him* was.

Can't wait. Are you sure you're ready?

This message was sent via the phone found in her underwear drawer…the one she held in her hand at this very moment.

Leah forced herself to keep reading, though the rock in her gut seemed to be trying to push upward into her throat.

Him: Oh yeah. We have everything we need.

Underwear-Drawer Phone User: How can I wait as long as this might take?

Him: Patience. The five mil will be ours.

The ability to breathe grew harder and harder.

Underwear-Drawer Phone User: Sand, sun and water...
forever.

Him: Just the two of us...

There were several more but nothing relevant, just the
mushy back-and-forth of two lovers planning some sort
of getaway.

She stared up at the man standing on the other side of
the island. His blue eyes watched her intently. He would
be analyzing her reaction...her every word. Deciding if he
should continue trusting her.

Leah swallowed. "I didn't send these messages. I have
never seen this phone before. This is not me." She shook
her head, the movement stilted. "Someone else did this."

Owen took the phone from her and set it aside. "Is there
anyone else who might have a key to your apartment? Besides you and Isla?"

Leah struggled to steady her respiration. She needed to
think rationally, which was difficult with her heart racing
and her thoughts in a tailspin. Who would do this? "No
one that I'm aware of. Isla said I was her first roommate."

"But she could have given a key to a boyfriend or long-
term lover," he suggested.

"I guess so, but she never mentioned having given a key
to anyone." Then again, why would she? Leah felt sick at
where this was pointing. "I didn't know Raymond Douglas before two weeks ago, and I had no idea he planned to
ask me on a date until one week ago." She searched Ow-
en's eyes. "How am I ever going to prove I'm telling the
truth?" She stared at the phone lying on the counter. "Everything keeps coming back to me."

"This phone—" he gestured to the one he'd found in her

drawer "—is commonly called a burner phone. I'm sure you've heard the term."

She nodded. "On television, but I've never known anyone who used one in real life." She frowned. "That might not be true. Chris…" She took a moment to ride out the uneasiness she always felt at saying his name out loud. "He and his thug buddies may have used them. I can't be sure, but it would make sense."

"That's a good guess," Owen agreed. "Whoever bought this one wanted to make it seem as if you were communicating with Raymond in a way that couldn't be traced. And it couldn't…not to you, except for the fact that the phone was hidden in your bedroom to do exactly that. Lead those investigating the case to you."

It couldn't be Isla. It just couldn't be.

"In my opinion," he went on, "the most telling aspect of what we have here is the fact that Raymond didn't use one. This suggests that whoever masterminded this plot wanted it known that the user of this burner phone—you, presumably—was interacting with Raymond. That step was deliberate."

Fighting a new bout of vertigo, Leah considered this for a moment. Owen was right. If the whole thing that went down on Saturday night was supposed to be some secret setup, all parties involved would have remained anonymous by using burner phones…*except* the one whom they wanted to get caught.

Bile stirred in her belly.

She struggled to articulate the fear pressing against her chest. "Are you suggesting that the person pretending to be me was actually setting Raymond up to be murdered, or are you saying they both wanted the police to believe he was being set up to be murdered?"

Owen's brow lined in thought. "This is where the situation could go either way. We have no definitive proof one way or the other."

"What about the life insurance policy?" Leah asked.

"Obviously, that detail would make it appear as though you were plotting to kill him, since you stood to gain five mil. This phone suggests the same. Except, if that is the goal, the rest of the plan seems counterintuitive."

"How so?" Leah's head was spinning. None of this made sense to her. It only proved to her that someone had set her up to take the fall for murder.

"If the goal was to get the five million," he explained, "you need a body or the patience to wait a very long time until there is irrefutable proof that the missing person is in fact dead—at least, for all intents and purposes. Why set up a scam like this if the payoff is going to be that far down the road? Or denied. There has to be an official determination that Raymond Douglas is dead before there is an insurance payoff to anyone."

"Are you saying the insurance policy is a ruse? Just something else to throw the police off…what?"

"We can't be sure at this point. But personally…" He gave her a critical look. "If I were Raymond Douglas, I would be worried. With what we have right now, I see no way anyone stands to win at this game without a body—*his* body."

Leah didn't want to believe what she was about to say, but at this juncture, what else could she believe? "The most likely scenario—for now, anyway—is that Isla and Raymond planned all this. She had access to my room, to my schedule…to my whole life." It hurt to say the words out loud. "And she knew Raymond. She downplayed her knowledge of him for my benefit. As much as I don't want to believe that's possible, I can't see any other scenario where this comes together logically."

"It's a difficult reality to accept," he agreed. "But, as you say, at this time it's the most logical theory."

"How could Isla and I have been friends all this time— shared all that we have shared—and none of it matter when she came up with this plan?" Leah wondered if Isla had ever really cared about her. Had her taking on a room-mate been a setup from the beginning? Surely she hadn't planned this three years ago.

"Bad people do things sometimes that shock us." Owen eased down onto a stool. "I do believe, unfortunately, that we should start digging even deeper into Isla's background, with the idea that she is—without doubt—involved, if not spearheading this unfortunate series of events."

"But," Leah countered, "based on the money aspect, for this to work, Raymond has to turn up dead."

Owen nodded. "It's the only way the insurance policy pays out without a long legal battle."

"But those messages and those calls were to his number." Leah didn't get this part at all. "Why would he go along with her plan if the only way for it to work out in an advantageous way was if he was dead? I got the impression he's a very intelligent man. I can't see him being this obtuse."

"She may have used his phone and sent the messages, then deleted them on his end. Accepted the calls and then deleted those. He wouldn't know. Which would mean they had to spend some time together over the time frame the calls were made and the messages sent."

"The police will be able to find out about the calls and text messages without his phone and without that one." She nodded to the burner.

"They will. I'm sure Lambert has already gotten a warrant and requested the records for his phone. Probably for yours and Isla's as well. Those records will show all calls, when and where they were made, and the duration. As for text messages, in some cases the content of recent text messages can be obtained. There's every reason to believe they will have all we saw on the burner available via Douglas's phone records. The burner phone may not have your name or any other attached to it, but its location at the time of a call or text will be available. If a call or text was sent from the vicinity of your apartment, for example, that information will be provided in the call record."

Leah understood. "In that case, in order to point to me, the calls and messages would have needed to originate from our apartment or the library where I work."

He nodded. "Or wherever you were at the time. If the mastermind behind this setup is as good as I suspect she or he is, then every aspect of the pieces of the puzzle will have been carefully thought out."

The ability to breathe escaped Leah temporarily. She would be a fool not to realize that would be the case. So far the whole sham had been very carefully orchestrated. There was no reason to believe this part would be any different.

"What can we do?" Tears burned in her eyes, even though she was suddenly fighting mad.

"How good is your relationship with your boss?"

The question surprised her. "At the library?" He nodded, and she shrugged. "Fine, I guess. I mean, she probably isn't really happy with me right now, since I haven't been at work in several days. But I called and explained the situation."

Owen picked up the burner phone and shut it off. "We have a small window of time, I suspect, before the call records for Douglas's phone make their way to Lambert. If he links that burner phone to you, I have a feeling he's going to want to start moving toward making an arrest. You have no family in the city, no permanent ties like a house or a business, which makes you a flight risk."

Leah's breath caught. "How do we prevent that from happening?"

"We prove that you weren't the only person who may have sent those calls and those text messages."

"Makes sense, but how do we do that?"

"If the library has security cameras, we talk to your boss. See if we can find Isla in the library or nearby, outside the library during the times the calls or text messages were made. If the time frames match up, then we can show doubt at the idea that only you could have sent them."

Anticipation fired in Leah's veins. "There are cameras. Two in the library and at least two outside."

"Tomorrow morning," he said, "we go to the library and see what we can find. For now, we put the phone up and don't think about it."

That would be about as easy as having teeth pulled without a numbing agent. "I can try," she admitted.

Owen suddenly reached for his own cell and checked the screen. "I need to take this."

Though there had been no ring, evidently he had gotten a call. Probably had his phone set to silent. Leah watched as he walked out into the back courtyard. She imagined it was a call from one of his colleagues at the agency. Could be a girlfriend or wife. She hadn't noticed a wedding band. They hadn't discussed his personal life. Part of her was disappointed at the idea that he might be married or involved with someone. It was ridiculous, but just about every aspect of her life right now was ridiculous. What was one more?

Her mind kept going back to the idea that her friend—

her best friend—could be responsible for all this. Why would Isla do such a thing? Leah had never once sensed that Isla was not honest with her or that she was only pretending to be her friend.

But then, Leah had never been particularly good at spotting duplicity. Look at how deeply she'd gotten involved with Chris before the trouble started. She'd had no idea just how far into the drug world he had been. She had ignored the rumors, too besotted to believe her parents or anyone else.

She had been a fool.

Had she been a fool with Isla too? With Raymond? The possibility that Raymond had misled her was far easier to swallow. They barely knew each other. But Isla…that was immensely difficult to fathom.

Yet the evidence kept pointing in that very direction.

Then again, the evidence regarding Raymond's disappearance led directly to Leah, and it certainly was not true.

Maybe Isla was a victim too.

But how had that phone gotten into Leah's room?

Owen came back into the house. "That was Jamie."

Jamie Colby. Not just a colleague. The head of the agency's granddaughter—someone high up the food chain. Leah's heart nearly stopped. "Is everything okay?" If there was an emergency and Owen had to be replaced on her investigation, she might just break down and cry like a baby.

"It's about the Chris Painter case."

If he had told her it was about Santa Claus, she wouldn't have been more shocked. "Are you serious? What about it?"

"Apparently, he has been found right here in Chicago."

Something like an earthquake shuddered through Leah. "Are you saying they found his body?" If that old case somehow got tangled up with this new one… Oh God, surely that wasn't possible.

"No," Owen said, his expression serious, his gaze searching hers. "He's alive. He claims to have been held prisoner here in Chicago all this time."

"Prisoner?" Leah didn't know what to say. This was surreal. She wasn't sure how many more revelations she could handle.

"He walked into the Fourth District precinct two hours ago. He's at Northwestern Memorial Hospital, being evaluated. What we know so far is that he is dehydrated and malnourished."

This was impossible. Leah couldn't grasp the ramifications... It was unbelievable.

"Walker here."

Leah's attention jerked back to Owen. He'd gotten another call. She tried to breathe, but the air just wasn't making it to her lungs. Chris was alive? He'd been alive all this time? Who had held him prisoner? And how ironic that he would be in Chicago as well. Or that he would be found in the middle of this other mess.

She closed her eyes, tried to slow the spiraling thoughts. The whole situation was outrageous and growing more so every minute.

"Leah."

She forced her eyes open and met Owen's gaze. The worry there almost undid her completely. If this latest news had him worried...she was doomed.

"Detective Lambert has asked that we come to his office in the morning at ten."

She moistened her lips. "Did he say why?"

"They found Douglas's body."

Chapter Eight

Owen had gotten up early for a conference call with Victoria and agency attorney Alfred Mannington. One of the agency's top criminal attorneys, Darren Brocato, had sat in on the call and provided the best advice for Owen going forward. If Lambert chose to move toward an arrest or even suggested as much at this time, Brocato would act as Leah's representative if she accepted the offer. Once the call ended and Owen heard Leah moving about upstairs, he started breakfast.

The toast popped up and Owen added it to the plates he'd prepared. Scrambled eggs, fresh fruit and toast. He was no master chef, but he made a mean scrambled egg. The secret was adding a little milk when whisking. He would let Leah be her own judge. It was doubtful that she would complain, even if she didn't like his efforts. She was too kind. He still found it difficult to conceive that she'd been involved with someone like Chris Painter as a senior in high school. He'd done his research on the guy. Painter and his crew had been serious trouble. Not to mention the thirty-year-old man, now forty, had been way too old to be dating a high schooler. Maybe not by legal standards, but in Owen's opinion.

Just then, Leah walked into the kitchen. "Coffee smells great." She mustered up a smile that didn't reach her eyes. "Good morning."

Assuredly, the effort wasn't one of her real smiles. He'd gotten a glimpse of the real thing a few times. Her whole face came to life with one of her genuine efforts. This one was nervous and for his benefit only. Not to mention her voice was a little over-bright. She was trying but couldn't quite pull off the *I'm okay* mask. She had every right to be nervous. The situation for her grew more complicated each day, as well as admittedly more disturbing.

"Good morning." He gestured to the plates he'd finished preparing. "This is my limited breakfast endeavor." He chuckled. "Hopefully, it's edible. If you like butter or jam on your toast, there's a nice variety available." The staff who maintained the safe houses were particularly good at stocking kitchens when guests were expected.

Her smile widened a bit, the expression prompting a little extra light in her eyes this time. "Looks great. Thank you for going to so much trouble."

They ate for a while without talking. He had spent a good deal of time last night considering how the setup mounting around her appeared to be a bit of an overkill. The end game seemed fairly clear at this point, and still the hits kept coming. This newest element—the resurrection of Chris Painter—really was over-the-top. Last night they hadn't talked a lot about that news or even the more painful reality that Raymond Douglas's body had been discovered. Leah had called it a night quite early. Owen understood she'd needed time alone to think.

She managed a few bites of eggs and half a piece of toast before diving into the questions he'd fully expected this morning. Her gaze fixed on Owen's. "Where did they find him? Raymond, I mean."

"They weren't liberal with the details," he clarified. "But it was near the lake house. In a car registered to him."

She nodded slowly. "No sign of Isla?"

"There was no mention of her." He understood the question she really wanted to ask but dreaded the answer even more than the previous two.

She sipped her coffee, then cleared her throat. "How..." Deep breath. "How did he die?"

This was where things got even stranger and considerably more murky. "He was shot, once, in the chest."

Another slow nod. "I guess that's where all the blood in the lake house came from."

The answer was not as cut and dry as that, and he only knew the few details at his disposal because the agency had friends in the medical examiner's office. Certainly Lambert had not shared the gritty details as of yet. The detective was far too convinced Leah was his best potential suspect.

"There's some question about that, actually," he explained, pushing his plate aside as well. He didn't look forward to relaying the rest to her. She was already hurt at the prospect of how she'd been fooled.

Her gaze searched his. "What do you mean?"

"The amount of blood found in the lake house was enough to suggest he died there," he explained, "but what the medical examiner found when examining the body was that the injury sustained with the gunshot would likely have caused far more internal bleeding versus external. The large amount found— outside his body, obviously—at the lake house is not consistent with his injury."

"Then the blood wasn't his?" Doubt and uncertainty clouded her expression.

"Testing confirmed the blood was his. The consensus we—meaning my colleagues from the agency and I—reached was that the blood was taken as if he'd given blood, like a donor, and then it was used to establish the appearance that he had died in that bedroom."

"Like the book *Gone Girl*," she suggested.

"Exactly like that, yes," he agreed. "But he was killed somewhere else by that single shot. What will help clear you of involvement is to know the actual time of death."

Sharing the other details wasn't exactly breakfast conversation, but she needed to hear the rest.

"The ME determined that the body was in the vehicle for some time before it was found. With temperatures in the high eighties, the heat inside the car sped up the decomp process and created some difficulty in determining a precise time of death, but the ME assigned to the case is very good. He'll pinpoint it as closely as possible. Obviously, the timing will not fit with you being the one who killed him, since many witnesses—employees of the Chop House—saw him, alive and well, around midnight on Saturday."

She considered all he'd said for a few beats, then asked, "Was there a head injury?" She touched her temple. "That's where the blood I saw was coming from when he was being dragged on that kitchen floor."

"No head injury. I specifically asked that question in the conference call with Victoria. Not even a scratch."

Leah digested this detail for a time. "So the blood I saw may have been planted to make me believe he was injured."

"Quite possibly."

Something changed in her demeanor. Her shoulders straightened; her lips set in a firm line. She was angry. Understandably so.

"Then it's true." Her words were edged with ice. "Raymond was part of whatever this scheme is to set me up. Most likely Isla, too, since the lake house belongs to her and her mother."

"There is good reason to believe as much, yes." Sugarcoating the situation or trying to lessen the blow at this point would be ridiculous. Her longtime friend was no doubt involved. He supposed it was still possible that she was a victim as well, but the idea seemed increasingly unlikely.

"I contacted her brother this morning."

Leah stared at him expectantly.

"He hasn't heard from her in years. Or their mother. There was a falling-out about six years ago. He was quite put out that I would even call him, and he wanted me to 'lose' his number."

"Wow. She mentioned they didn't keep in touch. But she never said a word about a falling-out at that level. Good grief, all she did was lie to me." Leah poked at the scrambled eggs with her fork. Took a bite and chewed far longer than necessary. "Is there any suggestion that some aspect of this is related to Chris?" She shook her head. "I mean, I don't see how that's possible. What happened with Chris was a long time ago—before I moved to Chicago or even knew Isla and Raymond."

"I can't answer that question," Owen admitted. "We don't have enough information to hazard a guess. We will, in time, find those answers for you."

"I can't keep waiting for answers." She moistened her lips. "I need to see him." She nodded as if only now, after saying the words, attempting to convince herself of the strategy. "I have a right to know why he left me to deal with all the fallout nine plus years ago. If we wait, some of the thugs he wronged will come after him, and then I may never know the truth."

Although Owen understood her reasoning, he couldn't help wondering if she wanted to see Painter because she still had feelings for the man. He had been her first love… Maybe on some level she was still in love with him. But then, that was none of his business unless it somehow affected the investigation. He understood this, but accepting it was a different story…for reasons completely unreasonable and inappropriate. Other investigators had told him about developing feelings for clients—some even married those clients—but Owen had not encountered that issue… until now.

Clearing his head of the thoughts, he opted to chalk her question up to mere curiosity whether it was precisely true. He liked Leah. More than he should, really. He'd felt a subtle attraction to her the moment they met. But being attracted to his client was not smart under the circumstances—never was, actually. Someone had gone to a lot of trouble to set her up, and he needed to find the reason and determine all the players involved. Hopefully to stop that person or persons and to see that Leah was not falsely accused or harmed.

"I understand," he said in response to her statement, "you feel the need for closure or perhaps for some sense of peace about what happened with Painter. But we need to proceed with caution when it comes to his sudden reappearance. We have no sense of his intent where you're concerned. At this point it's not clear if he was held against his will or if he was in hiding and is now pretending to have been a prisoner." Owen might be guessing on that aspect, but it was a valid possibility.

"You're right, of course." She frowned, then nodded as if needing to convince herself. "I would very much like to have some sort of closure, but until we understand how this happened at this particular time, I agree that it's not a good idea to barge into the situation." She scoffed. "After all these years and all I went through, I feel like punching him in the face…or worse. Still, I really am worried that the ones he double-crossed will show up. His friends were not the type to forget, much less forgive. Not that he deserved to be forgiven."

Owen smiled. "I would suggest that you not comment on your personal feelings when the reporters and Lambert start throwing questions at you."

She laughed. "I assure you, I will not comment."

The sound of her laugh made him smile. "Good."

"You cooked," she said, standing, "I'll clean up."

"I'll help," he insisted. It would give him something to do other than watch her.

For a while, they worked without speaking. The sound of clattering dishes and running water filled the silence. But there were things he wanted to know about her. Things that had nothing to do with the investigation. He ignored the urge for as long as possible.

"You must love reading," he commented.

She looked up at him, her hands sudsy. "I do." She shrugged and turned her attention back to the task of scrubbing the pan he'd used. "There was a time when I thought I would be a writer." She laughed and shook her head. "I was going to write the next great American novel. But I quickly realized I am not a writer. I love books and I love reading, but I'll leave the creating to those born with the talent."

The change of subject lightened the mood considerably. He confessed, "I don't always have as much time to devote to reading as I'd like, but I do enjoy a good mystery from time to time."

"Mysteries, romance… I love it all. My hope is to prompt that love in my students. Sometimes all it takes is reading the right book to ignite that love."

"I'm sure you'll be a great teacher."

She passed the pan to him and stared out the window, her hands resting on the counter since there was nothing more to wash. "That's if I get through this mess without ending up in prison."

He set the pan aside and put his hand on hers, gave it a squeeze. "The Colby Agency is not going to let that happen."

She turned her hand up and entwined her fingers with his, her gaze searching his face before settling on his eyes. "Thank you. I can't imagine going through this without you. And the agency," she hastened to add.

He managed a smile, when what he really wanted to do was lean down and kiss her. He sensed that she badly needed to be kissed. "I am really grateful I was the one chosen to help."

As if she, too, felt that sizzle of attraction, her gaze dropped to his lips. But then she looked away. "I should get prepared for the meeting with Detective Lambert."

Her fingers slid from his, and she hurried away, disappearing up the stairs.

He finished in the kitchen, taking his time in an effort to distract himself.

Whatever Lambert and his team had found that they hadn't shared so far, Owen was determined to keep Leah safe and ensure she walked away from this situation unscathed. He didn't have to wonder whether she was innocent. His instincts had never steered him wrong, and he was one hundred percent certain she was the victim in this twisty business of betrayal.

He suspected they might never know all the details unless they found Isla Morris alive.

But that was the problem. At this point, with Douglas dead…the prospect of finding her alive was growing dimmer and dimmer.

Chicago Police Department
Addison Street, 10:10 a.m.

LEAH REMINDED HERSELF to breathe calmly, evenly, though it was immensely difficult to do either. Panic nipped at her, wanted to rise and spread through her, but she fought it. This was no time for a panic attack. She'd had a few in her life, and she certainly did not want to deal with that right now.

Owen sat beside her. He was calm and steady, the very things she needed to be. In truth, he was the one part in all this that prevented her from losing it completely. The reality of what someone had done to her was shattering.

As soon as they had arrived at the department—five minutes before the designated time—they were escorted to a conference room. Leah couldn't decide whether that was good or bad. Were they meeting with others besides Lambert? Owen had warned her not to talk or ask questions about the case while they waited. Lambert or one of his colleagues could be listening.

Not that Leah had anything to hide. She was innocent in this bizarre chain of events. Her supposed best friend, it now seemed, had set Leah up for her own personal gain.

Although she couldn't see how Isla would be gaining anything—her name wasn't on that insurance policy. Leah was one of the beneficiaries. If she were charged with Raymond's murder, it was unlikely she would receive a dime.

So how did Isla expect to gain anything? Certainly Raymond Douglas wasn't going to.

Leah and Owen had not spoken in depth about this aspect of the case. She guessed he didn't want to go there until they had further confirmation that Isla was involved. He likely wanted to spare Leah's feelings. At this point, she was so far beyond being upset that her longtime friend may have betrayed her that she wasn't sure she could get past it even if it turned out Isla wasn't involved.

The door abruptly opened, and Detective Lambert walked in. He closed it behind him, so evidently this meeting would be only the three of them. Leah relaxed just a little. Maybe this wasn't as bad as she had feared. Then again, assuming anything could be a mistake. This eerie situation had taken several unexpected twists.

"Good morning." Lambert sat down, his attention fixed on the open file folder in his hands. "Thank you for coming."

"Good morning," Owen said. "I would hope that by now you will have found the necessary evidence to clear Ms. Gerard."

Leah stared at the man next to her a moment, hoped to God he was right. Then her attention swung back to the other man—the one who held all the cards, or so it seemed.

Lambert fixed his attention on her. "Your prints were found in the lake house. In several rooms." He said this without preamble or explanation of why he thought the find was relevant.

"We were there," Owen said. "We're the ones who found

the blood and called you. This was Leah's first visit to the lake house. I would think that the number of prints found that matched hers was few, no matter how many rooms were involved."

Lambert stared at Owen for a moment before turning back to Leah. "Mrs. Morris stated that you had been to the lake house many times with her daughter, Isla."

"That is not true," Leah responded. Owen had suggested she not answer any questions unless it was something very straightforward that they had already discussed. This one—a comment, actually—fit those parameters. He also warned her not to expand upon the most direct answer.

"You're saying," Lambert pressed, "that Mrs. Morris lied in her official statement."

"What Ms. Gerard is saying," Owen countered, "is that Mrs. Morris has never personally witnessed Ms. Gerard at the lake house. Her statement on the matter is mere hearsay."

Exactly. Leah managed a deep breath. She was so glad she had been smart and let Owen answer that one. She would never have been able to come across so emphatic and logical. All the more reason she was incredibly thankful for this man.

She stared at him now. Maybe more than she should admit.

Lambert considered the open file in front of him once more. Leah wished she could read the words and clearly see the images on the pages, but she could only make out enough to be worried all the more. This thing just kept expanding.

"In your statement," the detective said as he lifted his gaze to Leah, interrupting her worrisome thoughts, "from the incident at the restaurant, you said Raymond Douglas was being dragged across the floor and that there was blood on his temple, as if he had sustained a head injury."

"Yes." Leah bit her lips together to prevent saying more.

"Why couldn't you see who was dragging him? That person was surely taller than the stainless steel table that blocked Douglas from view once he was pulled fully behind it."

Leah waited for Owen to answer that one. She glanced at him. His full attention rested on the detective; the stony set of his jaw warned that he was losing patience.

"I visited the restaurant and viewed the window through which she witnessed the events that occurred in the kitchen that night," Owen said. "The only way to see between the two tables that stood perhaps eight feet apart was to be looking straight through the window in that swinging door. On the other hand, the only way to see the person dragging Mr. Douglas would have been for her to step to her right and lean against the door."

Leah nodded as he spoke. He was right. The view she'd had was limited, not only by the small size of the window but also by the shelving units flanking the door on the kitchen side. The window was designed to alert anyone approaching the door of someone about to push through it, not to provide a wide-angle view into the kitchen.

"My guess," Owen went on, "is that the reason she did not do this was because, obviously, she was in shock. It's a perfectly logical reaction. She saw Douglas on the floor, bleeding, and then his body being dragged along. It's human nature to stare at something so surprising or shocking for a few seconds to ensure that you are indeed seeing what you believe you are seeing. Then another moment is required to react. By that time, the person pulling the victim would have been blocked from view by the stainless steel shelving unit loaded with pots and pans and other cooking related items next to the tables. I'm sure you noticed this as well, if you had a close look at the scene."

Leah had not really thought about any of it at the time. She had been too busy staring at Raymond, unconscious or dead, on the floor. For several seconds she had been certain she was imagining it. She hadn't even thought to look at who was pulling him—if she could have seen him or her. Once she realized it was actually happening, her only thought—the one pounding in her brain—had been to run for her life…and call the police.

The detective looked from Owen to Leah. "The medical examiner has tentatively called time of death at some point on Monday. In the afternoon, he suspects. But there is a good deal more work to be done in order to narrow down that time frame."

His words echoed over and over in her brain before she could react. "Then you know it wasn't me," she said before she analyzed the prudence in doing so. Lambert had mentioned he had someone watching her after she went home Sunday morning. No doubt she was watched until she went to the safe house with Owen on Tuesday.

"In addition to watching Ms. Gerard," Owen said, "I'm confident you've monitored the location of her cell phone."

"We're aware," Lambert admitted, "that you did not murder Raymond Douglas."

The words struck Leah like a tidal wave washing over the shore. Finally. Did this mean the truth was emerging? She wanted to be relieved, yet she knew there was a *but* coming. She could hear it in his words, see it in his face.

"However, we still have questions as to whether you and your roommate have been working together. Planned and executed the event. Perhaps Isla decided to double-cross you, Leah. Have you considered this? It would be to your advantage to tell me all you know, and perhaps there would be a deal for you."

Every ounce of strength she possessed was required to prevent responding to that statement with all the fury building inside her. She wanted to shout her indignation, to rant at him for wasting time by being focused on her. Instead, she deferred to Owen. He would know how to best react to the man's ridiculous suggestion.

"In any scenario you can concoct," Owen began, "how would Ms. Gerard's participation in the murder of Raymond Douglas be believable, considering she would have known that the insurance policy would scream her guilt? You must be aware by now that she is a victim in this scam as well."

Lambert scrubbed a hand over his jaw. He looked from Owen to Leah. "Not once in three years did you suspect your roommate was some sort of scam artist?"

Leah shook her head. "Never. Honestly, I can't believe she would do this. Isla is brilliant. She's going to be a doctor. Why would she throw it all away—even for five million dollars—when she has so much future potential to lose? I'm confident her lifetime income potential is far more than that amount. She's young, with her entire life ahead of her. Think of all that would mean she was throwing away."

It simply did not make sense. Who would do such a thing?

Big exhale from Lambert. "The answer is quite simple. Because your roommate is not a student in medical school or anywhere else. Not legally."

Leah drew back at his words as if he'd slapped her. "What are you talking about? Isla is in her final year of medical school. I've watched her studying. Her schedule is insane."

"Isla Morris was a medical student, yes," Lambert confirmed. "But your roommate and Isla Morris are not the same person."

Shock shimmered through Leah, rocking her to the very core of her being. She somehow managed to turn her head and exchange a glance with Owen. Judging by the expression on his face, he was more than a little surprised as well.

Owen shifted his attention to the detective. "The agency confirmed the roommate's attendance at Northwestern as well as her employment at the hospital."

"Whoever this woman—your roommate—is," Lambert said to Leah, "she is not Isla Morris." He shifted his focus to Owen. "I have reason to believe the woman who invited Leah to move in with her is Alyssa Jones, and has been pretending to be Morris for just over three years."

"We'll need more details," Owen said, visibly unconvinced.

Leah couldn't speak. Her mind was still reeling.

"Isla Morris and Alyssa Jones were friends. They looked so much alike they could have been twins—even her mother said so. Olive, Isla's real mother, cremated her daughter after her tragic suicide three and a half years ago. In her grief, she foolishly allowed this Alyssa Jones to come and go in her home at will. She saw Alyssa as a sort of second daughter and firmly believed she could trust her completely. After Isla's death, she clung to Alyssa. Depended on her. Alyssa seemed to be a godsend."

Leah couldn't believe what she was hearing. Just when she thought this situation could not get any more bizarre. "You are absolutely certain this person I've known all this time is not Isla Morris? The woman I've met who gave us the key to the lake house is not her mother?"

"Correct," Lambert confirmed. "In fact, the woman you met who posed as Isla's mother has vanished. Her home looks as if it was ransacked and abandoned. We're still trying to identify her."

"I'm somewhat baffled," Owen admitted. "My agency found nothing in Isla Morris's background to suggest she was deceased. I'm aware the department has its resources, but none better than ours. Where is your in-depth knowledge coming from?"

"Frankly, I was confused myself when this thing with Douglas started," Lambert confessed. "You see, my wife and Olive Morris were friends back in high school. They hadn't seen each other in years, but when Isla died, Olive was devastated. She called my wife and begged her to persuade me to look into the girl's death because Olive was convinced her daughter wouldn't commit suicide. I conducted an unofficial investigation of sorts. Followed up on the coroner's report, that sort of thing."

He exhaled a weary breath. "And I spoke at length with the friend, Alyssa. She insisted the intense pressure Isla was under at school had her on edge. She went into great detail about the anxiety and other issues Isla hadn't told her mother about. She was so sincere. Damned persuasive. I bought the story hook, line and sinker. So you see, the mistake was mine."

"But you didn't say anything," Leah said, bewildered and feeling more hurt than ever. "You questioned me repeatedly, and you said nothing." He'd made her feel like a criminal!

"When I interviewed you," he explained, "early Sunday morning, I was stunned to discover that Isla's identity had been stolen. But I needed to let this thing play out in hopes of discovering the whole truth. I believe Alyssa Jones took over everything for Olive after Isla's death. Olive went into seclusion. Didn't talk to anyone. Didn't hold a memorial service for her daughter. She just stopped caring about anything, which likely left Jones with free rein…until she had everything she wanted. Birth certificate, family photos, money…whatever. If I'd had any doubts about my conclusion, those were gone when I checked with the medical examiner's office and no file for Isla Morris was found. This woman—Alyssa Jones, aka Isla Morris—may or may not be a professional, but she orchestrated the takeover of Isla's life like a professional."

Owen shifted in his chair, the move drawing Leah's attention. He asked, "Why are you telling us this now?"

Lambert studied Owen a moment, then looked to Leah. "I'm telling you this, and I shouldn't. If my commander learns about my personal involvement in the case, he'll take me off this investigation. I need to find the truth. I owe it to Isla and her mother. If you will work with me—play along—we may be able to draw this Alyssa Jones or whoever she is out of hiding."

Leah shifted her attention to Owen. "I would really like to help."

Owen nodded, then said to Lambert, "We'll need more information about what you have planned. Starting with, where is the real Mrs. Morris?"

Lambert's expression grew even more somber. "You have no idea how much I wish I could answer that question. I've gone to her home and gotten no answer. Her neighbors say they haven't seen her in ages." He shrugged. "I may have had a look around in her home, unofficially, and all appeared to be just as it should be. So, to answer your question, I have no idea."

"What is it that you expect of my client?" Owen prompted.

"Well, my official reason for calling you here today," Lambert said to Leah, "was to let you know that you're no longer a person of interest in the death of Raymond Douglas. I'll keep working the case, but I fear I won't find the answers I'm looking for without your help." He shifted to Owen then. "If you can protect Ms. Gerard, I believe I can draw out this Alyssa Jones, or whoever she is—bear in mind that according to all our databases, she does not exist. Anyway, I fear this is the only way I'm going to learn what has happened to Olive Morris. I'll start with a press briefing to tell the world that Douglas's body has been found and Leah Gerard is innocent of his murder."

Owen nodded. "This will lead the roommate to believe the life insurance will pay off. She'll be watching Ms. Gerard."

"Yes." Lambert nodded, his expression hopeful. "I believe this was her intent all along." He glanced at Leah. "But I worry that I can't prove it without your help."

Leah looked to Owen and nodded. She wanted to help. The person she had trusted the past three years had betrayed her and likely had plans to kill her. Leah wanted to see her go down, and anything she could do toward that end was fine by her. All she needed was for Owen to have her back.

"We can work with you on this," Owen agreed. "But we'll need assistance with another matter."

Lambert's expression turned guarded. "I'm listening."

"Chris Painter has resurfaced, and Ms. Gerard needs details. Perhaps even a visit with the man. It's my understanding the Chicago PD has him under guard at the hospital."

Lambert considered the request while Leah's heart thumped harder and harder.

Finally, he said, "I think I can arrange that."

Owen looked to Leah; she nodded again, then he turned back to Lambert. "Then we have a deal."

In light of the fact that Leah was now officially cleared of suspicion, she should have been happy. But what she felt was betrayed, used…and terrified—terrified that what she would learn would be far worse than what she already knew.

Terrified that Chris Painter would tell her secret.

Chapter Nine

Gerard/Morris Apartment
Chestnut Street, 1:00 p.m.

The press conference hit all the local stations.

Leah had been bursting with the need to do something since leaving the meeting with Detective Lambert. He'd asked her to return to the apartment she had shared with the woman who had called herself Isla Morris, and tomorrow she was to go back to work. She had done as Lambert asked and worked it out with her boss to have the evening shift tomorrow, which would include closing up the library. Bolling, the building manager, had ensured the apartment was ready. It was almost as if the explosion never happened, except every now and then, Leah got a whiff of a smoky odor. She supposed it lingered in places that were difficult to clean.

Lambert had made an official call to Isla's brother to inform him that his sister was deceased and his mother was missing. But the man hadn't wanted to hear it. He'd been just as curt and uncaring with the detective as he'd been when Owen called him. Leah wanted to judge him for the behavior, but honestly how could she? After what she'd done to her family, she had no right to judge anyone. No matter that she'd straightened up…she had hurt them badly.

Leah turned off the television and crossed her arms before turning to Owen. "Is waiting all we can do?"

He was so still and quiet sometimes. She couldn't help wondering what he was thinking. Maybe she didn't want to know.

"We've done a great deal already," Owen reminded her. He sat on the corner of the sofa back. "We changed the passwords on all your bank, credit card and other personal accounts. Same with the social media accounts. If Jones attempts to gain access to one of your accounts, she'll have no choice but to come directly to you."

This was true, but those efforts felt like nothing that was moving the investigation forward. As difficult as it had been to suffer through seventy-two hours of being made to feel as if she had committed some horrible crime, having to wait for the real person responsible for all this insanity to reappear was even harder. Maybe only because Leah had lost her patience already. Her entire life had been turned upside down, and now all she wanted to do was get this behind her. This wasn't the first time she'd had to right her life, but she sure hoped it would be the last.

"I know." She exhaled a big breath. "It's just hard to stand around here and wait." She had kept her life so carefully organized and in control for the past few years, to live with this uncertainty and total loss of control now was not easy.

She walked over to the window and scanned the street in search of the black sedan. It hadn't reappeared after Owen had lost it on their last trip to the safe house. And it certainly wasn't anyone Lambert had scheduled to keep her under surveillance. If the unknown surveillant had seen the detective's press conference, he would surely expect her to end up back at this apartment.

The Colby Agency was still working on tracking down his identity. The license plate had been traced to a leasing company. The car had been leased by one of Raymond Douglas's businesses, but the driver who'd picked up the vehicle had used a stolen ID. False identities seemed to be a theme in all this.

Leah had called first thing that morning and checked on her mother. She didn't generally allow three days to go by without talking to her mom, but this had been a week of doing things out of the ordinary, and any and all schedules had gone out the window. But Leah hadn't mentioned any of that to her mother. No need to worry her. There was nothing she could do, and upsetting her would not have helped.

"She went with me to see my mother once," Leah said, the memory only then occurring to her. Cold flowed through her veins at the thought. She turned back to the man watching her. "What if this Alyssa goes there and tries to hurt or use my mother in some way?" She should have thought of that possibility before. Her mother had no idea about any of this. Maybe Leah should have warned her about the pretend Isla. All her mother had ever heard was good things about Leah's roommate.

"We have eyes on the facility," Owen said as he walked toward her, then surveyed the street beyond the window. "She's not getting to your mother."

Relief washed over her, making her knees weak. "Thank you. I really should have considered the possibility as soon as Detective Lambert told us about Isla… Alyssa." She scrubbed at her forehead. "I don't know where my brain is."

"We should get out of here. Go to a restaurant you and

your roommate patronized regularly. Maybe later tonight, go to a club or other social gathering spot the two of you frequented. Being seen out will lend credibility to Lambert's plan."

He was right. "Okay. That's a great idea. We should go to Tempo. It's—*was* our favorite place. We'd walk there all the time for pancakes or burgers. I think we've probably tried everything on the menu at one time or another."

"Let's go, then. It's a nice day for a drive."

"Tempo is just up the block and across the street. We can walk."

He smiled. "Even better."

As they left the apartment building, Leah couldn't help feeling as if someone was watching. By the time they were on the sidewalk, she had shaken the feeling off. There was no sign of the black sedan. No reason, she supposed, for the police to still be monitoring her activities. Unless they hoped Alyssa would make a move to interact somehow with Leah. With effort, she forced the thoughts away and focused on the moment.

This tree-lined block was one of the reasons she had been so thrilled when the offer to share the apartment came along. She'd struggled so hard those first two years in Chicago to keep a decent roof over her head. Isla—she gave herself a mental shake; not Isla, Alyssa—had been a godsend. How could someone who had seemed so nice, so helpful, have been such a bad person? How could she be heartless enough to wreck someone else's life to get what she wanted? Not to mention a cold-blooded killer? It just didn't fit with the woman Leah knew. Then, on top of that, was the time period. They had been roommates for three years. Had Leah just been in the wrong place at the wrong time on Saturday night? Surely the plan had not been scheduled for three years. Maybe the friendship had been real in the beginning…until Alyssa Jones needed a scapegoat.

Any other idea made no sense. Whatever the case, obviously Alyssa had been instrumental in setting up Saturday night's fiasco.

Leah drew in a lungful of air, reminding herself to focus on the now. It was a little warm today, but the sun and the light breeze felt great.

"This was a good idea." She glanced up at Owen. "Thanks for suggesting it."

"You've been cooped up at one place or the other since this thing began. It's nice to get out." He smiled. "To think about other things."

That smile of his made her feel lighter. She focused forward. Getting too attached was a bad idea. Though they'd only been together for a few days, she felt so comfortable with him. More at ease than with any guy she had dated. This was the absolute wrong path for her thoughts. She felt confident his suggestion to think about other things was not that she should be thinking about him. Oh well, she couldn't turn it off with him right beside her, looking so handsome in his navy trousers and that sky blue shirt that highlighted his eyes. And smelling so…so good.

Maybe the distraction was sheer desperation or necessity, but it felt nice anyway.

As they approached the intersection of West Chestnut and North State Street, the towering buildings edged out everything else. The trees disappeared, save for the small ones sprouting from carefully planned squares of earth revealed along the sidewalks. Traffic lights and streetlamps took the place of the larger trees. The narrow, barely two-lane side street became a wide city passageway with turning lanes and crosswalks and ever-present traffic.

"Just on that corner." She pointed to Tempo. The lovely one-story painted building with its arched natural-wood windows was neatly tucked in amid the towering skyscrapers. The petite structure sat on the corner, the East Chestnut side flanked by an outdoor-dining space.

This was another one of the things Leah had enjoyed about living at Chestnut Place. There were so many shops and restaurants within a short walk. The hum of the city energized her. She refused to allow the betrayal of the past few days to take that away from her. This was home, and no one was robbing her of that feeling.

She would just have to see about taking over the lease and getting herself a new, trustworthy roommate.

They passed Leah's favorite coffee shop. She and Isla—Alyssa—had been there together many, many times.

A sickening sensation settled in her stomach when she considered how thoroughly she had been fooled. Pushing the thought away, she smiled and thanked Owen when he opened the door to Tempo. The café wasn't so busy, since the lunch crowd had diminished. Getting a table and ordering was quick.

Once the waitress had taken their order and drifted away, Owen asked, "Have you given any thought to where you go from here?" His blue eyes searched her face as she scrambled to figure out how to answer his question, since she really had no idea. "I mean, I'm sure you'll be finishing at the university. But will you be staying in the same apartment, or do you feel a change is in order?"

"Good question." She hadn't gotten that far with any sort of plan. "The lease has *her* name on it, so I'll have to see how or if I can change that."

"I imagine the rent is fairly steep for a student with only a part-time job."

"I have some savings." Actually, what she had was the remainder of the trust her father had left her. Not exactly enough, but something. But she really wanted to save that for anything her mom might need. "I would probably need to find another roommate."

She'd used the larger portion of her trust for her mother, and she did not regret doing so. With her whole heart, she was confident her father had expected his wife to be well cared for. The problem was, he hadn't noticed that the payment information hadn't been updated on the life insurance policy he'd purchase years ago to take care of her if something happened to him. In part, Leah had blamed the life insurance company for not trying to call a longtime customer, but there was no changing that sad fact once her father was gone. Instead, the policy had lapsed, and there was nothing for her mother. The savings her father had accumulated had already been established as a trust for Leah. He'd changed their will and set up the trust since, at the time, their only daughter had appeared determined to screw up her life. The trust only allowed for the withdrawal of a certain amount each year. Except for medical needs—which was how she had managed to use the money at a faster pace for her mother's needs.

"I have a friend," he said, "who owns a building not so far from where you live now who has great studios for really good prices. I can put in a word, if a move to something smaller and less expensive would help."

"I should do that," she agreed with a resounding nod. "The idea of looking for a roommate is…" She made a face. "Not something I really want to do."

"Understandable. I'll give my friend a call. We can go have a look when you're ready."

We. A rush of warmth gave her goose bumps. The very best part of this conversation was the idea that he antici-pated seeing her even after this investigation was finished. As foolish as it sounded since she hardly knew him, she really hoped that was a possibility. Maybe it was the hero-worship thing, but it felt like something more.

"Thank you." She smiled. "I really appreciate every-thing you're doing."

The smile he flashed back at her made her heart beat even faster. She really had to slow down. She was getting far too accustomed to having this man around.

They both ordered a cheeseburger and fries, which hit the spot. Leah added a vanilla milkshake to hers. She hadn't inhaled that many carbs in a while, and she desper-ately needed the boost they provided—however temporary.

Maybe it was all the sugar from that milkshake, but the words were out of her mouth before she could stop them: "Do you have siblings?"

She instantly bit her lip. In all the discussions about her personal life, he had never once offered any details of his own. Maybe it wasn't allowed. Whatever the case, the question was out there now.

"Two sisters," he said without hesitation. "Both older. I've spent my entire life being bossed around by them."

Leah laughed. "I thought you were going to say *protect-ing them* or *scaring off boyfriends*."

"That too," he admitted. "But mostly I've always done whatever they asked. Lauren got married three years ago and has the first grandchild on the way. Madilyn is en-gaged. But both still call me first when they're worried."

A smile tugged at her lips. "I love that they respect your input so much."

He inclined his head toward one shoulder. "Lauren is a psychologist, and she has told me many times that I'm far too calm and steady for a man just turned thirty-two. Madilyn insists that I take after our mother, and the wild child that never developed will appear when I least expect it."

"I'm not sure I want to know what that means." Leah grinned when he turned up his hands. "Wait, yes, I have to hear it!"

"The story goes," he explained, "my mother and father married very young—which is true. She was eighteen and he was twenty and still in college. By the time Mother was twenty-five, she had three kids. Our father had graduated by then and was working as an engineer in a coveted government position. So all was good financially. But then, at thirty, Mother suddenly experienced an early midlife crisis and took off for Paris."

Leah's jaw dropped. "Paris as in France?"

He nodded. "She said she'd never gone to Paris the way she always wanted. Father was forever too tied up at work to take any real time off, so she decided to just do it alone. She landed in Paris and then spent fourteen days traveling around Europe as if she hadn't a care or an obligation in the world. Both grandmothers were appropriately appalled and came to take care of the children. For the three of us, it was like a trip to Disney World. The grandmothers spoiled us entirely during her absence. On day fifteen in Europe, Mother woke up, spent the whole day in tears and trying to get the fastest flight back home."

"What a story." Leah grabbed another french fry from her plate. "What happened when she got back?"

"Father apologized for ignoring her and promised it

would never happen again, and just like that, life returned to normal, except for one thing." He held up one finger. "From that point on, no matter how busy work got, we took a real family vacation every year, and each year on their anniversary, our parents took a mini vacation, just the two of them, to wherever Mother wanted to go."

"I love it! Your family sounds wonderful." Leah supposed the way she had pined for siblings her whole life made her more vulnerable to someone like the roommate who had misled her so completely. Or maybe she just wanted to believe such a cool relationship could be real. Either way, she yearned for those close attachments. Too bad she'd always chosen the wrong people to form attachments to.

"I'm certain they would adore you," he said. "Both sisters and my mother are avid readers. You would have much in common."

Another stream of warmth filled Leah at the possibility of meeting his family. She smiled, though her lips tried hard not to shake with uncertainty. "I'd love to meet them one day."

His smile slipped and he reached for his cell phone. He looked at Leah. "It's Detective Lambert."

Leah held her breath.

Owen took the call but didn't put it on speaker since they were in a restaurant. He made several comments, but none that provided any inkling as to what Lambert was saying. When he finally ended the call, Leah found herself holding her breath once more.

"Two things." He pressed his lips together for a moment as if he wasn't looking forward to the necessary share. "The body of the real Isla Morris's mother was found in a freezer in the basement of the Morris home. It will take some time before the ME can determine cause of death."

The possibility that the woman Leah had trusted killed the poor woman tore at her like the claws of a rabid bear. "This just gets worse." She blinked back the tears of regret and frustration. "I'm afraid to ask what the second thing is."

"If you still want to see Painter," he said, obviously no happier about this part, "Lambert has made the arrangements."

The warmth Leah had been enjoying while listening to Owen talk about his family vanished. A cold flood of defeat and fear replaced it.

Another person was dead. And then there was the other. She didn't want to see Chris…but she had to.

Northwestern Memorial Hospital
East Huron Street, 3:30 p.m.

A UNIFORMED POLICE OFFICER stood outside the hospital room.

Owen showed his ID, and the officer nodded. "Detective Lambert gave approval for the two of you to go in."

Owen looked to Leah. "Do you want me to go in with you?"

She chewed her lower lip a moment before forcing the words from her mouth. "I should do this alone." She didn't want to do it alone, but she couldn't be sure what Chris would say… Oh God, how had she allowed her life to end up at this place?

So damned screwed up! She'd spent all these years pretending this day would never come. But here it was.

Owen nodded. "I'll be right here if you need me."

Leah resisted the urge to hug him. She wasn't sure there was a way to ever properly show her gratitude. This decision to see Chris alone, she hoped, would not make Owen doubt how much she trusted and appreciated him.

Still, this private meeting was necessary.

Leah took a breath and stepped up to the door. The officer opened it and she went inside.

The first thing to hit her senses was the beeping from the machines monitoring the patient's vitals. The lights in the room were dimmed a little. Then her attention settled on the bed. A sheet covered his body from the waist down. He wore a faded blue hospital gown. Since the gown had very short sleeves, it was easy to see that his arms were no longer the thick, muscular ones from all those years ago. The tattoos that had impressed her as a teenager had faded and shriveled to the point of being unrecognizable. But it was his face that really startled her. He looked far older than he had back then. A scruffy beard covered his jaws and chin. His blond hair was darker than before and on the stringy side. His closed eyes were sunken, leaving his cheekbones jutting out painfully.

This looked nothing like the guy she'd fallen so hard for. But then, she had been a kid. Barely eighteen. She had been desperate for excitement.

She had been immature and incredibly foolish.

Slowly, she approached his bedside. His arms lay alongside his torso, his left arm clustered with IVs and a blood pressure cuff.

She placed her hands on the bed rail and considered what to say. Maybe nothing. He seemed to be asleep. But then, she might never get this chance again. Alone, anyway.

His eyes fluttered open, taking the decision out of her hands.

Deep breath. "Hello, Chris."

She wondered if he recognized her. Her hair was the

same—same color, same length—and she was basically the same size. But she was older. Tired from juggling work and school, and from dealing with the strange things that had occurred this week.

She had gone from witness to a crime to a murder suspect to…whatever Lambert saw her as now in the space of four days.

"Leah."

A too-familiar sensation flickered through her. The way he said her name was the same. She had loved hearing her name on his lips. He was her first love, her first lover. She would have done anything for him.

And then he'd disappeared, leaving her heartbroken and alone and in the crosshairs of pure evil.

"You're alive," she decided to say. "Everyone thought you were dead."

He managed a small smile. It wasn't until then that she noticed his cracked lips. "That was sort of the point, apparently."

Part of her still wanted to punch him, but he looked to be in no condition to absorb the blow. "You double-crossed the wrong person." It was what everyone assumed. And it was true.

"I sure as hell did." He made a rusty sound that may have been an attempt at a laugh. "I guess I, as they say, got too big for my britches, and it cost me more than I was prepared to pay."

Now she was just flat-out pissed. "You?" She leaned forward to ensure he heard her words. "The man whose money and drugs you stole was going to kill me."

"But he didn't." His jaw hardened, lips formed a thin line.

"No." All the emotions she had expected to feel if she

ever saw Chris again were missing. All she felt was empty, sad. "He didn't because I gave him what he wanted."

"Yeah, I heard."

"Are you going to tell?" The one thing she didn't want to feel—fear—crept up her spine.

He stared at her for a long time before he answered. Each second that ticked off made that fear climb a little higher, until it coiled around her throat.

"No. What happened was my fault. I screwed up. I left you and the others to suffer the consequences. You did what you had to. Who am I to judge?"

Surprise radiated through her. She had. It had taken getting a beating like she'd never experienced in her entire life, but she'd spilled her guts in the end. "How did you get away?"

"He's dead—the one who held me captive all this time. His latest wife said she didn't want to take care of me, so she let me go."

"You killed him?" Leah wasn't sure she really wanted to hear the answer.

He moved his head slowly from side to side. "Nah, he had a heart attack—at least, that's what the wife said. Since she was the only one to give him a kid, she was expecting to get all his money and to take over the business. But she didn't want to deal with me, so she smuggled me out of his compound. First thing I heard when I got out was the trouble you were in. I figured the quickest way to find out about you was to turn myself in."

"Why didn't you just take off and keep going? I doubt anyone is even looking for you anymore." He wasn't making sense.

"I didn't want to leave Chicago until I knew you were okay. I figured I owed you that much. As it turns out, the only person who had anything on me is dead now. The feds wanted to question me, and I saw an opportunity, so I gave them an earful. They'll be taking me away as soon as I'm on my feet again. Witness Protection. I'll be starting over somewhere. A house, a job. I'll be set."

"Good for you." Leah meant it. "Perez held you prisoner this whole time?"

Lorenzo Perez had been a big fish in the world of drugs. Leah really was surprised he hadn't executed Chris. Her, too, for that matter.

"He said keeping me prisoner was worse than killing me, and at first he was right. But the more time that passed, the more lax he grew with his punishments. Eventually, it was just like being stuck in a really bad motel with an old friend who visited occasionally to brag about his exploits."

Leah laughed, couldn't help herself. "Only you could survive more than nine years of being held hostage by an infamous drug lord."

"My old man always said I could talk my way out of most anything." He looked away for a moment. "I'm sorry, Leah, for what I did to you. I hope you can forgive me."

"It doesn't matter anymore. You didn't do anything that I didn't let you do. Since I'm the one who told Lorenzo where he would probably find you, I suppose we're even… mostly."

She would never be even with her father's death, but that one was on her, not Chris.

"Guess so," he agreed.

"Well." She squared her shoulders, dropped her hands to her sides. "I should go."

"Take care of yourself, Leah. Make good choices."

She laughed. "You too."

She left knowing without a doubt that only one of them

would make good choices. The possibility that Chris would be happy on the straight and narrow was highly unlikely.

Leah, on the other hand, was never looking back, and she would do everything in her power to make the very best choices possible.

Chapter Ten

Owen couldn't help wondering, even hours later, what Leah and Painter had talked about. The meeting had only lasted seven minutes. Yes, he had ticked off every second in his head.

This case—this *woman*—had totally undone him on some level. He had been with the agency for ten years. He'd started fresh out of university. He'd spent the first four years in research. Then, six years ago, Victoria had asked him to become a field investigator. To say he'd been pleased would be a vast understatement. He'd completed the additional training and took on his first case six months later.

In all the intervening time, he had never once been physically attracted to a client. But Leah...he felt protective of her—sort of the way he felt about his sisters, but not in a sisterly way at all.

His phone buzzed, and he retrieved it from his hip pocket. Ian Michaels, one of Victoria's closest colleagues and a former US marshal, had responded to Owen's request for information.

According to Ian's contact, Painter would be moving into the Witness Protection Program. Although Lorenzo Perez was dead, Painter had considerable and quite valuable information about his network. Once word got out that he had cooperated with the authorities, he wouldn't be intruding into Leah's life again—not if he wanted to stay alive.

Another text message appeared, this one from Lambert. He had four members of his team in place at the Underground, Leah and Owen's destination for the evening. She and the woman who called herself Isla Morris had frequented the dance club over the years. No one expected Alyssa Jones to be hanging out there, but someone who knew her and who was there may have seen her since Saturday night. Leah was acquainted with most of her former roommate's friends. She had some idea of the faces to look for.

The club was the same place she'd run into Raymond Douglas that one time before the ill-fated date.

"I guess I'm ready."

Owen turned to Leah and for a moment he couldn't speak. Her hair was in a high ponytail, making her look incredibly young. She wore a short denim skirt and a pink scoop-necked tee. Her long legs flowed down to a pair of pink high heels. She…looked…great. And sexy as all get out.

"Wow." He took a breath. "You look very…*prepared*." The only photo he'd seen of her dressed this way was from ten years ago in her senior yearbook. She'd had the yearbook hidden in one of her dresser drawers. When he'd searched her room, he hadn't been able to resist having a look.

"I feel a little ridiculous." She shook her head. "Dressing for a night of clubbing after what's happened."

"Keep in mind it's part of the investigation." He grinned. "And you actually look…great. I like it."

She rolled her eyes. "You look pretty great yourself." Her gaze roved down, then back up his body, the move starting a fire deep in his gut.

"You said very casual. Do I meet the criteria?" He didn't generally wear blue jeans and a T-shirt on the job, but blending in tonight was important. Good thing he always packed a pair of jeans. The Guns N' Roses tee wasn't his; Leah had suggested he wear it. It belonged to her. She used the vintage tee as a nightshirt.

The idea that she'd slept in the tee, no matter when that might have been, had kept him on the edge of arousal for the past hour. Seeing her in that skirt was not helping.

"It's perfect." She gave him a nod. "That tee looks better on you than it ever did on me."

He doubted that was the case. "Thank you. Shall we go?"

She crossed the room, moving slowly, maybe because those heels were so high, or maybe just to make him more… Well, anyway.

"I have one question first." She stopped directly in front of him.

"If I'm lucky," he managed a smile, "I have the answer."

"If we're playing the part of a couple," she began, studying his face as if she expected the answer to appear there, "what exactly does that entail?"

She was going there, was she?

"I would think," he said, searching for the words that wouldn't sound so inappropriate, "that sticking together in the crowd would be essential."

She nodded. "I can do that." She tilted her head and eyed him expectantly. "Anything else?"

"We could hold hands." He nodded, thinking that was

a good idea. Reasonable. Not over the line. "Maybe share a toast at least once."

"What about dancing? I really like to dance."

"Sure." This one was a little more precarious. "Dancing would be expected, considering the venue."

"Okay." She smiled. "I think I've got it."

He was glad, because the way she was looking at him while she asked those questions was making him wild with need.

When had merely listening to a woman talk become such a turn-on?

Maybe it was just something about her...that touch of uncertainty and naivete that seemed absolutely genuine. She might be twenty-eight, but he had a feeling she had been holding herself back for a long while now.

The way she watched him as he locked the apartment door made him wonder if she was having the same trouble he was. If she was ready to let go, he was in trouble.

Then she took off toward the stairs at the end of the corridor, and the way she moved almost finished him off completely.

The Underground
Franklin Street, 10:00 p.m.

FINDING A PARKING SPOT had been an ordeal, but nothing Owen hadn't faced before. Living in the city, sometimes a car was a more of a nuisance than an asset. They had stopped at a favorite restaurant of his in the River North area, the Smith, for dinner. From there, they'd made their way to the club, which included round two of Find a Parking Spot Without Losing His Mind.

He and Leah held hands as they walked from the car

to the club entrance. It amazed him how soft her skin felt. Forcing his mind away from the thought to prevent other, more salacious thoughts, he focused on their surroundings.

As the name suggested, the place was underground, in a basement. The style inside was very European. An elevated DJ booth overlooked the dance floor. Tables hugged the walls all the way around the space. The music was loud, and the place literally vibrated with energy. The flashing colored lights kept time with the music.

Not too crowded, but that would change as midnight neared. Leah held on tightly to his hand as she threaded through the crowd in search of an empty table. She found one and moved in for the take. Most of the tables were pub-style and made for standing around. A few had chairs. Those, of course, were all occupied.

A waiter passed and Leah waved him down. "I'd like a vodka on the rocks with lemon." She turned to Owen.

"Whatever you have on draft," he said, loudly enough for the waiter to hear.

The waiter gave a nod and hurried away, weaving effortlessly through the growing crowd.

Leah leaned close and said, "Don't worry, I always nurse a single drink for the entire evening." She made a face. "I'm not much of a drinker, actually."

He'd suspected as much. Anyone who liked a good stiff drink from time to time would have been doing so after what she'd been through. He hadn't seen her go for so much as a beer. Just the wine that once.

For a while he watched her scan the crowd. Sometimes she stood on her tiptoes as if she needed to see over someone. She was far more relaxed than before. Made sense. She was no longer a murder suspect, and the man from her past who had still been haunting her was accounted for and wouldn't be unexpectedly appearing in her life again. Not if he was smart, anyway. Once they knew who was behind the setup that included her name on an insurance policy, the investigation, from her perspective, would be finished.

Closing a case was a good thing, but somehow this felt not so good.

He rested his crossed arms on the table, primarily to be nearer for conversation purposes. "Spotted anyone you recognize?"

"Not yet." She made a disappointed face.

She turned to him and he realized his mistake. His position put his face level with hers when she looked at him. As hard as he tried not to, he found himself studying her lips.

She smiled and his heart thumped.

"Come on." She grabbed his hand and pulled him away from the table. She wove a path through the crowd with almost as much ease as the waiter.

Their destination appeared to be a table where three women stood huddled together. Just as they reached it, Leah called out, "Maya!"

The other woman turned around and shock showed on her face for a split second before she dove at Leah, wrapping her in an enthusiastic hug.

"Oh my God." The one Leah had called Maya drew back and looked her over. "Are you all right? I can't believe what I've been seeing on the news. I started to call, but I wasn't sure if I should."

Which was code for *I didn't want to get involved.* Some friend. Owen recalled Leah mentioning that Maya was one of Isla's friends who hadn't really warmed up to her at first.

"It's okay," Leah said, talking loud enough for the other women to hear over the music. "But I'm really worried about Isla. No one has seen her since Saturday. She hasn't shown up for work, and her mother hasn't heard from her either."

Maya's expression turned apprehensive. "Are the police looking for her?"

Leah nodded. "I'm really worried she has…ended up like Raymond."

Maya's hand went to her chest. "No, that can't be. Maybe she's hiding. I can ask around. See if anyone has heard from her."

"That would be very helpful," Leah said. "I need to know she's okay."

Maya nodded, then glanced at Owen.

"Sorry." Leah shook her head. "This is my friend Owen." She turned to Owen. "This is Maya, Isla's friend I was telling you about."

Maya smiled at him, then glanced at Leah. "Where did you find him?" She waggled her eyebrows. "He's hot."

Owen opted to act as if he hadn't heard her comment.

"He's helping with the investigation," Leah explained.

Maya's expression blanked. "Is he a cop?" She stared at Owen with something like fear or uncertainty.

"Not a cop," he explained, leaning closer to ensure she heard him. "I'm a private investigator."

Maya nodded, her expression still obviously uncertain.

"We need to find Isla," he said. "We believe she is in danger and needs our help. If you or any of her other friends sees her, please let her know that we can help."

Maya shifted her attention from Owen to Leah. "Do you really think she's in trouble?"

Leah moved closer to the other woman. "Absolutely. You don't want to know what they did to Raymond. I have to find her and warn her."

Owen had to hand it to her, Leah was playing it just

right. He put his arm around her and moved closer into their huddle. "We will make sure she doesn't end up like that poor SOB."

Maya nodded slowly. "I'll get the word out to everyone who knows her." She frowned then. "Are you at the apartment?"

Leah nodded. "Where else would I go?"

"Of course. I don't know what I was thinking." Maya hugged Leah again. "You be careful too. I thought for sure you and Raymond were both done for."

"Me too," Leah admitted. She peered up at Owen. "But I had a secret weapon."

He smiled at her, but the look in her eyes made any amusement her remark had garnered vanish, and something entirely different settled in. Electricity was crackling between them, jumping wildly like the dance floor lights.

Rather than draw back, he kissed her. Slowly, briefly. The lightest of kisses. But the fire generated from his lips touching hers threatened to burn them both down.

Leah turned fully into him, stretched her arms up around his neck. His went around her waist, and the feel of her body pressing into his had his mouth deepening the kiss.

In the background, he heard Maya say, "See you around," but slowing this kiss down, much less stopping it for anyone, was out of the question.

Leah pulled back, her eyes wide with surprise and no small amount of desire. "We should mingle."

Before her words could filter through the haze of want blinding him to every single thing but her, she had grabbed his hand and was tugging him forward. He followed, struggled to relax the need roaring inside him.

Control…he had to regain control. This thing buzzing

between them made doing his job inordinately difficult. He could not compromise her safety...or the case.

For the next half hour, they wandered through the crowd, stopping to dance when a song Leah liked vibrated from the speakers. He spotted at least one of Lambert's people. The guy parked at a table looked far too uptight and watchful to be a regular patron.

By the time Leah announced she was ready to leave, Owen was incredibly grateful. He wasn't sure how much more he could take of this pretending to be a couple without making a serious mistake. His whole body hummed at the sound of her voice, the touch of her hand.

When they emerged onto the sidewalk in the night air, he relaxed marginally, sharpened his focus on their surroundings. A few people strolled the sidewalks on either side of the street. A car—not the black sedan—rolled slowly past. Lambert had people here. Leah's hand squeezed his, and she glanced up at him with a dreamy smile. This, he decided, was going to be a long night.

She held on to his hand until they were in the car heading back to Chestnut Place.

There was no talking...just the distinct sizzle of electricity still flowing between them. He had maybe fifteen minutes to regain some semblance of control.

Gerard/Morris Apartment
Chestnut Street, 11:45 p.m.

LEAH'S FINGERS FUMBLED twice in her effort to unlock the door. Though Owen waited behind her, the smell of his aftershave was driving her mad.

If they hadn't been in the middle of that club, she was certain that kiss would have ended up going way, way further. She had never been kissed like that. Ever. Even now, she could scarcely breathe thinking about it.

The truth was…she had wanted way more than just that kiss. Still did.

Finally, the key turned and the door unlocked. Owen placed a hand on her arm to remind her that he needed to go in first. If anyone was waiting inside, he wanted to be the one at the front of the line.

Leah closed and locked the door behind them and then sagged against it. Her body was on fire. She couldn't even remember the last time she'd had sex, but she wanted it now. Wanted it in the worst way.

When he was about to head into the hall toward the bedrooms, she couldn't take it anymore. "Wait."

He turned around, worry in his expression.

She pushed off the door she'd just locked, let her purse drop to the floor and walked straight up to him. Her arms went around his neck, and she rose onto her tiptoes until her lips locked with his. He hesitated, let her do what she would without reacting, which only made her more desperate. Her fingers threaded through his dark hair, her breasts rubbed against his chest—sending fire shooting straight through her.

Finally, his arms went around her and he pulled her tightly against him. She made a sound of want, and he reacted, lifting her off her feet and moving toward the bedroom. Her legs went around his waist, and he staggered to a stop, pressed her against the nearest wall. He glided one hand over her thigh, moving toward her bottom. She cried out. He deepened the kiss. She nipped his lower lip, and he repaid her in kind.

He lifted her away from the wall and moved through the door to her room. She wanted to rip that T-shirt off his body…wanted to feel his skin beneath her palms. When he reached the bed, her feet dropped to the floor and her hands went instantly to that tee, tugging it out from his jeans. He removed his belt, all the while kissing her.

They were doing this…yes, they were. If he stopped now, she would absolutely die.

His fingers went to her hair and worked the elastic from it, letting it fall around her shoulders. He traced the length of it down her back.

Her own fingers struggled with working his tee upward. His hands moved away from her long enough to pull the wad of cotton over his head and drop it to the floor. Her hands went instantly to his chest, glided over his skin… feeling the heat and the pounding of his heart.

Her tee came off next, and then he was easing her down onto the bed. She relaxed into the softness of the covers, and he climbed on top of her, his knees on either side of her hips, keeping his weight off her body.

But she wanted to feel the weight of him…she wanted to…

Her elbow brushed against something cool on the covers. She froze.

"You okay?" he whispered breathlessly.

"There's…" She tried to reach whatever it was with her hand but couldn't get in the right position. "There's something in the bed."

He was off her instantly and yanking her up and away from any potential threat. The bedside lamp suddenly came on, and she blinked her eyes to adjust to the light.

A faceted heart-shaped glass object sparkled red against the white covers. Another smaller piece, and then another and another, spread out around it. Leah rushed to her bedroom window and opened the curtains she kept pulled across it.

"The wind chime." She walked back to the bed and turned on the lamp that sat on the opposite side of where she slept. There was enough light then to see the near-invisible strings that connected all the pieces of colored glass. "It hangs in my window." She glanced back at the window, then at the bed once more. "It was in the window when I closed the curtains to get dressed before we left for the club."

"Where did the wind chime come from?" Owen asked.

"Isla—Alyssa. She gave it to me my first Christmas here."

Their gazes collided.

"She was here." His words echoed the thought that had just entered Leah's mind.

"Does the wind chime carry some particular significance?" he asked, not waiting for her confirmation.

Leah shook her head slowly, racked her brain—the one that was still whirling with desire. "No… I…" She thought of the day they'd bought it. A few days before Christmas, at the artisans' market. "We were shopping at that craft market on Ravenswood. I saw it and fell in love. She bought it and said it was an early Christmas present."

"Is the market open now—in August, I mean?"

Leah shook her head. "It's a seasonal thing. It probably won't open until October."

"But you know the place," he said.

She nodded. "We can go there in the morning." Leah stared at the wind chime for a moment before turning back to him. "Do you think she's trying to lure me into a trap? Or send me a message?"

He reached for the tee she had torn off him. "Either one

is possible. We'll need to be careful." He handed it to her. "Thanks for lending me the shirt."

She hugged it to her chest. Felt the warmth of his body that lingered in the fabric. "You're welcome. Thanks for helping me get word to her friends that we're looking for her." There was so much more she wanted to say, but instead, she asked, "Can we not tell Detective Lambert about this until we see what it means?"

"If that's what you want."

"I do." She looked away for a moment before meeting his gaze once more. "I'm sorry. I guess I got a little carried away tonight."

He reached out, swiped his thumb across her cheek. She leaned into his touch, wanting more, but it was his eyes and that smile that made her hungry to pick up where they had left off.

"If you're agreeable, we can do this again…soon," he promised.

"I am most agreeable."

He smiled. "Good."

When he'd left the room, she drifted to her bathroom and washed her face, then brushed her teeth. Instead of wondering what her lying roommate had in store for her now, she couldn't stop thinking about how it felt to be in Owen's arms. And those kisses. Mercy, the man knew how to kiss.

She tugged on the tee she'd lent him, reveled in the smell of him that had permeated the fabric. Next time, she was not stopping for anything. When she climbed into bed, she hugged herself and thought of how it felt to hug him, to slide her hand over all that muscled terrain.

The idea that he was so nice made her smile. The last time she'd been so taken with a man, he had been a total thug. She shook off thoughts of Chris and how old and weak he had looked in that hospital bed. No matter how he'd gotten himself where he was, she couldn't help feeling sad for him. He could have done so much more with his life. But what happened to him wasn't her fault. If Perez hadn't gotten the truth out of her, he would have gotten it out of someone else. All these years, she had felt guilty about telling Perez that it was Chris who had taken his money and drugs. But now she finally understood that none of that was her fault.

The alarm icon on the digital clock that stood on the bedside table dragged her from the past. The time was correct and wasn't blinking, so the power hadn't gone off. But she never used that clock for an alarm. Her phone was her alarm for everything. She sat up and checked the settings. The alarm had been set for ten in the morning. What in the world?

Then she smiled. She understood now. This was Isla's way of telling her what time to come.

Then her smile faded. Not Isla. A liar. A betrayer. Possibly a murderer.

Leah would see her at ten, and then she would have answers, one way or another.

Chapter Eleven

As certain as Leah had been about last night and what she and Owen had shared—those amazing kisses and, frankly, almost sex—the harsh light of day had her second-guessing herself.

He probably thought her a fool. Really, she was a cliché. A woman in jeopardy, falling for her protector. How sad was that?

The idea had prevented her from fully meeting his gaze that morning. He'd made toast—cheese toast and cinnamon toast. She'd forced herself to eat a slice. Not that it wasn't tasty—it was—but she just couldn't get any more down. She felt sick with regret for her actions. She was attracted to him, but she should have waited until this was done. Then, if they were both still interested… She had to stop thinking about it.

Not that she wanted to regret a moment of any part of their time together—and really, she didn't. She only regretted how foolish she probably looked. Detective Lambert had just told her she was no longer a suspect in Raymond's murder. Chris had let her off the hook after all these years. She should have behaved more like someone thankful for her freedom from accusation...not a lonely woman who had gone without a lover's attention for far too long.

She dropped her head against the car seat and fought the urge to groan. Instead, she stared out at the empty space that, in a couple of months, would be filled with artisans selling their wares and people excited to explore the many offerings.

Owen had parked very close to the entrance of the large warehouse where the market she had visited with her roommate was held. There was not a single other vehicle anywhere along the street. He had backed into a slot against the tree line opposite the row of warehouses.

"There's no need to regret anything about last night."

The sound of his voice filled the car, wrapped around her and made her want to reach out to him. Another groan rose inside her, but she tamped it back. How was she supposed to think clearly? And why was she so transparent?

"It's not necessary," he added.

She turned her head, met his gaze and her determination to be stronger melted. "I feel like I came off as a little too needy." She might as well be honest. She'd had enough lies for several lifetimes.

He smiled. "We were both a bit needy, but that's human, isn't it? We have needs, and sometimes, when we've ignored them for too long, they come on a little strong."

His words made so much sense. "I..." She swallowed back the doubt. "I enjoyed the *us* part of last night. I know it wasn't real, just part of this thing." She stared forward once more. "But I enjoyed being with you...like that."

He placed his open hand, palm up, on the console. "I very much enjoyed the *us* part as well, and it was very real."

She stared at his hand...his long fingers. She placed her hand there, their fingers entwined. Warmth spread through her, and her smile widened. "I slept in that tee you wore."

He smiled. "I'll hold on to that image, if you don't mind."

"I don't mind." She returned the smile.

They both looked forward then. Maybe to prevent the kiss that would no doubt have happened next. Even Leah understood this was not the time to get distracted. Focus. It was necessary.

The minutes slipped past, and she tried to think of something more to say. It was midmorning, and it was already hot. No, she wasn't bringing up the weather.

"I haven't noticed that black car again." Now, *that* seemed like an appropriate topic.

"Maybe because Lambert's people have been around. Since the detective doesn't know about this morning's rendezvous, it's possible our elusive follower will make an appearance." He turned to her then. "All the more reason to be extra careful."

She nodded. "Okay." The area was deserted. They were flanked by trees on one side and a long row of warehouse-type buildings—most of which were either closed at this hour or deserted for the summer—on the other.

"I keep asking myself," Leah said, the recurring thought suddenly pushing to the front of her mind, "if Raymond was a part of this in the beginning."

"How do you mean?"

She wished she knew. "I mean, he didn't die in the kitchen on Saturday night. According to the medical examiner, he likely didn't die until late on Monday. I'm aware that he may have been held hostage until then, but the part that makes me question his innocence on any level is that when I saw him being dragged away…his eyes were open and there was blood on his temple. If he was alive and unconscious, why were his eyes open? If he was knocked out, why was there no head injury the blood could have come from?"

"You make an excellent point," Owen agreed. "If he was a cooperating party, then perhaps your former roommate will know since she helped to set up the date. And we can't forget that he added you as a beneficiary to his life insurance policy."

Somehow she kept trying to block that part. "You're right. There's really no way he wasn't part of this well before Saturday night." Leah exhaled a frustrated breath. "It's ridiculous, I know, but I don't want to not be angry with *her*. A part of me wants to believe she would never do this. I mean, I've known her for three years. We lived together. I just can't see her doing this. Yet it appears to be the only logical explanation."

Owen turned to her. "Sometimes there is no logic to be found. Particularly if the action involved a strong emotion, like jealousy or revenge…maybe anger."

Another thought occurred to Leah. "Is it possible that Raymond figured out Isla wasn't really Isla? Maybe he was blackmailing her—forcing her to participate. That is motive, and it's oddly logical."

"I've considered that as well," Owen agreed. "Whatever drove her, whatever part she played, I believe it's imperative that we proceed with caution. If she feels cornered or that you represent a threat, your safety could be in jeopardy, and she certainly won't talk to us under those circumstances."

Leah recognized he was right. Whatever she thought she

knew about her roommate, all bets were off at this point. She couldn't trust her.

Alyssa Jones, aka Isla Morris, suddenly appeared behind the gate that led into the alley between two of the buildings. Leah's breath caught. She forced herself to raise her hand and wave.

"That's her," Leah said, though she imagined Owen was well aware.

Isla—Alyssa—stood so still, her coal-black hair hanging around her shoulders, her pale skin a sharp contrast to the black tee and slacks. Leah felt at once thankful she was alive and furious that she was.

"Remember what I said," he warned. "Caution is essential."

Leah nodded as she reached for her door.

She and Owen emerged from the car simultaneously. Even from across the street, Leah noted the change in the other woman's demeanor. She hadn't expected Leah to have someone with her.

Still, she waited while they crossed the street. Leah had worried that she would take off. The fact that she stayed put sent Leah's pulse racing.

"Who's he?" Alyssa asked as Leah neared the gate.

"He's a private investigator I hired," Leah said, anger suddenly igniting inside her. "I didn't really have a choice, since you set me up the way you did."

Surprise or something on that order flitted across the other woman's face. "I didn't set you up. I didn't do anything but get dragged into a situation that had nothing to do with me."

Leah scoffed. "I'm the one who was dragged into the situation. The police suspected me of murder!" She shook her head, worked to tamp down her anger before she scared this…this person off. "He's Owen," she said with a jerk of her head toward the man beside her. "He's helping me." She glanced up at him. "He's a friend."

Alyssa scrutinized him through a narrowed gaze. "Are you sure you can trust him?"

Leah laughed. "You're asking me about trust? Seriously? We're friends for three years. Roommates! And the whole time, you were lying. Your name isn't even Isla Morris. You stole a dead woman's identity."

Alyssa looked away then. "We were friends, Isla and I." She met Leah's gaze. "I was part of the janitorial team at the university. I was assigned to the library and the student center. But it was in the library where Isla spent a lot of time studying, and that's where we met. I helped her study sometimes. Eventually, I came to the apartment and helped as well. We were…" She met Leah's gaze again. "We were more than friends."

"Did you kill her too?" Leah demanded, ignoring the softer feelings that attempted to emerge.

"No." Alyssa's eyes were bright with emotion. "I loved her. But she had serious issues. Maybe her mother was in denial, but I believe Isla was bipolar. Rather than get the help she needed, she and her mother pretended the problem wasn't real. She wanted Isla to stay focused on school—to ignore her needs. Those last few months, Isla was miserable. She didn't want her life anymore. I tried to help, but it wasn't enough. I found her at the lake house. She had taken a whole bottle of her mother's sleeping pills. The next thing I knew, her mother had cremated her and gone into solitude."

"Did you kill her mother?" Leah demanded.

Alyssa rolled her eyes. "No. She took the same way out her daughter did. OD'd on her own medicine."

"So you, Alyssa Jones, put her mother in the freezer and stole the daughter's life."

She shook her head. "Maybe that was part of it, but mostly I wanted to *finish* her life. I wanted to keep her alive, and the only way to do that was to become her and to become the good person she was. Isla kept to herself —because of the disease, I think—so I made new friends for both of us, and I helped you because it was something Isla would have done." She shrugged. "Her mother never closed up her apartment or anything. Never ended her enrollment at the university. As far as I know, she never even notified anyone. They had no other close family other than that scumbag brother. It was just the two of them. There had to be a reason that happened."

Leah turned away, couldn't bear to look at her.

"How did you become acquainted with Raymond Douglas?" Owen asked, speaking for the first time.

Alyssa glared at Owen as if he were her enemy. Leah wanted to be furious with her. To hate her. But how could she, after hearing that story? Then again, maybe this woman was a master manipulator. A liar. A cheat. How could Leah believe anything she said?

Alyssa shrugged. "He was freshly divorced and hanging out at the same clubs as me and my friends. He was quite wealthy, had the right personality. I was drawn to him."

"You were drawn to him, or to his money?" Leah snapped. Those flashes of anger just wouldn't be tamped down.

Her former roommate looked at her, pain in her expression. "I guess I was his type and he was mine. He flirted and I flirted back. But—" she looked at Leah as she told her the rest "—the chemistry fizzled quickly. We saw each other from time to time to blow off steam. But that was it."

She drew in a deep breath. "Until a few weeks ago. He said he needed to disappear. He wouldn't say why. But he had a plan, he just needed a witness to…" Another big breath. "To his murder. Then he would disappear and never be bothered again. He gave me five thousand dollars. I needed the money. The funds Isla left in her account were running out, and I was getting desperate. I was never able to access the mother's money."

"He wanted a reliable witness," Owen said, "to his fake murder. Did he ask for Leah by name?"

Alyssa looked away a long moment, then nodded. "He'd looked into the backgrounds of my closest friends, and he thought the problem Leah had that summer after her high school graduation would be useful. It would lend credibility to what he needed the police to believe."

Leah's breath caught. "You told him?" She had shared her deepest secrets with this woman. How could she? Right. Of course. She did whatever was most beneficial to her.

"No," she argued, her fingers curling around the slats of the gate as if they were prison bars, "he found out about it through the background search. I never said a word."

"Doesn't matter," Leah argued. "You still betrayed me." Her dark eyes shone with emotion. "I did. I'm sorry."

"What went wrong?" Owen asked.

Alyssa blinked, turned her attention to him. "He wanted to stay at the lake house for a couple of days after his fake murder, so I said okay. It wasn't like I needed the place."

"You told the woman pretending to be your mother that you and I went there, but we didn't. Ever."

She looked away. "At first I couldn't face you. That's why I didn't come home on Sunday. I went to the lake house with the intention of telling Raymond that I had to tell you the truth. When I found the blood and the handcuffs, I panicked. I told the woman I hired to play the role of Isla's mother what to say and warned her that she should likely disappear too."

Leah wanted to shake her. "Thanks a lot."

"I knew you'd be okay, Leah," she said, her words urgent. "I never meant for you to get into trouble. I didn't know this was really going down. It was supposed to be insurance fraud, not murder."

If she expected forgiveness, she could forget it.

"Who killed him?" Owen demanded, his tone leaving no room for argument.

"That's the thing, I have no idea. Raymond planned this whole thing himself. I'm pretty sure he didn't tell anyone. He would have been damned stupid to do that. My best guess is that one of the other investors in his business figured out what he was up to and killed him. I really don't know. I just know he said he was in trouble."

"How would this investor know about his plan?" Owen asked. "Or where to find him?"

"I have no idea," she said.

"If you told anyone and caused all this," Leah warned, "you're an accessory to murder."

"No! I didn't. I didn't tell anyone. If you haven't figured it out by now, I'm really good at keeping secrets. Like I said, all I wanted was the five thousand. But then after he disappeared, I was too terrified to talk to anyone."

She shook her head. "But I knew I had to tell you," she said to Leah. "I couldn't have you believing I did this."

Leah met her gaze and lied. "I knew you didn't kill anyone."

Tears welled in her former roommate's eyes. "I'm really sorry this happened. I never meant for it to turn into this."

"What about Douglas's insurance policy?" Owen challenged. "Whose idea was it to put Leah as a beneficiary on his insurance policy?"

Alyssa made a face. "What insurance policy?"

"There is a ten-million-dollar life insurance policy on the man who hired you to help him fake his death," Owen explained. "Half to his ex-wife and half to Leah."

She looked at Leah. "What the hell, Leah?"

A blast of outrage that this supposed friend would dare accuse her roared through Leah. "That's what I've been asking myself all week. What the hell?"

"Are you prepared to turn yourself in to Detective Lambert?" Owen asked. "I'm sure he would be willing to offer some sort of deal for the information you have."

Alyssa drew back a little. "I'm not putting myself in the line of fire when it comes to a murder charge."

"Then help us prove you didn't do it," Owen suggested.

Leah felt like telling him they weren't going to bother, but that was her anger speaking. "He's with the Colby Agency. If there is anyone who can figure this out, he can. Let him help you."

Alyssa looked from Leah to Owen and back. "I didn't kill anyone. I don't know who did."

"The list of probable suspects is not that long," Owen told her. "You, the ex-wife or the investor you said he screwed over."

Leah wondered if Lambert had even looked at the ex-wife. The investor was a possible lead he might not have known about. But they knew now.

"What am I supposed to call you?" Leah asked before the other woman could comment on Owen's statement.

"Al," she said. "Alyssa Jones is my name, but my mom and the people who used to be my friends called me Al."

Leah nodded. "Did Raymond ever talk about his ex-wife?"

"He never said anything good, that's for sure," she said. "He complained that she was always having her lawyer go to a judge and demanding more child support and alimony. He wanted to be free of her in the worst way."

"Do you know her?" Owen asked. "I would think a person as intelligent as you would have looked into the situation before agreeing to the sort of deal you made with Douglas."

She shrugged. "I did a little checking up on her. Her family was poor. She met Raymond at a nightclub where she worked as a waitress. He always said that once she got her claws into his money, she wasn't letting go. He realized as soon as they had their first kid that he was never getting away from her. She proclaimed right from the beginning that she was never going to be poor again. He says he stuck it out as long as he could for the kids' sakes."

Leah wanted to throw up. What a jerk he'd been. She would never have accepted a date with him if she had known what sort of person he was. "You couldn't have told me this."

Alyssa had no answer, just stared at the ground.

"Did he ever say anything about how far she would go to keep his money?" Owen asked.

The woman shrugged. "All he said was, she would never let go as long as he was alive."

"We need to set up a meeting with Detective Lambert," Owen said. "Will you cooperate?"

Alyssa backed up a step. "I don't think I can do that." She glanced at Leah. "I'm sorry, but this has gone too far. I'm out."

"Please," Leah urged, "your life could be in danger."

Maybe she would cooperate if she feared for herself. She certainly cared for no one else. "Someone has been watching me."

"The black sedan," Al suggested.

"Yes." Leah grabbed the bars of the gate. "Do you know who it is?"

She shook her head. "That same car was watching me even before Saturday. I mentioned it to Raymond, and he said it was probably just some guy who had a thing for me, but I knew he was wrong."

"Let us help you," Owen urged.

"I can't." She took off running toward the other end of the alley.

Owen tried to open the gate, but it was locked. "Let's go. We can cut her off on the next block."

They ran to the car and climbed in. He shot out of the parking lot.

When he pulled out his cell phone, she put her hand on his. "Don't call Lambert."

He arrowed her a look. "You sure about that? We can't be certain she was telling the whole truth."

"I know. But we can't be certain she isn't either."

He left the phone on the console and focused on driving. They drove around several blocks but never spotted Alyssa. She was gone.

Leah hoped she stayed safe. As angry as she was at her former roommate for what she had done, she didn't want her to die too.

She just hoped they could both survive this…thing that was still somehow continuing even though Raymond was dead.

Then Alyssa could go to prison and suffer the consequences of her actions.

Leah felt like a seesaw. Up and down… One minute she was up and wanted to believe Alyssa, the next she was down and didn't believe a word she said.

How would they ever find the truth?

Chapter Twelve

As long as the weather was good, Leah almost always walked from her apartment to the library. It was a good half-hour stroll, but she enjoyed it. Other times, she took the Blue Line. Walking was her favorite, though. Approaching the iconic brick building with its big old owls always gave her goose bumps. Inside was equally amazing, with ten floors of incredible visuals as well as what you came to a library for—books and research material.

When Leah was offered the position, she'd felt deeply honored. She worked every hour possible between school sessions, and just as many weekends and other odd hours when in session. The past week hadn't worked out so well, but at least she still had a job. She'd worried about the negative publicity related to the investigation.

She'd spent the first half of this evening's shift on the fifth floor, working in the Assistive Resources Center, one of her very favorite things to do when not browsing and working with the books on the seventh floor.

Now she had moved to the Maker Lab on the third floor

to do some cleanup after an Open Shop preview class introducing those interested to the array of equipment available, from 3D printers to laser cutters and sewing machines. Such a great opportunity for the community. There was so much offered at this library. Leah never tired of seeing what was happening on any of the floors.

Owen had followed her from floor to floor. He stayed in the background, found something to appear busy, but his attention was always on her. Each time their gazes collided, she shivered.

She tidied the stack of sign-up sheets. Most participants were quite good at cleaning up after themselves, putting away supplies and tossing in the trash what should go there. The Open Shop classes had been fuller than usual tonight. No registration was required for most of them, which allowed bringing a friend at the last minute or opportunities for just showing up when you hadn't been sure you could attend. It was all very relaxed and user-friendly.

Staying busy had helped Leah to put the encounter with Alyssa out of her head for a while. All the things she had said made sense on some level, and yet the idea of trusting her after what she had admittedly done was difficult, at best. The notion of never seeing her again or sharing aspects of their lives was harder than Leah had expected. There she went with the up-and-down thing again.

As promised, Owen hadn't called Detective Lambert about the meeting. They had talked, but he didn't once mention Alyssa. Instead, he asked the detective about Raymond's ex-wife and a potential disgruntled investor. Lambert had, of course, interviewed the ex-wife numerous times. She had an alibi for Saturday night and all day Sunday and Monday. She'd gone to her mother's on Sunday and, after hearing that Raymond was missing, had decided to stay. The children, a fifteen-year-old boy and thirteen-year-old girl, had been with her. The whole thing was horrifying for the children. Leah couldn't imagine anyone hurting a child. Why in the world would Raymond be so uncaring about his own? To have them believe their father had been murdered just to get away from their mother?

It was awful, just awful.

The ex-wife claimed to have no idea about the life insurance policy or any investor problems. Both belonged to Raymond and he didn't share information with her. She did recall that he had taken out the policy a decade ago. She had nothing to do with it. The fact that she was a beneficiary had come as no surprise, but the detail of another woman being on the list of beneficiaries had floored her, according to Lambert. He hadn't given Leah's name, but the news had mentioned her on Tuesday, so the ex knew who Leah was. Leah was immensely grateful she hadn't shown up at the apartment, or here at the library, looking for her.

Mrs. Ward, the personnel director, had assured Leah that she had answered no questions from reporters or anyone else about her. Leah was relieved. The idea that she had been here since two with no lookie-loos or snoopy reporters seemed to back up the director's claim. Security would have escorted them out, but Leah was very thankful it hadn't come to that.

She glanced across the room to where Owen had taken another call. He'd been making and fielding calls all evening. He'd been trying to catch the agent who'd set up the life insurance policy. He was also still digging into the black sedan they, luckily, had not seen today. It was as if the driver had seen all he needed to, and now he was just gone.

Leah picked up a stack of manuals and headed for the storeroom. Each lab shared a very generous-size storeroom with its neighbor. The space was like a Jack-and-Jill, with doors on each end, one to the room where she was just tidying up and another on the opposite end to the neighboring lab. She tucked the manuals onto the proper shelf. Since a few supplies were out of place, she returned them to their correct space. She scanned the room once more, then turned to go. The lights went out.

Leah froze.

There wasn't a timer on the lights… Someone had to have flipped the switch. The silence had her trying to slow her heart's pounding, for fear whoever had turned off the lights would hear it.

Then she ran for the door.

A hard body slammed into her, trapping her against the wall next to the door. She tried to scream, but a gloved hand covered her mouth. He—had to be a man, tall, strong—dragged her backward…across the room and then through the other door into the neighboring lab. She blinked against the light.

He shoved her to the floor. Slammed her head against the hard tile. She tried to scream again, but the next bash of her head made the room spin and her vision darken.

Something wet hit her—her face, her arms—the smell vaguely familiar. Some distant, still-working brain cell had her wishing she could move, but she was fading into nothingness. The sound of Owen's voice calling her name followed her into that black place.

Chicago Hospital
Lawrence Avenue, 11:30 p.m.

SHE HAD A CONCUSSION.

Owen stood at her bedside, his forearms braced on the bed rail. His eyes closed against the images that haunted him each time he thought of what he'd found in the room right next door to where he'd been standing…on the damn phone.

Lambert had called him with the information Owen had asked for. He should have followed Leah into that storeroom while listening to the detective. But he'd been frustrated that Lambert had nothing new on the car, and he'd pushed Owen about where he and Leah had spent their morning. He wasn't buying the excuse that they were just driving around to help Leah relax. She was supposed to be, according to Lambert, searching for her former roommate in places they had frequented—like the club last night.

It wasn't until he'd heard a thumping sound that Owen realized Leah was still in the storeroom. He raced into the storeroom, found it dark but saw the light under the door in the next room. He rushed toward it, burst through the door just in time to see a man wearing a ski mask and holding a lighter. Three things hit him simultaneously: Leah was on the floor. There was a smell…something he had smelled before. And the lighter the masked man held was not the disposable kind but the old-fashioned type that kept its flame once you lit it until you closed the lid to extinguish it.

He charged the guy. The bastard ran, but not before throwing the lighter on the floor.

The instant that lighter flew through the air, Owen's brain identified the odor he'd smelled when he came into the room.

Gasoline…charcoal lighter fluid…something on that order.

Owen dove for Leah. He rolled her as far away from where the lighter hit the floor as possible. Flames lit, searing across the tile floor, then, out of fuel, dying as quickly as they'd started. The fire alarm blared to life.

Leah had moaned and Owen's heart had surged into his throat. He'd used the sleeve of his shirt to wipe the lighter fluid from her face. "Hey, Leah, can you hear me?" he'd asked.

When she hadn't answered, he'd gotten onto his knees and checked her body for injury. No blood. But then his fingers had traced the back of her head, and he felt the lumps there…and the dampness.

He'd sworn repeatedly as he felt for his phone. Where the hell was it? Had he dropped it? He glanced around the room, spotted it.

Scrambling for the phone, he had then recognized the call to Lambert was still connected.

"What's happening?" the detective demanded.

"I need an ambulance. Now!" Owen had roared. "And your people on-site should be watching for a man wearing a ski mask coming out of the library."

Half an hour later, they were in the ER.

The medical staff had removed Leah's clothes, which had all been doused with lighter fluid, and they'd cleaned her exposed skin. There was some redness, but so far nothing worse. The concussion was a grade 2. The doctor had insisted on keeping her in the hospital overnight even though she'd seemed fine by the time the ambulance arrived at the library. She'd regained consciousness within a minute or so of him finding her, and she'd seemed okay other than being a little dazed and unsteady on her feet.

A few minutes ago, she'd drifted off to sleep. Owen hadn't left her side since he'd found her, other than the time it took for the scan of her brain. And then he'd paced the corridor right outside the room. He just kept thinking of what could have happened if he had not rushed into that room when he did.

A tap on the door preceded Detective Lambert's entrance. He'd been at the hospital when they arrived. As soon as he was satisfied that Leah was okay, he'd returned to the library to oversee the activities there.

"She's asleep," Owen warned, meeting him near the door so as not to disturb Leah. The doctor had said she could sleep as long as she was watched carefully and roused occasionally.

The older man nodded. "No one we interviewed saw a man wearing a ski mask. We're viewing the security video, but we've found nothing on that footage so far."

"He was wearing black," Owen said. "I think the shirt was a button-up, not a tee or sweatshirt. Nothing so casual."

"A lot of people in Chicago wear black, apparently."

If the detective hadn't looked so exhausted, Owen might have snapped at his response, but he cut the man some slack. "Yeah, he probably pulled the ski mask off as soon as he exited the room."

"Strangely enough, the library doesn't have video surveillance on all floors. Just on the main floor and the tenth."

Owen heaved a weary sigh. "Which means we aren't likely to find anything. By the time he got to the first floor, he could have been wearing a different shirt and trousers, for that matter."

"That's exactly what he did," Lambert confirmed. "We found a black shirt and black trousers in a trash bin on the second floor. We've sent both to the lab for analysis."

Which would only help if the guy was in some database. Great.

"This is feeling more and more like a particularly well thought out plan from the beginning." Owen bit his tongue to prevent himself from revealing the details Alyssa had provided that morning.

"My money is on the roommate," Lambert said. "She still hasn't surfaced. She's either dead or is in on it. Maybe both."

"Leah doesn't believe she would kill anyone, but we're both confident she was in on it from the beginning."

"She has had trouble staying within the law off and on for the better part of her life," Lambert explained. "I've gotten access to more records, and it seems her legal issues started early with petty stuff. A woman who would assume someone else's life for three-plus years…" He shrugged. "I don't know. She might be capable of anything." He leaned closer as if to ensure Leah didn't hear this part, although she was asleep. "On the other hand, her GPA is at the top of her class. Keep in mind that she didn't do premed. She took up Isla's life in the first year of medical school. Comments in her file suggest she's some sort of genius. Anyway, there is no doubt in my mind she could pull off this whole scheme. Most of her adult life has been one scheme or the other."

Owen couldn't deny that Lambert had a valid point. The agency had discovered the same about Alyssa Jones. "But we can't be certain about anything. What about the ex-wife? She's the other beneficiary on the insurance policy. Or the investors who may lose money in all this?"

Lambert turned his hands up. "No issues with any investors that we've found so far, and the ex-wife has a firm alibi. Granted, she could have hired someone, but we haven't found the first indication that's the case. She hasn't dated in ages. According to her friends and neighbors, she is completely focused on the kids since Douglas isn't around much."

"Still," Owen argued, "she has the most to gain."

"About the same as Leah, based on the policy," Lambert pointed out.

Another thought occurred to Owen. After the brief meeting with Alyssa, it made the most sense—if anything the woman said was to be believed. "Maybe it is the ex-wife," he suggested. "Maybe she killed him—or hired someone to kill him —for the insurance payoff. And maybe that's why someone has been following Leah and has now officially attempted to kill her."

Realization dawned in the detective's expression. "Because if there are two beneficiaries and one is dead or is convicted in the murder of the insured, the other beneficiary would in all likelihood end up with all the proceeds."

"Leah has already been considered a suspect. It doesn't matter that she was cleared, there have been no other suspects or arrests. The ex-wife would have some legal standing, I imagine, to use that as leverage." Owen considered another thought. "Even if she didn't get the whole payout, maybe it was worth half the policy value to have a scapegoat. Particularly if the goal was to get him out of her life and the lives of her children."

That last part he'd taken from Alyssa's insistence that Douglas wanted his wife out of his life. The feeling was likely mutual.

"I see where you're going. And if the other beneficiary is dead—" Lambert looked to the hospital bed and Leah lying there "—all the better. She gets ten mil. Either way, the ex can walk away clean with five mil. The kids would get anything else he had left."

A sinking feeling tugged at Owen's chest. "Even if the full amount of money doesn't come for years because of the legal issues, it's like money in a trust for the kids. While the ex enjoys the five mil she will get any day now."

"I'll interview her again tomorrow." Lambert pursed his lips for a moment. "If I can get a judge to sign off on it,

I'll try for a search warrant of her home. I'll let you know how it goes. Keep me posted on how she's doing." He nodded toward Leah.

Owen assured him he would.

Lambert hesitated before walking out the door. "I've got a uniform outside the door. I'll have another one at her apartment."

Owen nodded. "Thanks."

The detective hesitated once more. "You know, I did finally get Douglas's cell phone records. There were some interesting text exchanges between him and someone using a burner phone. You haven't noticed one of those lying around, have you?"

"Maybe you should check the ex-wife's phone records," Owen suggested, rather than give him a direct answer.

The older man nodded. "On it already."

For a moment after the detective left, Owen stood by the door, staring at Leah in that hospital bed. She looked so pale, so fragile. The IV tube running down to her left arm made his gut clench. He crossed the room, took his place next to her bedside.

He wondered how he could have met her only a few days ago and already feel so close to her…so desperate to know her better, to spend more time with her. To protect her.

Her eyes fluttered open. She frowned, then dredged up a smile. "You look tired."

"Not so much," he lied. "Detective Lambert stopped by again."

"Did they find him?" The fear that lurked in her eyes twisted his insides into knots.

"They're still working on it." But he had a feeling they weren't going to find the guy who had attacked her in the library. Not unless he made one hell of a misstep they didn't know about yet.

"This is just completely out of control." She closed her eyes for a moment. "I do not see how all of this could have evolved from Raymond wanting to make his ex-wife think he was dead."

Owen had been mulling over that scenario as well. He was beating around another theory, but he wasn't sure he wanted to bring it up right now. Leah needed to rest.

"What?" she demanded, then grimaced as if she'd hurt her head by speaking so forcefully.

"You need to rest." The doctor had been clear on how important it was that she rest for a few days.

"Tell me what you know or what you're thinking. I will not rest until you do."

"Alyssa is apparently an expert at assuming identities. She's made up more than one in her life. Have you considered that her knowledge and experience may have been why Raymond asked her for help? If that's the case, then I'm thinking their relationship was something more than she has shared."

Leah appeared to consider the scenario. "It is a big risk, sharing that sort of self-incriminating plan with someone unless you really, really trust them."

"She said she didn't know about the blood or the life insurance policy. But what if she did? What if she killed him for real so she could claim the money?"

Leah's brow furrowed. "How would she claim any of the money?"

"By presenting herself as *you*."

"Except I was a murder suspect—my photo was on the news."

He shrugged. "Granted, that plan backfired, but I'm

guessing if it was her, there was a plan B. She's way too smart not to have a plan B."

Leah's expression suggested she was possibly buying into the scenario. "So she would need a way to get the money once it was paid out to me."

The fire in his gut had his instincts on point. This was a very plausible scenario. "I need you to think, Leah. Did you and Alyssa ever discuss your financial situation? Your bank account or savings? Anything along those lines?"

She nodded, her expression clouding with worry. "We talked about everything. She knows where I keep all my passwords, where I bank, how much money I have. Which is why we changed all those passwords," she reminded him.

"Did you ever add her to one of your accounts? You would have to go into the bank, the two of you, to do that."

Leah shook her head. "No. But I do my banking online. She could go on my account from my laptop and transfer money." She groaned. "Because even my new password is saved there."

"Then we can't be sure she isn't waiting around to do that," Owen suggested. "Think about it, she could have disappeared already. The woman pretending to be her mother is long gone. Why is Alyssa hanging around? Why does she care if you believe her? Or if you're still friends?"

Leah moistened her lips. "She wants that five million dollars. At this point, the only way to get it is for her to stay on my good side so I don't change anything that possibly gives her access to it."

"There are things we can do," Owen said gently. "Adding facial recognition to your laptop, for one."

Leah nodded. "Maybe I just need to start over in a new place."

Owen touched her cheek, noted the new bruise there. He

winced. "We'll find you a new place where you'll be safe, if that's what you want." Only this time he wasn't thinking of his friend who owned apartment buildings.

"I'll feel a lot safer—" she scooted over to her left a little, then patted the bed on her right side "—if you're next to me."

"I think I can do that." He lowered the side rail. "At least until a nurse comes in and tells me different."

He stretched out on the bed next to her. Kissed her forehead. "Close your eyes," he murmured. "Rest."

She closed her eyes and snuggled against him. He closed his and considered again how grateful he was that she was okay.

He'd let her down tonight, but that would never happen again.

Chapter Thirteen

The office was a small one. Nothing like Leah had expected, given the building where it was located and the many types of insurance sold. A soaring high-rise made of steel, glass and concrete. The office was on the tenth floor. She read a few of the Google reviews, and there was nothing bad mentioned about the owner or the business, only the surprisingly small office and the idea that it was basically a one-man operation. Owen's research had discovered that the company was actually part of a larger one that had small offices all over the country.

On the elevator ride up to the proper floor, Owen started in again. "You really should be resting in bed or on the sofa watching television."

"You've called this guy three times, and he hasn't called back. It's time for a face-to-face. You said so yourself."

He shot her a sidelong glance. "That was before someone gave you a concussion and tried to set you on fire."

There was that. "We're here." The elevator bumped to a stop, and the doors opened. "We might as well do this."

"Just take it easy," he urged as he waited for her to step into the corridor.

She headed for the office, and Owen followed. He opened the door, and they entered the tiny lobby. There were four chairs, a table with a couple of magazines and a sliding window behind which a receptionist likely sat. But not at the moment. Leah's shoulders sagged. If the man wasn't here, she was going to scream—except that would make her head hurt worse.

Though she would never admit it, she felt exhausted. Irritable. Her head ached. It was all to be expected, but that didn't make functioning any easier. "No one's here," she muttered.

Owen shrugged. "Maybe. We'll just see." He took the three steps across the dinky room and opened the only other door besides the entrance. On the other side was a narrow hall lined with three more doors. The first on the right was open, and it led to the desk behind the sliding window. The one across the hall was open as well and showed off a minuscule powder room.

At the end of the short hallway was the third. Owen glanced at her, held up a hand to knock but then heard a male voice on the other side. Had to be Hoyt Bechel, the owner; otherwise, someone else was using his office.

As Owen prepared to knock again, the man on the other side told someone he would be hearing from him soon and then said goodbye.

When the door didn't open with an exiting client, Owen knocked.

They waited, heard the man on the other side shuffling around his desk. The door opened and a frazzled-looking middle-aged fellow glared at them through his glasses.

"Can I help you?"

"Mr. Bechel?" Owen asked.

"That's me." He smoothed back the strands of hair that were sticking up as if he'd run his hand through repeatedly.

"I'm Owen Walker. This is Leah Gerard. We're here about the Douglas life insurance policy," he explained. "I've left you several voicemails."

"Ah, yes." He nodded, the movement exaggerated. "Sorry, it's been really busy."

"May we come in?" Leah asked when he made no offer.

"Ah, sure, sure." He backed up, rounded his desk and smiled in welcome. "Come on in and have a seat."

Leah sat down, but Owen remained standing. He braced his hands on the back of the other chair.

"So, how can I help you?" He looked from Leah to Owen and back. "You're one of the beneficiaries," he said to Leah.

"Yes."

"I," Owen interjected, "would like to know how my fiancée ended up being added to this man's insurance policy."

Leah stared at him. His statement startled her, but she recovered quickly. A great cover for the question.

Bechel's eyebrows shot up. "Well, now, I can't tell you the reason, because I have no idea. I met Mr. Douglas a few times. He took out the policy ten years ago. Right here in the office. But when he changed the beneficiaries, he did that online. He ordered a form for updating. It was mailed to his address of record. He filled it out, signed it and sent it back."

"Was it notarized?" Owen asked.

Bechel shook his head slowly, hesitantly. "We don't require that." He frowned. "If there is some question about whether this was an authorized update by the policy owner, then we'll have to look into it."

"But anyone could have requested the forms as long as they had access to his account," Owen argued.

"Well, I suppose so. But we compared the signatures to the original application. We always do that, and it looked proper. My secretary called to confirm. Those are our safeguards." He turned to Leah then. "I'm sure you're aware there won't be a payout until the homicide investigation is complete. But once all is sorted out, we'll get the money to you."

She held up her hands. "I understand. I'm just trying to figure out how this happened."

"You'll have to overlook my surprise. We rarely have a beneficiary come in with a question like that. Generally, they're very happy to be receiving money."

The man had no idea. "I understand there are two beneficiaries," Leah said. "What happens if one of them dies before the payout? What happens to the money?"

His gaze narrowed. "Well, there are two beneficiaries, and the benefits are fifty-fifty, as specified by the policy owner. If one of the beneficiaries passes away before distribution, the full amount of the policy payout will go to the remaining beneficiary." He held up his hands in surrender fashion. "I'm a little uncomfortable discussing this aspect of the benefits with you. Perhaps we should call Detective Lambert and make him aware of your concerns."

"Detective Lambert is well aware of our concerns," Owen said. "He was at the scene last night when someone made an attempt on Leah's life."

Bechel drew back. "Oh my. This has been a terrible, terrible situation. But I will leave it to the authorities to handle whatever is going on. Please take care of yourself, Ms. Gerard. Rest assured that the underwriters at Patriot Insurance are safeguarding the benefits Mr. Douglas purchased."

Leah stood, her legs a little wobbly. She really did need to rest, but how could she? Someone had tried to kill her, and that someone was still out there!

They were out of the office and back in the elevator, headed down, before she worked up the nerve to say, "I was surprised to hear you'd proposed." She laughed, tapped her temple. "I guess I lost that memory with this concussion."

Owen chuckled. "I thought about it all night while you were lying in that hospital bed."

"You were in that bed with me," she teased.

"This is true." He grinned.

"So you were busy thinking while I was sleeping." Her own grin tugged at her lips.

"It was either that or stare at you, and that may have caused issues."

Leah nodded. "I see."

The elevator stopped and the doors opened.

Owen stepped out first, had a look around and then put her arm in his. "Can I take you back to the apartment now?"

"Not until we see the ex-wife." Leah knew that had been on his to-do list. They needed to stick to the investigation. "I'm fine, really." She was tired, yes. But she could do this. It couldn't wait.

He scanned the sidewalk and street before they exited the building. Once he was satisfied, they began the walk to the car. "Are you certain you're feeling all right? Really."

"Really, I am. I'm a little tired, but that's normal with a concussion like this. As long as I don't try to run a marathon or get into a fight, I think I'm good."

He shook his head. "You are stubborn."

She'd gotten it from her daddy. "I'll rest tonight, I promise."

"You absolutely will," he vowed.

Somehow she had a feeling she was going to really enjoy tonight.

Louise Douglas Residence
Wolcott Avenue, 1:00 p.m.

THE DOUGLAS HOME was a multi-million-dollar residence ensconced comfortably between two other lovely high-end homes. According to Owen's research, Mrs. Douglas got the house and a car in the divorce settlement—as well as a very hefty monthly child support and alimony payment.

City records showed a mortgage on the house. With her ex-husband dead, those big monthly payments would likely be gone as soon as his remaining assets were dissolved or passed on according to his will. The house would be paid off.

Since Mrs. Douglas was a stay-at-home mother, any issues with the estate payout or the insurance proceeds was likely not good. She would need every dime of the five million, plus whatever else there was to inherit in order to maintain her current lifestyle.

A huge motive for murder.

Her ex-husband's and Leah's.

"What if she won't talk to us?" Leah's nerves were jittery.

"Curiosity will force her to talk to us." Owen turned to her. "You ready?"

She exhaled a big breath. "Guess so." She had insisted on doing this, after all.

Owen exited the car and was at her side of the vehicle before she could get the door open and climb out. That was the thing about this concussion. She felt like she was moving in slow motion. Losing time was another thing she'd noticed. Just when she thought five seconds had passed, she realized it was a minute or more.

They walked up the front steps, and Owen rang the bell. The brick-and-limestone house looked very much like a brownstone but was likely only a few years old. It was a style Leah loved, but owning one was about as likely as her winning the lottery.

The door opened, and the woman Leah had seen in photos on Raymond's social media accounts stood before them. Tall, slim, blonde, green eyes and dressed to the nines, as they say. The woman was gorgeous.

"You." She glared at Leah. "How dare you come to my home."

Owen moved closer to Leah as if anticipating throwing himself in front of her. "Mrs. Douglas, we're here to talk about inconsistencies in the events leading up to Raymond's murder. It would be very helpful if you could give us a few minutes of your time."

The fury in her expression made Leah certain she would say no, but then she backed up a step. "Fine. But unless you have something relevant to say, I'm not interested."

Leah relaxed. She tried to see the situation from this woman's perspective. Her ex-husband had been murdered—the father of her children. The source of her income. It could not be easy.

Then again, she was the one with the most to gain from his murder.

For that matter, she may have hired someone to come after Leah. After all, ten million was way better than five.

The entry hall flowed straight to the back of the house, where a large, open room served as a living, dining and kitchen space. It was beautiful, perfect for family living. Whoever designed the home had done a great job.

"Sit if you like," Louise Douglas said as she dropped onto the sofa.

"Let me start," Leah said to Owen. He gave her a nod, and she turned to the ex-wife. "I barely knew Raymond. I met him two weeks ago, just briefly. Then he called and asked me out. I was to meet him at the restaurant Saturday night. That, of course, didn't happen." Leah swallowed, her throat dry. She drew in a breath and went on. "I have no idea why he added me as a beneficiary to his insurance policy. It was totally out of left field and happened before I even knew him."

Louise stared at her for a moment before bursting into laughter. When she'd regained control of herself once more, she swiped at her eyes. "You, that Isla, your roommate, spent endless weekends at that lake house with Raymond. Don't even pretend you didn't know him. Please."

Leah looked at Owen. "I wish I could prove this to you, but I can't. Since we'd barely met, I have nothing to show you or to use as proof. I can only say that I am as stunned as you. In fact..." She probably should have run this part past Owen, but she'd only just thought of it. "I don't want the money. I'll gladly sign whatever necessary to ensure that it all goes to you."

Her gaze narrowed again. "I don't believe you."

"I will." Leah glanced at Owen. He gave no indication that she should stop with this line of discussion. "I can tell Mr. Bechel at the insurance company. I'll tell Detective Lambert. Sign whatever I need to sign."

"I'll have my attorney contact you." Her face warned that she wasn't completely convinced but was willing to see if it worked out.

"Someone," Owen said, "made an attempt on Leah's life last night."

The woman's heavily manicured eyebrows shot upward. "Why bring that up to me?" She glanced at Leah. "You know the saying, 'Live by the sword, die by the sword'? You can't go around sleeping with other women's husbands without finding trouble."

"First," Leah said, angry now, "I wasn't sleeping with anyone. Second, you and Raymond have been divorced for three years."

"I suppose you know the exact date the divorce was final."

"No. But it was part of the research we've done since the murder. I have a right to look into who might be involved in trying to kill me."

Louise smiled, a vicious expression. "You should probably talk to that roommate of yours. According to my research, she's the ruthless one. I suspect this whole scheme was her idea. It's just the sort of thing she would do to get ahead. Tell me, were the two of you going to split the five million?"

"Leah has already been cleared of any suspicion in Raymond's murder," Owen said. "Your alibi, on the other hand, hinges on your mother's testimony and that of your children."

Fury contorted her face. "Do you think my children would lie for me if I was MIA when their father was murdered? Please."

"I have no idea," Owen said flatly. "Would they?"

She shot to her feet. "I think it's time for you to go. As I told Detective Lambert, if you or the police have anything else to say to me or to ask of me, you can contact my attorney."

Owen stood. Leah did the same. The ex-wife led the way back to the front door. Leah's head was spinning a little.

She tried to think of what else she should say, but she really knew nothing relevant to this woman.

At the door, Owen hesitated, one hand on Leah's back, causing her to hesitate as well.

"Are you familiar with a company called After Dark?" he asked. "It's one of your former husband's investments. It appears to be an exclusive catering service."

"I recall some mention of it," she said, "but I'm not really familiar with any of his investments. What of it?"

"There's a black sedan that's been watching Leah. Following us at times. It's leased to that company."

"Knowing Raymond, he failed to follow through with whatever he owed the owner or other investors. Who knows which employee of his or of the business may be using the car?" She sent a look toward Leah. "Perhaps someone who isn't pleased that their boss or investing partner was murdered and who hopes to find the truth."

"Detective Lambert will be contacting you about the car," Owen warned. "Perhaps you'll be able to provide him with more information."

"I'm certain my attorney can answer the detective's questions."

She closed the door behind them.

Leah and Owen didn't speak until they were in the car, driving away.

"She made no bones about showing dislike for her ex-husband," Leah pointed out.

Owen glanced at her. "I'm not sure that *dislike* is a strong enough word."

"All kinds of motive there," Leah said, feeling very tired now.

"She didn't show any surprise when I mentioned the

car. She could have someone watching you. But the real question is, did she hire that someone to try and hurt you?"

"What about a boyfriend? She and Raymond have been divorced for three years. Could she have a secret boyfriend working with her?"

"She insisted to Lambert she wasn't dating and there was no one in her life. My research specialist found nothing on her social media accounts or any neighbors who mentioned seeing a frequent male visitor. No black sedan hanging around."

"Maybe she was still in love with Raymond." Didn't seem likely, but who knew?

"Or maybe she just doesn't want the children to know she has a social life. She might be concerned they would tell their father, and that would somehow be a problem for her."

"Possibly," Leah agreed. "She apparently took him back to court a number of times for more money."

"Maybe the money is more important to her than a social life."

"I can see that," Leah agreed.

Louise Douglas was angry and resentful of her husband, but did that mean she wanted to have him killed? Would she have gone that far? Would she have tried to have Leah killed for the other five million? She had seemed startled when Leah offered to turn it over to her.

The woman had suggested Alyssa was at the bottom of all this, but Leah wasn't convinced. Maybe because she didn't want to believe it.

She thought of the way that masked man had beaten her head against the floor and tried to set her on fire.

Would the woman she had believed to be her best friend—like a sister—have hired someone to do such a thing?

No… Leah didn't want to believe that.

But could she really be certain? Of anything or anyone in all this?

She turned to the man driving… She was certain of him. And that was almost worth having to go through this nightmare.

"I think I need to take that rest now."

He glanced at her, concern in his eyes. "Heading that way, then."

Leah relaxed in the seat and closed her eyes. She stopped thinking about all the horrors of the past six days and let her mind wander to those kisses they had shared. And the feel of his strong body next to her last night.

She couldn't imagine a better way to take her mind off all this than doing a little more of exactly that sort of therapy.

Chapter Fourteen

Saturday, August 16
Gerard Apartment
Chestnut Street, 7:00 a.m.

Her cell phone vibrating across the bedside tabletop woke Leah.

She was alone in the bed.

The distant scent of fresh-brewed coffee told her why. Owen was up, had probably been up for a while, making coffee and doing the job of keeping her safe.

She smiled. She'd really enjoyed the gentle way he'd made her feel all sorts of things last night. Safe. Warm. And utterly fulfilled. She couldn't think of any way she would rather spend her nights.

Her smile fell. But what would she do when this was over? Would he go back to his life and forget about her? She'd wanted to ask. While snug in his arms last night, the question had pounded in her brain. Then she'd decided that she would rather just not think about it until she had no choice. Enjoying the moment and the time they had together was more important.

Well, and finding the answers to who had tried to frame her up for murder—and tried to set her on fire, to boot.

Her phone started its insistent vibrating again.

It was probably her boss at the library, letting her know she was fired. She couldn't blame her if she did. She'd brought serious trouble to the library doors.

Her life was basically all trouble right now…except for Owen.

She checked the screen—unknown number—then cleared her throat and tapped the accept button. "Hello?"

Ignoring any call was out of the question right now.

"Leah."

"Isl—Alyssa." She frowned at the sound of her former roommate's breathing—too rapid, as if she'd been running. "Are you okay? Why are you calling?"

"I'm at the lake house," she whispered. "Someone's here… I need your help. Please."

Leah scrambled out from beneath the covers. The room spun with the sudden movement. "I'll get there as fast as I can. Is there a place you can hide? In the woods? Somewhere?"

She staggered to her closet. Grabbed a pair of jeans from the closet, then a tee. No time for a bra.

"I think so. Hurry, Leah."

The call ended. Leah threw the phone down and quickly dressed. "Owen!" She stuffed her feet into a pair of slides and rushed out of her room.

Owen was headed to her door.

"We have to go. Alyssa is at the lake house and someone's there. She's afraid and hiding."

He nodded. "Let's go."

Leah had started to panic by the time they were in the

car. The idea that it would take them at least fifty minutes to get to the lake house had her nerves tattered.

"The police would get there more quickly," Owen said, reading her mind.

Leah hated the idea of feeling as if she had given up her friend to the police. No, Alyssa—Isla, whatever she called herself—was not really her friend. Leah should know that by now.

"You're right. Should we call Detective Lambert?"

"I'll call him," he said, understanding her hesitancy.

At the next traffic signal, he made the call. When he'd hung up, he glanced at Leah. "Someone will be there in the next ten minutes."

Leah breathed a sigh of relief. No matter what happened, that call was the right thing to do if her former friend's life was truly in danger.

"There's something else."

She turned to him, her heart nearly stalling with worry. "I'm listening."

"The black sedan leased to Douglas's company that has been following you," he said.

"The one with the driver who could be the same person who tried to set me on fire?"

"Considering what they found in the car," Owen said, "I would say so."

"Did they catch him?" She mentally crossed her fingers. Maybe he could provide some answers about who hired him or who else was involved.

"They found the car. He was inside. Dead."

Her hopes sank. "Who was he?"

"They're trying to run that down right now. There was no ID on him. His wallet was missing. The registration in the glove box shows After Dark."

"How do we know he was the one in the library?"

She wasn't sure she would ever feel completely safe again until he was found.

"His prints. He wasn't in the system until the incident at the library, and since he didn't wear gloves, his prints were on the container of lighter fluid and on the lighter. They matched the ones they took from the dead man. Those same prints were all over the car."

Having anyone be murdered was not something she would ever want…but the idea that she no longer had to worry about that threat was a relief.

But what about who hired him?

Morris Lake House
Fox Lake, 8:15 a.m.

THREE POLICE CRUISERS were in the driveway. Owen parked behind them. One uniform waited at the house, and five others were combing the woods and knocking on neighbors' doors.

Detective Lambert was there too. Leah spotted him getting out of his car.

"I think I'll stay in the car, if that's okay." She didn't want to answer the questions he would have. She didn't want to see her former roommate's body if they'd found it. Leah just needed to stay back for a bit.

Owen glanced toward the back entrance of the house and the officer standing there with Lambert. "I'll leave the car running for the air-conditioning but lock the doors when I get out."

She nodded. "Sure."

Her stomach was tied in knots. This just kept going and going, and she was so, so tired of it all. She released her seat belt and closed her eyes. It was probably the concussion making her feel so weary and irritable. She'd forgotten all about that last night, but this morning had brought the whole nightmare back.

A rap on the glass of the driver's-side door made her eyes snap open. She turned, expecting to see Owen at the door already—not Owen.

Alyssa stared at her through the window, eyes wide. She tugged at the door handle. "Please," she murmured.

Without thinking, Leah hit the unlock button. A glance forward showed Owen and Lambert looking at something on the uniformed officer's cell phone.

Alyssa dropped into the driver's seat, hunkering down as if she feared being seen. "Thank God you came."

Leah sat up straighter. "What's going on?" She looked forward. "I should get Owen. Everyone's looking for you."

"No!" She grabbed Leah's arm. "Please, just listen to me first."

Leah relaxed a tiny fraction. "All right, but I need to know what's really going on. Right now."

Alyssa glanced forward. "If they see me…" Rather than finish the statement, she shoved the gear shift into reverse and barreled out of the driveway.

Leah reached for her door.

"Don't."

She glanced at the woman behind the wheel. There was a gun in her hand, and it was pointed at Leah.

She spun onto the road. "Just relax," she ordered, struggling to control the car with her one free hand.

The beeping sound warned them that the car's fob was with Owen. How far would the vehicle go without it? The warning signal for the fact that neither she nor the driver were wearing seat belts grew louder as well, creating a building staccato.

"What are you doing?" Leah demanded. "Stop the car now. Owen and I are trying to help you."

Her former roommate laughed. "I swear." She whipped the car left, heading down a side road.

Leah slammed against the door, grimaced at the ache in her head, then righted herself.

Alyssa hit the brakes then, and Leah almost slammed into the dash but caught herself. Her aching head screamed in protest. "What the hell are you doing?"

The sound of the door locks disengaging had Leah reaching for her door again. Alyssa nudged her with the gun. "Do not even think about it."

The back door behind Leah opened, and someone got in. Leah turned to see and gaped.

Louise Douglas.

"What is going on?" Leah demanded of the woman behind the wheel.

Alyssa handed the gun to Louise. "Better buckle up."

She slammed on the accelerator. Leah braced herself, hands against the dash, rather than bothering with the seat belt.

"Did you send that man to kill me?" Leah demanded, turning to look over her shoulder at the woman now sitting in the middle of the back seat.

"I did." She grinned. "Too bad he failed. I never could tolerate a man who failed on the follow-through."

The two of them, Louise and Alyssa, laughed.

"Did you kill Raymond too?" Leah asked, fury pounding inside her. She should have been afraid, but instead she was furious. Her head didn't even hurt anymore, or maybe she just couldn't feel it.

"No," the driver said, "that was me." She grinned at Leah. "Don't feel bad for him. He deserved it. He was a womanizing pig."

Leah suddenly realized one thing with complete certainty: they weren't sharing all this information to build comradery...they intended to kill her.

"They'll know it was you." She looked from her former friend to the woman in the back seat.

"Not me," Louise said. She showed off her gloved hands, the gun in one of them. "I was never even here."

Alyssa slowed to look back at her accomplice. "What does that mean?"

Leah took the opportunity to open the door and launch herself out. The jump might gravely injure her, but at least she'd have a shot at surviving. If she stayed in the vehicle, she was certain to end up dead.

She hit the ground hard, rolled to a stop. Then she scrambled to her feet and started to run. Her head was spinning, but she didn't slow down.

Tires squealed as the car started to back up.

Leah had to find a way out of its path before—

Her thought was interrupted by the sound of a gunshot.

OWEN BRAKED TO a stop. "They turned off somewhere?"

Lambert looked over the seat to stare out the rear window. "Back that way, on the left."

Owen slammed into reverse, and the car rocketed backward. When they reached the turn off, he hit the brakes, then shoved into drive, lunging down the narrow road.

The first thing he saw was Leah diving for the ditch.

Then a bullet struck the windshield.

"Get down!" Lambert shouted.

Owen pushed into park and shot out of the car before it

stopped rocking. He skirted around to the back of the vehicle for cover. Lambert did the same.

"Cover me." Owen went for the ditch.

Lambert laid down fire to keep the shooter on the other side ducking.

The air didn't fill Owen's lungs again until Leah was within reach. "Keep down and move toward the car. I'll be behind you."

They headed for the car.

A round of shots hit the ground.

Owen was on top of Leah instantly. When Lambert started firing again, he moved, urging Leah forward. They scrambled up the bank and behind the car where Lambert was still spraying bullets toward the other vehicle.

Owen's stolen car suddenly barreled forward.

Lambert stopped firing.

Owen raised his head above the trunk and watched as his car faded into the distance. But it was the woman left in the middle of the road, clambering to her feet, that held his attention. She shouted at the fleeing vehicle.

Lambert stepped away from the vehicle, his weapon aimed at the woman. "Put your hands up!" he shouted.

"Stay down," Owen warned Leah. "Do not move unless you see my car coming from the other direction."

She nodded, her face pale.

Owen stood and followed Lambert.

"She kidnapped me!" Louise Douglas stood in the middle of the road, hands up in surrender. "She was going to kill us both."

Leah was suddenly next to Owen, swaying precariously. "She's lying. She was going to kill me. The two of them are working together."

Before Owen could grab her, Leah stormed up to the

other woman. He was right behind her but didn't catch up fast enough to prevent what happened next.

Leah punched the other woman in the face. Louise hit the ground.

"That's for having that guy try to kill me." She rubbed her fist.

"You got this?" Lambert asked, backing toward the car.

"Got it," Owen assured him.

"I'll send a patrol car for the woman, and the rest of us are going to find the one who got away."

Owen helped Douglas to her feet. "If you resist," he warned, "the next punch will be from me."

In the five minutes that followed, a patrol car arrived and took custody of Louise Douglas. Another uniform offered to give them a ride; Owen declined and told the officer to help the others find his car and the fugitive driving it.

When the police were gone, he called the office and ordered a car to pick him and Leah up. Then he draped his arm around her shoulders and pulled her close. She looked ready to drop.

"You okay?"

"I guess so." She leaned her head against him. "I guess I held out hope that Isla—Alyssa, whatever, was telling the truth. That the friendship we shared was real on some level."

But it wasn't. Owen understood how difficult that must be to accept.

"You up to walking for a few minutes?"

"Yeah. I just want to get out of here."

"I can make that happen," he promised. "In fact, I think we're both due for a vacation."

She peered up at him, the new bruise on her cheek making his gut clench. "A vacation sounds amazing."

"Don't you want to know where?" he asked, grinning at her eagerness.

"I don't care where as long as I'm with you."

"Same," he murmured as he leaned down to press a kiss to her forehead.

They walked until their ride arrived, and then they relaxed and started to plan.

Chapter Fifteen

Leah packed the last of her things into a final box, then glanced around the living room.

Her few pieces of furniture, as well as the ones that had belonged to the real Isla Morris, were being donated to charity. With Isla's mother dead—of an overdose, as Alyssa had suggested—there was no one to take possession of anything. As for the clothes and personal belongings, they had been boxed up for donation as well.

Leah sighed. She was glad to be finished with this part.

She glanced at the time. Owen would be here in a few minutes to pick her up. He'd rented a small moving van for hauling her boxes to the new place. His friend had come through with one of the studio apartments Owen had mentioned. Leah was excited about the move.

She couldn't deny having some regrets about walking away from the last three years of her life, but what else could she do? The friends she'd made had been friends of Alyssa's. They hadn't really cared about Leah. And that was okay. She didn't need those people. She'd recognized their self-centeredness from the beginning, but they were her roommate's friends, so she'd ignored their shortcomings.

Lambert and the Chicago PD had caught Alyssa. She and Louise Douglas were in jail, both charged with murder. The Douglas children were with their grandparents. Leah would never understand how a parent could do this to her children.

Alyssa was spilling her guts in hopes of a deal. Louise had said nothing since her outrageously expensive attorney had counseled her to keep her mouth shut.

Leah had given her statement to Lambert, and she, of course, would have no choice but to testify at the trials as a witness. But until then, she was not looking back.

The woman who had pretended to be Isla Morris's mother had gotten scared and turned herself in. Alyssa had admitted that she and Louise had gotten intimately involved and devised the entire scheme. Now they would both be going to prison. No matter the deal Alyssa wrangled, she was not getting out of a murder charge.

Leah regretted that she had ever believed the woman. But she was a good person, and she'd always believed the best in people. She would have thought she'd learned her lesson with Chris, but apparently not.

She had contacted Bechel at the insurance company and signed over her portion of the insurance proceeds to Raymond's children. Whatever kind of selfish person he had been, he would have wanted his children cared for, Leah felt certain.

The sound of the buzzer announced that Owen had arrived. She rushed to the door and was just about to press the necessary button to grant him entrance when she remembered that there was a possibility it wasn't him. She pressed the intercom button instead. "Yes?"

"It's me," he said.

A smile broke across her lips. She pressed the button that would release the entrance-door lock and then waited just outside her door for him to arrive. When he hit the top of the stairs, her heart started to pound. Watching him walk toward her had the organ racing. She loved the way he walked. Loved every part of him. During their week-long vacation, he had explored every inch of her and she had done the same to him. Her smile stretched even wider at the beautiful bouquet of flowers he carried.

"You're here," she said, sounding breathless.

"I am." He stopped directly in front of her. "You ready?"

She nodded. "I am so ready." She looked at the flowers. "Are those for me?"

He smiled. "They are. You said no one had ever sent you flowers. I intend to do that as often as possible."

She kissed him, almost crushing the flowers in the process.

They spent the next few minutes carrying boxes to the rented van. When she locked the apartment door for the last time, she turned to Owen.

"I'm glad this is behind me."

He smiled. "Me too."

"But the best part—" she reached for him, slid her arms around his waist "—is what's in front of me."

He leaned down and kissed her.

She could not wait to see where their journey took them next.

The Colby Agency, 7:30 p.m.

VICTORIA SHUT OFF the light to her office and closed the door. It had been a long day, but a very good one. Several investigations were settled, and all investigators and clients were safe.

This was always what she hoped for. When love bloomed between an investigator and a client, it was all the better.

The Colby Agency had a long history of solving the most difficult cases as well as bringing some amazing people together.

Victoria was very proud of her agency and of all who'd worked here, past and present. They were all such great people. In all the years she had been at the head of this agency, she had only ever lost one investigator and that was one too many. The many, many clients they had helped often sent postcards or letters of thanks even years later.

Victoria truly loved the agency and the work they did.

She smiled as she reached the lobby. Lucas waited there for her. She should have known Jamie would call him. She hadn't wanted to leave this evening without Victoria. Everyone else had gone. But Victoria had needed some time alone at her beloved window, watching life on the street below. Not that she had any troubles to worry about. No. Life was well within the Colby family. But there were times when she just needed to stare out that window and remember all the times she had done so before.

This evening had been one of those times.

The sight of Lucas waiting for her lifted her nostalgic heart. No matter that they were both getting up there age-wise, she still saw him as the dashing man who had stolen her heart when she had been certain her heart would never again feel that kind of love.

Like James, her first husband, Lucas had been a master spy, his work the darkest of dark operations. He, James and Victoria had been dear friends for a lifetime before tragedy stuck so very hard. First, her son had been abducted, and then her husband had been murdered. Before James's death, they had desperately searched for their child. She regretted so that James had not lived to see their son returned. Jim was a good, strong man.

He hadn't returned to Victoria that way, however. Jim had been horribly abused and brainwashed. He had come back to her as a killer, determined to murder her. But somehow she had reached him and he had changed. Over the years since that time, he had married and had two beautiful children. One of which, Jamie, now worked with Victoria, running the agency. Luke, the younger of the two, was in medical school.

Life was as perfect as could be expected in this changing world.

"I thought," Lucas announced, "that I would take you to dinner, my love."

Victoria put her arm in his and turned to the elevator. "I think that is an amazing idea." She grinned. "Jamie called you, didn't she?"

He grinned as well. "She did. She said you were looking a little sad."

Victoria rose onto her tiptoes and gave him a kiss on the jaw. "Not sad, just lost in memories."

The elevator doors opened and they stepped into the car.

"I hope I was present in those memories."

"You, my dear husband, are in the very best of all my memories, going back to the night we met."

"The night James stole you away from me," he teased.

Victoria laughed. Lucas swore to this day that he had been smitten with Victoria, but it was James who had swept her off her feet that long-ago night when they were all so young.

"But you were always there," she reminded him. "Always a part of our lives, for better or worse."

He nodded. "I was, indeed."

"Thank you, Lucas." When he met her gaze with a questioning look, she explained, "For being the man who helped me love again."

"No thanks necessary, my dear. I was happy to wait for that moment."

The doors closed and the elevator swept them down to the lobby.

When the doors opened once more, rather than finding an empty space where only the security guard manned the information desk, she found a room full of people. She gasped. Not just people. Everyone from the agency…even some she hadn't seen in years. And the massive lobby was decorated beautifully with balloons and flowers and streamers.

"What on earth?" she murmured.

"Happy birthday, Victoria," Lucas said, turning to her. "I hope this one is the best one yet."

Jim and Tasha, Jamie and Luke, they hurried forward and hugged her. Despite her best efforts, tears filled Victoria's eyes.

"You didn't say a word," she said to Jamie.

Jamie grinned. "It was a surprise, Grandmother." She gestured to a small stage that had been erected with a waiting microphone.

Victoria surveyed the clapping crowd as they urged her to speak.

"Come along," Lucas said, ushering her toward the stage. "They're all waiting to hear from you."

Victoria stepped up onto the stage and scanned the crowd. She smiled. Lucas didn't have to worry. This was certainly the best birthday ever.

* * * * *

Look for Striking Distance *and read the suspense-filled story of Jim Colby's return.*

COMING SOON!

We really hope you enjoyed reading this book.
If you're looking for more romance
be sure to head to the shops when
new books are available on

Thursday 20th November

To see which titles are coming soon, please visit
millsandboon.co.uk/nextmonth

MILLS & BOON

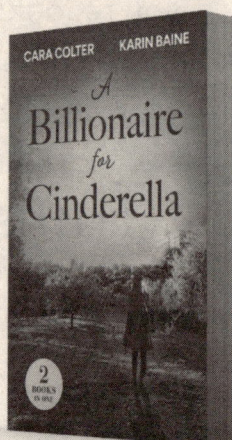

A STYLISH NEW LOOK FOR
MILLS & BOON TRUE LOVE!

Introducing

Love Always

Swoon-worthy romances, where love takes centre stage. Same heartwarming stories, stylish new look!

Look out for our brand new look

OUT NOW

MILLS & BOON

FOUR BRAND NEW BOOKS FROM
MILLS & BOON MODERN

Indulge in desire, drama, and breathtaking romance – where passion knows no bounds!

2 BOOKS IN ONE

WANTED: A FIANCÉ

PIPPA ROSCOE   CLARE CONNELLY

2 BOOKS IN ONE

Business Meets Pleasure...

Louise Fuller   Millie Adams

2 BOOKS IN ONE

Christmas **Baby Bombshell**

Sharon Kendrick   Caitlin Crews

2 BOOKS IN ONE

Bound to a Bride

NATALIE ANDERSON   ANNIE WEST

OUT NOW

Eight Modern stories published every month, find them all at:

millsandboon.co.uk

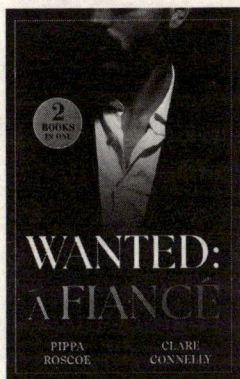

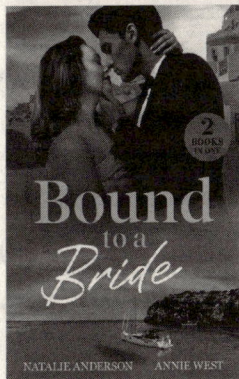

LET'S TALK

Romance

For exclusive extracts, competitions and special offers, find us online:

- **f** MillsandBoon
- **X** @MillsandBoon
- **O** @MillsandBoonUK
- **♪** @MillsandBoonUK

Get in touch on 01413 063 232

For all the latest titles coming soon, visit
millsandboon.co.uk/nextmonth